Could Have been Us

Could Have Been Us
Copyright © 2021 Corinne Michaels

All rights reserved.
ISBN—paperback: 978-1-942834-58-8

This book is a work of fiction. Names, characters, places, and incidents
either are products of the author's imagination or are used fictitiously.
Any resemblance to actual events or locales or persons, living or dead, is
entirely coincidental and beyond the intent of the author or publisher.

Cover Design: Sommer Stein, Perfect Pear Creative

Editing: Ashley Williams, AW Editing

Proofreading: Michele Ficht & Julia Griffis

Cover photo © Brian Kaminiski

Model: Charlie Matthews

Formatting: Alyssa Garica, Uplifting Author Services

Could Have been Us

NEW YORK TIMES BESTSELLING AUTHOR
CORINNE MICHAELS

To Aly Martinez, I'm sure you've done something nice at some point, even if I can't remember it.

One

STELLA

"You don't have to do this, Stella. We can . . . we can find a way," Jack says as I wipe the tears from my cheeks.

"We don't have a choice."

"There's always a choice."

"Not an easy one." My eyes are on the tiny baby in my arms.

No matter how much I wish I could keep her, I won't. There are a million reasons neither of our options are great, but to change our minds now would end disastrously. My father has made it clear that, if I keep her, I'm cut off completely. No family. No friends. No help from any one of my siblings or he'll cut them off. I am not to be *that* girl. The one who has a baby at eighteen, not his daughter. Then, when I cried, said I didn't care, he went for the only other thing that could've hurt me—Jack.

He'll destroy his future, make sure that he can't get a job in the town. He already has no family, so seeing everything he's worked for taken from him isn't something I can endure.

We were stupid that night. We made a mistake, and this is our penance.

Jack touches her fingers. I've already counted all ten, kissed them too. She's a perfect little girl who fits in my arms, just as she was designed to do.

"No, but this isn't about what's easy."

I look up at him. His dark brown hair is in disarray because he raced to get here in time from his college, and his hazel eyes are filled with confliction over having to do what we agreed on seven months ago.

"No, it's not about what's easy, it's about her," I say, hating the words as I speak them.

"She's our daughter. I'll leave school, and we can figure out how to raise her."

A new wave of tears comes. I thought this would be easier. How naïve I was. I've been in Georgia the last four months, not able to see anyone from Willow Creek Valley as I hid the pregnancy. All I've done is plan for how I would survive this, and now that it's here, I don't think I will. Not without a lifetime of pain, at least.

"I'm eighteen," I remind him.

Jack gets to his feet, pacing the room. "I know that. I know all of it, but now she's here."

"And you're in grad school. We've talked about this, Jack. We've gone over this because . . ."

He looks at me with heartache. "We'd have to tell Grayson."

Yes, my brother. His best friend in the whole world. The one person who has always been there for him but who can never know the truth.

We're lying to ourselves.

Lying that it was just a kiss, which became so much more as we were both lost, searching for someone else to make it okay. And now, the biggest lie of all, a baby that we are going to give to another family to love.

"Grayson isn't the only reason. Do you want this? Do you want to be a father right now?"

He pinches the bridge of his nose. "No, but we made a baby."

"We did, and we made the choice to have her and give her the life she deserves. Just outside there are two people who will love our daughter. People who have their lives together, a family, a home, and can give her a future that we can't. People who aren't two kids who aren't dating but got carried away and forgot a condom. Not to mention, my father will take everything, Jack. Everything and . . . I'm just . . . I need to do what's right for her and not think about us. It's not about our wants."

Even though I want him to just love me.

Jack sighs deeply. "They have no idea the gift they're getting."

Misty and Samuel Elkins are nice people who already have a nursery set up, complete with pink bumpers and an elephant mobile. They've bought clothes, a car seat, and diapers. We've been to their house and they have spent hours talking to us and creating a plan that Jack and I could live with. They are well aware of what we're giving up.

I close my eyes, nuzzling the baby and kissing her forehead. "Misty will love Kinsley. She'll be the mother I can't be. This may break me, but it's the best thing for her. We both know it." I place my other hand on her chest, feeling her rapid heartbeat.

Jack comes to my side, his large hand resting on mine. "If it's right, why does it feel so hard?"

"Because we love her. Even if we can't keep her."

Three hearts beating, two breaking with the knowledge of what is to come. I will hand this little girl over to another family. I'll give her a chance that she'll never have with me. I start college in a few weeks, Jack is in his second year of grad school, and we don't love each other. Well, at least he doesn't love me.

"I'll do whatever you want, Stella. I told you that. I'll go against your father, your brother, the world if that's what you need."

He would too. He's been great through it all. Jack offered to help me in whatever way I needed and supported my decision when I said I wanted to give her a better life than we could. The hardest part has been hiding it all from my brothers.

"I know, but I think we need to make the most unselfish decision we can ever make."

No matter how it breaks us both.

There's a knock on the door. The nurse peeks her head in. "Are you guys ready?"

I look down at my daughter again, my heart feeling as though it's been torn from my chest. Is anyone ever ready for this? I don't know how to do it. Jack stares down at me. "It's time, Stella. If we're going to do it, we have to do it now."

I know he's right. The longer I hold her, the more my head and heart war with each other.

My watery gaze goes back to the door. "We're ready."

The door closes again, and I tell my daughter everything. "I love you. I love you so much, and that is why I'm doing this. I will always love you. I'm so sorry, Kinsley. I'm sorry I'm not strong enough. Don't ever think this was easy or that it was because I didn't love you." I glance back up to Jack. "Take her from me. Please, it has to be you. I can't . . ."

Jack's tears are brimming, ready to spill over as he reaches out, pulling Kinsley into his arms. "No matter what, I hope that someday you understand that this is the hardest thing we've ever done. Your mother is right that we love you, which is why we're letting you have a better life."

The door opens back up, and I turn my head, unable to witness this. I hear Jack's footsteps as he carries our child across the room. Misty and Samuel are talking to Jack, and I turn on my side. I cry. I cry so hard that I worry I'll drown. I cry so I don't have to hear their words. I cry so I don't have to watch them take this little girl out of my room.

I want to scream because none of this is fair.

One night changed every possibility I could ever have.

Jack doesn't know how much I'm giving up. He can't understand that I'm losing my daughter and probably the only piece of him I'll ever have. I love him so much, and this finalized that we will never be.

A hand touches my back. "Stella." Jack's deep voice reverberates in the small space.

I sob harder, and he pulls me into his arms. I clutch him, knowing that this will be the last time he ever holds me. I try not to think about all that's fading from my grasp or how I'll endure the rest of my life like this.

Pretending I never had a baby.

Pretending I don't love Jack.

Pretending it all is fine when I'll feel empty.

Jack rubs my back, holding me close as I try to let it go. When I emerge from this room, I won't be the same again because I no longer have a heart.

STELLA

Twelve Years Later

"You should get this dress," Winnie says as she holds up a scrap of fabric she pulled from the rack.

"That's a dress?"

She checks the tag. "Sure is."

"I'm not twenty-one anymore," I remind her.

"No, but you're not dead either. Plus, neither of us is married or in a serious relationship. We need to at least look hot when we go out."

"Because the options out there are anything to get excited over?"

Winnie raises one brow. "Do you even look? When was the last time you went on a date?"

"I don't remember."

She shakes her head, the disapproval layered in her reply. "Which is the damn problem. Seriously, you're a gorgeous heiress who refuses to be in any kind of relationship. It's like you refuse to even date."

I date. Kind of.

I've known Winnie since we were five years old, and while she's normally content not to talk about this, when it does come up, she's relentless.

"Because I am an heiress, that's why I don't date." It's not entirely true, but it's close enough. Grayson and I run the flagship inn here in Willow Creek Valley and our brothers are scattered to various locations, but our father still holds the reins. Just my last name alone attracts a lot of . . . money-seeking men.

"You could be a little nicer. Maybe that would land you a boyfriend."

I roll my eyes. "None of these guys are worth it, and I'm not going to waste my time."

Because the only man I have ever loved pretends I don't exist past being his best friend's little sister even though we have a child together.

"I just want you to be happy."

I push the clothes on the rack and sigh. "Well, same goes for you, Win."

"Difference is that I'm willing to date, you're not."

The sad part is that I've tried. I've found men—ones I thought were good—and not one of them stood up against Jack.

It's the most pathetic thing in the world. Why I can't seem to get over Jack O'Donnell, I'll never understand.

One glorious night was all I was meant to have with that man, and it ruined me. Absolutely took every damn chance away for another man. Because no matter how great a guy is, what he does or thinks, he's never going to be as wonderful as Jack.

"Then we'll both die alone." I grab an outfit, pulling it to my chest. "What do you think?"

"I think you're in need of Jess's shrink."

I grin. "You might be right there."

Jessica is Winnie's older sister, and she's been through a lot. She came back to Willow Creek Valley not too long ago and has been getting help to heal. I always loved Jess and, I'm really hoping she and Grayson straighten their shit out. They're destined to be together and just need to stop being so stubborn.

Winnie tilts her head, looking over the outfit, and then scrunches her nose. Well, that's a no.

"Will you at least go on a double date with me once I get a date set?"

I groan and put the garment back where I took it. "Why do you do this to me? I'm happy, Winnie. I love my job. I have a great home. I have a crazy but fantastic family if you ignore my asshole parents. I've got you and Delia and Jess now that she's back in town. My life is *fine*. Why do you think I need to date?"

"Because you're my best friend, and part of what we love about each other is the torment we inflict?"

She's a damn mess. "Fine, but tell this guy to tell his friend I'm a bitch."

"Oh, don't worry, there's not a man around here who doesn't hear your name and shudder."

"I'm like Mufasa."

She does the shiver from the movie, and we both start laughing.

"I love you, Win."

"I love you too. I only ride you because I know the truth."

"What's that?"

She chews on her lower lip and then answers softly. "You want what Grayson and Jess will hopefully have. You want the marriage and kids and love."

"They don't have that," I say quickly.

"I said *hopefully*. But they're trying to find a way. I think we know our siblings will figure it out sooner rather than later."

I nod. "I hope so. Grayson has loved her his whole life."

"And Jess loves him, but we're not talking about them. We're talking about you and what you want. I remember your dreams when we were kids, Stell. You forget that we don't have secrets."

My chest pangs because I do have one. A very big one.

"I appreciate you caring, and who knows, maybe one day I'll meet my prince."

Her face lights up. "Maybe it'll be this guy."

"Yeah, maybe."

But probably not.

Tonight is pizza night at Grayson's house, which I normally skip because I can only handle being around Jack so often, but since he's out in the wilderness, pretending he's some kind of bonding guide, I'm going to get some Amelia time.

I change out of my work clothes, tossing on a pair of leggings and an oversized sweatshirt, and then check the mail.

When I see the letter stamped from Georgia, I smile and rush to open it.

Dear Stella,

I hope this letter finds you well. We had a really exciting day today. Kinsley was accepted into the summer math program she applied to, which she says is, "Super cool." How anyone can think math is fun is beyond me. She grew another inch—I swear, I can't keep this girl in clothing more than a few weeks—and also asked if she could try out for the soccer team. I'm not sure how long this attempt will last, though. If you remember, she tried soccer last year and found that she really hated running. However, her father and I can't deny her anything.

Samuel just took a new position at the company he's with. It's longer hours but the pay is better. For now, we are focusing on the fact that, in a few years, he can retire with a fabulous pension and health insurance, which helps with my treatments. That's the mantra, at least. Things are well. Having cancer the first time was much worse than this go. My doctors are very hopeful about the prognosis.

How is Jack? Is he still being MacGyver in the woods? (Your words, not mine). It makes me smile knowing you both are doing so well. I have been debating writing him again. I know he doesn't respond, I don't even know if he opens them, but well, I don't know, maybe it's being sick again and seeing how precious time is that makes me keep wanting to try.

Anyway, I'm enclosing a few photos of Kinsley. She's so much of you and Jack, it's crazy. When she was a baby, she was more you, but as she's growing, I see so much of Jack in her.

I apologize for this letter being so short, but lately I've been so tired and don't have much to report. I await your next letter, and as always, we thank you so much for allowing us to be her parents. It warms my heart to know that should the day come that she wants to know about you and Jack, I can tell her how special you both are.

Love,
Misty

I sit at the counter, looking at the photos of Kinsley. Her hair is long and the same deep brown as mine, but her eyes are all Jack. Hazel with flecks of green mixed in and the thickest black around the iris. She's stunning. Even at twelve years old, it's clear she's going to be a very beautiful young lady.

And smart, which is even better.

Her love of numbers definitely doesn't come from me. Jack was an accountant before he became a wilderness guide.

I release a heavy sigh, laden with the guilt that still haunts me. While Kinsley is thriving and doing well, I've gotten older and even more listless.

She's growing and becoming someone I will never know. Of course, Misty and Samuel have always been open in the spirit of what we asked for, but that was just the luck of choosing them. When the sixty-day period expired, we lost all rights to her. The fortunate part was picking two people who don't have an ounce of malice in their hearts and show their appreciation by honoring an agreement we all know they don't really have to. If Kinsley ever wants to know more about us, the option is there, but until then, I get photos and letters.

I've never asked for more, and I never will, mostly because of Jack. He chooses zero contact, and I understand it. It's incredibly difficult being on this side. To see this girl in photos but never hear her voice or see her smile.

My phone pings with a text from Grayson.

Grayson: Are you coming? Pizza is here.

Me: You bet.

Tonight, however, is not a night to make any other choice other than how much pizza to consume.

I grab my purse and head out. The drive to his house takes about five minutes. When I was looking for my own place, I knew I wanted to be close to my other brothers. I don't understand why, but Grayson is my favorite sibling.

Mostly because he has Amelia, the most precious little girl

who I love with my whole heart.

"Auntie!" Amelia yells and runs to me as I exit the car.

While I may not have my own daughter to hold and love, I have her. No one but Jack will ever understand how much Amelia coming into my life saved me, and I do whatever I can to help my brother with her.

"Look at you," I say as she stops in front of me. "You grew."

"No, I'm the same size."

"Well, you look bigger."

Melia smiles brightly. "Then maybe I am."

Grayson comes out, carrying her doll and looking haggard. "Hey."

"Hey yourself. You look like crap," I tell him.

"Gee, thanks."

"You're welcome."

He rolls his eyes. "Pizza is here, and I'm starving."

"Aww, you waited for me," I tease him.

Amelia tugs on my hand. "I made him."

"Which is why you're my favorite Parkerson."

"I'm everyone's favorite," she informs us.

Grayson scoops her up and lifts her above his head. "You're a monster. That's what you are."

I smile at the effortless love the two of them share. My brother hasn't had it easy with Melia. Yvonne and he had plans. They were going to get married, raise their daughter, and my brother would've been miserable. However, when Amelia was two weeks old, Yvonne brought her and all her belongings to Grayson and then left.

While I grapple with the idea of being anything like her, I, at least, care. Yvonne wasn't a kid. She was a grown woman and walked away, never looking back.

I follow them and hear a booming laugh from inside the house.

Immediately, my body tenses. I feel the tingles of each nerve ending lighting up, knowing whose laugh that is.

Usually, I'm able to control myself. To push aside the feelings that haven't subsided in over twelve years. You'd think I'd be a master at it. That I could get over this childhood love because, surely, it can't be a real thing anymore, but here I am, trembling inside.

"Are you the monster or the food?" Jack asks as Grayson and Amelia enter the living room in front of me.

Amelia laughs. "I'm the food. Daddy is the monster."

Don't think about it. Do not let yourself imagine a life that never could be.

"Do you need saving, my precious?" Jack asks as he approaches them.

"Save me, Uncle Jack!"

He moves forward, pulling her out of Grayson's grasp and clutching her to his chest.

And I imagine a very different scene with a very different girl. One who would have been loved and protected by him. A little girl with hazel eyes and dark brown hair.

As the laughter subsides, Jack's eyes meet mine and a flash of something like regret passes before his easy smile replaces it.

"Hey, Stella."

"Hey, Jack. I thought you were lost in the woods," I say, clearing my throat and swallowing the emotion that vision brought.

"Thankfully, the trip ended early."

"They realized you were too inept to lead?" I joke.

"Now, we both know that's not true. The main guy was covered in poison ivy."

I shake my head with a smile. "And the inept thing rings true."

Grayson walks over, tossing his arm around my shoulders.

"Now, Stella, don't forget that Jack is inept in everything. Dating, firefighting, football . . ."

"I'm capable where it matters."

"And where is that?" Grayson challenges.

"I've never had a woman complain about my prowess in the bedroom."

Gray rolls his eyes, and I use every ounce of self-control not to flinch. "Well, since neither Stella nor I can attest to that, we call bullshit."

I laugh and move out of my brother's hold. I can attest to it, but I sure as hell won't. "Let's have pizza and watch the movie before I no longer have an appetite," I suggest.

We eat, laughing and talking about the last group Jack took out in the woods. The entire point is team building and survival skills, but most of the time, we hear more about how miserable everyone was. Jack had a cushy job as an accountant for one of North Carolina's biggest firms. He was able to work remotely and made a killing.

Then, one day, he was just done. He left the company and started this venture.

He's done well, but it still doesn't make sense to me.

Amelia is curled up against my side as the movie plays. I hear her soft snore and smile, pushing her sandy blonde hair off her face.

"She's out," I tell Gray.

His smile is automatic as he sees his daughter. "She always falls asleep during the movie."

I kiss the top of her head. "And I love that she usually does it while I hold her."

While I have always been somewhat of a mother figure to Amelia, I've been extremely careful not to let myself be more than her aunt. I love her immensely, but it would be incredibly unfair to both of us to consider her a replacement to the daughter I gave up. Amelia isn't mine. She's Grayson's, and I'm just lucky enough to be here for her.

He gets up, lifting Amelia to his chest. "I'm going to put her to bed."

Leaving Jack and I alone.

What is wrong with me? Seriously. Since the one night we slept together, nothing has ever been romantic between us. I've seen him a million times, and we've talked and hung out, and yet, I still feel this way. It's absolutely fucking sad, that's what it is.

I'm that sad, stupid girl who loves a guy who will never love her back.

"So, how is work?" he asks after a minute.

"Good. Busy, but good."

He nods. "How is Jessica working out there? I know she just started the other week, right?"

I settle back against the couch. "Jessica is amazing. She picked everything up really quickly and has already made some great changes to the way we're running the front office. The fact that Grayson is so clearly in love with her still makes it a little more enjoyable as well."

Jack chuckles. "You didn't see them at the beach house."

"Them and that damn house."

"Seriously, it's magical for them," he agrees.

I've always known my brother's heart belonged to Jess, and when she left, he took it hard. He closed himself off for a bit and then allowed his pain to blind him to Yvonne's bullshit. I never thought they were good together, but trying to tell Grayson something he doesn't want to hear is like talking to a brick wall. I've learned it's best not to even try.

A weird lull falls between us, and the words tumble from my lips before I can stop them.

"I got a letter from Misty today." Damn it. I should not have said it.

His eyes widen. "Stella . . ."

I shake my head quickly. "I know . . . I . . . I'm sorry. Forget I said anything. Please."

Jack rubs the back of his neck. "It's not that I don't—"

"Jack, stop. I know where you stand, and I was being stupid. Please, let's drop it."

After we had given Kinsley over and I had finally stopped crying in his arms, we made promises. We both made our decisions, and Jack wanted to move on. He needed to be able to go forward with his life, putting this behind him. He said he couldn't look Grayson in the eyes, lie to him day in and day out, if he had any relationship with Kinsley.

I chose a half-in model that Misty seemed okay with. I talk to Misty every six months. Sometimes, it's a letter, and other times, it's a phone call from her, but I've never once brought it up to Jack. I have no idea why I did now.

An awkward and painful silence falls around us, and I know that Grayson will sense it. I do my best to shove it down and smile at him to avoid questions neither of us want to answer. The one thing the two of us have become exceedingly good at is pretending.

At least I have.

"Are you coming to the charity dinner this week?" I ask, needing to break this tension.

"I'm not sure."

I nod. "My mother went all out this time."

"Doesn't she always?" he asks with the classic Jack smile in place.

"She does."

Jack turns to me, his elbows resting on his knees, wringing his hands. I can't remember the last time I saw him so nervous. "Stella . . . I need to—"

Grayson enters, breaking off whatever Jack was about to say. I resist the urge to take a pillow and throw it at my brother to make him leave. Damn him and his horrible timing.

"Am I interrupting something?"

I smile, leaning back against the couch. "No," I scoff.

He looks to us. "You just look serious."

Jack's voice is controlled and even. "We were talking about you and Jessica. You know the fact that you're both in love with each other and won't admit it."

Oh, the irony in that statement is comical.

Grayson sits on the couch, looking a little lost. "I wish I could deny it, but I can't. I love her, want her, and yet, I know I can't have her."

Jack and I look at each other, and my heart aches. Then his voice breaks the very small part of my heart that was still living. "I know the feeling, but it's best not to let yourself hope."

Three

JACK

Stella Parkerson is off fucking limits.

I say it for the one-hundred-millionth time. She's not for me. Never has been and never will be. The night we made love was the only time I was ever stupid enough to think I could walk in her light.

The darkness is where I belong.

It's been twelve years since Kinsley was born, and I've done a pretty good job of pretending it never happened. I think about her randomly, but I force it away before I can ever wonder.

But now, Stella spoke our daughter's name into the murky water of the present, and I'm drowning from it.

"Well, you look worse than I feel," Danny, the bartender, says as he puts a beer in front of me.

"I'm fine."

He laughs once. "Yeah, convincing."

I lift the bottle, taking a long pull, letting the liquid slide down my throat. How the hell did I get here again? I have been fine. Doing just fine ignoring the way Stella walks, the sound of her voice, the way her breathing reminds me of a night long ago. It's been . . . fine.

And now it's not.

"Keep these coming," I tell Danny.

He nods once and leaves to help someone else.

I reach into my pocket, touching the sealed letter I got two weeks after Kinsley was born.

I have never been tempted to open it until now.

No. I'm not doing it.

There is no point. Reading it won't change anything, and neither would talking to Misty and Samuel. They are her parents, not us.

Someone sits beside me, but I don't need to look to know who it is.

"What are you doing here?" I ask Delia, Jessica's best friend and also one of mine.

"I could ask you the same."

I turn my head slightly. "Bad day."

She waves her hand to Danny and he brings her over a vodka and cranberry. She turns to me, lifting the glass. "To bad days."

"Are you sure we should toast to that?"

Delia shrugs. "Might as well. They happen anyway."

"That they do."

We both take a drink and then she turns her chair to me. "What's got you coming two towns over for a beer?"

Because drinking anywhere in Willow Creek Valley means I may run into Stella. And I do not need to run into Stella.

"Just needed a change of scenery."

"I see."

"You do?"

She takes a sip and then smiles sadly. "Well, I know that look."

"What look?" I ask with a bit of ice in my voice.

"The one that says it isn't about scenery at all and all about trying not to care about someone you can't stop caring about."

Delia is the only person who ever alluded to thinking something happened between Stella and me. Even then, it took her over a decade to hint at it. We were walking, giving Grayson and Jessica some alone time to work out their shit, and I mentioned the color of the sky being like Stella's eyes.

One stupid slipup, and it seems Delia caught it.

"You're talking about Josh?"

"Please, my love for that man isn't a secret. I've just gotten good at pretending otherwise. It helps with not feeling like a total idiot." She nudges me with her shoulder. "What I'm wondering is how long you've maybe had feelings for someone else."

I shake my head, staring at my beer. "I don't have feelings for anyone. You know that."

I can feel her assessing each word and debating if she's going to call me out. Admitting it will never happen. That would be the dumbest thing I can do. The only reason that I'm still breathing is because Grayson has no idea I've ever looked at Stella in that way.

He's my best friend—a brother more than anything—and I betrayed him once. I'll never do it again.

Not because everyone knows you don't fuck your best friend's sister but because our actions broke Stella and me and we don't need Grayson doing more damage.

Delia releases a long sigh. "I guess I thought differently."

This mood has to stop. I can't walk around Willow Creek with my head all messed up. I need to get back to being the fun guy. Being the character who laughs, doesn't let shit bother him, and is a take-it-on-the-chin kind of friend. I'm who people come to for a laugh.

"What brings you here?" I ask her, changing the topic.

"I got stood up."

"Oh?"

She laughs. "It happens more than I care to admit."

"I'd never stand you up," I tell her honestly. Delia is beautiful. She's smart, has a great sense of humor, and would do anything for those she loves.

"Aww, be still my heart. However, here we both sit, drinking in a bar that smells like piss and beer."

"I'm not sure it's piss, I think it's the beer that's spilled so much."

Delia scrunches her nose. "Either way, it's gross."

"It is."

Delia and I have always had an easy friendship. It was nice being friends with a girl who didn't want anything more than just that. She never lusted after me and while she was incredibly attractive, the feelings never grew to more. We've been able to share secrets, well, some of them, and never have to worry. I could tell her about what has brought me so low. At least I could confide a part of it.

But I won't.

A secret is only that when it's only yours.

No one knows how I feel about Stella.

Not a soul alive has a clue that I lust for, dream about, or crave the girl who I should never again touch.

And that's how it has to stay.

"You can be my date tonight," I offer.

She grins. "You always were a gentleman."

"Is that what they say?"

"No, they say you're an idiot."

I laugh, the first real one in three days. "They're not wrong."

"Jack . . ."

"Yes?"

The emotions filter across her face as she struggles with

her thoughts. "Is . . . are you . . . ugh, I don't know why I'm hesitating to ask you, but here it is . . . is there something with you and Winnie?"

Now I'm stunned. "Winnie? As in Jess's little sister?"

She raises a brow. "Do you know another Winnie?"

I shift in my seat. "No, and to answer your question, also no. I don't have feelings for Winnie. She's . . ."

"She's beautiful."

"Yeah, I mean, I guess she is."

"Well, she's single, and you're single."

Wait, is she trying to set me up with Winnie Walker? "Deals, are you serious right now?"

Delia tilts her head with wide eyes. "Duh. You're getting on in age, Jack. It's time to settle down, and Winnie is a catch."

"I'm thirty-four. She's turning thirty this year."

"And I'm thirty-two. I'm glad we're all aware of our ages. My point is that she's young and pretty and has a great job. She laughs at your *awful* jokes. Plus, young is good, right? You'll have someone to change your diapers when you're ancient and decrepit."

"You can change my diapers."

She laughs. "Ha! I will be single forever."

"Because you're unwilling to let go of Josh."

Delia doesn't deny it. And, honestly, I shouldn't judge. I'm the same fucking way. It's Friday night, and I'm at a bar with a letter burning a hole in my pocket because Stella reminded me of it all.

It's true what they say, I really am an idiot.

Four

STELLA

Being a Parkerson means weathering disasters and cleaning up messes that others make. Mostly, my father's messes.

"I have to go," Grayson says as he tosses things into a bag.

"I get it, but why you? Why the hell aren't you telling Dad to fuck off?"

He sighs. "Because Oliver asked me to come, that's why."

"Oh, because once again, Dad fucks up and we're stuck doing damage control."

Apparently, there's a problem at our Wyoming Inn, which isn't even fully operational. My father bought it—without talking to anyone—and pushed Oliver to go out there to make it worthy of the Parkerson name.

Instead of allowing my brother to actually . . . do his job . . . Dad spent a lot of time around there, watching over the refurbishing. Which translates to him spending time with a new girlfriend. I can only imagine what has Gray going out there.

"It's either I hang Ollie out to dry or I go help. Which

would you rather?"

"I'd rather none of us be saddled with his piss-poor decision making."

"Yes, well, that's not an option, Stella, so . . ."

I get it, we do what we can with the options we have. "I know. I'll keep Melia. It'll be a fun weekend and we'll do all kinds of girl things."

He kisses my cheek. "Thank you."

"While you keep acting like you're not a complete and total mess about Jessica, which is why you volunteered to go instead of letting Josh or Alex, who don't have a kid or any responsibility, handle it." I add that last part on for good measure. Grayson may be using Dad as the reason he's going, but I'm not an idiot.

"That's not why I'm going," Grayson denies.

"Oh?"

He glares at me the way that only older brothers do. "It's not."

I raise my hands. "If you say so."

"I do."

"You sure do."

"Anyone ever tell you that you're annoying as fuck?" Gray asks with a note of admiration under the words.

"Only my four older and *stupid* brothers."

He laughs and then hoists the bag onto his shoulders. "Yes, I'm in love with her. Yes, I'm pretty sure she's in love with me, but we won't work, Stell. We are two different people who want different things. I have to think about Amelia."

"Who is madly in love with her," I point out.

"Yes, she is. She loves Jess and asks about her daily, which is why I need to keep my distance."

I touch his cheek and press my lips into a thin line. "Oh, Gray, you're a wonderful dipshit. You and Jessica can't stay away from each other any more than two magnets. But I admire the effort. Go kick my twin's ass and tell him I miss him."

He looks away. "Don't let Melia eat KitKats for dinner."

I shrug with a playful smirk. "You won't be here, and you can't stop us."

He groans and then heads out the door.

I gather Melia's things, making sure I have enough clothes for two nights, and then bring the bag to my house. I'll pick her up from daycare that she goes to once a week later because I have learned all too well that one does not remove that girl early.

She loves her friends and her food and doing art after nap time.

I rank rather low on her list of priorities come to think of it.

I head into work, smiling at everyone as I walk through the front grounds.

The Park Inn is a five-star in a town of nothing but twos. When I took it over, it was already great, but Grayson and I made it into a diamond. There have been small renovations to the interior that keep with the charm but add to the opulence, but it's the outside that is the showstopper.

We've worked relentlessly to make the views stunning.

The biggest improvement we made was to the staff. Our chef is renowned, making this a perfect location for a date night or a corporate event. We hired a new gardener, who has made this place gorgeous, and we brought on a new activities coordinator who gave us more appeal to families.

My office faces the back of the property with a tree line and mountain views for days. I spend the next six hours going over paperwork, addressing complaints, and doing some billing. It's a nice day, filled with very few issues thanks to Jessica.

Hiring her might have driven Grayson crazy, but it is the best thing we have ever done. She's smart and has taken a lot of the burden off me. I get up, stretching my arms over my head and gazing at the sun, which is starting to move behind the bigger mountain top. I hear the buzzing on my cell and smile when I see it's my brother.

"Hey, Meatball," Alex's deep voice says on the other line.

"One day, you're going to stop calling me that."

He chuckles. "Not likely. You were shaped like a meatball as a child."

"I'm not a child anymore."

"You'll always be our meatball."

I roll my eyes. I hate brothers. "What do I owe the pleasure of your call?"

Alex launches into his concerns with the property he manages. It's doing well, but there's been a steady decline in bookings. The Savannah is beautiful, but where Dad put this particular inn makes it very destination oriented, especially since the main road leading from town to the property washed out over a year ago.

While the views are stunning, the drive is a nightmare, and it has led to a lot of complaints and the reviews online aren't favorable.

"Have you spoken with the mayor again?" I ask.

Alex has worked very hard to get the road repaired. None of us are sure why the mayor there is so against it, but he's blocked the funds each time.

"Yeah, he said that there are more pressing matters the town needs than a road that only benefits one proprietor."

"He's not wrong."

He groans. "He's not right either. It's going to be my ass that has to listen to why revenue is down."

"Do you want me to come out there? Is that what you're asking?"

My brothers are great, but their ability to just ask for help is sorely lacking.

"No, I don't need you to fix this. I just need you to tell me *how* to fix it."

I roll my eyes even though he can't see it. "Of course. First you need to figure out—" As I'm about to launch into the ways he needs to try to get this situation rectified, my phone beeps. "Hold on."

I look down at the number and my heart stops. It's Misty. She never calls.

"Alex, I need to call you back," I say quickly.

"Wait I need—"

I don't hesitate to click over.

"Misty?"

There's a sound at the end that I can't decipher, and then it's Samuel's voice. "Stella, I . . . I wanted to call because we just got your letter."

"Is everything okay?" I ask because his tone is off.

"No, it's . . . we lost her a few days ago."

My heart stops. Everything inside me is tight as the words roll around my head. "Lost who?"

Each breath feels as though someone is pulling razors from my chest and slicing me from the inside out. One. Two. Three. I wait, needing him to tell me he doesn't mean Kinsley. I can't . . . I can't live in a world where she isn't at least out there.

I plead with God, begging him not to let him say her name.

And then Samuel speaks between a sob. "Misty."

I shouldn't feel relief.

I shouldn't, but I do.

"What do you mean?" I ask, feeling breathless and uneasy.

"She went into the hospital because she was weak and her head hurt. It wasn't . . . she was . . . she's gone."

Even though there's a slight part of me that is grateful my daughter is fine, I'm shocked and heartbroken that Misty is gone. I don't understand how this happened. Her letter made it sound like she was okay. Why didn't she tell me?

We shared a kinship. An understanding between two

women who loved someone so much they put everything else aside. While she didn't birth Kinsley, she was her mom. While I wasn't her mom, I'm her mother.

"I don't know what to say. I'm so incredibly sorry."

He sniffs a few times, and when he speaks again, his voice is raw. "I don't know what to do without her. We were together thirty-six years. She was my world."

"Oh, Samuel, I don't know what to say."

"I don't either. She was doing better, and the treatment was working, but . . . here I am—without her and a single parent now."

He's a single parent. That thought sobers me. Their entire world is different now.

"How is Kinsley doing?" I ask, both hesitating to do it and knowing there is no way I could not ask.

Samuel clears his throat. "She's not holding up well. As much as I need Misty, Kinsley needs her more. Well, that's a lie, right now, I'm just in denial."

"I wish I could say something to make this better."

"Me too, but I wanted to tell you immediately."

"I'd like to—" I pause and then forge on. "I'd like to come pay my respects. I don't want to intrude or make things worse, so if you don't want me to . . ."

"No, please, come. Misty would've wanted you here."

"Just let me know when Kinsley won't be there. I don't want to confuse anyone."

"Of course, tomorrow is the first service. Kinsley will be at the morning one but not the evening service."

"I'll leave tonight so I can be there," I say quickly.

"She loved you, you know."

I do know. Even though I never went to visit, Misty became a great friend. Someone who I got to know a lot about over the years and who became more than just my daughter's adoptive mother. She was the only person in my life, other than Jack, my parents, and grandmother, who knew of Kinsley's existence. I could tell Misty about things, talk with her, feel like I was even somewhat a part of Kinsley's life, even if just from a distance.

My heart is breaking because I'm going to miss my friend.

A tear trickles down my face, and I wipe it away.

"I loved her too."

"As did I. And now," Samuel's voice shakes, "I have to learn to live without her, and I'm not sure I know how."

"I know you're in pain, but you have your family and friends to support you. Lean on them when you feel weak and of course, you can always talk to me. I know we weren't close, but you're extremely important to me, Samuel. I will always be here."

"Thank you, Stella."

"Of course, I'll see you tomorrow."

We hang up, and I sit here, looking out at the horizon that seems foreign to me. She was doing fine. She said that the doctors were happy with her prognosis. Misty had plans and a life, it wasn't fair that they were taken from her.

Dread and a mix of something else starts to take root. I am going to Georgia for the first time since that night. I'm going to see the town where two loving people took my daughter and loved her as though she came from them.

How am I going to handle this?

My phone pings with a text from Alex.

Alex: Thanks for hanging up on me, Meatball. Call me after you get Amelia to bed so we can talk through this.

Amelia.

Shit. I have Amelia for a few days.

I pace my office, trying to think of what to do. I have to

leave in an hour if I'm going to make it down there at a reasonable time. My mother is out of town, so she can't watch her. Jack has another wilderness tour going out tomorrow, so he's off the table.

There's really only one other person, and she owes me.

I text Winnie.

Me: Can you watch Amelia for me tonight? It's an emergency.

Winnie: I wish I could, but I have two client meetings that I can't reschedule. Is everything okay?

Me: I'm fine. I just need someone to keep Amelia. I have to go out of town, and it's important.

Winnie: I'm assuming you already went through the short list. You could always ask Jessica. She loves Amelia.

Of course. She'd be perfect. Amelia adores her and Grayson trusts her. Regardless of the dance they're doing, he knows she would never do anything to hurt his daughter. Still, the guilt of having to ask her eats at me.

I don't want to put Grayson in this predicament, but this isn't just some random thing. It's a funeral for the woman who has been a mother to my daughter. No matter how uncomfortable I am, I need to go.

Me: I know I said I'd watch Melia, but something has happened with a friend. I need to go out of town tonight. If this weren't an emergency, I wouldn't ask, but it is. Do you mind if I ask Jessica to watch Amelia tonight at my place?

The reply is immediate.

Grayson: *I have a million questions, but I know that you wouldn't be asking me if it weren't really important. So, yes, I am okay with that.*

I really love my brother. No matter what I've said in the past, he is an amazing human and I am so very lucky to call him family.

Me: *I love you. Thank you.*

Grayson: *We'll talk when I get back.*

I'm sure we will. I rush out of the room, suddenly propelled by the need to get out of town as fast as I can so I don't change my mind and hide.

I enter her office. "Oh, good! You're here. Thank God."

"What's wrong?" Jessica asks with wide eyes.

"I *need* you to help me."

She stands. "Of course, what's up?"

So much, but I can't tell her anything. I need to come up with something that makes sense and that she can't refuse. "I have to watch Amelia this weekend, but something has come up . . . an emergency with an old friend, but she has dance tonight and can't miss it."

"Okay . . ."

"I promise, I wouldn't ask you this if there were any way around it. If there was another option, I swear, Jess, I wouldn't do this. But I'm desperate, and I have to leave right away. I know it's a lot, but can you please take her for me?"

A moment passes between us, and I see the hesitancy in her gaze. "Where is Grayson?"

"We had a huge issue out in Wyoming with Oliver's property, and he flew out first thing this morning."

"Oh."

My heart is racing as I search for another angle, a way to reassure her. "Look, I know it's a big ask, and I wouldn't ask if I hadn't already cleared it with Grayson and he said it was fine if I had no other options, and I don't."

"What about Winnie?"

"Winnie said she's bogged down at work."

Please, Jessica. Please, I need you.

"You really have no one else?" she asks.

"I promise, I wouldn't ask if I did. I swear, if I didn't need to leave within the hour, I wouldn't do this."

"I can't drive," she says, the defeat in her voice makes me want to cry.

She's going to do this. She's going to help.

"I know. It's fine. I will drive you to my place and you can hang out with Melia there since it's in town and a block or two away from her dance studio. She has her own bedroom, and there's a guest room, so you'll be completely comfortable. *Please.*" I beg with my hands folded in front of my chest and then I go for the only thing that might sway her. "If you say no, I'll have to take her with me, and she'll be crushed that she's missing dance."

"I guess, but I still get nightmares and don't want to scare her."

Victory. Jessica is in, and I can get out of Willow Creek without anyone knowing what's going on.

"You won't. I promise. She would sleep through an entire army marching through her room."

"All right. As long as you swear Grayson is fine with it."

Five

STELLA

There's a hole in my chest, one that's getting larger the more it settles on me that Misty is gone. I got home, packed a bag, and made sure all the letters were in the safe. As I placed the last one in, tears fell relentlessly.

It's the last one that I will ever get from her.

I'm going to miss her.

Now, I'm standing on Jack's doorstep, turning to the one person who will understand. The only person in this town I can come to, and I pray he doesn't turn me away.

After a few seconds, I gather my courage and knock.

"One second." His deep voice booms from the other side of the door. There is some shuffling and a bang before he curses loudly.

Then the door opens, and my breath is stolen from my chest.

He's glorious. A God among men as he stands here, hair wet from the shower, chest bare, and basketball shorts slung low on his hips.

"Stella?" He tests my name as he stares at me.

"I . . ." I stumble over the words, not only because he seems to have scrambled my brain but also because the reason I'm here breaks through. "Misty, she . . . she died."

His eyes go wide, and he pulls the door open wider. I enter, and then as the door clicks and I turn, Jack's arms are around me.

I sink into his embrace, my head resting against the center of his chest as I listen to his heartbeat in my ear. I clutch at him, knowing that he's the only person alive who can understand the myriad of emotions racketing through me.

"She died, and I . . . I don't know what to do," I confess.

His hands move up and down my back as I inhale his clean soap and spice scent. God, he smells so damn good, feels so damn perfect, and I want to stay here *forever*.

The word whispers around my heart, but I push it down.

Jack isn't my forever.

He was my once.

"How? When?" he asks.

"The other day, but Samuel called me about it a few hours ago."

Jack releases me, taking the warmth of his body with him and leaving me colder than before.

He moves toward the window, running his fingers through his thick brown hair. When he turns to me, his eyes are filled with questions and hesitancy. "Are you okay?"

I shake my head. "I don't know. Are you?"

The sound of a half laugh and half sigh comes from his lips. "No. I don't know what to think."

"I'm going."

"Going where?" he asks.

"To Georgia. I need to pay my respects."

Jack's breathing grows labored as he stares at me. "What about her?"

After all this time, he still struggles to say her name. When we gave her away, he had to release everything about Kinsley. He has never mentioned her to me since. Part of me has hated him for it.

I've wanted him to live in the grief of giving her away the same as I have. Each year, her birthday passes, and each year, I spend it alone, crying and thinking of who she is. I've looked at her beautiful face in photos, always there, just on the cusp of my life but never a part of it.

Another part of me has envied him. How he's been able to just go on with life, pretending as if we never held her, loved her for those brief moments, and then clung to each other as we dealt with the pain of losing her. We both agreed to never speak of it. Not because we worried not only about my father's threats, but because it would change nothing.

All it would do is hurt people in our lives for lying and us for the fact we don't have her.

"I won't see her. I've already spoken to Samuel, and I'm going there now."

He shakes his head. "This is wrong, Stella."

"What?"

"You going there. It's a risk. What if she sees you?"

"Misty was my friend, Jack. I . . ."

"You're going for you."

I snap back at his words as though he's slapped me. "What?"

He closes his eyes, looking away as shame creeps in. "I shouldn't have said that. It's just that it feels like everything we've done is crumbling. We've spent years convincing ourselves that giving her away was the right thing, and now you're going to where she lives?"

"Screw you, Jack. If that were the case, I could've asked Misty if I could meet her anytime over the last twelve years. I've stayed away because it was the right thing, but going and paying my respects to the woman who has raised *our* daughter, well, that's the right thing too."

If there's nothing else I know in this world, at least I know that. Had we kept Kinsley in the lives we were living twelve years ago, nothing would be this way. I wouldn't have been able to give her anything. My father made it clear that, if I kept her, I wouldn't have any support. He would ensure my family cut me off and I would know exactly what it was like to be a single teenage mother. I would've been working in the factory, barely making ends meet. Jack would never have gotten the job he did out of college or risen up the corporate ladder as fast as he had.

Kinsley would've learned poverty and hunger, and I would've hated myself.

"I know."

"And so is this," I tell him. "Misty was more than just the adoptive mother to me, Jack. While you have gone on and forgotten, I haven't."

Anger flares in those gorgeous hazel eyes. "You think I've forgotten?"

"Haven't you?"

"Not a single fucking moment."

The statement threatens to derail me. "Well—" I stop, trying to gain my composure. "Well, she was my friend, and I'm sad, and I want to pay my respects to the woman who gave me a gift."

"And that's fine, but you're opening yourself up to destroying everything we've done this for."

My breath comes out in a loud huff. "The fuck I am. I already told you I wasn't going to see her, so what are you so worried about?"

"How about the fact that we've sacrificed everything for her. We've been fucking miserable for twelve years. When is the last time you dated? When is the last time I had . . ."

My heart begins to race and the question comes out, even though I wish I could stop it. "Had what?"

"Nothing."

I step toward him. My hand lifting just a fraction before I pull it back. I can't touch him like that, not the way I want to. The way my body craves him each time he's near isn't something I would be able to curb if I gave in to it. I've learned to live around a man I love, need, desire more than anything. I have refused to allow myself so much as a whisper of hope that he felt this way, and now I'm confused.

Being around him, watching him smile, and acting like I don't know what his lips feel like against mine, has been a millimeter away from impossible. I'm so tired of struggling to forget how his eyes were warm as we made love on my birthday.

Jack pinches the bridge of his nose and avoids the question. "I think this is a mistake. What if you see Kinsley? What if she sees you?"

"I'm going to do everything I can to avoid that. Samuel said she was not going to the night service, which is when I'll go."

"And again, if she sees you?"

"Then I'll do what I've been doing the last twelve years . . . I'll lie."

The only person I am lying to is myself.

The parking lot of the funeral home is packed, and there's a group of people by the cars, hugging and dabbing their eyes with tissues.

I look around, hoping to see a little girl with long brown hair and eyes like her father's just as fiercely as I hope I don't.

What a fool I am.

I exit my car, smoothing my dress, and draw a steadying breath.

I can do this. She's not here, and if she is, I need to act casual.

Walking to the door, I keep my gaze down. Misty was a school teacher before she left to raise Kinsley. I will just use that as my reason if anyone asks who I am.

When I enter the room, there are almost a hundred people milling around. There are some wiping their eyes and others smiling. I'd like to imagine they're remembering stories of Misty.

I get in line, still keeping my head down as I move closer to the casket. There, on thick velvet chairs in the front row, sits a man, staring at the casket. Samuel's grief is so deep that I feel it in my soul.

When I get up there, I rest my knees on the hassock and look at the woman who has meant so much to me.

"Oh, Misty," I whisper, ensuring no one else can hear me. "I'm so sorry. I wish I had told you more times how much I loved and admired you. I should've thanked you more for all you did. There is nothing I can ever say that would be enough." I lift my hand to my lips and then place it on the edge of the casket. "Goodbye, my friend. Please watch over us all."

I push to my feet and make my way to Samuel. When he sees me, he stands. "Stella."

I give him a sad smile as tears brim against my lashes. "I'm so sorry."

He nods, his own tears spilling over. "I can't live in a world without her."

The pain in his voice is almost too much to bear. "She loved you very much."

"I was a lucky man."

Misty often spoke of how hard things were for them before

Kinsley. They had tried for years to have a baby, leaving them broke and also broken. She suffered through six miscarriages, and each one stole more hope from them both. Samuel took each loss as though he were at fault and Misty couldn't do it anymore. They had been passed over three times by other pregnant mothers, which drove distance between them. Still, their love was strong enough to get through it, and then, when they thought they'd learned to live without a child, they got the call that I wanted to meet them.

"I think you were both lucky in that regard."

"It seems my luck ran out." His gaze returns to Misty's body.

He's wrong, he still has something precious to love.

He forces a smile as he looks to me. "Did you come alone?"

I hear the real question: Is Jack here?

"Yes, I have to return tonight."

"I understand. It's good that you came. Misty would've wanted you here."

I settle a hand on his shoulder, smiling softly. "There's nothing that could've kept me from paying my respects to a woman I cared so much for."

"I appreciate that. I really do." Samuel sighs after a moment, looking weary. "I don't know what life is going to be like anymore. Kinsley . . . she . . . she's struggling, and I don't know how to help her."

A pang in my chest keeps me from speaking. I know he's struggling, but being here, thinking about Kinsley, is almost too much. "You're a great father. I'm sure you'll give her what she needs."

He shakes his head. "She needs her mother."

I'm right here.

No.

No. No. I am not her mother. I am nothing to Kinsley. I'm a stranger who gave up any claim to that girl.

"I should go," I say as self-preservation kicks in. I don't belong here, and the sooner I leave, the better it will be for everyone.

He gives me a quick hug before the next person waiting to pay their respects to him steps forward. I start to walk out the door, looking back one last time at Misty.

My heart aches. Everything about this is wrong. She was the best of us, and she's leaving two people who need her.

When I turn back, leaving to head back to my life, I see her.

A little girl.

Twelve.

Brown hair, hazel eyes, and long, dark lashes. She's staring at me as if she knows me.

Jack was right. Coming here was a mistake.

I force a smile, as though I don't know who she is . . . as if she didn't come from my heart and soul, and start to walk. My lips press tight, refusing to speak to her because, if I do, I have no idea what I'll say.

Does she know who I am?

Does she suspect I'm her mother?

Did she show up tonight, wondering if I would come?

I should've stayed in Willow Creek.

I exit the funeral home, drawing shallow breaths as I move quickly but not so fast that I draw attention, and get into my car.

Keeping my eyes down, I start it, and then as I pull out, I see her standing there watching me, and I leave her again, hating myself even more.

Six

JACK

The woods usually offer me peace from my thoughts, but this trip has been hell. Twelve days out there did nothing to quiet the chaos in my head.

I wondered, worried, wished to call her, but I couldn't. There is no reception where I take these people. If they could get ahold of someone, then the entire point of a survival trip would be moot.

So, I also endured the struggle.

I wash away the dirt that seems embedded in my skin, scrubbing and trying to get clean, all while debating whether I should've gone to see Stella first.

Once clean, I drive over to her loft, climbing the steps two at a time, not wanting to waste another second.

She opens the door, surprise in her eyes. "What are you doing here?"

"Can I come in?"

Stella sighs deeply and takes a step back as the door opens wider. Stella's house is warm. That's the word that always surrounded her anyway. It's vanilla and cookies and campfires. She's the comfort when everything is a mess, and still, she's not for me.

"What's wrong?" Her voice is distant, showing me her hurt.

"Nothing. I came to check on you."

I've thought of little else since she left that night. I've wondered if going had hurt her. If she saw our *daughter*. All of this went around in my head, hating that she was there. That she might get to look at her, hug her, talk to her. Just that thought makes me clench my fists, needing to control the emotions that build because I don't have a right to be jealous. I made my choice to erase Kinsley from my mind in order to fucking breathe.

She swallows and then turns from me. "I'm fine."

"You're not."

She whips around, eyes blazing. "Of course I'm not. You've been gone! Gone again. And I'm . . ."

"You're what?"

Her lip trembles, and my fucking heart breaks. "Stella?"

"Samuel just called."

"What did he say?"

"He's struggling. He's alone with a little girl who wants to know who her birth parents are."

I don't say a word, mostly because I'm not sure what the hell to say. "How did they handle it before?"

"Misty never said, but she saw me, Jack. She looked into my eyes and . . . God, she saw me, and I ran."

There's shame in her eyes, and I wish I could take it away from her. "I'm sorry, Stella. I'm sorry for all of it."

I never should've touched her that night. I've apologized countless times, and it still isn't enough. Stella wouldn't have had to bear the fallout from it. Every conversation with her parents. Every appointment I missed because I was stuck in college and couldn't be there. Then she was sent away to live with her grandmother while she waited to give birth.

I haven't suffered even a quarter of what she has. And I'm so fucking sorry for it.

Stella rubs her face, moving away. "She's beautiful."

"I always knew she would be." She came from Stella, after all.

Tears form in those beautiful brown eyes. She's in so much pain, and I'm helpless to save her. "She looks like you."

I close my eyes, imagining a version of Stella and me, hating the vision as it appears. "What did Samuel say?" I ask again, needing to get to a topic I can actually focus on.

"He was drunk. I don't know that he even knew what he was saying. He's in pain and he's lost."

I imagine how I would feel if Stella was taken from this world. How I would want to rip my heart from my chest because it wouldn't be worth anything anymore. I would want to be in that hole beside her, and I haven't spent thirty years by her side. I've just loved her from afar.

To anyone who knows us, we're indifferent to each other. I like her fine enough as my best friend's little sister, but nothing more.

She definitely doesn't feel anything for me. I've taken from her, and she will never forgive me. Not that I would ask her to.

Yet, here I am, unable to stay away from the one person I should leave in peace. The woman who makes me weak because my love for her is so strong.

"He'll be okay after some time has passed."

Stella shrugs. "Hopefully." After a few seconds, she speaks again. "Why did you really come here, Jack?"

"I told you."

Because I hate when you suffer.

"You don't want to talk about her."

"I can't."

"Why?"

I look into her brown eyes, wishing I were a better man. A stronger one. One who could say fuck everyone and everything and lay my heart out for her, but Stella made up her mind a long time ago about us when we realized the mistake we made. Then we sealed our fate the day we gave up Kinsley. Thinking about Kinsley makes me remember too much about how much I love Stella, and God knows I need to forget.

"It was the worst day of our lives, Stella. Do you want to live it again?"

She sits on the couch as if the weight of the world is too much. "Some days, I feel like it was a dream or maybe more like a nightmare. Either way, it doesn't feel real. It's easy to go on with my life, pretending that we don't have a child. And then—" She pauses, her eyes glistening with unshed tears. "I see you with Melia. I watch you lift her into the air, kiss her cheeks, and love her. I . . ."

"I know." I stop her, needing her not to say it. "But Amelia isn't our daughter."

"No, she's not."

"It wouldn't have been that way for us," I remind her of why we did this.

She nods, looking away. "Probably not."

"Definitely not, Stella. Your father threatened to take it all away from you. We would've been completely on our own. Your brother never would've forgiven me. We would . . ."

"We would what?"

Have loved.

In a perfect world, we would've been together. I would've said to hell with Grayson, her family, that was essentially my family, and school. I would've married her, given her whatever life I could, and we would have been together. But we don't live in a perfect world. We live in this tragically imperfect one.

"We would've struggled," I finish.

"We could've had each other."

"Could we, Stell? Could we have really had each other without destroying everything? Would you have wanted that? We were kids, and we didn't have a fucking clue."

"I would've wanted the moments," she confesses. "I would've wanted whatever we could've had." Stella gets to her feet, wrapping her arms around her stomach. "I wanted them. I was too young to fight for them, but the moments, Jack, they're what matter."

And with that, she opens the door, clearly asking for me to leave.

I go because I have spent the last twelve years walking away from her, letting the action steal one more sliver of my heart as I do.

But when I get outside, I stop and turn. "What would our moment have been?"

She leans her head against the door, a sad, wistful smile on her lips. "I don't know. I guess maybe we had our moment, didn't we? We loved each other one time. One night. That moment is all we'll ever have. I'm tired and need to get some sleep. Good night, Jack."

I want so badly to pull her into my arms, to hold her close to me, kissing her until neither of us can fucking breathe, but I don't. I return her smile, hating how easy it comes. "Good night, Stella."

"Those boots can't get much cleaner," Grayson notes as I wipe the toe harder.

"They can always be cleaner."

"To go back into the fire?"

I shrug. It's giving me something to do. Something to stop

myself from replaying the conversations I've had in the last week.

I was a fucking idiot. I said too much, and while he thinks it was Misty I was talking about regarding moments, it wasn't.

I want the moments with her.

With Stella.

Tonight's fire took a lot from me. I didn't realize how much I needed to expel this energy.

Then there's the fact that Stella disappeared again today, and I have a feeling she didn't tell anyone because she's in Georgia—again.

Grayson puts his hand on my shoulder. "Listen, about the other night . . ."

Fucking hell, he knows. He knows that I was at Stella's late at night or he heard something from Delia and Jess.

"I can . . ."

"No, listen, what you said about taking a chance and living in the moments instead of the end was some profound shit coming from you." He laughs, and I nod. "But you were right. I've been so worried about Jessica leaving that I forgot to focus on the fact that she's here now."

Relief that it's not what I thought ripples through me. This is a topic I can manage. If one of us can be happy, then it should be him.

"Did you talk to her about this?"

He nods. "She told me she loves me. Before I got in the car to come on this call."

I laugh because he seems surprised. The two of them have been in love since they were freaking teenagers. "And?"

"And . . . I don't know, maybe she won't go. Maybe . . . maybe I'm a fool."

"Isn't that the saying about being in love, it makes us fools?"

Grayson snorts. "That's the fucking truth."

"Well, we've known that about you for a long time."

"Enough about me and love, what about you? You've been distant and missed a few pizza nights."

I have been. I'm missing my usual fuck-it-all type attitude. The last few weeks haven't allowed that.

"I'm fine. It's been crazy with work and just . . . memories."

That's the closest I'm getting to confessing anything.

He sighs deeply. "I get it. Sometimes they creep up on us."

"Yeah."

"Lately, I've been thinking of Yvonne," Grayson admits.

My head jerks back. He never mentions her. "You what?"

"Amelia is growing, becoming more and more of her own person. I don't know." He runs his fingers through his hair, nervous energy around him. "I wonder if I'm fucking it all up. I'm a dude. What the hell do I know about raising a daughter?"

"You think her mother would do a better job?"

Grayson looks away. "No. I don't, and she proved that when she left almost five years ago. How could she ever walk away from her? How could a woman give up her daughter without giving a shit? It blows my mind."

I work extremely hard to keep my voice even. "Maybe she believed she was doing the right thing?"

He laughs without humor. "Yeah, the right thing for her. Not Amelia. She needed her fucking mother. She needed her, and Yvonne walked away. She's a piece of shit, but she still is her mother."

The fact that he's unaware of the parallel he just drew between his ex and Stella makes me want to rage and defend her. While I don't think Yvonne, who literally walked away from Grayson and Amelia because she wanted a job, and Stella, who was a kid trying to do the right thing for her daughter, are the same thing, it pisses me off.

Also, I've never once defended Yvonne, and I can't start

now.

"Yvonne was selfish. She doesn't deserve Amelia."

"No, but . . . I don't know that anyone who walks away from their kids do."

"What about adoption? Don't you think there are valid reasons?"

Grayson seems surprised. "Of course there are. Yvonne didn't give her daughter up for adoption. She abandoned her because she wanted a career and Amelia didn't fit into that."

I rub the brush against the tip of the boot a little harder. "In the end, I think her walking away was the best thing that happened to you and Amelia."

He claps his hand on my shoulder. "I think so too because, if not, I wouldn't have Jess and I wouldn't be taking them to the beach house."

I glance up at him as he smiles. "You're going away, the three of you?"

He nods. "It'll allow me to show Jessica what we could be if she'll stay."

"She'll stay," I tell him.

"I hope so, but if she won't, then I'll let her go and hope she returns."

"Which is all any of us can do, right?"

"Yeah. I guess it is."

It's all I've been doing the last twelve years—letting Stella go and hoping one day I'll be good enough for her.

Seven

STELLA

"Samuel?" I shake him, careful not to jostle him hard enough to knock him from the bar stool he's passed out in. "Samuel, wake up."

He moans, and the bartender looks at me. "He kept saying someone was coming," he explains.

"How long as he been like this?" I ask.

"Weeks. His wife died, and he's been here daily. He cries a lot, more than anyone I've ever seen, and drinks until the tears stop."

Jesus.

"And how does he normally get home?"

The bartender hands me a sheet of paper. "This is his version of an emergency card. The first number was his brother, who lives in Arizona. He usually called him a cab. Today, he wouldn't pick up, so I called the only other number listed, which is yours."

I let out a soft breath and look down at Samuel. He's a mess, and I'm not sure what the hell to do. Clearly, he needs help.

"Samuel," I say again, a little more forcefully.

His eyes open, and the smell of alcohol on his breath when he speaks is enough to make me drunk. "Stella. You came."

"Yes, but what is going on?"

"She's dead."

"Yes, Misty is gone, but you're drunk at five on a Thursday. What are you doing?"

He closes his eyes, resting his head on his fist. "I'm forgetting."

"Are you?" I say as more rhetorical than anything.

His head wobbles from his fist and falls forward, hitting the hard bar, causing him to snap back upright. "You can have her."

"Have her?" I ask with a mix of fear.

"Yeah, you can have Kinsley."

"Samuel, stop. Where is she?"

"At a friend's for dinner. It doesn't matter. I can't do it. I'm done now."

"Yes, you're done now. We need to get you cleaned up and sober."

Samuel shrugs and looks at the bartender. "Mickey, can you get Stella something to clean?"

Mickey's eyes fill with sympathy. "Do you need help?" he asks.

"Please. I don't know where to go, but he's . . ."

He nods. "Are you his daughter?"

"No." I struggle to explain because the way Mickey is looking at me makes me think he assumes I'm something else. "I'm a friend who was close with his wife."

"I don't judge," Mickey says, a hint of disbelief in his voice.

"I'm not that. I promise, it's complicated, but his wife was a good friend and . . . whatever. I don't need to explain myself to you."

There are bigger issues than some random bartender in Georgia thinking I'm Samuel's mistress. Things like trying to get a two-hundred-and-fifty-pound man back home without my—his—daughter recognizing me.

Thankfully, it's only five, so it should be a few hours before she's home.

"Again, I don't judge," Mickey says, trying to help me lift Samuel off the stool.

"Samuel, we need you to help just a little," I say as I try to pull him up.

He groans and then stumbles a bit.

"Once you get him into the car, I doubt you'll get him out," Mickey notes.

"Want to make five hundred bucks?" I ask, knowing this is my only option. I need help getting him home, into his house, showered, and into his bed before Kinsley shows up.

"What?" he asks.

I tell him my plan, and he looks at me like I'm insane. I might just be, but I'm desperate and Samuel and Misty were—are—important to me. If she were alive, this would not be happening, but she's gone, and I owe her.

The least I can do is get him sobered up.

"You can't be serious."

"One thousand," I say, upping my initial assessment of how bad this could be. I need his help, and I'm willing to pay for it.

"Sweetheart, you got yourself a deal." He calls back to the other bartender, explaining he has to help me, and the other guy agrees to cover for him.

With that taken care of, Mickey and I work quickly to get him into the car. Then comes trying to figure out how to get into his house since there's no house keys on his set.

I did not think this through.

Mickey is at the car door, looking at me as I search around for a key. "You can't get in his house?"

I sigh. "Clearly not."

"You're a very bad mistress."

"Well, that's because I'm not a mistress," I reply as I swipe my fingers along the top of the door.

Misty was a practical person, she'd have a spare key somewhere.

"Do you know the garage code or the front door one?"

I turn, glaring at him. "If I did, I would've opened it." Of course he has one of those fancy keyless entries.

However, most codes are birthdays, and there's one birthday that's important to them that I know. It's worth a shot. I walk over and lift the lid to the keys. "Please let this work," I whisper.

Sure enough, the hum of the motor revs and the door lifts.

Mickey walks over, his voice in my ear. "Impressive."

I roll my eyes. "I'm paying you for help, not comments."

Thank God the door to the house is unlocked. After a lot of effort, we get Samuel inside the house, but his legs give out when we enter.

"Stella, she's gone," he says from the floor. "I need you . . . I need . . ."

Mickey and I look down at him, and the smug bartender is grinning as he turns back to me.

"Think what you want." I shrug. "He needs to shower and to eat before he passes out and sleeps it off."

In a move I've seen my brother and Jack practice a million times, Mickey hoists Samuel up over his shoulder. "Where's the shower?"

"I have no idea."

That's the moment it hits me. I'm in their home. The place where Misty and Samuel have raised Kinsley. In all the years I've imagined her life, I never once thought I would step into it.

Their living room is quaint and cute. The couch is old, well loved, and clearly, a place where they watched movies or snuggled as they opened Christmas presents.

The kitchen is right off that room. It's dated but still gives an air of comfort. The oak cabinets need to be replaced, and the countertops are not in fashion, but it's clear that cookies were baked here and Thanksgiving dinners were cooked in the oven.

Misty is everywhere. Her touch, warmth, and spunky personality fills the rooms around us.

"Let's try the back," I suggest.

The house is a modest ranch home, and from where we entered, the only way to go is straight, so that's where we head.

We walk through the home, opening doors and closing them when we discover it's not the master bedroom. There's a spare room that doubles as a sewing or craft room. Another empty bedroom, a hall bathroom, and then we get to where the house bends to the right and leads to a short hallway with two doors. I open the one to the right, thinking it has to be the master.

It's Kinsley's.

The light gray walls are covered with posters. Most of them are of some soccer player who I don't know, and there's a board with push pins securing various flyers. There is also a white desk in the corner with books stacked high on top of it, a full-size bed with a sage-colored comforter.

"Stella?" Mickey calls my name, pulling me from the room.

"Yes?"

"He's fucking heavy."

I shake my head, closing the door as I exit and forcing myself back to the task. "Only one door left."

We push through, and thankfully, it's his. The bedroom is a

mess—clothes strewn all over the floor and the pillows tossed off the bed. Even though I've never been in this house, I know this isn't the way the room usually looked.

"Oh, Samuel," I say on a sigh.

He's in pain. So much so that he's drowning himself in alcohol. I understand, to a point, wanting to ignore the pain of loss. It's deep and can take you under, but he has to remember why he can't.

He needs to clean himself up and handle this.

For Kinsley.

Mickey and I enter the master bathroom. I turn on the cold water, and he doesn't hesitate before dropping Samuel down onto the bench. Samuel jerks awake, trying to move out from under the spray.

We block him, forcing him to sit under the water. "You're drunk, and you have to clean yourself up before your daughter gets home," I tell him.

His eyes focus on me for a moment. "Stella?"

"Yes?"

A sob rips from his chest. "She's dead, and I can't do this."

"You've said that already, and I'm telling you now that you *have* to do this." There's no room for another option. "You have to pull yourself together."

I've dealt with drunk men before. I have four older brothers who I've sobered up many times, and Samuel needs the same treatment.

"I'm done."

I turn the handle to warmer now that he's at least semi aware. "Shower first, then we'll talk. I'll be back in twenty minutes, get dressed with the clothes I put out."

Mickey and I leave the bathroom, and I lean against the wall. "What now?" he asks.

"Now, I need to clean up this room, get him to eat and drink, and get the fuck out of here before his daughter comes home."

I start on the bedroom since the rest of the house didn't seem too bad. I put some clothes away, change the sheets, and make the bed, leaving the side that appears to be Samuel's down. Mickey is in the kitchen, searching for something to help absorb the booze in Samuel's system.

Twenty minutes pass before I hear the water shut off, and I knock. "Samuel?"

He grunts.

I really do not want to go in there. Mickey comes back in with some bread, water, and Tylenol. "This will help a little."

"Yeah, it's something. He's not coming out."

He raises his brows. "You think I should get him?"

"Yes. I don't want to see him naked."

"And I do?"

I shrug. "Better you than me."

Before we can argue about it more, Samuel pushes the door open. He still is a mess, but at least he doesn't smell like a dumpster soaked in alcohol. I guide him to the bed, thankful he listened.

"Here, eat." I shove the plate into his hands.

"I'm sorry, Stella." Samuel's voice breaks. "I wish I was stronger."

"You are stronger," I remind him. "Misty loved you. She always had faith in you. You have to stop drinking and start taking care of things."

A tear falls down his cheek. "I don't know how to do this anymore. She handled everything. She was my everything and now she's dead and I can't do it."

He keeps saying this, but he's forgetting why he has no choice but to pull his shit together. "Kinsley needs you to do it, Samuel."

Samuel puts the food on the side table and sinks into the bed, his eyes closing as he clutches a pillow. "I . . . just . . ."

"Shh," I croon. Not wanting him to repeat what he seems to think is his new mantra. He can. I know he can. He just needs to sober up and try again.

"You're going to be okay," I tell Samuel while we sit at the diner.

After Kinsley left for school, I went back over, picked him up, and we started the mission to get him back to the Samuel before Misty's death.

Samuel called his boss, who lost his wife two years ago. Thankfully, Samuel was granted a bit of time to get himself together. The job is shut down for a permit issue anyway, so it works out. He needs to heal and find a way through his grief.

Then I hired a cleaning company that will come twice a week for the first month and then weekly after that. Mickey, my new Georgia best friend, has agreed to call me if Samuel shows up at the bar again, get him home, and sober him up. For a very nice price.

As much as I hate the idea of asking someone else to look out for Samuel, there isn't much I can do from five hours away.

The worst part is that he's alone. He has no family close by, and no friends outside of work. Everything that Samuel has was Misty's doing. She knew everyone's name, birthday, and anniversary. She ran their home, always taking care of life, and he doesn't know what to do now.

And they say men are stronger than women.

"I'm not the same as I was," he says, taking a sip of the coffee.

"No one is after they lose the love of their life."

I would know. The girl I was who thought money and fairy tales were possible died the day I gave up my child. I learned that nothing I had was worth anything in the end. My father made me believe I had no choice, forced my hand, and in doing so, he changed me.

"I just want to be numb," Samuel admits.

"This isn't you. This isn't the man Misty talked about. You're the man who worked for everything and was always there for her. Now, your daughter needs you."

He shakes his head. "Your daughter."

I blink, unsure of what he means because Kinsley is his. "I'm . . . I'm not . . ."

"No, you are. She needs a mother. She needs someone who will take care of her. Do you know who cleaned the kitchen? The bathroom? Do you know who made sure there was breakfast last week? That's not what a father allows. That's . . . I can't."

I shift in my seat. This conversation isn't going where I thought it would. "You are the only father she has ever known. I came here to help, but I gave her to you, and you *are* her parent."

His gaze is far away when he answers. "I know."

Relief fills me because, as much as I want the girl I gave away in my life, it's not what's best for her. She needs the man who has been the constant in her life to continue to do that.

"Then you'll get some help? You'll talk to someone to get through this?" I ask.

Samuel reaches his hand to mine, squeezing. "I'll try."

And I pray that will be enough.

STELLA

This date is a disaster.

Winnie is a damn maniac for making me come along on this crap. I'm pretty sure this guy is over fifty, and he keeps talking about his kid, who is about my age.

On top of that, I'm exhausted and ready to sleep for a week. I got home from Georgia a few days ago, and I haven't been able to sleep because I've been waiting for Mickey to call me. So far, it's been quiet, which makes me hopeful.

"And I told my kid I wasn't paying for his college. I've noticed that most of your generation all think life should be easy. Well, it's not."

I nod and take a sip of my drink. "Nope. It's not."

"So, did your parents pay for your college?"

I grin, knowing this is going to chap his ass. "They did. They paid for all five of their kids to go to school."

It was the one thing my father was adamant about. He thought that if he paid for school, we'd be indebted to him to work, regardless of whatever other aspirations we had. The rule was that, if he paid for our education, we were to work for Parkerson Enterprises for at least seven years after college or we pay every penny back.

The sad part is, we are all well past that obligation and all still work for him. With the salaries we make, it's hard to walk away.

But, oh, I wish we would.

His face falls. "You're one of those?"

"I'm not sure what that means, Tripp."

"You know, you don't work. You probably live at home like my leech of a child."

"Well, considering I'm the general manager of an inn, I think I work hard. Also, I bought my own house."

That seems to mollify him slightly. "Oh, good for you."

I don't mention that my parents own the inn I work for because it doesn't matter. I still bust my ass and make sure I earn every penny I make. I scrimped and saved for my own down payment on the house. I didn't take any help from them, and the very nice nest egg I have now is from putting aside money and not being wasteful. I refused to accept anything that would land me indebted to my father ever again.

"Yes, I guess it is."

Winnie and her date, who I'm starting to suspect is Tripp's son, come back, her hand on his chest as she laughs. "Oh, Stella, Easton here was just telling me about this concert he went to."

Easton's grin is mischievous. "We snuck in the back to meet the band."

"And then they were mistaken for the crew," Winnie finishes.

"Oh?" I say, feigning curiosity. Although, maybe I'm not faking it because anything out of Easton's mouth is going to be better than whatever good ole Tripp here has to say.

"Yeah, so we had to help, but then we drank their beer and

hung out the whole night without anyone figuring it out. Free beer and the band without actually buying a ticket. It was a good night."

Okay, I know my best friend, and she does not find this story amusing. Winnie works harder than I do, and she absolutely hates when people steal.

"So you saw a concert—free and then drank their beer and lied?"

Easton's face falls slightly. "It wasn't like that."

Winnie gives me a look that screams *shut up, asshole*. She must really be lonely. So, I smile at her as she rolls her eyes.

"I'm going to grab a beer," I explain as I get up.

Tripp looks at me, lifting his. Is he kidding? "You don't mind, do ya?"

"Nope. I love leeches," I say as I walk away.

Asshole.

Here he is going on and on about his kids taking his money and he expects me to pay for his shit. Some freaking date.

I get up to the bar and order a drink.

"You look happy," Jack says from beside me.

His voice causes me to jump a little. "Jesus, you scared the shit out of me."

He laughs as he takes a drink from his beer. "I figured you saw me."

"I've been stuck talking to someone all night, I didn't know you were even in town."

"I haven't been the one missing. Grayson said you were gone again?"

This time, I hadn't told Jack about my trip. There was no need because no matter what kind of crap he would have said, I was going.

"I was."

"Where were you?"

I shift, facing him more head-on. "Why do you care?"

"I don't."

At that, I grin. "Sure you don't." His hand rests on the bar in front of me, close enough that, if he extended his fingers, he could touch me. Oh, how I wish he would. I lean forward, unable to resist. "If you didn't care, you wouldn't be asking."

"How is your date?"

Horrible. I should say it. I should be honest and let him know that I'm fucking miserable and would like to punch this dude in the face, but I lie.

"I don't know, we'll see if he passes the test."

Jack's eyes move to where Tripp is. "What test?"

My voice is low. "The one where I see if he comes home with me."

I grab my drink and walk back to the table, forcing my face forward. Jack may not want me. He may think I'm still a little girl who is untouchable, but that doesn't mean I don't want to piss him off.

I settle back onto my seat, and Tripp tosses his arm around the back of my chair. I end up giving him my beer since I forgot to get him one and there isn't a chance in hell I am going back over to where Jack is.

But I can feel him. In this tiny bar, he is looming and large. His presence, the way he pulls the air, commanding it to form around him, makes me feel as if the oxygen is missing. Each breath leaves me dizzy, and I hate him.

Why? Why do I feel like this?

I want to scream at the injustice of it all. I *know* better. I'm not an idiot. I know how this works.

Tripp and Easton get up, leaving for the bar to get another round or talk how they think they're going to get laid, who knows, and Winnie flops down beside me. "I owe you."

"That's an understatement, my friend."

"I really like him."

"Easton? Really?"

"I know, he's kind of a dork, but he's sweet, and it's been a really long time since I've gotten laid."

I laugh because no matter how long she's gone, I've got her beat. It's not that I don't have offers or that I haven't hooked up with guys here and there, but it never goes further than that. It's not that I don't lie and pretend that I'm getting it constantly. It's that I can't seem to get myself there. I'm terrified of getting pregnant again. I'm more afraid that I won't feel like I did that first time.

Safe. Loved. Needed by a man who cared for me.

Jack.

As though we're planets, being pulled by a force greater than us, our eyes meet.

A million things go through my mind. Things I wish I could tell him.

I love you.

I need you.

I'm sorry for everything. Please, let's try . . . just try. Love me, I'm right here.

But those things will never be spoken because Jack doesn't love me. He doesn't want me or need me.

Winnie looks up at me. "Hey, Stell?"

"Yeah?"

She looks over at Easton, her bottom lip between her teeth. "I think I'm going to be leaving in a few, but are you okay to drive?"

"Yes, why?"

"I think . . . I won't need a ride."

"Be safe," I tell her.

"I will."

"Call me tomorrow so I know he didn't kill you with an ax and bury you in the woods somewhere."

Winnie laughs. "Well, hopefully he'll kill me in another way."

I roll my eyes. "Please, if he had those skills, you wouldn't have a chance with him. The girl before you would be dying in his bed tonight."

Winnie grins as she stands. "I'll be sure to let you know."

Yeah, I'm sure she won't.

She heads over toward Easton, and I take this moment to head into the bathroom and splash water on my face, grateful I can tell Tripp to get lost and head home. There's a pint of ice cream and a book waiting for me on my ereader. My favorite author released this week, and I've been dying to see if the heroine forgives the hero from the last book.

I nearly groan as I look at myself in the mirror. My eyes are puffy, the shade of blue under my eyes does nothing to help, and I look like shit. Seriously, I should've stayed the hell home tonight.

Well, no time like the present to do just that.

I exit the bathroom and slam into someone. "I'm sorry!" I say quickly as I stagger back, but a pair of arms wrap around me.

Arms I know.

Arms that I will never forget.

And then there's the scent. Warm, clean, with a hint of spice . . . Jack.

I look up into the hazel eyes that always make me feel safe.

There is something in his gaze that keeps me from moving even a muscle.

"Fuck it," he says, and then my back is against the wall. His body, hot and pressed against me, keeps me there. Before I can gasp or think, Jack's lips are on mine.

His kiss is hard and full of want—I'm floating toward heaven. My hands are trapped against his chest, giving me nothing to hold on to but him. I moan into his mouth, savoring the taste of whiskey, oak, and vanilla on his tongue.

His heart is pounding against my palm, the steady thrum

my talisman that he is real. I'm not dreaming because dream Jack doesn't feel this good.

And it feels good. It's too damn much.

I want this kiss to never end. I don't care that we're in the hallway of the bar and anyone can see. I want him. Every muscle in my body is screaming that this is right and perfect.

Jack's tongue swipes against mine again, pushing deeper into my mouth. His hand moves down my side, leaving a trail of heat as it passes. Then he hooks his hand under my thigh, pulling the jean-clad leg up around his hip, letting me feel his erection.

Yes. The word screams in my head.

He wants me, and God how I want him.

His lips move down my neck, and I force myself not to speak. If this is all I'll ever get again, then I'm not going to do anything to break the moment. However, he's freed my hands, and I move them up his chest, over the scruff on his cheeks, and then tangle them in his hair.

"Stella." Jack's voice is gruff. "God, what you do to me."

I arch my back, giving him better access to my neck as he continues to kiss down it. "Tell me," I speak, knowing it's a risk but not caring.

"I'm not supposed to like you."

Supposed. The word hangs there, and I cling to it.

"I shouldn't be touching you, but . . ."

"But what?" I say so quietly, I'm not sure he heard.

He keeps kissing me, now moving back up. "You taste like sin, and touching you makes me the devil, but I can't stop."

"Don't," I beg.

His mouth is back on me, hands clutching at my back, pushing his hardness against my core.

"I don't even want to like you," he says again, his warm breath against my ear this time. "I want to forget you. I . . . fuck . . . I—" Jack steps back, as though he were just suddenly awoken from a dream.

The loss of his heat causes me to suck in a breath. My thoughts are jumbled as we stare at each other. I want to say so much, beg him to come back, to love me, just for tonight. But, as though he can read my mind, he shakes his head.

"This. You and me." His lips are a thin line before he turns his back to me, slamming his hand on the wall. "Fuck!"

I step to him, my hand on his back. He flinches. "So, this is how it is?" I ask, suddenly no longer confused. Now I'm just angry.

"What?"

"You and I keep doing this dance. We pretend, we fake it, we act as though we don't even like each other, and yet . . ."

He shakes his head. "Yet what?"

"Coward," I spit the word at him.

"No, I'm not afraid, I'm the opposite. I know better than anyone what it's like to take a chance on more."

I laugh once. "Sure you do. Tell me, do you want me right now?"

Jack's eyes roam my body, the heat telling me that no matter what he says, the truth is there. "Any man would."

As Winnie always says, a drunk man's words are a sober man's thoughts. The alcohol just allows the words to finally be free.

"I'm not asking any man. I'm asking you. Do you want me?"

"Like the fucking air I breathe."

Well, I'm going to take full advantage of this then. "For how long?"

His eyes widen, and then he leans against the wall. The movement seems to change something in him. He's no longer out of control. Instead, he's steady, confident, as he presses the sole of one shoe to the wall behind him. "Go home, Stella. We're done making mistakes for tonight."

"That's what I am? A mistake?"

One shoulder lifts and then falls. "Not you, but this? Us? It's all we ever make."

Nine

JACK

Fucking hell the sunlight is loud.

I know that thought isn't coherent, but there it is. Everything is loud from the way my body is moving against the sheets to the dull noise of a television in the background. Wait. Where the hell am I?

Slowly opening my eyes, I see the familiar view from Grayson's guest room.

Great.

All I remember is watching Stella walk away last night, her back straight, the arrow I shot landing exactly as I needed it to. She was so hurt by the words I threw at her that I hated myself for them.

Then I went back to the bar and drank until I couldn't remember the look she gave me after what I said.

I lie here, arm slung over my eyes, and try to think about how I got here. It's clear someone called me a cab or gave me a ride. Was it Delia?

No. I don't think I called her. At least, I hope I didn't because that's one more person I might have said some stupid shit to.

God only knows what I said to Gray.

The door flies open, and Amelia flies into the room, a huge smile on her face.

"Uncle Jack, are you awake yet?" she asks softly, but it still feels like she's screaming.

"Nope."

She laughs. "You just answered me."

"I'm sleep talking."

Amelia climbs onto the bed. "You stink!"

If the taste in my mouth is any indication, she would be correct.

"How about you give your uncle a second to clean himself up?" Grayson says from the doorway. "We can get all the answers we need after he doesn't stink."

The one thing that Grayson has always been good at is hiding what he's thinking. It doesn't matter that when we were seven, I saved him from getting his ass kicked. Or at ten, when I warned him that he was being set up by two football guys to walk into an ambush. It doesn't matter that I have saved his ass a million times, probably more, he never shows me what he's thinking.

He's a master at it.

It's a trick I've tried to emulate when it comes to wanting to sleep with his sister.

Or I should say, when I *did* sleep with his sister.

Not that there was much sleeping.

So, here I am, not sure what the hell I said last night. Not sure if I told him that I pushed his sister against the wall in the bar, rubbing my dick against her and shoving my tongue into her mouth. How I thought of something else I'd like to stick there. Nope. He just waits for Amelia to exit and then shuts the door, leaving me to wonder.

Dickhead.

As much as I'd like to hate him, the medication on the nightstand and bottle of Gatorade is a nice gesture. If I did say any of those things, Grayson would've killed me. He didn't, so there's some hope.

I take the pills, chugging the electrolytes I desperately need, and climb out of bed.

The pounding in my head doesn't relent as I shower, get dressed, or walk to the kitchen.

"Tough night," Gray notes as he grabs the bag of bread.

"You could say that."

"You all right?"

Three words that let me know I did not, in fact, talk about Stella.

No one in this world is more protective of their sister than the Parkerson brothers. They have spent their entire lives making sure no one could hurt her. Little do they know that I did that and more.

I broke her.

And last night, I did it again.

I push the bread away, not feeling much like eating.

"I've known you my whole life," Grayson says, his back against the counter as he watches me. "I've never seen you that fucked up. Well, not since we were in college."

Since the night I lost my fucking mind when I found out Stella was pregnant.

"Yeah," is the brilliant reply I come up with.

Grayson laughs. "You're an idiot and a liar. You kept saying shit like, 'I don't even want to like her.'"

I scratch my head and then sigh. "I don't."

"Like who?"

Your sister.

"No one. It really doesn't matter because I was drunk and don't remember much. I must've met someone at the bar."

And because I put the proverbial nail in the coffin last night when I called us a mistake.

Stella won't take that lying down. She will never look at me the same after that one.

Good.

I'd like it all to stop. If she hated me, this would be a hundred times easier. I wouldn't have to see things I'd rather not when she looks at me.

"You? You never meet anyone at a bar and then get drunk like that."

I lay my head down on my arms to stop the pounding. "Clearly, I was a mess."

"Was it Misty?" he asks.

If Grayson knew Misty, he wouldn't be asking that. A long time ago, I must've said something about her, and he's clung to it. In order to make it be plausible, I've run with it. Lies upon lies stack around me regarding this. In so many ways, Misty has become Stella. When I was sad and alone, he assumed it was because of Misty, which in reality, was his sister.

Some days, I wish I could just tell him.

Everything.

It would be so much easier, but the deal we made with Stella's father is that no one knows. We keep the secret or he'll ruin me. And he could—easily.

My prospects would shrivel up. My friends, especially the Parkersons, would disappear and that would ruin me.

"No, it's not Misty. She's not . . . well, it's nothing about her."

"You said as much last night."

I glare at him. "Have you always been this annoying?"

"Pretty much."

"I must've blocked this part of your personality out."

He grins. "You're an asshole when you're hungover."

"You're an asshole when I'm hungover."

"At least we're consistent."

I flip him off. "I'm going home."

Amelia comes running into the kitchen. "Uncle Jack, will you play dolls with me? Jessica showed me a new way to make their hair feel soft. We didn't brush it right the last time."

I look to her father for help, but he has that stupid fucking grin as he drinks his coffee.

She tilts her head, batting those long lashes. "Please, Uncle Jack? I love you *so* much."

"Women learn this really young," I note aloud.

"Learn what?"

I lift her up, eliciting a squeal of delight. "How to get men to do what they want."

She giggles and squirms in my arms, and then I spend the next hour playing dolls because at least I can make one woman happy.

Ten

STELLA

The last two and a half weeks have been interesting. Since that kiss, I've been a mess. I can still feel his lips on mine as though it just happened. The taste of him lingers on my tongue, and the smell of his cologne seems to be embedded in my nose. I hate him and love him all at the same time.

But I am done being a mess, damn it. I have other things to worry about.

Two days ago, I got a call from Mickey, saying that Samuel came in this week. He said it wasn't bad, but he could tell there was a chance it was going that way. He knows the signs, sees guys who come in, thinking they have it under control, only to realize they don't. It's a vicious cycle, and Samuel is stuck in it. It also doesn't help that Samuel isn't returning my calls—or his brother's.

Until he does, there isn't a whole lot that his brother or I can do.

All of that has resulted in my being exhausted and done. I

want my life to move forward, and it feels as if I'm in neutral.

"Auntie?" Amelia calls my attention.

"Yes, Monkey?"

"Is Daddy going to marry Jessica?"

Oh, so not going there. "I don't know, why?"

"Because I like her." She takes a heaping spoonful of her ice cream and crams it into her mouth.

At least my brother is happy, that's something. "I like her too."

"Daddy does too."

"I think you're right."

My sweet and loving niece is the only thing that could pull me out of my black mood.

"Do you think my mommy loves me?" she asks, causing me to jerk back.

Amelia has never asked me about Yvonne before, and I have no idea what my brother has told his daughter about the woman. "I didn't really know your mom," I tell her honestly.

I don't think any of us did. I know Grayson wanted to believe they would work, but she was never content. There was never enough money or enough time. She always wanted more, and when she got pregnant, it was as though someone had stolen everything from her.

The worst part was that she gave Amelia up so easily. I know what it is like to make that impossible choice, but she seemed almost happy to make it. I don't know if she saw having a child as a burden, but Amelia is not a burden. Not ever.

"I asked Daddy if Jessica could be my mommy."

I smile because I can only imagine how uncomfortable that was for him. "And what did he say?"

She shrugs. "I don't remember."

I would bet my ass it's because he didn't answer.

"You all finished?" I ask when she starts licking the bowl.

Amelia looks up with the sweetest expression on her face.

"Can I have more?"

"Not a chance."

"Then I'm done."

I lift her off the tall counter seat and kiss her cheek. "Go get ready for bed."

She rushes to her room, which is a guest room that might as well be hers, and a second later, there's a knock at the door. I'm not expecting anyone, but if the dinner at my parents' went the way I'm guessing it did, Grayson may want Amelia.

I open the door, expecting to find an annoyed sibling, only it is not my brother.

"Hello, Jack. What can I do for you?" I ask acidly, not feeling very kind.

Jack has done everything he can to pretend I don't exist and the kiss never happened. I have not been able to do that.

No, instead, I'm reliving it. Over and over like a damn movie stuck on the same scene.

"I owe you an apology."

Wrong thing to say. "No, you owe me an explanation."

He seems taken aback by that. Good. "A what?"

"An explanation. You know, where you explain why you're such an asshole."

"I know you're pissed."

"Yeah, I am." There's no point in denying it. "But more than that, I'm hurt. You do this to me, you know that? I get to a point where it doesn't hurt, and then something happens, and I'm right back to being that eighteen-year-old girl again."

"It's no different for me."

I roll my eyes. "Please, you couldn't give two shits about me. Anyway, go ahead, I'm waiting for this explanation of how it's so damn easy for you to care so little. I'd like to know your secret so I can do it myself." My arms cross against my chest as I wait.

"Okay, well, I guess it's because being around you makes

me lose my mind. I see you, want you, and know that there's not a fucking universe that exists where I should have you. I push you away because, if I don't, I'll go crazy waiting for something I will never allow myself to have. You want to know why I do this? Because I have never wanted something so badly as I do you. So, I'm here to apologize because you deserve better."

"Better? Better than what?"

"Than me!"

I shake my head. "What the hell makes you think there is better? I want you. I have always wanted you. You keep saying better, but you fail to see that you are what's better for me."

Jack runs his hands through his hair, turning before looking into my eyes again. "Are you serious, Stell? You were eighteen and I fucked up your entire life. I took advantage of you that night, and then we had a kid. One we had to give up."

"Yes, we had a kid, but you weren't the one at fault. There were two of us there that night."

"I should've been a better man."

I huff. "Then be the better man now, Jack. Tell me what you truly want." I step forward. "Tell me how you feel."

Jack's eyes close, and I see that he won't. "You deserve a man who will slay the dragons, Stella. Not the dragon himself."

I open my mouth to say something, anything, but only air escapes. My heart is racing, and I want to grab him and kiss him until he sees that he is the one who slays my dragons.

"Uncle Jack?" Amelia's voice is soft, and when I turn to her, she's running forward, arms wide without a care in the world.

I step back, giving her room.

Everything he said is what I've wanted to hear from his lips, and I don't know what to do. I know he wants more, but now the question is . . . can I convince him to do it?

Jack catches her, kissing her cheek. "What are you doing here?"

She beams at him. "I'm sleeping over. You should too. We can have a party."

"I don't know that your auntie would like that."

Oh, I would very much like a slumber party, without the kid—or clothes.

"Do you want to?" Amelia asks.

Please don't answer that.

"I'm not sure about sleeping over, but I'd like to stay for a while."

Amelia clasps her hands together, her eyes wide with excitement as she turns to me. "Oh, can we?"

Damn it.

I know letting him in tonight is the forgiveness he showed up to get. As much as I'd like to push him, punish him the way he's doing to us, I won't. Staying mad at him is something I've never been good at.

"Sure. He can come watch a movie."

She shimmies until he lets her go, and then her feet are moving at warp speed to get to the couch.

Jack stands outside the loft. "Are you sure this is okay?"

I nod. "I'm sure."

He moves toward me, and I tense as his lips brush my cheek. He smells so good. His fresh scent fills me, and I stay still, absorbing it.

"Thanks, Meatball."

I groan at the stupid nickname. Not just because I have to hear it from my brothers but because it solidifies what Jack thinks of me. I'm that kid. The little girl who is annoying and likes to tag along whenever I can. I can't bear hearing it from him.

"No," I say, leaning back. "You don't get to do that."

"Do what?"

"Make me your little sister. Make me that girl. I've never been that, Jack. I won't be tonight."

He waits a beat, looking at me, and I can almost feel his thoughts rioting through him. "No, you're not."

I want to say more, but Amelia is waiting, and hopefully, after she falls asleep, we'll be able to talk about everything that's happening.

We're only an hour into the movie, and Amelia is out, leaving Jack and me to suffer through the princess movie she had to watch because she can't get enough of it. To be young and believe that princes exist.

Jack moves the blanket up over her a little higher. "She's so cute when she's sleeping."

"She's cute all the time."

He smiles. "She is."

My stupid heart sputters watching him with her.

"Jack, we need to talk," I say softly.

"If it's about the other night—"

"It's not. It's about Samuel."

"Samuel?" he asks, his head pulling back.

I nod. "Let's get her to bed first."

Jack carries Amelia to her room, and we tuck her in. Jack and I putting a little girl to bed after we watched a movie is so domestic, so perfectly simple of a thing, and it feels natural.

It could have been us. It should've been us. But it isn't, and I'd do well to remember that.

As I pull the door closed, I turn to find him already pacing the living room. "What about Samuel?"

I tell him about my last trip down. He sits, listening as the information pours out. There's been so much in my head, and

I've been dealing with it the best I can, but by unpacking all that stress on someone, it's as if a small weight is lifting with each word.

After a moment, he lets out a long puff of air and shakes his head. "And he has no one down there?"

"No, his boss seemed like a great guy when I talked to him, but I don't know what is going on or if he's working. He's not answering my calls. I feel like . . . like we have to do something."

"We're not her parents, Stella. We can't go down there and make demands or do anything. I'm not sure what exactly you're expecting."

"We have to do something."

"No, no we don't," he says and gets to his feet. "I haven't seen that little girl since the day I put her in their arms. I've lived and wondered and fucking acted as though this never happened. I did it because I knew we were doing what we had to."

"And now? Now she needs us!" I remind him. "She needs someone because she lost her mother and her father is falling apart."

Jack's gaze turns to me. "And you're going to, what? Sweep in and be the mother she needs? Do you hear yourself, Stella? She doesn't know you."

I fight back the tears and hold on to my anger. "No, but we aren't those people. The ones who let others suffer because we're afraid."

"Afraid," he says through a laugh. "I'm past afraid. I'm fucking terrified. Do you understand what we've done? Truly. How all of this unravels? Do you get that not only did I sleep with Grayson's sister on her eighteenth fucking birthday but I also knocked her up?"

"I was there for it all, in case you forgot. I remember how all of it was."

I remember the way he looked at me that night. Like I wasn't a little girl, but a woman. I remember how he stood there, watching me as I walked to him, placed my hand on his chest, and asked him to kiss me.

There isn't a single moment of that night that I don't remember. The two of us at the inn, escaping the party that I didn't want to be at.

But Jack was there, and I would go anywhere he was.

The feel of his hands on my skin as he pushed the straps of my dress down to kiss me is something I'll never forget.

"What are you doing out here?" Jack asked, and I gasped, clutching my hand to my throat.

"Jack, you scared me."

He smiled. "It's your birthday party, and you're hiding?"

I looked back out at the tree line, feeling sad and alone. "It's quiet out here, and I don't really want to be at a party with my parents' friends."

I asked for a night with friends. One where we could dance, laugh, and enjoy the fact that Oliver and I turned eighteen. My mother had other ideas and threw me something akin to a coming-out party or whatever she called it.

Instead of my friends, it was all high-society people who had big money and wore far too much perfume.

Oliver was off with my brothers, doing God knows what in the woods as some sort of Parkerson boys birthday tradition. I hated them for leaving me behind.

"Mind if I join you?"

I swallowed deeply and used all the tricks I had acquired to appear indifferent. "If you want."

Jack sat on the bench next to me and handed me his wine glass. "Want some?"

"Look at you, corrupting your best friend's little sister."

"I have a feeling that ship sailed."

I laughed and took a sip.

My lips just touched where Jack's had been.

I might die.

Relax, Stella, keep it together, you're an adult now and starting college soon. Play it cool.

"So, how is college?" I asked.

"Good. Ready to start my master's program."

I nodded. "Yeah, Gray told us he's staying in Charlotte."

As though he didn't know that . . .

Jack chuckled. "I guess he doesn't like coming back here."

"Reminds him of Jess."

He sighed deeply. "I guess so. And what about you? You graduate this month and then where are you off to?"

"South Carolina."

"It's crazy that you're going to college."

"Why?"

Jack shrugged. "I don't know, you've just always been so young to me, Meatball."

I glared at him. "Seriously, I hate Josh for giving me that stupid nickname."

"It's not so bad." He nudged me playfully. "It could be worse."

"I don't doubt that."

Jack wrapped an arm around me, pulling me close as my teeth chattered. "You're freezing."

I was willing to become a popsicle if it meant Jack's arm stayed around me. "Temperature dropped fast."

He rubbed his hands up and down, trying to warm me. I'd dreamed of this—of Jack realizing that he wanted me. His arms would wrap around me before he admitted to having always wanted me, and then our lips would touch.

Of course, it didn't happen, but a girl could dream.

I leaned into his chest, absorbing the warmth. "Better?" he asked with a chuckle.

"Much," I said and bit my tongue to stop from saying

more. Like how he smelled like spice, whiskey, and heaven.

That would be a bit much.

The music played on behind us, stars twinkled above as well as the string lights around the property. It was beautiful and magical, even if it wasn't what I had wanted.

"Good. So what did you get for your birthday?"

"This stupid party, my brothers leaving to do their boy thing, and stood up."

"That sounds like you got screwed."

I laughed once. "I guess we could say that was *supposed* to happen."

"What does that mean?"

I broke up with my boyfriend two weeks ago. Before then, we had decided that my birthday was going to be the night. The night we gave ourselves to each other—finally. It would've been perfect because the idiots known as my brothers would be gone. The house would be empty and there would have been very little chance of being caught, but . . . I didn't know, the closer the date got, the less I wanted it to happen. I didn't want it to be him, if I were being honest.

I wanted Jack.

I'd always wanted Jack.

I sat up and gave him a sad smile. "I had plans, that's all, and they are all gone now."

Jack's hand lifted, tucking a strand of hair behind my ear. "What plans?" he asked, barely audible.

Our eyes were locked, his hazel ones staring into my brown, and I wondered . . . did he feel this? Could Jack hear the pounding of my heart or feel the way I shook, not from the cold but from my need for him to touch me?

I was literally trembling with anticipation.

Our breaths mingled, and if this were a dream, I never wanted to wake. "He was going to be my first."

That seemed to shock him a little. "He didn't deserve you."

My lips quirked a bit. "He wasn't who I wanted anyway," I admitted and prayed that, just this once, I'd have the courage to tell him the truth if he asked.

But Jack didn't ask. He just watched me, his strong hands glided up from my wrist and held the back of my arm.

"Stella?" Jack's voice broke the silence.

"Yes?"

"If you could have anything for your birthday, what would it be?"

There was a note of something in his voice, something I'd never heard before, and my pulse quickened. I pulled from every fiber of courage I had in my body, willing my lips to say what was in my heart.

"For you to kiss me."

And then, like a scene from a movie, Jack's lips moved to mine, and he kissed me. We didn't stop there . . .

I walk toward him, keeping my voice even. "I didn't forget. I wish I could. God, how it would make things easier if I didn't have to remember."

"I have tried! I have done everything I could to erase that night, your kiss, the way you breathed my name that night. How it was so fucking perfect and so goddamn wrong. You, standing there"—Jack cuts the distance between us—"with your hair coming down and how it felt between my fingers. I want to forget you, Stella, but you're always there."

My heart is racing, and I'm struggling to breathe.

I go to him, stopping just a breath away, but not allowing myself to touch him. "Why are we doing this?" I ask. "Why are we fighting against this?"

"Because we can't ever be. It's the penance that I'm going to pay for the rest of my fucking life for what I did to you. No matter how much I want you. No matter how much I know my life would be better if I could just . . ."

"Just what?" His eyes close, and I rest my hand on his

chest.

After a few seconds, Jack's warm palm settles against my cheek. "You were always so sweet. So innocent and perfect."

"I'm not perfect."

"You are, though. You always have been."

"I'm perfect for you, Jack. Always you."

Please tell me you want me. Please let yourself see that we're fighting the wrong battle.

A knock on the door, which is more like someone pounding, causes us both to jump.

Neither of us says a word, and then it sounds again. "Stella. Please."

Jessica's voice breaks over the words and has Jack dropping his hand and stepping back. The loss of his warmth is almost painful.

"Stella! I need you." Jessica's tone is frantic.

"Go," Jack says.

I move quickly, pulling the door open. "Jess, what's wrong?"

Tears are falling down her face. "I need to go."

"Go?"

Delia is behind her, hand rubbing her back. "She keeps saying she needs the keys. Jack?"

"Hey, Deals."

I move forward, pulling Jess into my arms. "Are you all right?"

She wipes her face and shakes her head. "I just need to go to the beach. Please. Can I have the keys?"

I look to Delia, who shrugs. Whatever happened at dinner tonight must've been bad and my brother was being a dick.

"Maybe you should stay the night here," I offer.

She shakes her head. "No, I need to leave and think. I can't . . ."

"Is it my parents?"

"It's everything."

I know more than most about how sometimes you just have to escape. There have been so many times I've retreated to the beach house, where the air is filled with the brine of the ocean and it doesn't remind me of here.

I walk over to the drawer and pull out the keys to the beach house.

"Here."

She inhales deeply. "Thank you. I just need some time, and . . ."

"You don't have to explain. I understand needing to just go."

"Thank you," she says again, pulling me in for a hug.

Jess and Delia leave, and when I turn back, Jack is standing at the door. He closes his eyes for a second and then exhales. "I can't be involved with whatever you're doing in Georgia."

"I see."

"I know that you think I'm wrong, but when we gave Kinsley up, we gave her up. Meddling in her life now would be unfair to all of us."

"Okay."

I don't see, but even though this is what I expected from him, a small part of me hoped for something different.

Jack continues to explain. "If Samuel needs us, he would tell us."

"Right."

"I won't do this to you again, Stella."

"Do what?"

He comes closer, and his fingers tip my chin up. "Hurt you."

Little does he know that I'm hurting every minute that I'm near him. That my heart cries out for him regardless of where we are or who we're near. He hurts me because we will never be despite us both wanting to be each other's everything.

"Too late." I say the only two words I can.

"Don't say that."

"What? Say the truth? We've been dancing around it for a long time, why not just be honest for once?"

"And what's the truth?"

I step back three times, forcing distance between us because him touching me is too much. The contrast between how it makes me feel and how deeply his words wound me is breathtakingly painful. "That it hurts me that we will never be more than this—two people who want each other but one is too afraid to reach out."

"I see."

I hope he does because I'm not the one who is afraid.

He nods once and then leaves. When the door shuts, I sink to the ground and cry because there's nothing else I can do.

Eleven

JACK

"What can I do?" I ask Grayson as he exits his room after settling Jessica in.

"Nothing, just . . . I appreciate everything you've done already."

As if there's nothing in this world I wouldn't do for him. I literally would walk through fire for this guy, which I've done a few times. The last week has been hell for him and Jessica, so we've rallied together, doing whatever they need us to. And while what happened to Jessica is a tragedy and has us all waiting to find out if she'll really be okay, the distraction of focusing on them has allowed me a break from the pain of hurting Stella.

"You'd do the same for me."

Grayson flops onto the couch. "Absolutely."

"Is she okay?"

"She seems it, but I can't imagine she actually is. You've lived through it, were you okay after?"

I think about the fire at my house, the flames and how

I screamed relentlessly for my mother. All she did was yell back, telling me to get out the window. My father was frantic, trying to reach us both. He couldn't. She demanded he come to me and help me out. My mother died so I could live. I was fifteen when it happened, and I can still smell the smoke all these years later.

While it wasn't the same scenario for Jessica, it will never leave her.

"No, but she has you. Just like I had people. People will help."

Grayson was there for me every day. He was the best friend any kid could ask for. He didn't force me to talk. He was there. Anytime I felt alone, Grayson was there, reminding me I wasn't.

When my father started to disappear, I wasn't alone.

I had him.

I had them all.

Josh, Alex, Oliver, and Stella. God, Stella. She was always smiling, bringing me things to cheer me up. She made me cards and drew pictures for me. She was eleven at the time, and I will never forget how she went from being a sweet little kid into this gorgeous girl. Then when I was a senior and she was a freshman, that girl walked down the hallway of the high school as though she were the new queen—and she was. I wanted to fall to my knees.

It was the most confusing emotion ever.

She was Stella. Stella. Grayson's little sister.

Instead of being shy and a little sheltered, she walked right up to me, smiled, and kept going past me.

I don't know that I was the same again.

Grayson's head falls back. "My parents. They . . . my father."

"They've always been this way. They've done nothing but manipulate you and your siblings."

He laughs. "You don't know the half of it."

Neither does he. Grayson's father makes my father, who eventually ended up taking off after my mother died, look like father of the year. The shit he did to Stella and me, the things he threatened to do if we chose to keep our child, was cruel. She was eighteen, afraid, and I was broke with no family to fall back on for help.

He made sure we knew we were at his mercy and there wasn't a chance we were going to fuck up his precious family name.

I get up, grabbing us both a beer from the fridge.

"What happened?" I ask as I hand it to him.

Grayson fills me in on all that happened at dinner. I'm . . . floored. If I didn't know him as well as I do, I would have called him a liar to his face because what he's telling me is disgusting and incomprehensible. His father has always been a piece of work, but sleeping with Grayson's ex is a little much, even for him. Although, I'm not sure why I'm surprised after the ultimatum he gave to his daughter.

"Wow."

"Yeah." He lifts the bottle toward me. "How about that."

"So, you fought with Jess?"

He nods. "I was pissed and took it out on her."

"Which caused her to run."

"And almost die," Grayson adds. I can hear the pain and fear in just those three words.

"She's here. She survived."

"I'm going to marry her."

I grin at that. "You should."

"Soon."

"I figured. You never were one to wait once you made up your mind."

"We've always been that way. You and I were reckless for a long time . . . and we made lots of mistakes, but also had a lot of fun."

I lean forward, forearms resting on my knees. "I've definitely made my share of mistakes."

Grayson sets the beer down. "I want you to be my best man."

My eyes widen. "What? You have three other brothers."

"I know, but you've always been more family to me than anyone. You're my best friend, and when I marry her, I want you standing next to me. Will you do it?"

Guilt like I've never known before rises, filling me until I feel like I might choke. I nod, unable to speak without being sure I won't tell him about Stella.

"Yeah?" he asks.

"Yes," I croak and then drain my beer, the feeling of betrayal too much to handle.

Twelve

STELLA

"So, we're going into business together," my brother Oliver says as he throws his feet onto my table.

"I feel like we've always been in business together."

"Yes, but now we're going to take all our life's savings and toss it in. It's a good thing none of us—well, other than Gray—have a relationship or kids."

Right. None of us.

Oliver is my twin. He knows me sometimes better than I know myself. But he has never asked a direct question about why I went to stay with our grandmother.

I've waited for him to call me out on why I didn't go to South Carolina and went to Georgia instead. Because as wonderful as Ollie is, and he is truly the kindest and most wonderful of the Parkerson brothers, he's not timid . . . not with me.

"Listen, if you're going to live with me, you shouldn't do . . . that." I point to his feet.

"You know we'll kill each other before the month is out."

"If I don't kill you by the end of the week."

He grins. "You can try."

I sigh and sit beside him, nestling into him like we were kids. "Ollie, what's wrong with me?"

The deep rumble of his laugh makes me smile. "So much, Meatball."

"I'm serious. Why don't I have a husband and a family?"

Oliver shifts, causing me to sit up. "What in the hell made you ask that?"

"Nothing."

"Liar." I should've known he wouldn't let me back away from the question. "Is there . . . someone you're not telling anyone about?"

This is the most he's ever asked. "No. Yes. I don't know. There's always been someone."

Oliver's eyes narrow slightly. "Stella, you know you can't."

And there it is. Oliver knows something.

"I can't what?"

He sighs through his nose. "He's Grayson's best friend, and he's about to go into business with us."

"So you know."

"About the fact that you like Jack? Yeah, I've known."

Do you know more? Do you know about my daughter?

The question hovers in my mind, and I stamp it down. "It doesn't matter."

"I doubt that, but in a way, you're right. It doesn't because Grayson will flip his shit."

"Why though? Why the hell do I give a shit what Grayson wants? I'm thirty years old. I'm not some stupid little girl."

"I know, but you have to see it from his perspective. Jack's his best friend, and if shit goes wrong between you, then what? He loses someone he's known since childhood."

"Why would he lose him?" I ask, feeling frustrated.

"Because you're our sister. No matter what the hell happens, we will always be on your side."

I roll my eyes. "There doesn't have to be sides."

"Stella, I'm not trying to be a dick, but there are always sides. Look at Devney and me, we ended things, and do you think I've talked to anyone from Sugarloaf since then? I was friends with Sydney, but she, of course, sided with her friend. It's the way shit goes. Now imagine if I was with Winnie and it went bad, how are you going to handle that when she broke my heart by leaving me when she realized what a dickhead I am?"

"You are a dickhead."

"Besides the point, but nice try."

I hate it when he's right. Probably because it doesn't happen often.

I lean back, wanting to cry again. "It's been a long time that I've felt this way, Ollie."

He nudges me. "I know it. I think Grayson does too and pretends he doesn't. I don't know, maybe he doesn't because I can't see him not saying something."

I turn my head, looking into the brown eyes that mirror mine. "You haven't."

"Because I know better than to talk boys with you."

I laugh softly. "I did it *one* time."

"And it was enough to scar me for life. Who wants to answer their sister's questions about cocks and what they do?" He shudders.

"You told me to ask you!"

"I *lied*!"

"Four brothers, and I got stuck with the worst as my twin."

Oliver shrugs. "I may be an ass, but I'm not in love with our older brother's best friend."

There's more, Ollie, ask me.

I look into his eyes, begging him to please give me someone to unburden myself to. If there's anyone, it can be him.

Oliver would keep my secret. He has to know I have one. He had to feel the pain I was in twelve years ago.

"Oliver . . ."

Oliver gives me a sad smile. "Don't, Stella. Don't open a box you can't close."

A tear falls down my cheek. It's clear he is asking me not to force him to lie too.

If he doesn't know, he never has to betray our brothers.

For him, I will continue to harbor this alone, drowning in the sea of grief and sadness.

I lean in, kissing his cheek. "I won't. You're a good-ish brother."

The pain fills my chest. I hate that I still have to keep the secret, but I understand it at the same time.

"I could've done without the ish."

"I could do without a lot of things."

He nudges me softly. "Well, just think of all the fun we'll have living together."

I groan and lay my head back on his shoulder. "Fun. That's a word."

And definitely not the word I would use, but then nothing has been fun for a long time.

"Are you excited?" I ask Jessica as we look through the rack of wedding gowns.

"Of course I am. I love your brother."

I smile. "I do too. I just can't believe you're getting married in a week."

Her hand moves to her stomach almost instinctually. "I want this to be as easy for Amelia as possible. I figure if we get married first, then we have some time to settle in before the baby comes. There's also no point in waiting, we've done enough of that."

"Yeah, you guys deserve to be happy."

Jess pushes a dress and looks at me. "What about you, Stella?"

"What about me?"

"Don't you deserve to be happy too?"

I look away, not wanting to think of all the ways I am definitely not happy. "I'm sure someday I'll meet the right guy."

We get to the end of the dresses, which prevents me from hiding. "Look, I know that you have Winnie and your brothers, but I'd like to sort of just say this and not overstep. I'm always here too. If you ever want to talk, your secrets will never be shared, not even with Grayson."

I always wished I had a sister. Four brothers made for horrible playmates and even worse confidants. They were protective to an extreme and sucked at girl talk.

Winnie was the closest thing I had, but she had Jessica.

"As a kid, I always wished I had you as my big sister. Winnie would talk about how cool you were and how you always shared things."

"Winnie hated me," she says with a laugh. "I pulled her hair, told her to get lost, and tried to lock her in a closet once— okay, twice."

I laugh softly. "She mentioned that one."

"I know you're best friends with Winnie, but you're my friend too. You helped me so much with Grayson and coming back here—not to mention with your parents. And now, we're all going into business together."

"We are."

"And we'll be sisters."

I smile. "I'm glad for that. There have been enough boys around to last me a lifetime."

"Me too," Jess says as her hand grips mine.

"Can I tell you something and you not tell Gray?"

"Of course."

My heartbeat accelerates, and I know that this will be that moment for me. The one where I will open the box that can't ever be closed again.

"I'm in love with Jack."

Her lips form into a soft smile. "I think Jack is in love with you too."

I nod. "I think you're right on that as well."

"And yet, you guys aren't together. So, I'm guessing Grayson is part of it?"

A tear trickles down my cheek. "He's part of it."

"There's another part?" she asks.

Here it is. The chance to tell someone about Kinsley. She's not asking me to keep it. She's offering me a gift that she'll never fully understand the meaning of. It's the gift of sisterhood and understanding. Well, at least I hope it is because it could go very wrong.

"Yes."

She tilts her head just a little. "You can trust me."

"It's just that I've never told anyone."

"Not even Winnie?"

I look around for my best friend, ensuring she's not close. "No, not even Winnie. There are a total of seven—well, six now—who know."

Jessica blinks a few times. "If you don't want to tell me—"

"No," I cut her off. "I do. It's that I'm terrified to say it."

Jessica steps closer. "Did he hurt you?"

I give her a look, letting her know she's nuts to think that. Jack is not that man. He hurts me, but not like that.

"We have a daughter."

And just like that, the box is opened and the truth is exposed.

Thirteen

JACK

I've survived days in the wilderness with very little food, a wet sleeping bag, and a broken arm. I would like to consider myself a tough man, but today, I'm weak. My best friend in the world is dancing with his wife while I stare at his sister.

What a fucking joke my life is.

Josh comes up behind me, clapping his hand on my shoulder. "What a fool."

"What?"

He laughs. "Grayson thinking he was ever going to resist Jessica when she came back. There are women we love and never get over, right?"

I clear my throat. "I wouldn't know."

"No? I remember Gray talking about some girl."

I shake my head. "Nope."

"Huh, well, I have one."

His eyes follow over to where Delia stands with Winnie and Stella, all three of them dabbing their eyes as they watch the happy couple.

"Delia?"

Joshua shrugs. "It's complicated."

"How?"

"She wants things I'll never give her. It's better this way."

Delia is a catch. I'm not sure what his issue is because he'll never find someone who is more devoted and kind. And yet, he won't allow himself to even think about it.

"I doubt she agrees."

Josh rubs the back of his neck. "We've been through some crazy shit in our lives."

"Meaning?"

"Just that life isn't always kind to people. We love. We lose. We fuck up, and we're the ones who have to accept it. We live with it, knowing that another blow is right at the corner of happy."

My eyes narrow as I try to understand what the hell he's saying. "So, you're saying that staying away from Delia is better for her?"

"Absolutely. I'm not going to fill her head with bullshit about a future that can't be."

"Why can't it be?" I counter.

"Because there's no way I'm ever going to be in a serious relationship. I keep my distance to keep her heart from being destroyed."

I swear I've heard all this shit before in my own head. I wasn't going to love Stella. I wasn't going to kiss her. I was going to stay far away from her. And here I am, watching her and feeling my heart rip from my chest because there's not a chance in hell I can keep this up much longer.

"If you say so."

He exhales deeply. "Are you ready for the business?"

"Yeah, I appreciate you guys bringing me into the fold."

"It was Stella's idea."

At that, my eyes cut to Josh. "It was?"

"Yeah, she said offering something like wilderness training would give us an edge to start. We'll help bring new clients to you, and your clients will stay at the inn once they're done with your weird wilderness shit. It's kind of a great scenario on both sides. Plus, you're like a brother to us, so it makes sense."

Right. "Well, I appreciate it."

"Of course." He looks back at his brother. "I never really thought I'd be moving back to North Carolina."

"You've been gone a long time."

Josh took the New Orleans location the second he could and hasn't spent much time here since. That is going to change.

Soon, they'll all walk away from their jobs at the same time, leaving their father in a position he's not prepared for. He's relied on his kids needing to remain in his good graces, too caught up in his own hubris to see what is coming. He's about to be slapped with a healthy dose of reality that they're not kids anymore.

To be honest, I'm going to enjoy every second of his discomfort.

He looks over at his mother, who is standing on the fringes. "I do feel bad for her."

"She gets half of everything."

Josh lets out one laugh. "But half of nothing is nothing."

"I can't imagine your father was stupid with money."

He shrugs. "Maybe not, but he's going to need to come up with a lot of money to buy us all out."

The song ends, and we all clap. Josh sets his glass of champagne on the table. "If you'll excuse me. I'm going to dance with the bride."

It's as though the universe is trying to kill me because Jess dances with Alex, Delia and Oliver pair up, and Winnie and Grayson are taking a turn. It leaves Stella on the side, staring at me.

She's so stunning that it's hard to breathe.

When she gives me a small smile, I dip my head toward the dance floor and she lifts the hem of her dress, walking toward me.

We are at a wedding, filled with family and friends, so there is no hiding. We have zero privacy, and yet, it feels as though we're alone.

It's us, two people with baggage that would sink a ship, moving toward each other.

I extend my hand, and she places hers in my palm. Her other hand rests on my shoulder, and I pull her close.

No words are spoken because we're saying it all as we move as one.

The music is slow, and Stella and I watch each other the entire song. This is our dance. It's where there's no past or future, only now.

I'm holding her, and no one will ever think twice about it. They don't know that I never want this song to end. They don't understand that the melody will never leave me. They can't see that each second that Stella's body is against mine is the most painful and wonderful feeling.

They don't see that I love her more than any man has loved another woman.

And yet, I can't have her.

The music stops, and we linger for just a heartbeat on the dance floor. "Thank you for the dance."

Stella's lashes flutter, and her gaze drops. "You're welcome."

We break apart and the loss of her, God, it kills me.

I don't know how I'm going to survive working by her day in and day out. How I'm going to endure the constant heartache that comes with being near her.

Grayson's mother rests her hand on my arm, and I dance with her. Mrs. Parkerson has never been my favorite person, but she's always been nice to me. Even during everything with Stella, she wasn't cruel so much as she was sad.

Her baby girl was pregnant, and I was the irresponsible asshole who did it.

"You and Stella would've made a beautiful couple," she notes quietly. "If everything had gone just a little . . . differently."

I try not to let that sting, but it does. "Right."

"I know you don't believe me, but I didn't have the same objections that Mitchell did. I just wanted you both to have a chance at a life."

I turn her a little farther away from her other sons who are dancing. "It is what it is. Stella and I made choices, and we've lived with the consequences."

She looks at her daughter and sighs. "We all have. I've spent thirty-eight years married to a man who I don't love. I've watched him use our children as pawns, destroy their hopes for his own gain, and have said nothing about the countless affairs he's had. And for what? We all live with our choices, Jack."

"And you think I'm making the wrong choice?"

The song ends, and she takes a step back.

She smiles up at me. "You are a smart man, figure it out."

Mrs. Parkerson walks away, leaving me feeling off-center and dazed. What the hell does that mean? Suddenly, Stella's mother thinks I should be with her daughter? Weddings and funerals bring out the crazy in people.

I walk over to the bar and grab a drink while I do my best to forget the last three minutes of my life. I've been handling things with Stella. I've learned that love isn't for me. I don't get the girl in the end, she's not for me.

She's meant for love and happiness and a family.

I toss back the drink the bartender set in front of me. Then, as fate would fucking have it, I feel her beside me.

"I thought weddings were supposed to be happy," Stella

says as she grabs a glass of wine.

"They are."

She laughs once. "Neither of us looks very happy."

"We both know the truth about it all." I turn to her, my elbow resting on the bar.

"And what's that?"

"That love and happiness don't go hand in hand."

Stella shakes her head. "And I thought I was the jaded one." She brings the glass to her lips and takes a long sip. "That's where you're wrong. They are happy because they're in love."

"And what about the people who are in love but are miserable?"

She drains her glass and places it down. "Follow me and you can find out."

There's no pause before her exit, she just walks out of the tent.

I look around to see if anyone notices, but everyone is drinking, laughing, dancing, and smiling, not paying attention to Stella and me.

So, like a dog with a bone, I follow her. My feet are moving before my mind can think better of it. I trail along the path she took, and when I get to the tree line, she calls my name softly.

I move into the forest, finding her in a small clearing where the sun is coming through the leaves, making her look like an angel.

"What are we doing here?"

She lifts her head, a beam of light catching her dark brown hair and causing it to shimmer. "We're breathing, Jack."

"Don't we pretty much do that each minute?" I ask, moving closer to her.

Like a magnet, she pulls me in.

Her eyes meet mine, and she smiles. "No, I don't think either of us do. I think we fight it." She steps toward me. "I think that if we didn't, if we really inhaled, we'd find that it hurts."

"I don't want to hurt you," I tell her.

"I know."

"Everything I do is to avoid that."

Stella takes another step. Slowly, her hand lifts to rest on my cheek. "I know that too, but you avoiding me, Jack, it hurts. I've been in love with you for . . . God, fifteen years."

The restraint I'm using to keep from grabbing her causes my arms to shake. I can't move or I'll fuck everything up. I'll take her in my arms and kiss her until the only breath she knows is mine. I'll . . . No. I can't. I won't.

"This is why love and happiness don't exist," I tell her.

"No, it's because you're afraid. Tell me you don't want me right now. Tell me that, when I touch you, you don't wish it would never end." She moves closer, her chest brushes against mine, and I swear I'm going to fucking die. "Tell me that you don't love me the way I love you."

I have to lie because if I say the truth, then we will just be back where we started. Even if I tell her the truth, it won't change our circumstances.

I take her wrist, pulling her palm away from my face. "I don't feel that way."

Anger flares in those brown eyes. She knows me too well. "So, you're going to pretend? Like . . . it's nothing?"

"It's better this way," I tell her.

My heart is pounding, and when I try to let her go, she grabs the lapels of my jacket. "We have to deal with this. We can't . . . we can't pretend anymore. You still have feelings for me, I know you do!"

Yes, I do. I fucking love her enough to stay away because we will never work.

Instead of telling her that, I dig deeper into the lie. "I don't."

She shakes her head, tears starting to fill her gaze. "Lies," she whispers. "Tell me the truth for once."

"I do . . . I *can't*."

Why can't she fucking see it? If I let myself love her, then we won't be able to go back. We'll have to tell everyone the truth. The number of lies we've told over the years will unravel and it will destroy everything.

"You can't pretend with me, Jack." Her hands fall away, and I make a grave mistake.

I reach for her. She comes to me instantly, her hands on my chest as I hold her close, making one last attempt. One chance for her to see what I'm saying before I do everything I said I wouldn't. "We can't. God, Stella, we can't."

Her eyes flutter, and her lips part. And then, like the bastard I've always been, I stop fighting and kiss her.

"Get your fucking hands off my sister," Grayson says from behind us.

Fourteen

STELLA

Of all the damn people to catch us, it had to be him.
"Grayson . . ." I say quickly, moving toward him.
My brother doesn't look at me though. No, his rage is centered on Jack. "How could you?" he seethes.

"It's not what you think," I cut in, hoping to defuse this.

Grayson's hands flex as he glares at Jack.

I look to Jessica, who shrugs. Great, I finally get a sister, and she's no help.

Jack takes a step toward Grayson's direction. "I know you're pissed, and I get it, but you have to know . . ."

Gray doesn't let him finish. His hand goes up, and then Jess grips his arm. "Come on, love, let's dance and let them talk."

"Talk? Did you see that? It didn't look like they were talking when he was *kissing* her."

Jessica gives me an apologetic smile and then turns back to her stark-raving-mad husband. Her voice is calm and soothing. "Yes, and it's not our business. Your sister can handle it."

And I now love this girl. Yes, his sister can handle it. Thank you. Finally someone sees I'm not a fourteen-year-old. "Go with your wife, Gray. We'll talk tomorrow."

He sends a dagger-like glance in Jack's direction again before he allows Jessica to pull him away.

As soon as he's out of view, Jack runs his hands through his hair and practically growls. "This is why!"

"Why, what?"

He gives me a look, one that is clearly not affectionate. "Why this was a mistake."

"Yes, the sky will fall and the ground will crumble now that Grayson saw us kiss." I roll my eyes.

"This isn't funny."

I turn back to him. "No, it's not. It's sad. Did Grayson ask you for permission to date Jessica? What about Yvonne? Did you two discuss the who's and what's about dating? No. You didn't."

"Neither Yvonne nor Jessica are my little sister."

"And that's the fucking issue!" I yell at him. "I'm not *little*, Jack. I'm a grown woman who doesn't need her brother's permission to be with someone. You don't need it either. I love you. I love you and you love me." I throw my hands up. "This is insane! Don't you see that? Grayson knows now. There's nothing to hide. We're found out."

He starts to pace, his head shaking the entire time. "He saw us kiss once."

"Yes, and he'll be upset, but you know what will piss him off even more? You breaking my heart. So, here's an idea, don't do it. Don't make me walk out of this clearing with tears streaming down my face because, once again, you let me go."

Jack stops moving, his eyes on me. "You think I let you go?"

"Haven't you? Each time you choose not to kiss me, love me, hold me, and tell me the damn truth, you let me go."

His strides are steady and sure as he closes the space between us. In a few seconds, I'm hauled against his chest, my arms trapped between us as he looks down at me. "I've never let you go."

"Prove it."

He kisses me. His lips are soft and yet unyielding. I close my eyes and get lost in his touch. It's as though all the world is right, the birds are chirping, and the sun is streaming down around us, illuminating the truth that has always been—we belong together.

Jack is the other part of my heart, and for so long, I've been desperate for it. I've needed this—us.

The kiss ends, but he doesn't release me. "Are you sure about this, Stella?"

"I'm sure about how I feel."

"I am too. I don't want to live like this anymore. Your brothers aren't going to like it. There's been years of lies."

As much as I've been yelling about my brothers, he's right. When they find out that we aren't some new thing, they're going to be furious and feel betrayed.

"Let's do this slowly," I suggest.

"How do you suggest we do that?"

"We don't rush into this. Let's give Grayson and the other idiots some time to adjust."

He pulls back a little. "You don't want to tell them about our past?"

"Do you?" I ask with brows raised.

"No, but I don't want to keep lying either."

I squirm out of his grip so I can see him better. "I don't want to tell any of them about Kinsley. That's . . . well, she's not ours. She's Samuel's, and it will only hurt everyone more if they realize the amount of time we've been keeping this from them. Grayson is your best friend, and I want to protect that."

"So we keep lying?"

"No, but let everyone get used to us together before we drop that bomb on them. We can let them see how much we care about each other first. Everyone has a lot on their plates with the resort plans, quitting the company, and moving. Besides, this isn't their story to know, so we don't ever *have* to tell them if we decide not to."

Jack's thumb grazes my wrist. "I'm not sure I agree, but if you want to keep her out of it, we can."

"It's going to be hard enough dealing with questions about us, and adding in that layer, I just can't do it. I can't look at their faces, not when I know what it's been like for Grayson to raise Amelia. I can't see his disappointment."

I wasn't as strong as him, and I've struggled with the idea of Grayson looking at me the way he does Yvonne.

I'm not ready yet.

"You think he'll judge you?"

I nod. "Of course he will. Gray kept Amelia."

"That's different. You were eighteen."

I take a step back, not wanting to think about it. "Just . . . let's wait. Kinsley is our secret, and, honestly, there's no reason to share it."

His arms wrap around me from behind, and I close my eyes. I've wished for this to be my life so damn often. Jack, holding me as his lips touch my neck, is a gesture so sweet I could cry.

I turn my head back. "I guess weddings aren't so bad after all."

He chuckles once. "Let's see if we both think that when we have to face your family."

I twist around, my arms resting on his shoulders. "For now, let's pretend they don't exist and make up for lost time."

Jack's hand is on the small of my back as we walk to the dance floor.

He sweeps me into his arms, and I ignore my brothers, focusing only on Jack. "Is anyone glaring at you?" I ask as he looks around.

"Only Grayson."

"He'll get over it."

Jack laughs. "Yeah, after he punches me in the face."

That's probably true. "He's never been good at fighting. I bet you can take him."

He smiles a little.

"Joshua, on the other hand . . ." I warn.

"Has other things on his mind."

"Really?" I ask, turning to see what my eldest brother is focusing on. Ah. Yes, Delia. "I guess it's a man thing."

Jack's head jerks back. "What is?"

"Being stupid and letting the woman you love pine for you."

"Sometimes there are reasons."

"None of them are good enough."

"Life with you is going to be interesting, isn't it?" Jack asks as if he doesn't already know the answer.

"Always."

"Good."

I smile and slide my fingers through the hair at his nape. "You have no idea how much I've wanted this. Us. I've waited and hoped for so long that we would figure it out."

There's a slight tinge of hesitation in his eyes, and I know this thing with Grayson is weighing on him. Jack doesn't have any family, the Parkerson brothers have basically adopted him, and I know that being with me is a risk he's struggling with.

"Jack," I call his attention back to me, "I promise that if Grayson or any of them . . . well, if they aren't . . ." The words lodge in my throat. I'm going to offer him an out because the only thing worse than not having Jack is hurting him. "If they won't support us, I won't let it destroy your friendship. I'll walk away."

"No," he says with an air of finality.

"I'm serious."

"And so am I. You were right when you said that we weren't doing anything wrong, Stella. Once Grayson gets over this, it will be fine. We will be fine. For twelve years, we've stayed apart, and I'm not doing it anymore. Christ. I'm not even sure I could if I had to."

My lips turn up, and I want to kiss him right here in front of everyone, but I don't have to make that choice because Jack does. He kisses me quickly and softly while my entire family watches.

I hear Oliver's voice above the rest. "And so it begins."

Fifteen

STELLA

Jack and I are official. I'm still struggling to wrap my head around it, but there's no going back now.

As soon as the kiss ends, I can actually feel the stares of my brothers. I've dealt with their overprotective bullshit since I was born, and as much as they'd like to think I give a shit about what they think, I don't.

I wrap my arms around Jack's middle, rest my head on his chest, and walk to the edge of the dance floor where Oliver stands. I might not care what they think, but I also know Oliver is the least likely to be a complete asshole.

He laughs as I approach. "Chicken shit."

"I went with the safest option."

"You just want me to take them on."

There is some level of truth to that. "Which you'll do because you love me the most."

Oliver can't deny it.

"Jack, I have to admit, that took balls."

"I just figure we get it all done at once," he says, gazing

down at me.

I hope he knows what he's asking for because before we can say anything else, Joshua and Alex approach.

"Did I see what I thought I saw?" Josh asks with his arms crossed.

"If you mean that Jack and I are together now, then yes," I answer first.

"And you kissed her?" Alex goes next.

I don't know how anyone who has brothers survives their nonsense. They're incredibly stupid and intrusive.

Jack's hand rests on my hip, and he clears his throat. "I know this may come as a surprise, but Stella and I have feelings for each other, and we've decided to date."

Oliver comes to my other side. "Let's not pretend we didn't see this coming."

He's definitely my favorite brother.

Josh's eyes turn to me. "Does Gray know?"

"Yes, and like I told him, I don't need any of your permission. I'm not a kid."

"No, but we're going into business together," Alex reminds us.

"It'll be fine. We're not stupid, and we know what it all means," I assure him.

Josh's lips are in a thin line. "I hope so." There is a small pause before he shrugs. "I'm not surprised. I've thought there was something for a while, but I figured you guys would never really act on it."

"We tried," Jack says. "I don't suggest it."

Josh looks at him, eyes wide, and then he turns away. Oliver extends a hand to Jack. "Be good to her."

Jack shakes his hand and nods. "Of course."

I turn to Alex, who releases a heavy sigh before doing the same gesture. "She's the best of us."

I shake my head. "For God's sake, he's not stealing me

away. We're going to date."

Joshua pinches the bridge of his nose. "If that's what you think, Meatball, you're the naïve one."

I don't care what they say, I'm not getting my hopes up. If this progresses, then great. If it doesn't, I won't be shocked.

Gray, who is standing on the fringe, catches my eyes, and I look up at Jack, who nods before his hand falls away. I love my brother. Whether he's wrong or right, he and I are extremely close. I don't want to see this tear any of us apart.

I walk to him and offer him a cautious smile. "Will you dance with your sister?" I ask.

He glances over at the four other men I love with my whole heart and then gives me his hand. "Come on."

For the first part, we don't talk. He seems lost in his thoughts, but then he looks down at me. "How long have you been going behind my back?"

"Gray, it's not like that."

"I saw you, Stell."

"We've been fighting it for a long time, but what you saw in the clearing was the tipping point, I promise. We haven't been sneaking around. That was us being unable to pretend anymore."

"And you love him?"

"I do."

A low sound rumbles from his chest. "I'm going to need some time to get my head on straight."

I smile softly. "I figured."

"I'm sure I'll get over it."

"I hope you'll find a way to be happy for me," I tell him, removing a piece of lint from his shoulder.

"You're making me feel like an ass."

"Okay, how about a turd?" I counter.

He smiles—reluctantly. "Jack? Really?"

"I know he's your best friend, and if you really don't want

me to date him, then I won't. It might break my heart, but for you, Gray, I will."

"Don't do that," he says, defeat in his voice. "I just need a few days, okay?"

"Okay."

"What did Josh and Alex say? I bet they were shocked."

"No one seems surprised."

His voice gets higher. "What?"

"Did you really never see it? The way we avoided each other? How hard it was for me to be around him, and the excuses I made to avoid him? Come on, Grayson, not even you are that oblivious."

"Maybe I am."

I give him a soft smile. "Or maybe you just wanted to be."

"If it goes bad . . ."

"You won't have to choose."

If there's anything I can promise, it's that. I won't make Grayson pick between us. Oliver said it would be the hardest part for him to reconcile, so I'm taking it away from him. I know that, no matter what happens, Jack would never make Grayson choose either.

I'll do whatever I have to do so that neither of them has to bear that burden.

"There wouldn't be an option. You're my sister."

"And he's like a brother to you." Gray looks over at Jack, a scowl on his face, and I laugh a little. "You're being stupid."

The song ends, and he kisses my cheek. "I know you say it wasn't like that, but he lied. He had opportunities to tell me and didn't. For that, he deserves to sweat it out."

Men. "For how long?"

"Until I'm not ready to rip his head off."

Jack and I are sitting in his car because Oliver is inside my condo.

"Are you okay?" he asks.

I turn quickly. "Why wouldn't I be?"

"You didn't say what happened with your brother."

"Grayson will be fine. I think he just wants to make you worry," I say with a grin.

"Sounds like him." Jack pauses. "So," he says, tilting his head to the side as our eyes meet.

"So."

He clears his throat and then takes my hand in his. "I won't lie, I'm not really sure how this all goes. For so long, I was pretty much convinced that, if this were to ever happen, it would be a dream."

I know exactly what he means. It's intimidating. Being with Jack like this, out in the open and where there's a real possibility of love, really isn't something I thought would ever happen.

It's weird and amazing and scary as hell.

"I don't either."

He smiles. "So, we're both unsure?"

"It would appear that way."

"I know one thing I'm sure of." Jack's voice is low.

"And what's that?" I ask softly.

"I want to kiss you."

My lips turn up, and I lean in a little. "There's nothing stopping you."

His fingers brush my cheek, leaving a trail of warmth in their wake. I fight back the sigh as his hand cups the back of my head. "No, there's not."

The heat of his breath fans across my face before his mouth is on mine. I push myself forward, eliminating any space I can without actually crawling over the console. A low moan escapes his lips as our tongues touch. It's different kissing Jack this way. When there's no reasons we shouldn't or fear of what would happen if we did.

It's freeing, and I never want it to end.

I push his suit jacket down and press my palms against his chest. He pulls my face closer, tilting it and kissing me deeply.

"I want you so much, Stella."

"You have no idea," I say between kisses.

He dominates my lips, pushing and pulling back as though it's a game. After what could be hours for all I care, he pulls back, resting his forehead against mine.

"But the first time we make love as a couple isn't going to be in this car with your brother up in your apartment."

I look up at my loft, and to punctuate why this is a bad idea, the curtain gets pulled back.

I groan when I see Oliver there.

"Great," I mutter.

Jack ducks down, seeing what I do, and laughs. "He's definitely the smartass of you all."

There my dumbass twin stands, staring at the car, tapping his finger on his wrist. "I'm surprised he hasn't knocked on the window."

"So am I."

I plop back down in my seat and sigh. "Do you know how much I want to invite you in?"

Jack grins. "Not as much as I want to accept the invitation."

"I wouldn't bet on that."

His thumb rubs against my lower lip. "We have time. I'm not going anywhere, and I've waited way too fucking long to complain about having to wait a little while longer."

"I just feel like we've lost so much time."

"We have, but we have so much in front of us. Who knows what would've been if we'd done this sooner? I don't know."

I sigh. "Me either, but I don't want to waste any of the time we have now."

"We're not wasting anything. Maybe being forced to go slow is a good thing? It will give us time to make sure we don't fuck anything up because we were being impulsive."

"What about this is impulsive?"

Jack looks up at the window where Oliver was. "Not impulsive, but there are things—or people—slowing us down and maybe that's a good thing. I don't want to fuck this up. I have a lot to lose if this goes bad."

"I think we both do, but I know that I'm willing to risk it all for you, Jack." He's quiet. I can see him trying to arrange his thoughts as he looks out the windshield. I give him a few minutes and do my best to stay calm since it seems Oliver has moved away from the window. The past would suggest that this is how Jack is when he's getting ready to run.

Finally, he turns to me. "You hold all the cards, Stella. When my family fell apart, your brothers were who held me together. If things go south between us, I'll not only have to deal with losing you, which I promise will fucking wreck me, but also your brothers. In the end, I'll be totally alone."

"Jack . . ."

I want to reassure him that is not the case. I won't let my brothers shun him. I know what it's like to feel alone. After we gave Kinsley up, I had no one. I couldn't talk to Jack. I couldn't talk to my family. It was horrible, and the pain was so bad that, at times, I wanted to die.

"I'm not asking for you to say a word. I know the risks, and there's nothing you could say or do to make it different or make me change my mind. You're worth the chance, Stella. You're worth losing it all for, but that's the reality of my situation. I want us to be sure. I want to make love to you more than I want air, but I need to talk to Grayson first. We have to iron this shit out before I do something I can't undo. Does that make sense?"

A part of me, the very stubborn and insubordinate part, wants to tell him that's ridiculous. I'd like very much for him to back out of this driveway, take me to his cabin, and screw me six ways to Sunday. That part of me would be wrong. Jack is the one who is risking the most.

I need to make sure that he doesn't lose anything.

"It does. As much as it pains me to get out of this car and go upstairs to where Oliver has probably done something that will piss me off, I know it's the right thing to do." I lean toward him, my voice soft and throaty. "Once you talk to Grayson, though, and you're both fine . . . I expect a very, very long and orgasmic night."

The sound that comes from him is almost a growl. "You can count on that."

"Good."

"Now go before I change my mind," Jack says, his hands gripping the steering wheel.

"Talk to him tomorrow," I whisper and give him a brief kiss. "Or I may have to take matters into my own hands."

I exit the car, smiling as I hear him groan.

JACK

"So, you and Stella?" Grayson asks while I stand outside his door.

"Can I come in?"

Jessica appears next to him, pulling the door open. "Of course you can."

Grayson huffs. It's been two days since his wedding, and hopefully enough time has passed for him to have cooled off.

"Thanks, Mrs. Parkerson."

She grins. "You were always my favorite, Jack O'Donnell."

"Seems he's a favorite among a few women in this town."

"Get it out now," I say, knowing he's got more.

"My sister?"

Jess groans. "You need to stop."

"No, he's always been this way," I tell her. "He thinks he knows what should and shouldn't be, so let him say his shit so we can get it over with."

Grayson walks toward the kitchen. "You came to my fucking house drunk, talking about how you didn't like her. You went on and on about some girl, and it was Stella?"

"It's always been Stella." There's no point in hiding that now.

He blinks a few times. "What about Misty?"

"Misty was never someone I dated."

Misty is the woman who was something else entirely.

"Are you kidding me? There's no fucking girl named Misty who you've been pining over?"

"It's complicated, but Stella is the only woman I've ever loved, and out of respect for you, I . . ." I can't say I never acted on those feelings, and I refuse to add more lies onto this. "I did my best to stay away from her. The two of us have fought it and tried, but I have been in love with her for a long time."

Grayson leans against the counter, fingers gripping the granite. At least they're not around my throat.

"Years?"

I nod.

"And have you . . ."

My throat goes dry because I know that if I tell him we've slept together, he's going to lose his fucking shit. If I lie, then I'm doing everything I promised myself I wouldn't do. "Do you really want to know the details or do you just want to know what I feel for her?"

Jessica comes beside him and takes his hand in hers. "Your sister is a grown woman who is entitled to live her life however she wants, and Jack is your best friend. Do you really think he'd do anything to hurt her?"

Grayson looks at me and shakes his head. "No, but you've both lied to me."

"It wasn't something either of us wanted to do."

"You could've told me, Jack. You could've sat me down and said you were in love with Stella and wanted to date her."

"I should have done it, but I wasn't ready either."

"Ready for what?"

Ready to let myself release the guilt of the past. In some ways, I'm still not. We have a daughter, and she never would have happened if I weren't being a selfish asshole. I went to that party because Grayson asked me to. I went to watch over her, be a friend, and I took advantage of her.

"For her."

He releases a heavy sigh. "I don't know what to say. I was so ready to tell you to fuck off, but I'm being ridiculous. It's not entirely about the fact that it's Stella, either. It's that you both had some big damn secret that I don't know about. I would've never stood in your damn way. I might not have been excited, but I wouldn't have stopped you."

"I'm sorry for that. I've tried to stop feeling this way—I really did, but then we were arguing at the wedding, and I'm not strong enough to stay away anymore."

Gray looks at Jess and smiles with a roll of his eyes. "I get that part."

"Yes you do," she says with triumph in her voice.

"No more lies," Grayson says, turning back to me.

I feel like I'm skating on fractured ice. I can twist a justification for keeping Kinsley from him, but a part of me knows it's still the lie he will see it as.

But Kinsley is Samuel's and telling Grayson and the family will do no good. They'll never know her any more than we will. So how do I answer this?

Jessica looks at me and links her arm around Grayson's. "Let's all agree that we're going to behave like adults, okay? You know about him and Stella, and I don't really think you want to know all the details, do you?"

Grayson makes a face that has me holding my breath to stop from laughing. After a few seconds, he sighs deeply. "Fine, I won't punch him."

I smirk. "Please, you hit like a girl."

Jessica slaps my chest playfully. "I resent that. I'll punch you in your junk, and we'll see what a girl hits like."

Grayson extends his arm. "By all means, I support this."

Just like that, the mood changes, and the restrained hostility melts away. "I take it back."

Jess laughs. "Good, because I'll do it."

"I have no doubt."

"Now, let's have a drink and toast to love." She lifts her hand to Grayson. "Relax, I will have apple juice."

She grabs us each a beer and then fills her glass with sparkling juice. Gray speaks first. "To never breaking my sister's heart so I don't have to break your face."

Jess huffs. "To love of friends and family."

"To finding the girl who makes you willing to take a beating."

Grayson smirks and clinks my bottle. "You have no idea."

I head right to Stella's after leaving Gray's. I promised her I'd let her know how it went. When I knock on the door, it's not her beautiful face I see, but Oliver's ugly mug.

"You here to shack up with my sister?" he asks with a smirk.

"I have a feeling we'll be hanging out at my cabin more than anywhere else," I note.

"So, you did want to get in her pants?"

"Ollie? What the hell?" Stella yells from the other room. "Is someone at the door?"

He turns to see her coming toward him. "Just an unwanted visitor."

She huffs. "Already you have a girl coming here? I thought I told you that I don't want you bringing random girls to my apartment. I don't care if you're single and still nursing your broken heart from Devney."

I laugh once, and Oliver opens the door. "I'm definitely not here for him, babe."

Her eyes widen as her smile grows wide. "Jack."

Just the sound of my name on her lips causes everything to click into place. The way she's looking at me, the tone of her voice that sounds as though her whole world just righted itself, are things I don't deserve. I have loved this woman for almost fifteen years, and I've never once felt good enough to stand in her shadow, let alone in her light.

She rushes toward me and jumps into my arms. "This is one hell of a hello."

"It's been two days."

"Two very long days," I say as I carry her inside.

"This is going to be unbearable." Oliver's voice cuts in from beside us. "If you two are going to be making these sighs and doing God knows what else, I'm not staying here."

Stella turns to him with a grin. "By all means, go stay with anyone else. I'm going to kiss my boyfriend."

He shudders and then walks away. Stella fuses her lips to mine, legs wrapped around my waist as she clings to me.

I carry her deeper into the loft to where the table is and rest her ass on it. My hands move to her back, tightening her body to mine. Two days of knowing she is mine but I still couldn't have her has been hell.

She pulls back. "Did you talk to Grayson?"

"I did."

"And?"

I kiss her again, giving her the best answer I can. Her fingers tangle in my hair, and she smiles against my lips.

"I like that answer," she says, her eyes filled with desire.

"Me too."

"He's fine?" Stella's voice is layered with concern.

"He's fine."

"So, now what?"

Now, if we were alone, I'd strip every piece of clothing off her and make her scream. But we're not alone, so I'm going to have to be patient. And by patient, I mean getting her back to my place where I can do just that.

"You get your shoes on, that's what."

Seventeen

JACK

My cabin is exactly eleven minutes and twenty-nine seconds from Stella's apartment.

We get into the car, smiling at each other. I've been waiting for this for years. I've dreamed a million fucking dreams about how it would happen. Now it's here and it's real.

I start the car, and after I turn onto the main road, Stella leans in, her hand on my thigh. "You know, I've wondered about this so many times," she says, verbalizing my thoughts. "I've hoped you'd do just this."

I shift in my seat, using all my focus not to embarrass myself. "Stella . . ." I warn.

She grins as her hand moves up. "I've imagined you coming to my house and telling me you couldn't stand it anymore."

"I can't."

"That you'd be so . . . overcome with your feelings that you'd toss me over your shoulder, carry me inside, and make love to me for hours."

She's trying to kill me.

"I promise, that's exactly what's going to happen."

We have one light in this town. One fucking light, and sure enough, it's red. I push my foot down on the brake harder than I mean to, holding it and the wheel with every ounce of control I have.

Seven more minutes. One long stretch and two turns. That's all we have left. I can do this. I will not look at her or think about her hand moving a little higher. How her dark hair will look against my pillow or the sweet scent of her perfume as I kiss every inch of her body.

I won't let myself imagine her laid out like a fucking goddess for me.

I won't.

Stella leans closer, her lips against my ear. "I want you so much, Jack." I close my eyes, clamping my jaw shut. "I have loved you for so long that I don't remember a time when I didn't."

The light turns, and I gun it. If Jeremy is out patrolling, he'll have to follow me to the house and cite me there. Nothing is going to stop me.

Three more minutes.

I start the ascent to my cabin, driving faster than I normally would, but I've never been in such a rush to get home.

One more turn.

When her fingers creep higher, I clasp her hand, stopping her from touching me.

She laughs softly. "Are you anxious?"

"You're playing a dangerous game, baby."

Stella's smile is sly. "I like games."

"I always win."

"I think we're both coming out victorious here."

She would be right.

I pull into my driveway, making it here in eight minutes flat, and throw the car into park. Before she can get her seatbelt off, I'm out of the car and opening her door. Once she's out of the passenger side, I grab her face and kiss her, shoving her back against the door. Stella matches my enthusiasm with her own. Her tongue meets mine, pushing her way into my mouth as though she's claiming me. I've never been anyone else's. Stella has owned my heart from a young age.

This girl, who is funny and sweet, has always been what I wanted. I took her once when she wasn't mine to have. This time, there's nothing holding me back.

"I want you inside," I say, lifting her and tossing her over my shoulder.

Stella giggles as I carry her toward the house.

"I want you inside too," she says, slapping my ass as we get to the door.

"You're going to kill me, woman."

"I sure hope not. At least not until after."

This is why I love her. The playful, fun side that is all mischief and smiles.

I get the door open and climb the stairs to my bedroom. When I toss her onto the bed, she laughs as she bounces softly.

Stella takes a second, looking around. "I've never been up here."

"You haven't."

I would never have been able to handle it. Stella in my bedroom would've ended exactly like this, which wasn't an option before.

She takes her lower lip between her teeth as her eyes move. The cabin is small, but nice. I've worked hard at remodeling it and modernizing it when I could. While I may work in the wilderness during my tours, I don't want to live like that constantly. The cabin is basically a large studio downstairs with a bedroom loft. From up here, you can see the entire place.

There's a nice-sized kitchen and a huge fireplace against the southern wall. The television is off to the side of the big windows that look out at the mountains.

Her eyes meet mine. "It's very you."

"How so?" I ask, suddenly feeling like that is a question I don't want to know the answer to.

Stella lifts her hand, touching my face softly. "It's strong, masculine, and tucked away where it thinks it's hidden, but I see it."

My heart is pounding as her words sink in. "And what do you see?"

"That it's perfect."

I move, climbing onto the bed and crawling toward her. She falls back, looking up at me with desire in those brown eyes. "You're perfect."

She shakes her head. "I'm far from it."

"Allow me to show you how wrong you are," I say. I push back a strand of hair that lies across her cheek, running my finger down her jawline. "First, you are beautiful beyond words. When I look at you, I want nothing more than to touch you. I dream of how my hands would skim every surface of your skin."

Her chest rises and falls a bit harder. "I dream of it too."

"We don't have to dream right now." I take the hem of her shirt and lift it over her head. God, she's so fucking gorgeous. "Besides, my imagination failed. You're better than I could ever imagine."

She smiles. "And what about my imagination?"

"What about it?"

"Do I not get to see if my mind remembers as poorly?"

"By all means," I say as an invitation.

Stella tugs my shirt off. Her fingers trail back down my chest, moving against every muscle. Her long lashes lift as she stares up at me. "It seems both our imaginations have failed us."

I move back over her, forcing her down onto the bed, and kiss her.

Because I can.

Because I've wanted to and have years of missed opportunities to make up for.

Because Stella is here and there is nothing keeping us apart anymore.

Our tongues slide against the others as her hands sink into my hair. I love how she holds me as though I'm anchoring her and she needs me as much as I need her.

My mouth leaves hers and trails down her neck and then lower. Stella pushes up a little, unhooking her bra but leaving it there. One brow lifts as if she's asking what I'm going to do about it.

Well, I know exactly what I want to do.

I pull it off, exposing her to my gaze. "So fucking beautiful."

"Touch me, Jack. Please."

The please does me in. I can't deny her anything. I lean down, tongue gliding around her nipple. She draws in a deep breath, and I take the bud into my mouth, sucking. I knead her breasts as my mouth worships back and forth.

Stella makes breathy sounds, and I focus on each one, trying to repeat the motion to make her moan.

"Jack," she says on a groan. "Don't stop."

It's not even a possibility.

I want to do this over and over until the two of us can't move. I want to make her scream, cry out, and beg me to stop. I plan for this night to last until the sun goes back down tomorrow. I'm going to pour twelve years' worth of love, desire, and need into the time I have now.

I kiss down farther, over her flat stomach, which was round the last time I touched it. Her hand moves to the back of my head. "Jack."

It's as though she's in the same memory as I am. I lift my head, seeing the emotion welling in her eyes. "I loved you then."

"I loved you too."

"I'm sorry, Stella."

There's so much that I'm apologizing for—all the pain we endured, the years of secrets and loneliness. I should've been stronger. I should've gone to war for her so that we didn't have to suffer because of the choices we made.

Her hand moves to my jaw, cupping my chin. "You have nothing to be sorry for. Tonight isn't about the past."

"I hate that I hurt you."

"I hurt you too." Stella's voice breaks. "We both hold blame, but we can't build the future on the regrets of the past."

I kiss her belly again. "I'm going to give you a future," I vow.

"With you."

"For as long as you want me."

"Forever."

Eighteen

STELLA

The word slips out as though it wasn't even a thought. He smiles down at me, and I breathe a sigh of relief. I'm going to need to put that back in check before I scare him off.

Jack pulls my pants down. He moves my legs apart before settling between them.

"Let's see if I remember how you taste."

I close my eyes, trying not to make a fool of myself. Jack was the first boy to ever do this to me. I remember the mortification I felt when he did it. Winnie told me about her boyfriend doing it to her, but mine never had.

That night with Jack, he was insistent. He said he had to or he might never forgive himself for not tasting me.

I was scarlet red, but once I got over the shock of it, I thought I might die.

Now I want nothing more than the feel of his mouth again.

His tongue swipes over my clit, and I arch my back. The pleasure running through every vein in my body.

"Even better," he says and then his tongue is there again. Jack licks, alternating the pressure, driving me insane. He moves in circles, then flicks, and then sucks as the climb to my orgasm moves faster than ever before. He finds a new rhythm, one that has me panting and crying out his name.

I have no idea what I'm saying other than one word here and there. There's a sheen of sweat forming on my face, and I can feel the tightening in my muscles.

"So close. So close. Oh, God," I pant.

He does it again, increasing the pressure on my clit, and as though we've reached the end of the music, I explode. I cry out, head thrashing back and forth as he holds my legs apart, continuing to lick and suck. The orgasm is wave after wave that drags me under.

When I catch my breath, Jack is on his knees, pulling his pants down. I watch as his cock springs free, and he grins at me.

Yeah, my memory has totally failed me. He's bigger—so much bigger—than I remember. His body is different, more defined. He's like a damn God who is chiseled in all the right places and hard as stone where I want him most.

Needing to explore him, I shove him back against his pillows. "I want to touch you," I tell him.

Jack puts both hands behind his head. "I'm all yours."

"Yes," I say with a smirk. "You are."

I kiss his neck, his shoulder, and his chest, letting my lips linger over the scar from a fire he was in four years ago. I kiss it again. "I remember this night." I remember every second of fear from not knowing if he was seriously hurt. All I heard from Grayson was that Jack needed care after being in an on-scene accident. I was terrified as I waited for the news that he was okay.

"The fire?"

I nod. "What happened?"

Jack moves a little. "One of the new guys was in a weak spot in the house. I saw the ceiling starting to come down, so I dove after him."

"And you got hurt."

"There was something between us that cut me. It was nothing."

I look up at him. "It wasn't nothing to me. I remember worrying so much. Gray said you're always the one who takes the risks. I don't want to lose you, Jack."

He sits up, taking my face in his hands. "I didn't have you then."

"You did. You just didn't know it."

Jack's head rests on mine, his eyes closed. "I didn't. Not really."

I kiss his lips, pouring all my fear and love into him. He had me, whether we understood it or not. He has always had me.

If he didn't understand that before, I'm going to make sure he does after tonight.

I shove him back down, and he resumes his relaxed position. Let's see how long he can stay like that.

My lips return to the place I last kissed, moving down his body. I don't wait or tease him, I want to make him lose his fucking mind. My tongue rings around the head of his cock before I take him deep.

"Fucking hell." Jack grunts, and then his hands are gripping the comforter.

I bob my head as I watch his thigh muscles tighten.

"Stella." He says my name as a plea to stop, but I don't.

I suck him deeper, moving at a pace I know will drive him wild. I want him to be out of his mind. I want to do for him what he did for me. He didn't allow me to reciprocate that night, and I've dreamed of taking him in my mouth so many times.

I'm going to live this fantasy out now.

My hand cups his balls as my other hand pumps in time with my mouth. Jack's fingers tangle in my hair while his other hand still clutches the bedding.

I love this. The power I have over this man right now.

"You have to stop." Jack's breath is coming faster. "Stella, fuck. Stop, baby."

I lift up, and Jack has me on my back before I can blink. He reaches toward his side table, grabbing a condom.

This time, at least, I have an IUD as well and we don't have to worry about forgetting a condom. He slips it on and braces above me.

His eyes tell me everything I need to know. Not only does he want me but also that he loves me. There's a slight lift of his lips as we allow this moment to pass between us.

I rub my finger down his strong jawline. "Make love to me, Jack."

He moves his hips, and I feel the tip of him at my core. "I won't be able to let you go, you know that?"

I nod quickly. "I know, and I'm counting on it."

He slides in deeper, and it's almost too much. The pieces of me that have been empty are whole again. He fills the gaps with each thrust. The passion and love we give each other as we make love borders on overwhelming.

Tears fill my vision as I wrap myself around him—legs bracketing his hips, hands clutching at his back. Jack pushes deeper again and again.

"Stella," he murmurs. "Stella, God, baby."

I look up through blurry vision, and a tear slips down. He wipes it away. "Don't cry."

"It's just so much," I explain as the tears keep coming. "I love you so much."

He leans down, lips touching mine sweetly. "I can't hold back," he admits. "God, you feel too good."

I know what he means. It's the culmination of time coming together with the promise of tomorrow. We don't have to hold back anymore. We can love each other and finally allow our feelings to grow.

"Let go," I urge him.

His lips are on mine a moment later, and he pushes harder, faster, and deeper than before. I fall apart again, Jack following seconds later, and I know that nothing will ever come close to that again.

It's nightfall, and I'm lying in his arms on the couch. The television is playing some movie that neither of us is watching. Dinner was . . . inventive. Jack is in desperate need of some food shopping.

I was able to put together some type of snack board with the crackers, salami, and cheese sticks he had. It wasn't elegant, but it was perfect for us.

He shifts a little, tucking me closer into his side. We are naked under the blankets, being warmed by each other and the fire.

"What are we watching again?" he asks after a few minutes.

"No clue."

"You put it on."

I shrug. "It's a movie channel."

He studies the television a little longer. "No, it's a chick movie channel."

I laugh at the face he makes. "It's all about love."

"How the hell did you even find this channel? I thought I only got sports."

"Yes, Jack, you get only sports channels on your television."

"Well, it's all that's ever on."

I shake my head. "Look, they're snowed in together."

"It's almost summer, why would we want to watch this?"

"She's the local farmer's daughter, and he's a grumpy business mogul who got stranded. Fifty bucks says they fall in love and he wants to stay there because he sees the simple life with her is worth more than this company."

Jack sighs deeply. "Are you implying this is somehow about us?"

I grin and nestle closer. "You do love me and are grumpy."

"I was grumpy. Today, I'm definitely not."

"Why is that?" I ask playfully.

"Some dark-haired beauty let me do very dirty things to her."

I laugh as the heat fills my cheeks. "She sounds like a keeper."

"I think she is."

I look up from under my lashes, batting them a few times. "Do you think she's worth more than a company?"

"She's worth everything."

My chest gets tighter. "She's scared," I confess.

"Of what?"

"Waking up tomorrow and losing her grumpy man."

Jack lifts my chin, waiting for my eyes to meet his. "She doesn't have to worry about that."

"It's easy to say."

"I know, and it'll take time for you to see it's true."

He gives me a brief kiss before I rest my head on his shoulder. This feels right. The two of us together, watching a movie on the couch. It's easy and effortless.

The movie keeps playing while Jack comments on how ridiculous the guy is. I try not to roll my eyes, but he keeps making me laugh.

"Seriously, if he can't make a choice, how does he run a company?"

"I don't know, how do you do it?"

Jack's face scrunches up. "Hey, I'm not a millionaire with nothing standing in my way."

"Yes, this is true."

"Besides"—he wiggles his brows—"I got the girl. This dude hasn't even gotten a kiss yet."

I shake my head. "You're a mess."

"No, I'm lucky. I have the most beautiful woman naked on my couch and under my blankets so I can do this . . ." His hand moves, rubbing the side of my breast.

Warmth spreads through me as his fingertips move across my nipple. "We've had sex three times already, you can't possibly want to do it again."

Jack pushes me flat on my back. "Does it feel like I don't?" He rocks his hips forward, and I can feel his erection through the blanket.

"I might need a better look."

He tears away the blanket between us, leaving no question as to exactly what he wants. "What do you think now?"

I grip his cock in my hand. "I think you should show me."

And he does—again.

Nineteen

STELLA

"Thank you, Winnie," I say as I hug my best friend. She's saving my butt.

Tonight, Jack is taking me on a date. A real one, but the instructions he sent are a little worrisome.

"I have no idea what the hell you need this for." Winnie hands me her backpack and a rain jacket.

"Me either."

She laughs. "You know this is usually gear you bring when you go on a hike."

I already thought of that, but Jack wouldn't be that stupid, right?

"I'm pretty sure he's just bringing me somewhere and is concerned I might get dirty so he's taking precautions," I say while opening the box of hiking boots I bought yesterday, per his instructions.

Winnie leans against the doorjamb and grins. "Yeah, that sounds like Jack—worried about you getting in the mud. He told you to bring hiking boots, which you didn't even have and needed to buy." She looks down at the box. "Are those heels?"

"They're cute, right?"

I lift one shoe out and marvel at it. It was the only fashionable pair of boots they had. They are fur-lined with thick laces that go up around the calf, but the heels make them look more like regular boots than hiking shoes.

Winnie bursts out laughing. "Stella, you bought heels! To hike!"

I groan. "You don't think he's going to make me hike, do you? I wanted to be sure I looked cute."

"I think it's pretty obvious that he means to take you out in the woods."

Damn it. "Maybe he'll surprise me."

"Oh, he's going to surprise you, all right," Winnie says with a laugh. "With a hike."

"It'll be fine. I love hiking."

"You're a liar." She shrugs. "But then again, you're dating a wilderness guide, what the hell do you think is going to be his idea of a date?"

I shake my head as the reality of this starts to hit me, and I look at her in horror. "Oh my God, do you think he's going to ask me to camp?"

Winnie almost chokes on her laughter. "You should see your face! Oh, Stella, it's priceless. I wouldn't discount the idea. He loves being outdoors, and I'm sure he wants to share his passion with you."

I'd much prefer passion without any chance of bugs or animals.

"I'm going to hate this."

"Probably, but you love Jack, so this is sort of a good compromise."

I roll my eyes. "Not that much."

"Liar."

Fine. She's right. I do love him, but Jack knows me. He

knows I don't do anything outside and camping is an absolute no.

"There's no way I'm sleeping outdoors, not even for him."

Oliver decides to come out of the guest room, which I refuse to let him repaint because Amelia picked the shade of pink she wanted. "Winnie!"

"Hey, Ollie."

My brother pulls her in for a tight hug.

"Are you going hiking?" he asks when he sees the boots.

"Not me, Stella is."

He bursts out laughing. "Stella?"

"Jack is taking her."

"He's not taking me hiking!" I say.

Oliver laughs harder. "Oh, it's like he wants this relationship to fail before it's even started."

"Right!" Winnie agrees.

"Maybe he doesn't know about the time we all went out in the woods."

I glare at Winnie. "Really?"

"What? You were a damn mess."

"She almost started a forest fire," Oliver offers.

I flip them off. How was I supposed to know that I needed to make a ring of rocks when I put almost the entire bottle of lighter fluid on the wood? No one told me anything, they just said to make a big flame, so I did.

"I'm so glad we're taking this trip down memory lane." The sarcasm in my voice can't be missed.

"Well, I'll send him a text to warn him that he may be in more danger than with the city people he's used to dealing with."

The people in my life suck.

"As much as I'd love to listen to you guys, I have a date to get ready for and you have to get to work." I point at Winnie.

Oliver elbows me. "Yeah? And how are you going to get

rid of me?"

"Jack is going to sleep here tomorrow."

His face falls a little, and I giggle. "And, on that note, I'm getting out of here," Winnie says.

"Thank you again." I give her a hug and lift the backpack.

"Call me when you get back . . . from camping!" Winnie calls from over her shoulder.

"Is he really sleeping here?" Oliver asks as I head into the kitchen.

"Yes, this is my place and we're going to have nights where he stays here and we have lots of loud, headboard-banging sex."

Oliver rubs his forehead. "I'm going to call Alex."

"Why?"

"I need to move out."

I pull into the driveway of where the resort is going to be out on Melia Lake. Jack is there, still in the same spot where he took the selfie he sent me moments ago to let me know he was waiting and I was late.

He's smiling as I walk to him.

"Hi there."

"Hello, gorgeous." He gets to his feet and then wraps his arms around me, kissing me sweetly.

This. This simple, easy, hello is everything. It's the little moments that have my heart feeling light. I pray we always have these moments.

I lean up, wanting another kiss. "So. What are we doing?"

He grins. "We're going to have fun, that's what we're doing."

"How?"

"We're going to hike first."

Jesus, Winnie was right.

All right. I mean, I was somewhat prepared for this. While it may not be what I want to do, relationships are about sacrifice, right? Jack may not want to go shopping one day, but when I book us a trip where I plan to do nothing but walk around and fill his arms with bags, he'll endure. I must do the same.

Or I can kill him.

I'll go with option one.

I plaster on a smile. "Hiking sounds great."

Jack bursts out laughing before pulling me into his arms, rocking back and forth as his shoulders bounce. "Oh, baby, that was almost priceless."

"What was?" I ask, forcing myself not to smile.

"Your face. You really tried."

I slap his chest. "Jerk."

"Stella, I've known you for a really fucking long time, and you have never once gone hiking, have you?"

"No."

"I am not going to force you to start now."

Now I almost wish we were going hiking so I could prove myself. "I could hike."

"If you were dying and needed to."

I shake my head. "I mean for fun. You do it."

"I like the outdoors, nature, and the land."

"I could too," I counter.

Of course, as luck would have it, some kind of flying object streaks by me, getting entirely too close to my face as it passes. I fall to the ground, letting out a very . . . loud screech as I go down.

Jack resumes his fit of laughter as he drops down on his haunches. "That was . . ."

"Shut up."

He tries to cover another laugh with a cough.

"Jack, if you ever want to see my breasts or any other part of me again, I really urge you to choke on your laughter before anything else escapes."

He clamps his mouth closed and nods. "All right, for the boobs, I'll do it. And those . . . whatever we're calling your boots."

I roll my eyes. "I didn't think we were hiking."

"We're not."

Jack rises and extends his hand, helping me up. "Well, if we're not hiking, what are we doing?"

"I didn't say *I* wasn't hiking."

"If this is a riddle, you really suck at it."

His fingers brush my cheek. "I'm going to be the only one hiking."

"You're leaving me here?" I ask with a hint of panic.

Instead of answering, he bends down and lifts me up over his shoulder. "I'll never leave a man behind."

I giggle as he moves through the woods, carrying me as though I weigh nothing. We go over a few rocks, but his gait never wavers. After we cross over a brook, he stops and puts me down.

"Get on my back," he instructs. "We have a little way to go."

"I can walk."

He turns to me, his eyes moving across my face. "I want to feel your body against mine, Stella. Let me carry you."

Well, I don't know that I am going to turn that down.

I lift up on my toes, pressing my lips to his. "You are a very sweet man."

"Remember that."

"Why?"

He winks. "Just remember."

"All right," I say warily.

He squats, and I wrap my arms and legs around him. As ridiculous as it feels to be getting a piggy back ride, it's sort of fun. We move through the woods with ease. I push a branch aside as he moves, and we spend the time laughing and talking, when I briefly mention my best friend's assumptions about our date.

"Winnie isn't wrong," Jack says as he hoists us over a fallen log.

"What do you mean?"

"We are camping."

I close my eyes and groan. "Jack!"

"You'll love it."

"I promise I won't."

Not unless the tent has running water and a bath.

Oh, maybe that's it. Maybe he got the RV from my brothers. That I could do. Glamping is a thing that I could get on board with.

Before I can ask another question, we push through to a clearing, but there is no damn RV.

Instead, it's a big white tent with a pallet in front of the door. The campsite is already set up with a pile of firewood to one side, a grill and coolers on the other, and a fire pit and chairs in the middle.

I slide off his back, looking around. As much as this isn't what I would've picked, I know that he worked hard on this.

Jack's hand slides in mine. "I want to share with you, Stella. I want to give you glimpses of the things we would've done if things had been different."

I look up at him. "What do you mean?"

"Had I been able to love you all those years ago, I would've taken you to the woods, and we would have shared a night under the stars. I would've begged you to let me make love to you in a tent with the fire glowing outside." He moves us so we're facing each other and settles his hands on my hips. "I would've spent countless nights beside you, showing you that the outdoors has advantages too."

"Like what?"

He leans close. "Like no one around us for miles. The stars above, twinkling as I kiss you. The way the air is clean, and I can inhale, taking in the smell of the wildness that is mingled with your perfume." Jack's lips move to my ear. "I want to feel like we're the only people in this world. I want to love you like this night is all we'll have so when we wake in each other's arms tomorrow, we see the sun rises for just us."

He pushes my flannel shirt down my shoulders, kissing my neck.

"And what do you want to do now?" I ask, already knowing where this is going.

I feel his grin against my skin. "Whatever you want."

I take his face in my hands, staring into his eyes. "I want you to show me the bed."

There is no cell service out here. That's the first thing that has me going a bit crazy. The second thing is the absolute silence.

I have no idea what time it is, but it's pitch-black and the fire has died to embers. Or, at least, I'm pretty sure it has since I can't see it anymore. Fuck if I know what the hell the fire is or isn't.

Jack and I are cocooned in the sleeping bag, his strong arms wrapped around me. As much as I didn't want to come camping, it's been fun.

Kind of.

Well, it hasn't sucked to the extent I thought it would, which is the first step toward thinking it could be fun.

However, I have to pee and this part doesn't seem so fun.

I reach for my phone to get the flashlight, and Jack's arm tightens. Great, now I'm going to pee in the sleeping bag. I try again, and this time, he rolls onto his back. The loss of his heat is immediate, and I shiver, but I need to move.

I pull my flannel shirt around me, throw on my boots, and rush out.

He showed me the spot on the left of the tent that he cleared so nothing would poke me as I squatted.

Seriously, he is going to pay for this.

Using my flashlight, I find the spot and internally groan.

I can do this. I am a smart, successful woman who has accomplished great things. Taking a piss outside is . . . easy.

I don't even believe myself.

An owl hoots from somewhere deep in the woods, and I take a deep breath, ignoring the fact that nature is all around me.

I sink down, and then I hear it.

A branch breaking.

I stand quickly, shining the flashlight around.

I don't move.

Silence.

It is probably nothing. I start to drop again, and then it's louder.

Leaves moving and another crack of the branch.

That's it. I am going to die.

I am that girl in those scary movies who thinks all is fine and goes outside where the murderer is waiting.

Only this time, it's not some serial killer, it's a bear or a lion. I don't think we have lions here, but if we do, I'm about to be dinner.

My legs are trembling, and I'm dangerously close to peeing on myself instead of behind a damn bush.

"Jack," I whisper-yell. "Jack!"

I can feel something's eyes on me. "Oh, please don't eat

me," I say to the creature that is probably licking its chops. "I'm bony and you'd much rather eat Jack, he's meatier."

I don't feel bad that I'm going to sacrifice him. *He* is who brought me camping. *He* should die first.

Although, I'm not sure I want to watch him get eaten.

I would miss him.

"Okay, I take it back, I'm a good appetizer," I tell the ferocious beast lurking in the woods.

"Jack!" I say louder this time. "Jack, something is going to kill me."

I start to back toward the tent and the shotgun I'm pretty sure Jack told me is in there.

I probably should've asked more about why he felt the need to carry a gun out here, but I was trying to put on a brave face.

Stupid that.

I take another step, listening to the sounds behind me too. "Jaccccck!" I say again.

Finally, I hear the tent zipper open, and Jack emerges with a lantern. "Stella?"

"Jack, there's something in the woods." I rush toward him.

He pulls me to his chest. "Where?"

"In the woods! I don't know where."

"Did you see it?"

I nod. "It was huge. It has to be because it was breaking trees down as it walked."

"Trees?"

It sounded like it. "Maybe small ones."

He looks around, scanning the area with an intensity that would be sexy if we weren't about to be eaten by a bear-lion thing that knocked down trees. He pushes me behind him, head turning to me. "Are you wearing pants?"

"Are you seriously asking that when Yogi is out there, wanting his version of a human picnic basket?"

"Stella, I've been on hundreds of camping trips and have only seen a bear once."

"What?" I screech. "You brought me out here when there are bears?"

"Go in the tent. I'll look around."

That would be great, but I still really have to pee. "Jack, I . . . I need to use the restroom."

He laughs once, and then the sound of something in the woods happens again. Within a heartbeat, Jack has me behind him and is walking me backward toward the tent. The light slashes through the inky darkness, and I can feel the tension in his muscles.

The light reflects, and I tap his shoulders. "There!" Two eyes are shining back at us. "I love you. I'm sorry I had to pee," I say as my last words.

It moves closer. It's a bear or a wolf or a lion or maybe some mutant version of the three. That's it. I'm going to die the first time I experienced nature.

The animal stalks closer as he moves us back with each step.

Then three things happen almost at the same time.

The killer emerges.

I scream.

And Jack bursts out laughing as I realize my killer is a deer.

I really hate nature.

Twenty

STELLA

My four siblings and I are seated in my father's study. It's the day. The day we're going to all walk out of our jobs, inheritance, and his life.

Alex's leg bounces continuously. Josh looks calm, Grayson is furious, and Oliver seems indifferent. It's insane that he's able to stay so carefree when the tension in the room is enough to make me feel ill.

Our father enters, looking us over before taking his seat behind the huge mahogany desk. "I see this is a family meeting. I'm sure it's about your mother."

Josh speaks first. "It's not. It's about you."

"Ahh, yes, I'm the villain. Go ahead, have your say." Dad leans back, arms over his chest.

Alex, the one closest to our mother, laughs. "You're incredible. You cheat for years. You play games with all our lives, and you think that we want a say? Do you really think all five of us came together just to let you have it? Come on, Dad, you're smarter than that. Or maybe you're not."

Dad's eyes narrow, and he sits straight. "Then what do you want?"

"I would've liked a good father, but clearly, that didn't happen," I say.

"Yes, you had it so hard, Stella. You've lived in luxury, owned a home before your friends were out of college, got a free education, and have a job that supports a life that most people would kill for. I'm a horrible father."

"You know what that cost me," I remind him of Kinsley. While no one else will know, I see the flash of emotion in his eyes that lets me know my barb hit.

Good.

"Everything comes with a price."

Grayson leans back in his chair, crossing his leg over the other. "And what is your price, Dad?"

"So, this is retribution?"

The slow smile that forms on my brother's lips is chilling. "It will be."

"What did I teach you about threats, Grayson?" Dad asks.

"Oh, don't you worry, Father. I will make good on my promises today."

For the first time since he entered, the confidence and manner of ease slips away. He assesses us, and I hope he's scared. He did this to us, trained us to be ruthless in business when we needed to be. While none of us have ever followed in his footsteps regarding other areas of his life, when it comes to this part—we're going to prove our mettle.

And this is going to come hard and fast.

Joshua drops a folder onto his desk. "We all plan to."

"What is this?" Dad asks, his voice filled with anger.

"This is what you taught us," I say with a smile.

Alex nods slowly. "It's what family does."

"Well, what a real family would do, not what he does. No, not our dad, he fucks around on Mom and sleeps with

Grayson's ex, who happens to be his granddaughter's fucking mother," Oliver speaks, his voice hard, which is a total contrast to his outward appearance. "But the thing is, we're not like you."

My father does his best to look unaffected, but it's clear he's not. The tic in his eye and the way he keeps shifting in the chair give him away. I really expected better of him. "Then you're weak."

I laugh this time. "Maybe we're weak apart, but together, we're stronger than you."

Josh grins at me. "You made an error." Dad doesn't say anything, and as he opens the file, Josh continues on. "At the age of twenty-five each of us was granted partial ownership of the company. We have shares and a seat on the board."

My father inhales and looks around. "This is what you're play is? To force me out?"

Grayson grins. "No. We don't want you to go anywhere."

"Then what?" My father finally snaps, getting to his feet.

Then Alex puts his folder down and walks over to Josh. "Nothing."

"You too?"

Oliver and Grayson do the same, giving them the paperwork we all have. My four brothers stand in front of me like a wall of power. When we talked about this, they were clear that I was to be the one to land the final blow. As his little girl, there's nothing that would hurt him more than it being me. I'm not really excited about it, but they're right. I am his only girl, the one person he thinks will always love him more than anyone else. And for a time, that was true.

I thought he walked on water. I believed in him because he was my daddy. The one man who I was supposed to always be able to count on. Then I learned that there's no such thing. He's a man. A flawed one who has a cruel streak as wide as his selfish one.

He forced me to give up my child because it didn't fit his appearances. He used power, family, threats, and money over me and Jack.

He broke my fucking heart, and I'm going to do the same.

Slowly, I place my hands on the arms of the chair and push myself up. I take two steps so I'm beside my brothers. "We're going to make you pay, Daddy." He swallows deeply, and I paint a sly smile on my lips. "You buy back all our shares or we'll use our other buyer. You see, the five of us no longer want to be in business with Parkerson Enterprises. You have a month to come up with the money to buy us all out or . . . we find someone else to do it, and then your precious company will crumble."

I walk out of the room, my brothers following after me, and none of us look back.

Twenty-One

JACK

"Let's stop here and get some water from the stream," I instruct the small group with me.

Today is the last day of our two-night bonding experience. The boss thought this would be a great way to help with office tension.

The boss is unglued.

All they've done is complain or criticize each other.

"How much longer?" Denise, the receptionist, asks.

"Just a few more miles."

She nods. "And how did we do?"

I smirk. "As expected."

"So we sucked?"

"No, you guys just aren't working as a unit, and I don't know that two days is enough to fix that," I explain.

Originally, they wanted a five-day exploration, but after talking to their boss, I convinced them to just do two. Five days is a lot and better suited for a group of people who don't blatantly hate each other. Not to mention, Stella and her brothers had the talk with their father yesterday. I really didn't want to be out in the woods during it so I could be there for her, but I couldn't convince Stella to wait, and I couldn't cancel this trip.

Having the trip shortened made it easier on my conscience.

She kept reassuring me it would be fine. I haven't been able to relax, and I won't until I know she's okay.

The boss walks over, wiping his forehead. "I tried."

"You did, but what you guys need is a reason to trust each other."

"I hoped this would do that."

It's clear he had their best interests at heart. "Then rally behind something. A common goal that the entire group cares about. When we set out, we had a plan, but that went to shit when members of the team broke off from the group."

Mike sighs and looks over at the two people I was talking about. "He thought he was going to get the promotion."

"So, he's working to create a divide."

Mike nods. "He's been with the company for years, and I haven't."

"Your boss clearly thought you deserved it."

"Yes, I work hard while Jim just screws around."

"Well, a two-night camping trip won't bring them all around, but creating meaningful relationships with the five who didn't exclude themselves might be a good start."

"Thanks," Mike says with sincerity.

"No problem." I clear my throat and address the group. "We have about two miles before we're back at camp. If we get a move on, we can make it back within an hour. I want to just say this before we start back up. I've been doing this a long time, and I've seen a lot of companies come out here and go back without having learned much. You're a team, and when you work as one, you'll accomplish more than you will divided. Grab your packs and let's go."

It's a last-ditch effort.

Everyone moves to grab their stuff, and one of the women is struggling with her pack. Before I can get there to help her, Mike takes it from her. He puts it on his chest, with his on his back, and carries it for her.

Right there, I see that maybe they'll find a way.

When we get back to base, everyone scatters, hugging each other before getting into their cars. I'm freaking beat, but I want to clean up before going to see Stella.

I go into the cabin that doubles as my office, check the messages, make a few notes of who to call back, and text Stella.

Me: Hey, baby. I'm back, and once I'm done showering, I'll head to you. Are you okay?

Stella: I'm good. I'll tell you about it when I see you.

Me: Okay. I'll see you soon.

I toss my phone onto the bed and enter the shower. Two days of no showers and bathing in the lake we usually swim in isn't so fun. The hot water sprays down on me. I rest my head against the cool tile, letting the steam release the tension in my muscles.

I'm not used to my trips leaving me feeling this way. Usually, I don't want to get back to civilization. I love the wilderness and the serenity that comes with it. This time, I was antsy. All I wanted was to be with Stella. I thought about her every fucking minute. This woman has crawled her way inside me, and I'll never be the same.

I sigh, eyes closed, and then I feel a hand on my back.

I jump, turning as my fight or flight spikes my adrenaline.

"Stella."

"I missed you," she says softly, moving her hand on my chest. "I need you."

"God, baby." I groan and pull her to me. "I always need

you."

The water comes down around us, and she's so gorgeous I can't breathe. She robs me of air and the only thing that will give me life is her.

My lips are against hers as I tighten her naked, wet body against mine and swallow her sounds. Her finger moves up my chest and into my hair, gripping the strands and holding me where she needs me.

I challenge her as we battle for control. I can feel her pain, her hurt, and there is a primitive urge to take it all from her. She is always so strong, and with me, Stella can let it go.

"Baby," I say as I move my mouth down her neck. "Tell me. Tell me what you need."

She sighs deeply as my hands move down her back to cup her ass. "You, I need you."

"What do you need me to do?"

"Take it away."

Those three words break my heart. "Always. I'll take it all, give it to me, Stella. Let me carry it for you."

Her head falls back as my tongue licks her nipple. I push her back against the wall, arms caging her in. Our breathing is labored, but I want her to see that, right now, I'm in control.

"Lift your arms." She does. I use one hand to hold them above her head. "You're so gorgeous. So strong and beautiful," I assure her. "I'm going to kiss every inch of you and then make love to you until you can't think of anything else but me."

She whimpers softly as my teeth bite down on her neck. "Jack." Stella's arms twitch, but I hold her in place and slide my other hand down to her clit.

Gently, I rub, making my circles slow and deliberate. "Today, as I was walking back, I thought about how much I wanted to touch you. For the last two days, you've been the only thing I've cared about. Not food, water, sleep, or the peace around me." I push against her body, my cock sliding against her heat. I want to sink into her. To take her over and over until she's screaming my name, but first, I want to make her as crazy as I've been.

"I've wanted you too."

"Good." I reward her by increasing the pressure. "Keep your arms up, Stella. If you move them, I'll stop. Do you understand?"

"Yes."

I kiss her, wanting to feel her tongue against mine because it's a gift I don't deserve. She was made for me.

I move down her body, sucking on each nipple and then moving lower. I lift her leg, pulling it to the side as she looks down at me, keeping her arms up. My position has never been more fitting. I'm on my knees before a woman I plan to worship.

My tongue slides up her pussy and around her clit. Her hips move, but she keeps her arms up. "Jack, I can't."

"You have to," I tell her before my tongue pushes against her clit.

I hold her thighs open and devour her. Every scream, cry, and plea makes me go harder. I want her incoherent, falling in my arms from the intense pleasure.

"God. I'm so close," she says over and over. "Jack, please!"

I flick her clit faster, harder, and I don't care when I feel her hands in my hair, holding me as she grinds her hips in the rhythm she needs. Stella rides my face, and it's fucking heaven.

She screams as her legs give out, but I catch her and lift her. With her back against the wall and the hot water falling over us, I thrust once, filling her while the very last pulses of her orgasm squeeze me.

"Yes!" Stella's cries echo as I pump harder.

We are past talking. All I want is her. I need to fall apart inside her, to have her climax again as I give her everything I am.

She takes my face in her hands, pushing her mouth to mine. I kiss her as I take her over and over.

"I'm close," I warn her.

"Me too."

We both climb, and I know I'm going to lose it. I hold on, wanting her to go before or with me.

"Jack. Yes. Jack."

"I can't . . . I need to . . ." I try to speak, but she clamps her legs tighter around me. "Stella, inside." It's all I can say, and I pray she understands. "Time. Now."

Her eyes lock onto mine. "It's okay. It's okay. I want you to come inside me."

I don't have another second. I thrust once more, a groan escaping me, and we sink to the floor. "I love you."

She sighs. "I love you. Never leave me."

I kiss her forehead. "Never." Stella giggles, and I stare down at her. "What?"

"Nothing, just that you may regret saying that after you hear about our plans for this weekend."

"Plans?"

"Most definitely. See, you owe me for that camping crap."

I have a feeling I'm about to pay for it greatly. "What exactly are you planning?"

She touches her finger to my lips. "It's nothing bad. I have to check out something for the resort plans before I meet with the contractors."

That doesn't sound too bad. Then I remember that Stella, when mischievous, can be a handful.

I narrow my eyes slightly. "Why do I not trust this?"

She grins. "Because you're a smart man, Jack O'Donnell. A very smart man."

Twenty-Two

STELLA

The last five days have passed like a whirlwind. I've been meeting with all kinds of designers and contractors and people who I had no idea existed but all needed a meeting.

It's crazy how much shit my father went through to get each inn up and running. Now it's our turn, which means it's mostly me doing it because my brothers are handling other things, like talking to possible buyers in case my father doesn't come up with the money. Jacob Arrowood agreed to invest if we needed him to, but my brothers and I decided he would be our last resort.

Today, though, is partial research and partial retribution for Jack dragging me camping.

Jack's car pulls into my driveway, and I grab my things to meet him out front. If he comes inside, chances are we'll end up naked and miss the appointment.

When in the car, leaning over to kiss him, his eyes sparkle with curiosity. "Where are we going?"

I could tell him, but turnabout is fair play. I grab his phone and punch in the address. "Follow the GPS."

"I really don't have a good feeling about this."

I grin, leaning my head back. "Trust me."

"Oh, I trust that I'm going to be in big trouble."

"You're being a baby."

He tilts his head, giving me a warning glance. "A baby?"

"I didn't know where we were going on my date, and I didn't cry about it. Hell, I hiked! I slept in the damn woods, for Christ's sake."

Jack lets out a low groan and puts the car in reverse.

The drive isn't long, and we chat about the last few days and what's going on with his end of the Firefly Resort. We all felt it was best to use the same contractors to do all aspects of the property, so Jack is working on his requests for his space. Joshua believes the larger bid will keep the contractors incentivized to finish the work on time and I think he's right.

When the directions tell him to turn right, I have to work hard to hide my glee.

He is going to kill me, and I can't wait.

"What the hell is this?"

"It's a spa."

"A spa?"

"Yes."

Jack glances at me with horror clear on his face. "You're taking me to a spa? Do I look like I do spa things?"

I look him over, pretending to ponder the question. "You look like you *need* to do spa things. What is with those eyebrows? There should be two."

His fingers grip the wheel, and I grin. "I knew better than to trust you."

I roll my eyes. "You made me pee outside . . . where I could've died . . . from a bear attack. Each time you want to gripe about a spa, let's remember that, shall we?"

Jack grumbles under his breath about women and love.

I take this as a win and exit the car. When we meet in the front, I grab his hands. "I love you, and this will be fun. We're going to get pampered and scrubbed. Plus, this is research."

He huffs. "Research for what? How to lose your man card?"

"You have one? Can I see it?"

"Stella." Jack groans around my name, and it's adorable.

"Oh, stop being such a turd. I didn't complain this much when you made me hike in heels."

His head falls back. "I carried you, so you didn't hike much. Plus, you're the one who bought hiking heels. I didn't even know they made that shit!"

"A woman must always be cute," I retort.

"Is that so? Even when the man wants that woman so much that he couldn't care less if she was wearing a sack?"

I step closer, lifting onto my tiptoes and pressing my lips to his. Such a sweet man he is. "What if I was wearing nothing?"

"Then I definitely wouldn't care."

I play with the neckline of his shirt. "Did you know that, when you get a massage, you don't wear any clothes?"

"Really?"

I nod. "And we are scheduled to have one . . . together."

He grins and wiggles his brows. "Let's go get naked then."

Oh, if he only knew what I planned to make him suffer through first.

Twenty-Three

JACK

I'm in a room, separate from Stella, wearing some flip-flop things that don't fit and a robe that leaves very little to the imagination.

The host? Worker? Spa person? Whatever we call her, led me here and gave me a glass of champagne while I waited for my first service.

I'm a little scared because, when I asked exactly how many services I was due to have, she grinned and told me to take a seat.

The room is nice, a little cold for my liking, but I'm not wearing shit under this robe because I thought we were going to get naked and rub each other down.

That sounded like a good time.

Sitting on this weird chair that is deep in the bottom, my legs feel like they're in the air, making it impossible to be comfortable with my bare ass practically hanging out. There are two doors, one that says 'Men' and the other 'Women'. I keep staring, waiting for my woman to show herself and explain why people think water with cucumber in it is appealing. Stella comes out wearing her robe that fully covers her chest and ass, a smile on her lips.

"Hi, honey. You look comfy."

I raise one brow. "Far from it."

She grins. "Imagine what it's like to hike in heels and then sleep in a tent."

Oh, I see where this is going. "So, this is payback?"

Stella's eyes widen, and she gasps. "Never. This is research."

"And you needed me?"

"I need a man's perspective on what things we should offer at the spa. It's important that we have every angle covered."

"And your brothers, who are also owners, aren't inclined to help?"

Stella walks toward me, a slow smile spreading as she moves. "I knew my amazing boyfriend would be the best at this."

"I see."

She laughs. "Oh, Jack, stop. I promise it will be great, and you'll still be brimming with testosterone at the end."

I grab her by the waist, pulling her onto my lap. My hand moves to her thigh, sliding up. "And naked?"

"If you behave." Her voice gives her away at the end. She wants me, us, just as much as I do. "Jack," she warns as I inch higher.

"Hmm?"

"You can't . . . not . . . this is a real spa, and I don't want to get kicked out. Wait, are you naked now?"

I laugh and stop my ascent to where I really want to touch her. "Yes. You said not to wear clothes for a massage."

"Oh, but . . ."

"But?"

She bites her lower lip. "Nothing."

"Uh-huh. But can we be clear that, after this, we're even. Right?"

Her lips touch mine briefly. "Okay. If you say so."

We sit like this for a little longer as she takes in the room. Stella's head tilts as she stares at something in particular.

"What is it?"

"Oh? Nothing. I'm just curious as to why they set this room up this way. If this were our space, I would want the wall of windows to be the focal point so I would have chairs over there instead of here."

I turn because I am seated facing away, which at the time seemed fine because I didn't care about the view. I wanted to look at Stella. Also, I never put my back to a door, but most women don't think about that.

"Maybe people want to talk?"

"Maybe. Just something to think about. Also, I like the color palette they used, but I think there is a more soothing color than this green. Green is so much of the mountains, so I'd like to have the contrast be a little stronger."

"No idea what that means."

She turns to me, brown eyes bright, and I see how much she really loves doing this. "What about you? Do you like this room?"

"Umm, it's fine. If you are a chick."

"Yeah, that's a great endorsement. I think we need to consider all our guests at our resort. If we're to be a destination for weddings, we need to have an area where guys can chill while they wait or have their own things done."

"Sweetheart, I can promise this will be the first and only time you have my ass in a spa."

She shifts, nudging me. "Want to bet on that?"

I chuckle and move her over on my lap more. "Maybe I should make that declaration after we're done."

Stella's smile is as bright as the sun. "You may like this

pampered life instead of the dirt and sweat outside."

"Remember I had a cushy office life once."

"And you gave it all up to be eaten by a bear. Listen, I love you and all, so I'm thinking maybe I should warn you . . ."

"Warn me about what?"

"Just that maybe you should go put something on under that robe."

Before I can say anything else, the spa person walks in. "Hi, I'm Kami, and I'm going to be your nail technician."

I look to Stella as I help her up. "Have fun. I'll wait here until it's our time."

My girlfriend doesn't hesitate. "Oh, no, my love, she's *your* technician."

My smile falters. "Mine?"

Kami watches us as if this isn't the first time she's witnessed this conversation. "I have you down for a manicure and a pedicure. Come right this way, Mr. O'Donnell."

Stella is trying to hold back her laughter. "Is this what your warning was for?"

She doesn't say anything as she grins.

"You're going to owe me, sweetheart. So much."

"I look forward to it."

"So do I." I lean into her, pulling her body against mine, and then kiss her passionately. Her fingers grip my hair as she returns the kiss. Kami clears her throat, and I pull back. Stella's eyes wild and breath ragged. "So do I."

"We will never speak about this again. Ever." I am fucking horrified.

As is Kami.

I think she's probably far more scarred than I am.

"Please, tell me what happened," Stella says with a smirk.

"You already know. Look at your face! You are fucking giddy."

She laughs. "I mean, I only heard what was said as we passed by. I figured you went back and put your boxers on before the pedicure."

I turn to her as she sits at the foot of the chair. "You failed to stress that was necessary, *Stella*. Instead, I was naked."

I didn't really know what the hell a pedicure was until I was being escorted over to a chair. Poor Kami and I shared a look as I pulled that robe a bit tighter when I had to sit down.

"We are only naked for the massages."

"I thought that's what this whole day was supposed to be!"

Stella can no longer control herself. A laugh so deep and loud practically explodes from her. She clutches her stomach. "You really flashed her?"

"She touched my foot!"

"So you showed her your dick?"

I groan, dropping my head back. "Not on purpose!"

"You shouldn't be embarrassed, you have a very nice dick."

If this situation were less humiliating, I would be happy she thinks that. However, poor Kami couldn't look at me after the unintended peep show.

"Can we go now? I think you've had your revenge."

Stella snorts. "Not a chance in hell. We have a lot more research to do."

"You can do it, I'll wait in the car."

I start to get up, and she rushes in front of me. "Jack, wait. I'm sorry. I didn't mean to laugh. I didn't know which order we were doing things or I would've warned you—more emphatically. Just think," she says with a soft lift in her voice, "you probably made her day with her surprise."

Stella's arms rest on my shoulders, fingers toying with the

hair on the back of my neck. "I'm pretty sure Kami turned purple."

She smiles awkwardly, obviously trying to stop herself from laughing again. "I really did want this to be fun for us. I love coming to the spa and wanted us to relax and be lost together. Please don't go. Not before we have our couple's massage. I swear it'll be amazing and relaxing with no horrifying surprises."

I sigh deeply. This woman has me whipped already. I can't and don't want to say no to her. Seeing her like this, after years of imagining this as a reality, has me tied up. For her.

Always her.

If she asked me to walk across hot coals, I would. Asking me to do this is nothing.

Even if Kami got a peep show she didn't ask for.

"Only a massage," I warn.

"Okay," she agrees far too quickly.

"I'm serious."

"I know. I'll cancel the waxing appointment."

"What?" I try to step back, but she clings tighter to me.

"I'm kidding. Kind of. I mean . . . I thought we could wax your balls or something, but I see now that was a bad idea."

Is she fucking insane?

I don't speak because I can't guarantee that what would come out would be coherent or kind.

Stella shifts, and the tops of her breasts peek out of her robe. "I wouldn't have made you do it. It was just a fun way to torture you."

"This is torture. You being in a room with me alone, practically fucking naked, while I can't touch you."

"Well, I'm always naked under my clothes."

I laugh. "Believe me, love. I know."

Each time I see her, it's an exercise in restraint not to rip her clothes off and make her scream my name.

It's like a dam that's been broken, the water rushing toward me that speaks her name.

She consumes my thoughts, and I'm not strong enough to resist her.

Two different spa employees enter. "I'm Jodi and this is Amy, we are your massage therapists for today. I'll be working on you Jack," Jodi says.

Seems Kami has left me.

"And I'll be your therapist." Amy smiles at Stella. "Are you both ready to go in?"

Stella's brown eyes lock onto mine. "Will you do the massage with me?"

I sigh in resignation. "Yes. I'll do the massage."

She walks backward, pulling me with her as she moves toward the door.

When we get into the room, there are two tables in the middle and candles everywhere. Some instrumental music is playing in the background, and Stella sighs deeply.

"You can both get undressed, lie face down on the table under the sheet, and we'll be back in a few to get started."

This isn't what I was expecting.

The door closes, shutting us away in the softly lit space. "This is supposed to be relaxing? I thought that *you* were giving me the massage."

"How would that be relaxing for me?"

There are rules for dating, and I didn't think another chick rubbing me down with oil in a room with sex music and incense was cool, but Stella is the one who set this up.

"I don't know, but I'm not going to be in trouble for this later?"

She squints, shaking her head at the same time. "Why the hell would you be in trouble?"

"I'm about to get oiled up."

Stella laughs softly and walks to me. Her hands rest on my

chest, long brown hair falling down her back, making her look insanely attractive in the candlelight. "There is nothing sexual about them touching you. I promise, you'll probably hurt afterward because they're going to work out all the tension in your body."

And she said this was supposed to be relaxing . . .

"Good to know. I'll carry the memories of this day with me always."

Stella sighs deeply and takes a step back. Her hand moves to her robe, untying the belt, allowing the terrycloth fabric to gape open. "Fucking hell."

"You can go now or you can take your robe off and get on the table. If you stay, when we get home, I'll let you wash all the oil off me. How does that sound?"

I do as she says, dropping my robe and loving how Stella's eyes take me all in. "Enjoying the view?"

She grins. "Absolutely worth it. Don't you think?"

"Yeah, you are. You're worth everything."

Twenty-Four

STELLA

"It'll be fine," I tell Jack while we stand outside of Grayson's house.

"It's going to be weird."

"Yes, but it'll be fine. Gray will give us shit, we'll ignore him, and then we can go back to my place."

Jack gives me a side eye. "Where Oliver is waiting?"

I sigh. "He'll move out after the first night we have sex at my place. It's time to rip off this Band-Aid so we can move past it."

Jack and I have been living in a cloud of happiness. I survived camping and he endured the spa. We've had dinner together almost every night, worked on a few business plans, and have spent countless hours making love. I've been able to confide in Jack the way I always dreamed of doing.

He's a partner, a friend, and one hell of a lover.

Jack squeezes my hand a little, shaking out his arms. "No backing out now. If you can attempt camping, and I didn't kill you after the spa day, then we can handle dinner with your brother."

He knocks on the door, and it opens suspiciously fast, as if my niece had been waiting for us. "Auntie!" Amelia yells and launches herself at me. I barely have time to catch her.

"Hey, Monkey!"

"I've missed you. It's been forever since you came to see me."

Grayson is married, so there's very little need for me to watch her anymore, but that is no excuse. "Well, I'm just going to have to steal you away then."

"Tonight?"

I smile and tap her nose. "Not tonight, but soon."

She lets out a dramatic sigh. "Fine."

Jack drops down and grabs her hips. "Hey, what about me? I don't get a hello?"

Amelia's eyes brighten. "Of course you do." Her little arms wrap around his neck, and he squeezes her tight as he stands and carries her inside.

We find Grayson in the living room, sitting on the couch. "I'm told I have to behave."

"That'll be a first," I toss back.

"The punishment I'll endure will be a form of torture I don't subscribe to."

I grin, imagining what my sister-in-law has threatened him with. "I really love your wife."

"She apparently loves you."

I grin and kiss his cheek. "Hello, brother."

"Hello, sister."

Jack comes up behind me, wearing Amelia like a necklace as she dangles while giggling. "Gray."

He grunts. "Jack . . . ass."

Before I can chide him, Jessica's voice comes from the kitchen. "I heard that!"

"It's what we call a donkey," Gray yells over his shoulder.

"Am I not allowed to refer to animals now?"

"Nice try. Let that be your warning."

He huffs and extends his hand to Jack. "Good to see you again, even if I'm still not sure I *like* you."

Jack lifts Amelia up, gives her a kiss on the forehead, and then takes Grayson's hand. "I haven't been sure if I've liked you for a long time."

"You both love each other in a bromance kind of way." Jessica yells again. "Exactly. Now hug it out so we can eat in peace."

"It's a good thing we have women in our lives to let us know what we think," Grayson says with a laugh.

"I have a feeling they will let us know a lot more than that."

"Gray?" I call as I'm heading into the kitchen.

"Yeah?"

"Be sure to ask Jack all about how fun pedicures are. He really loves showing things off."

Jack lets out a curse, but I walk away before hearing the rest, leaving Jack to my brother's mercy as I seek out Jessica.

She pulls me in for a tight hug. "You're happy?"

I nod. "Very."

"Good."

It is. Life is good right now. Jack and I are figuring things out, and Grayson has Jess to make him not be an idiot. All in all, things are exactly how I always hoped they'd be.

The only big obstacle left is my father. His time to get the funds together to buy all of us out is ticking away. If he can't manage it, then Jacob Arrowood, Jessica's friend who just happens to be my favorite actor, is willing to buy them. He'll take over everything and force my father out and either sell off the properties or maybe enter a new business venture. Either way, all of us will have the capital we need to get the Firefly Resort off the ground.

"I'm glad you guys could come tonight."

I smile at Jess. "There's nowhere else we'd rather be."

Jessica snorts. "Oh, I'm sure there's somewhere else."

I let out a laugh and try to hide the blush warming my cheeks.

"I know that look." Her voice drops to a whisper. "Is it everything you hoped?"

I nod. "More."

"Good. You deserve more."

Grayson walks into the kitchen, and his eyes narrow. "What are you two whispering about?"

Jessica replies before I can. "Sex."

His face is priceless. He turns, leaving as quickly as he entered.

"Jess," I hiss.

"Please. He is the one who said he didn't want any more lies when it comes to you and Jack. I'm just reminding him that sometimes we leave things out to spare others. He doesn't really want to hear about you and his best friend and not everything is his business."

The *not everything* Jessica means is Kinsley. Telling her was a risk. I trusted that she wouldn't tell Grayson, and so far, she hasn't.

In fact, this is the first time she's even eluded to suggesting that maybe she means more than what she's saying. She hasn't mentioned her or asked questions, content to let me get it out how I needed to.

For that alone, she's become a friend I would do anything for.

"I don't want to ask you to lie to your husband."

"You're not."

In a way, I am. "He won't see it that way," I say as I trace the patterns in the wood countertop.

Jessica stops chopping the vegetables and places her hand

over mine. "You have a right to your secrets, just as he has to his. We all do."

I force a smile and shove down my emotions. There's guilt, like always, but there is also shame because my brother would never have done things the way I did.

"No more thinking about this. Let's talk about you and the baby. How are you feeling?"

Understanding fills her eyes, and she smiles back. "I'm good. No sickness and the regular checkups keep me from being anxious."

Jessica wasn't very far along when she was trapped in the fire. She is lucky, and Grayson has insisted that she have a team of doctors to monitor her pregnancy. The last ultrasound showed the baby is healthy and everything looks like it should.

That was a huge relief right before the wedding.

"You have no idea how happy that makes me."

"I think that's why Grayson was such a lunatic about you and Jack. It was just one more thing for him to worry about."

"And the fact that he felt blindsided."

"Well, sure," she says with a shrug.

Jack enters the kitchen and wraps his arms around me from behind. "You okay?"

I nod, my smile instantaneous.

"Want a glass of wine?"

I turn my head so I can see his profile. "I would love one."

"Coming right up."

He goes back into the other room, and I turn to find Jess grinning like a fool. "You guys are so cute."

"Stop it."

She laughs. "I'm serious. You guys are perfect, and I'm so happy you got your heads out of your asses and finally made it happen."

"It's not weird?"

"No. In fact, I don't know how the hell none of us ever

saw this."

"You were all worried about other things, which is sort of what we banked on."

If everyone had been able to tell that Jack and I were in love and struggling, it would've been terrible. We were too young and dealing with too much.

The timing wasn't right until now.

Well, I hope that's the case anyway.

Jack returns with a glass of wine, and I get a brief kiss. "I'm going to get my nails painted once she's done doing Grayson's."

I giggle. "Oh? And what shade are you going for?"

"Amelia is picking."

"I hope she does pink."

"I'm sure she will."

As am I. Amelia loves pink, and her favorite thing in the world is going to get her nails done. My mother takes her every other week when she goes. They make her feel like a princess, and she's always excited to show off her new polish.

It's adorable, and I love that Grayson and Jack are allowing her to paint their nails without argument.

Although, I'm pretty sure they'd let that little girl do just about anything to them. Putty in her hands is what those men are.

Jessica and I bring out the plates of food, putting them on the table and laughing as Grayson blows on his nails.

My phone rings, and my heart stops. It's Mickey.

"I have to take this," I say to Jess.

"Sure. Of course."

I walk outside and swipe the screen. "Mickey?"

"Hey, Stella, I . . . I wanted to call you because it's bad again."

I let out a deep sigh. "How bad?"

"I was out of town for the last five days, and my buddy

ended up calling Samuel a cab because he was too drunk to drive. The drain he was circling, well, he's down it now. He needs help that I sure as hell can't give him."

"I'm not sure what to do. Samuel hasn't replied to any of my calls or emails. I took it as a sign that he wanted distance to deal with things. I understood and didn't push, but this has me worried.

"I've been trying to get in touch with him."

"He was doing better for a while there, but . . . I don't know."

"Did he say anything?"

"Yeah, he asked me to call you, which I was going to do anyway. I'm at his place, and he keeps saying he has to go in. I don't know what that means, but you should probably come down."

I bite my thumb, looking through the window at my brother and Jack with Amelia. "Is his daughter there?"

My chest is tight as I wait for his answer. "There's a note saying she went to stay at a friend's house."

A note. Jesus. She's still young, but she's old enough to know her dad is spiraling. Kids are young, not stupid. "I'll . . . I'll leave tomorrow. I have to deal with a few things before I can go."

"Okay. I'll check on him in the morning, make sure he's okay before you get here."

"Thanks, Mickey."

His deep laughter fills the phone. "Don't thank me, princess. You haven't gotten my bill."

I roll my eyes, and the phone goes dead. This is a mess, and if Samuel is asking for me, then I have to go. Still, I know it won't be easy. Jack won't want me to do it, and once again, I'll have to lie to the people I love about where I'm going.

Blowing out a deep breath, I work on calming myself. I need to get through tonight and then I can deal with the rest.

The scene through the glass is picturesque. My brother is on the floor with Amelia, and Jessica comes around the corner to take a seat on the couch behind him. Jack is there, laughing as Amelia swipes another coat on Grayson's nail.

Jack looks up, and our eyes lock. My going down there is not something I can keep from him, but I also know how he feels.

Jack's smile is wide as he jerks his head, indicating I should come inside.

I nod once, swallowing the emotion that's churning inside me, and vow to do whatever I can to get through tonight.

We pull up to my apartment, and Jack puts the car in park. "Are you going to tell me what's going on now?"

"Am I that obvious?" I ask.

"Well, I know you, and after that phone call, something changed."

"Do you remember when I told you about the bartender in Georgia? The one who helped with Samuel?"

Jack's hands clench, but his voice stays level. "Yes. You said he'd call you if Samuel was in trouble again."

"Yes, well, he's in trouble."

"Drinking again?"

I nod. "He said it's bad and that Samuel asked me to come."

"And what are you going to do?"

I can hear the censure in his voice. Jack may not want me to get involved, but I feel like I have to. It's not just that Misty was a good friend. It's also because that's our daughter whether we have any rights or not. I didn't raise her, but I still love her, and I don't know how he doesn't see that.

I promised myself that I would never abandon her again,

and that's what turning my back would be.

"I'm going to go," I tell him.

"No matter what?"

I swallow and then clear my throat. "Yes. He asked me to come."

"What part of this seems like a good idea, Stella?"

"None of it, but it is what it is. Samuel needs help, and I'm sorry, but that means Kinsley does too."

He runs his hands through his hair. "We've survived this for twelve years because we agreed then when we gave her up, that was it. We aren't her parents. We are complete strangers to her."

"That may be, but Misty is dead, Jack. She died and things changed. While I understand your feelings and respect them, I can't pretend that call didn't come in. I can't pretend as if it's okay that Samuel is falling apart and getting drunk in bars while she is alone."

"I'm not asking you to."

"No, you're just asking me not to go."

He pushes the air from his mouth. "If you go, then what?"

"I'll figure it out."

There is no way to answer that. I could get down there and find that Samuel is totally okay. This last week could have been just a hard day for him. Or I could find a totally different scene. From what Mickey said, it's more likely to be the second. No matter what, that little girl has lost enough, and I won't hang her out to dry.

Jack's voice is low. "You're setting yourself up for heartache. And don't take that as me not caring, because I do. I . . . I care, Stella, but I also know that this doesn't end well for you. You who has the kindest heart and there's no way to protect her. You aren't her parent. You have no rights. We gave those away. Misty was who *allowed* you glimpses into her life. If she hadn't, there was nothing we could've done and we knew that.

We were told, when we signed the papers, that it was the spirit of the agreement, nothing was mandated other than our names weren't hidden on the birth certificate. Remember?"

I'm well aware of that. I know that after the sixty-day period, I lost all rights to that girl. I'm aware that even though we had an agreement for updates, it wasn't legally binding. I just had to trust Misty and Samuel, the same as they trusted us during my pregnancy.

Still, the fact remains that he asked me for help and I'm not going to turn my back.

"I didn't forget that, Jack. She's still our daughter regardless of the paperwork."

He leans toward me. "She's not. She's a child we had, but fuck, Stella. How don't you see what lines you're crossing?"

All I see right now is that he's willing to let her suffer. "I can't see this your way."

Jack sighs, his shoulders drop, and I can see this is wearing on him. "I love you. I want nothing more than to change all of this, but our only *legal* option is to call child services. Is that what you want?"

"Of course not! I want to help."

"And what if you being there makes it worse? What if you go there and Kinsley wants nothing to do with you? What if she rails about how you're the worst mother because you left her with another family? What then? How the hell will you handle that?"

I start to tremble, fear making it hard to speak, so I don't.

Jack places his hand on mine. "This is a mistake."

"Maybe it is, but it's one I have to make. With or without your support."

Twenty-Five

JACK

I can't lose her. All night long I felt her slipping away as that argument went on.

Stella is asleep—head on my arm and legs entangled with mine. At some point during the night, I went from holding her to having her suction cup herself to my body. I don't complain, though, because having her beside me at night is the only way I want to sleep.

In a few minutes, she'll wake up and then she'll leave.

I understand her reasoning, and I don't blame her for going, but I know it will change things. I've spent twelve years pretending that Kinsley wasn't real in some way. I built walls to protect myself and in a matter of a few months, they've come crashing down. My heart is breaking for what she's going through and there's also a level of self-preservation screaming inside of me.

There won't be a way out of this that doesn't devastate everyone. Samuel is a mess, Kinsley might be hurt, I know Stella and I will. Nothing about this is going to go in a direction that isn't a catastrophe.

My fingers brush her long brown hair down her bare back. She nuzzles closer and makes a mewling noise.

The only thing I do know, is that she won't do this alone. Even if we end up crushed, we'll do it together.

Slowly, she pulls herself from sleep, lashes blinking slowly as she tightens her arms. "Good morning."

"Good morning."

"I like this."

"Me too," I say, not caring what part she's referring to because I like it all.

"Did you sleep well?"

I didn't sleep at all. My mind was going in circles, which led me nowhere but back to the thought that if she goes, everything would change because I would've done the exact opposite of what she needed—be there.

All I would've had was one month.

Not that I would trade it. It's been the best month of my life, but still, this would be all we'd have, and that is how our story has always seemed to be.

Not meant for forever.

Stella's fingertips slide against my jaw. I take her hand in mine and bring it to my lips. "I had you snoring in my ear, what do you think?"

Her jaw drops. "I don't snore."

I grin. "You do."

"Jack! You're not supposed to say it."

"Why?"

"Because . . . you're supposed to pretend." She rolls her eyes dramatically and huffs.

"Well, you snore, and it's adorable. I would listen to it every night if it means you were here."

Her lips turn into a tentative smile. "Do you think I won't be here?"

"I don't know," I answer her honestly. "What time are you leaving today?"

She lowers her lids and shifts her body closer. "I don't know. Soon."

A mix of dread and panic fills my chest, making breathing difficult. I grappled all night with what the right thing to do is. Losing Stella isn't an option for me and I will support her no matter what, even if I don't agree.

There are really only two options. I let her go, stay here and hope it goes well, or I go with her. I stand beside her like I should've done all those years ago.

"I want to go with you," I tell her.

Stella's eyes open wide. "What?"

"I'd like to come. I want to be there and help you get Samuel through whatever he's dealing with."

"But . . . Jack."

"I know. I know the chance of seeing Kinsley is there, and I know what all of it means, but I love you, Stella. I love you, and while she's not our daughter, she came from us. You and I can do this together, and we'll figure it out. You shouldn't have to do this alone."

Her lip trembles. "I don't know what to say. I feel . . . a lot."

"I have been feeling it all night."

Stella releases a shaky breath. "Jack, are you sure? You don't have to do this."

"No, I do. I thought about it all night. We may not have rights, but we have to help them. We sacrificed when we gave her up and we survived, we'll do it again."

Tears fill her eyes. "You're a good man."

"Only because of you."

And it's true. She makes me want to be better. While I would rather not deal with any of this, we have to. Samuel is struggling, and when we were drowning, he threw us a lifeline.

We entrusted Kinsley in his care and I can't turn my back on what's happening to her now.

She rests her head back on my chest, and I feel the tears pool there. "Don't cry, baby."

"I'm not sad." Stella lifts her head and wipes her cheeks. "I'm overwhelmed, and I was worried that this was going to break us."

"It won't. I won't let it."

"Me either."

"Then we go down there with a plan. We help Samuel and Kinsley and come back home."

"I agree. I'm scared," she admits.

"Of?" There are a million things that she could be worried about, most of which are probably the same things I spent all night agonizing over. The biggest is seeing Kinsley. I don't know what she knows. I don't know how I'm going to see her and then leave her again. I'm not sure I'll be able to get through it again.

When I gave her over, it was the worst moment of my life. Giving the sweet little girl, who I loved even though I'd just met her, to another family is a feeling I'll never forget.

I handed her to another person to love.

I gave her away.

I just don't know that it won't destroy me if she hates me for giving her up.

But for Stella, I'll find a way to do what we can to help Samuel because I would rather endure the pain of having to never know Kinsley than allow Stella or our daughter to feel even a fraction of sadness.

"Seeing her this time. And if we do, leaving her or having to answer questions that I either can't fully explain or I don't want to."

"You didn't see her the last time, though?"

"No," Stella says, looking away. "I didn't, but she was at

a friend's house and I have no idea. I was scared when I went the last time."

"Well, if we do see her, and have to go down that road, hopefully she'll understand that we were kids."

Stella shrugs a little. "We were, but we're not now. We chose never to push the door open and ask for Misty to let us in further."

Where I didn't even see a door. I put studs, drywall, and a fucking steel cage around that door.

"You did what you had to."

"We both did," she says with understanding.

I push back the hair that clings to her lips. "All we know is that he needs help. We don't know what kind of help or how bad it is. Whatever situation we walk into, we'll handle it. Hopefully, this is like the last time."

She smiles softly. "Right, we'll go down, clean him up, help him with whatever, and be back home without anyone knowing."

"Exactly."

I'm really hoping this bartender friend is overexaggerating. Maybe he had a few drinks and just needed to sleep it off.

Her phone rings, and she reaches for it. "It's Samuel," she says. There's hesitation as the ringer goes again.

"Answer it. I'm right here."

Stella does, and they talk while I only hear the one side of the conversation. "I understand. Jack and I are coming down, and we can talk then." After a second, she nods. "Okay." He talks again. "That's good, Samuel." Her breath hitches, and her eyes dart to me. "We'll figure it out. I . . . we'll be there in a few hours. Just stay home and try to see if she can stay at her friend's house until then."

"What did he say?" I ask as she hangs up.

"He's not doing well."

I push up and rest my hand on her back. "We'll do what we

can, and I'm sure it'll be fine."

Her head shakes a little. "No, Jack, I don't think you understand."

"Okay, tell me."

Stella turns to face me. "I think we're going to have to bring Kinsley home with us."

And just like that, all my fears have come true. We will never be the same again.

STELLA

Jack has barely spoken for the entire ride. I think I can count on one hand the words exchanged. I understand his silence because there's not much I really want to say either.

The GPS continues to direct us, and I thank God for that because I know I can't focus on anything other than Samuel saying he might need me to take her.

Now we're here, turning onto his road, and I feel like I might be sick.

Mickey's car is parked in the driveway. I sent him a text when we left, and he said he'd wait until I got here.

We pull up, stopping in front of his house.

Jack looks out the window. "No going back now."

I take his hand, not just because he might need it but because I do as well. "We'll find a way through it, won't we?"

His hazel eyes are filled with a mix of emotions. I try to piece them out, but mostly I see his worry. This is as hard for him as it is for me, but Jack has spent the last twelve years living as though this never happened.

At least I saw photos and got letters.

Jack's fingers tighten a little. "We will."

We get out of the car, and Mickey opens the door. "Sad to see you again."

I smile. "Same. This is Jack."

Jack shakes his hand. "Thanks for helping."

"Are you his brother?"

"No, I'm Stella's boyfriend."

I step forward before this gets stupid. "What happened last night?"

They eye each other, and then Mickey nods. "Samuel is bad. He's on a bender like I haven't seen in a while. He needs help, real help. Before I called you, he got in touch with his brother, who said he can't come or do anything. I guess Samuel borrowed money or something from him and he's mad. I don't know. The daughter called and said she'd be home later."

"I don't know what to do."

Mickey lifts one shoulder. "It's his call. I've been around long enough to see this go bad. He's . . . out of control. I think he lost his job. There are bills stacked up in the kitchen."

I look to Jack as he rubs the back of his neck. "We should go in and see what we're dealing with."

"Thank you," I say to Mickey.

He gives me a sad smile. "I'm going to stick around while you talk to him in case you need anything. Whatever tipped him over was bad. I like the guy, and well, we've sort of become friends."

"Of course."

We head into the house, and it's so much worse than the last time I was here.

In the living room, the television is on low and Samuel is wrapped in a blanket. He turns when we enter.

"Stella."

I walk over and sit beside him, pulling him in for a hug. "Are you okay?"

He starts to cry. "I can't do this. I tried. I tried for her, but I can't. I lost it all, and I'm drowning."

I rub his back, trying to calm him. "Talk to us. We're all here to help."

Samuel pulls himself back up and takes a good look at Jack. It takes him a second, but then he gasps. "Oh my God. Jack?"

Jack looks to me and then to Samuel. "Hi, Samuel. It's been a long time."

Samuel rises, his legs wobbling, and he extends his hand. "It has been, and I wish it wasn't like this now."

Jack nods once and helps Samuel back down.

Mickey clears his throat. "Why don't you tell them what's going on?"

"I lost my job," he starts. "I was doing fine. I wasn't drinking, and things were getting better. It was hard because I missed her, but I was staying strong. Kinsley was happy and . . . then they let me go."

"So you drank?" I ask.

Samuel's eyes fill with tears. "It was just one drink. That was all, but . . . I don't remember going home. The next day, it was the same."

The shame in his voice shatters me. "Tell us what we can do."

"You have to take her," he says, tears falling down his cheeks.

"Take Kinsley?" I ask, needing the clarification.

He starts to shake. "I have no one, Stella. Her mother is dead. My brother is in Phoenix and wants nothing to do with me. I need to get help." Jack stands and starts to pace. "If you don't take her, she'll go into foster care while I'm in rehab. You're her parents, and . . ."

My eyes lift to Jack, and his shoulders sag. I know he doesn't want this, but there's not a chance in hell I'm letting her go into foster care.

I turn to Mickey, his eyes wide as he looks between Jack and I.

I lick my lips and let out a deep breath. "I . . . I don't . . ."

Jack steps in. "Give Stella and me a minute."

I get up and walk over to him. His hand rests on the small of my back as we go into the kitchen area. Jack takes a step back, and his head falls before his gaze meets mine. "You want to take her."

"Want? No, but I'm not letting her go into foster care."

"I'm not saying I want that either, but you can't just bring her into Willow Creek Valley and expect no one to notice."

"Of course it wouldn't be a secret. We'd have to deal with it."

"Deal with the fact that you and I have a twelve-year-old daughter who we've never told anyone about. Are you prepared to do this?" Jack asks.

I'm not prepared for any of this, but it's the hand we were dealt. "We're her parents."

Jack shakes his head. "We're not her parents, Stella. Samuel and Misty are. If you do this, you're going to be fucking crushed at the end. Do you get that? You're going to have your heart destroyed when you have to give her back, which you'll have to do."

Tears well in my eyes, and I force them back. "I know that."

"Do you, baby? Do you know it is going to be ten times harder this time? She's going to know we are her biological mother and father. That we gave her up twelve years ago. That she has uncles and a cousin. She's going to see that . . . God, Stella, this is . . ."

Impossible.

Everything he's saying is right. My heart and my head hear it all, and yet, it changes nothing.

I step forward, placing my hand on his chest. "I'm going to be devasted giving her back, but once again, I have to put my daughter's needs first. We made a choice years ago to do the best thing for her, and we'll do it again. She needs us, Jack. This time, it's Samuel asking for us to help him the way they did for us. Now, if you can't or don't want to do this, that's your choice. I won't . . ." I want to say that I won't hold it against him, but I will. As much as I hate it, this is a defining moment for us. "Well, I will respect your decision. So, you can walk away, but I am going to take Kinsley home. I'm going to take care of her while Samuel gets the help he needs. We can do this together or you can walk away."

He turns, pushing his hair back and cursing. "Look at me, Stella. I am not going to walk away from you and let you do this on your own. I'm just as responsible as you are, and I will never be okay with her going into foster care. I just . . . I don't know how to do this. How to act like a guardian or whatever we'll be."

"Neither do I, but you're a great man."

"No, you are the good one. Jesus. Don't you see? You made the choice for her. You struggled and . . ."

"And you didn't?" I challenge. "I know that you're scared, and I'm absolutely terrified, but there's only one option here, and it's what's best for that little girl. We have to do the best thing for her, regardless of our own feelings."

His eyes close, and I can see the pain when he opens them again. "I know. The worst part of this entire thing is that there really isn't any way either of us would abandon her. But it's going to cost us, Stella. It's going to break us in so many ways, and I'm not at all sure that we're prepared for that."

I walk over to him and rest my hand on his cheek. "We've survived worse, we'll find a way through it again, only this time, we'll have each other."

His forehead rests on mine as we breathe each other in. "I hope so. I really fucking hope so."

Twenty-Seven

JACK

After a lot of phone calls, preparing documents, and tears, Stella and I are the legal guardians of Kinsley Rose Elkins for the next thirty days.

My hands are shaking, I keep clenching them in an effort to stop, but it doesn't. She's going to be home in the next hour, and her entire world will change.

"What does she know?" Stella asks Samuel as he rocks back and forth on the couch.

"Misty and I promised we would never lie to her. She knows she's adopted. She knows her mother was young and her father was too. We always gave her the option to ask whatever questions she wanted, but she never did."

I swallow deeply as Stella's fingers lace with mine. "We just want to help her get through this without complicating it."

He nods. "I think today is going to be the worst day of all our lives. Kinsley will face the fact that I'm not as infallible as she thinks I am, and she'll have to come to grips with having to go somewhere new for a while. It will be a lot for her."

That's the understatement of the year. I know what it's like to lose your parents at the same time. When your mother is taken away and your father falls apart. I've been where she is, and it will fuck her life up in so many ways. The things she thought she knew will become false.

"I've been where she is," I speak for the first time in a while. "It's going to be extremely hard for her. She'll be taken from the life she's known and everyone she loves. I don't know that any of us are remotely prepared for how she will react."

Stella turns to me. "What if we stay here for a few days? We can help her get through the first part in the comfort of her own home, and when she's ready, we can bring her back to Willow Creek."

I nod. "I think that's a good idea."

It's something, at least. Plus, it'll give Stella and I some time before her family has to learn the truth. As much as she's trying to pretend she's strong, I see the cracks in her armor as she trembles.

We fear the same things. What if Kinsley refuses? What if the answers we give make her loathe us? There is no way to know how she'll react. She has never met us, and now we're in charge of her life. Not a single thing regarding this is okay.

Not one.

And yet, we all know that this is the best option. Her going into the foster care system with a bunch of strangers for thirty days makes my stomach churn.

Samuel's neighbor, who is a family practice lawyer, asks, "Are you all sure you don't want to give her the illusion that you are foster parents? It may be one less thing."

Samuel shakes his head. "She's the smartest kid I know. She'll take one look at Jack and know he's her real father."

Stella wipes at her face and then turns her head. "She's the spitting image of him."

"Not to mention, lying to her was never something Misty

and I did. I won't start now," he says. "I have always prided myself on being honest, even if she may not have been old enough to understand."

"Jack and I don't want to lie either."

We fall silent as headlights pull up to the front of the house. A car door closes, and I hear her voice. "Bye, thank you!"

My hand grips Stella's a little tighter, and she does the same. I can feel my chest tighten, and a tingling sensation races through my veins. She's going to walk through this door and nothing in the world will be the same.

I'll be someone's father. Her father. I'll have to see what I gave away, look into her eyes again and know that, for so long, she's been walking this world without us.

Guilt like I've never known before settles in my gut. I'm not good enough for her. I'm not the strong man I've tried to be. I'm just like my father. I ran from her when things were hard and stayed away because it was easier.

The door opens, and Samuel gets to his feet. He meets her in the foyer while Stella and I sit here.

"Jack?" she whispers. "I . . . I don't know what to say."

Her lip trembles, and the tears in her eyes break me. The look, the fear on her beautiful face, takes me back to that hospital and how powerless I felt.

"We'll let Samuel lead it."

She nods.

After another minute, he guides Kinsley into the living room. Stella and I stand, and my hand settles on her back, steadying her and also needing to keep ahold of something for my own sanity.

My mind races as I see Kinsley for the first time. Her dark brown hair with hints of light brown falls around her shoulders, and her hazel eyes, which are the exact same shade as mine, stare back at me.

She has Stella's nose, and when she smiles, it's like a time machine.

She's equal parts of us. The beauty of Stella in her youth. A keen eye, measuring the room the way I did.

Samuel's hand rests on her shoulder. He sighs deeply and then speaks. "Kinsley, this is Stella and Jack."

Her eyes move between us, and then her soft voice fills the silence. "My biological parents."

"Yes," Samuel says. "We need to talk."

She looks back to her father. "Are you giving me back?" Her voice goes high with panic.

Samuel moves fast, his hands cupping her face. "No, not like that. I . . . I need help. Come, let's sit so we can talk."

He leads her to the couch, but her eyes continue to look back at us. I can't begin to imagine what's going through her mind. Stella sits beside me, her hand on my thigh, and I cover it with my own. The room is filled with a million questions, emotions, and everyone is trying to hold it together.

Samuel begins, taking Kinsley's hands in his. "Losing your mother has been . . . difficult for me. I'm not okay, Kinsley. I need to get help before it's too late. Do you understand?"

"Daddy, I can help. I'm trying to do what I can around the house."

He shakes his head. "You've been the only thing that has been able to keep me together until now. You are the reason I haven't . . ." He trails off, and I squeeze Stella's hand. It's far worse than I think we thought. Samuel is killing himself slowly, and if it weren't for Kinsley, he probably would've done far worse than just drink. "I can't hold it together. I'm falling apart, and if I don't get help, I'll never be able to survive. And I can't lose you."

A sob escapes her throat as she throws herself into his arms. "Please, Daddy, you can't go too."

"I have to, baby. I have to get help so I can come back and be the daddy you need. It's what I should've done before. You shouldn't be taking care of me, Kinsley. It's my job to take care of you."

"I can do it, though. I can take care of everything."

"You can't, and that's why I called Stella and Jack."

Stella wipes her face, and I do as well. It's incredibly hard seeing the two of them in this much pain.

She looks to us, tears running down her face, and then back to Samuel. He wipes them away and says, "There are two other people in this world who love you more than their own lives, and they're here, willing to help. While I go away to get myself better, they're going to take care of you."

I want to scream about how unfair it is for her to have to go through this. Her life has been upended, and now it's becoming worse. We gave her up to avoid causing her pain, and now we're sitting here, inflicting it.

"I want you!" she cries out.

"I know, and I'm sorry I'm not able to do this on my own. I wish I were—God, I wish I could do what your mother would want, but I can't."

Samuel looks to us, and I'm not sure what to say, but I'm going to try. "I can't imagine what you're thinking. You don't know us at all, and now you're being told we're your biological parents and are here to help. I'm . . . I'm not sure what to say, and I'm an adult."

Stella clears her throat. "Whatever questions you have, we'll answer."

She looks at Stella. "I saw you. You were at Mom's funeral."

"I was."

"So, you knew who I was?"

Stella nods. "Yes, I talked to your mom frequently. She would write to me and send me photos. But her funeral wasn't the right time to talk to you. I knew you were grieving, and I came just to pay my respects to someone I loved."

Kinsley's eyes turn to me. "Were you there?"

My throat goes dry, and I answer her honestly. "No, I didn't . . . I didn't really talk to your parents. When I had to let you go, it was . . . well, it was the only way I could survive it."

"Right. And now I'm supposed to stay with you? Pretend that this is okay?"

Samuel takes her hand again. "I'm asking you to temporarily go with two people who love you enough to be here right now. Who came, without hesitation, to do the best thing for you. I can't do this. I have to go, and none of us want you to go into foster care."

Her eyes widen. "What about my friends? Why can't I stay with them?"

"Because this is the right choice," Samuel tells her. "You have to trust me."

Kinsley gets to her feet, tears still falling down her cheeks. "I don't! I want Mom! She would never let this happen!" she yells before running out of the room. The sound of her door slamming reverberates around the room as we all sit here in silence.

Twenty-Eight

STELLA

Watching Mickey drive Samuel away was incredibly heartbreaking. Kinsley cried continuously— hell, we all did. The next thirty days will be a testament to our fortitude. Jack is quiet, doing his best to appear strong, and I'm dying inside.

I try to think of how I would feel at her age. She knew she was adopted but knows nothing about us. Now, she's forced into this while the only parent she has left checks himself into rehab.

I'd be angry, scared, and inconsolable. Which is what I imagine she is.

She's been in her room the last hour, crying and breaking my heart. If she were Amelia, I would be in there, holding her as she let go of all her pain, but I don't have that right. So, I'm standing outside her door, debating the right move.

Jack enters the hallway, jerking his head to the side as an indication that he wants me to follow him. I touch the wood panel, sighing and then moving away.

"She needs time."

"I know, but I hate that she feels alone right now."

Jack looks around, seeming lost. "We just have to do what we can. We also have to talk to your family."

I step toward him, and he wraps his arms around me. "I didn't ever want to do this."

"I know."

"I'm not ready for them to know."

Jack kisses the top of my head. "It's time we deal with it. Kinsley has been a secret hanging over both our heads for a long time."

"Grayson . . . he's going to be so angry."

I'm not ready for his ire. Not just because Jack and I lied, I can handle that part of his anger, but because I'm afraid he will see me in the same light he sees Yvonne. A woman who walked away from her child. It's what I did. Regardless of my reasons or my age, I let her go for someone else to raise.

Jack lifts my chin so our eyes meet. "We did what we thought we had to. If he hurts you or says anything . . ."

"He's your best friend."

"And you're the woman I love." The statement says more than he'll ever know. "I won't let anyone say something to hurt you. That much I can promise."

A tear falls, and my heart both hurts and is full at the same time. I know my brothers will be upset. I know they'll make assumptions. But, when they hear that my father was part of the reason we gave her up, the anger will shift. They'll just never understand what it was like for Jack and me.

They can't begin to know the guilt, heartache, and pain we've struggled with all these years.

Still, Jack is right about my not being able to avoid telling them. "I'll call them," I say.

"Why don't we do it now? She's in her room, so we can go outside to talk to them."

I lean on Jack, taking whatever strength he's lending me and hoping I can make it through this.

The first person I want to tell is Oliver.

The two of us walk outside to the covered porch, and with a shaky breath, I hit the call button.

"Hey, Stell, we're out of milk. Are you able to get some from Jack's house?"

"Ollie, we . . . we have to talk."

"What's wrong?" His voice instantly shifts. "Are you okay? Are you crying?"

My brother knows me too well. "I'm okay, and yes, I'm crying, but I need you to listen and let me get through this, can you do that?"

Jack wraps his arm around my shoulders, holding me tight.

"I can try," Oliver says, which is the best I can hope for.

I explain it all. The night with Jack when I was a kid. The day we found out I was pregnant. The pregnancy, our father's ultimatum, going to stay with our grandmother, and the birth. I talk about Kinsley, and what that was like for us to give her up. Through it all, he's silent. Telling Oliver first was the right move. He's my twin. He knows my heart and how difficult this is for me.

When I'm finished, and the tears are like rivers, Oliver finally speaks.

"Whatever you need from me, I'll do it," he says, and his voice breaks at the end.

I cry harder as Jack holds me to his chest, and I feel like maybe I'll be okay.

Maybe.

I'm completely spent. There is nothing left in my heart, but we still have one call to make. I've spoken to three of my brothers, who all handled it much better than I thought they would and offered their unwavering support.

Next is the call I'm dreading and still not ready to make.

"Do you want to call Grayson now?" Jack asks.

"No."

"You can't avoid it."

I can't, but I only have so much emotional bandwidth and I'd rather use the rest of it on Kinsley.

"I want to check on Kinsley," I tell Jack. "It's been almost an hour, and I don't want her to think we don't care."

The disappointment is there, but he doesn't push me. "All right, but we have to tell him tonight. If he finds out from anyone other than us, it would be unforgivable."

"I know. We'll tell him."

Jack leans over and gives me a kiss. "I love you."

"I love you too."

I don't know that I've ever loved him as much as I do in this moment.

We head inside, and Jack motions me forward before moving to the kitchen. She's still hidden away behind a shut door, and if anyone is going to be able to reach her emotionally, it'll be me. I knock twice and wait for the door to open.

Her eyes are red, wet trails go down her face, and I imagine we match more than we'd like.

"Are you hungry?" I ask.

She shakes her head.

"Would you like to watch a movie or . . . anything?"

I see her debate it a little and then she pulls her door open a bit more. I take the olive branch and head inside. Her room is the same as it was the last time I saw it with the exception of the box of letters on the ground.

My letters.

She sits on the edge of her bed. "My mother gave me these

before she died."

There are photos, letters, and small gifts I sent to Kinsley through the years spread out. It's tangible proof that I thought of her, wondered, and worried. If I told her how often I looked at babies as they passed and imagined what she was like, I'm not sure she would believe me. Each time Amelia would do something, my mind would go to Kinsley and how I wished I could've been there for those moments.

It was hard at first, but eventually, I found a sense of peace when it came to her. As though the more I allowed her into my heart and mind, the more I knew what we did was right.

"I remember sending pretty much everything that is in that box."

"You wrote to her, but never me."

I exhale deeply. "I didn't really know what to say. Misty was a friend, someone I loved and thought was a hero. She took care of something that was more precious to me than myself."

Kinsley's eyes meet mine. "You were young when you had me?"

"Yes, I was eighteen and Jack was twenty-two." I move toward her bed but hesitate before asking, "May I sit?"

She nods. "I have a lot of questions."

"I'm sure you do, and we'll answer whatever you ask."

Kinsley grabs a tattered blanket from her bed and pulls it onto her lap. It's the blanket we gave Misty and Samuel to bring her home in. I didn't know if they would throw it out, but I wanted Kinsley to have one thing from us. Something that maybe told her we were wrapping her in our love. Jack and I spent hours in the store, searching for something perfect. I wouldn't allow myself to buy anything other than this one thing.

Jack appears in the doorway, not entering, and she looks at him and then back to me. "So you're together?"

"Now we are, but we weren't when you were born and not until recently."

She plays with the edge of the blanket. "So you're not married or have another kid?"

Jack answers. "No, we've spent every minute apart until about two months ago."

"What changed?"

I smile. "Time."

"Time?" Her voice squeaks.

"Yeah, we fought it for a lot of years before we gave in. However, we were both in love with each other before that, we just stayed away."

"Why?"

"Well, a lot of reasons. We both struggled with your adoption and the secrets we kept."

"Oh." Kinsley releases a heavy sigh. "This is really weird, and I'm not sure what I'm supposed to do."

Jack enters the room and leans against the dresser. "You're not supposed to do anything. If you want one or both of us to let you have time, just tell us. If you need to ask questions, we'll answer. None of us know what to do right now. Stella and I are just as stunned by how this has gone as you are."

She looks down at her fingers. "Why don't I see letters from you?"

Jack grips the back of his neck, watching Kinsley with apprehension. "The only way I could live with the decision we made was to let you go completely. It may not make sense to you, and I know it'll probably sound horrible, but after I placed you in your mother's arms and you were gone, I couldn't look back. I had to go on with life, knowing that the decision I made that day was irreversible. It was the hardest thing I have ever done, and if I could see you, know you, I would've wanted you back, and that was never an option."

Kinsley's eyes mist over, and her lip quivers again. "I want to be angry, but then I don't know how to be. I loved my mom. I love my dad. They love me and have been good parents. I thought . . . I don't know . . . that you didn't love me, but now I've read these letters and you're talking and I don't know what to think."

I clench my hands together to keep from pulling her into my arms. "We love you more than we loved anything else, Kinsley. I know that it's hard to believe that when you think we abandoned you."

She shakes her head, not able to meet our eyes. "They didn't talk about you guys much, and I never asked. But they did tell me that you loved me and that's why you gave me to them. I've had great parents."

"We know," Jack says. "It's why we chose them."

The day we met Misty and Samuel, we knew instantly that they were the right people. We could feel how wonderful they were and were positive that they would raise our child the best way possible.

He walks toward the two of us. "Today has been really intense, so why don't we get some food, and tomorrow we can all figure out a plan that works?"

"Okay."

I take a few breaths and nod.

Now to figure out the plan.

Twenty-Nine

JACK

Stella and I are sitting in the living room, staring at the cell phone on the table. We've put it off as long as we can. Kinsley is asleep, and we've run out of excuses.

"We have to call," I say, lifting my phone.

"Wait. I should tell him." Her hand grabs mine and then she trembles.

"No. This time, it has to come from me."

I've thought about this, and I'm not going to let her be the one who deals with this brother. Grayson may not handle this well, but I'll be the one he yells at, not Stella. She's done enough today.

"It should be us both." Stella's voice cracks at the end.

I lean in, kissing her gently. "It should've been me twelve years ago. It should've been me, telling him the truth about how I felt about you, a hundred times after that. All this time, Stella, I've been putting off this conversation, and I'm going to have it, man to man."

She sits back, pinching the bridge of her nose. "I want to

argue, but honestly, I don't have it in me. I'd like to be here though."

That request I have no problem granting her. "Okay."

I dial his number and wait for the video to kick on. After a few rings, Grayson's face is there. "Hey, where are you? We got a fire call last night, and you weren't there."

"I had something I needed to take care of." I'm unable to hide the strain in my voice.

"Everything all right?" Gray asks.

"Are you alone?"

He looks over and then back to me. "Jess is here, but Amelia is asleep."

I nod. "I have to talk to you about something, Gray."

He sits up straight before propping the phone against something so we see Jess in the screen too. "Okay? What's wrong?"

Stella's hand moves to my back, and her head rests on my shoulder. "Stella and I are in Georgia. We had to come down here to deal with something, and I want you to know that not telling you about this hasn't been easy for either of us. We've struggled with it each day, but we both felt it wasn't something we were ready to talk to anyone about."

"What the hell are you talking about?" There's an edge to his voice, and I know this isn't going to be like when Stella told Joshua, Alexander, or Oliver.

I take Stella's hand, grateful that he'll be directing his anger at me even if it'll hurt her all the same.

As I blow out a long breath of air, I begin. "Your sister and I have had feelings for each other for a long time. We weren't going behind your back, but we were together once."

"I figured as much. When?"

"Her eighteenth birthday. That night, we slept together. It was something that just happened, and it never happened again." Stella's fingers grip mine tighter. Grayson's jaw clenches, and Jessica shifts to rest her hand on his shoulder.

"We had a daughter."

"You're fucking kidding me."

"No, I wish we were. Kinsley is twelve. Her mother died recently, and her father is struggling. He's asked us to keep her for the next thirty days while he gets help. Stella and I are here now, making all the arrangements."

Grayson's face is frozen in anger. He doesn't speak or move other than to draw in heavy breaths through his clenched teeth. This is exactly what I was afraid of. He hates lies. He hates deceit. It is his unforgivable sin, and we committed it twice.

"I guess no lies wasn't the same promise I thought it was."

"I didn't lie to you, Grayson. I kept something that neither of us wanted to ever tell anyone else. We gave Kinsley up, she hasn't been ours since the day she was born, and we had no intention of that changing. You didn't need to know."

"She's my fucking sister. You slept with her, got her pregnant when she was a kid, and then let her give that baby away?"

I let out a long sigh. "And I've lived with that daily. I've punished myself more than you ever could have. It hasn't been easy for anyone, and I didn't enjoy keeping this from you."

He runs his fingers through his hair. "It's like I don't even fucking know you. You're the guy who . . . Jesus Christ."

Stella takes the phone. "Grayson, Jack and I have had a really hard day today. If you can't be the supportive and wonderful brother I need, then I don't really need to hear your voice. I understand that, right now, you might feel a bit blindsided, but I don't give a flying fuck about that. We called because we're . . . well, we're drowning. You think this is hard for you? Imagine how it is for the three of us. Imagine how it was to have to meet a little girl that we let go as a baby, watch her cry as her life is literally flipped. For one second, just think about how difficult it was for Jack and me to have to call Josh, Alex, and Oliver. Then to know we had to call you and face this reaction.

You're supposed to be Jack's best friend, the one person he can rely on. Be it, and stop being a selfish ass."

She hangs up the phone and collapses against my chest. Sobs wrack her body as her emotions release.

I hold her as tight as I can. Each shudder of her body causes my heart to break. After a few minutes, she lifts her head. "I'm sorry."

"Don't you dare apologize," I tell her. "I'm just as . . . done . . . as you are."

"The hard part of telling my brothers is over. Now we can focus on the next step."

"We have to remember that this is temporary. No matter how special, beautiful, and wonderful that little girl is, she's not ours. She's Samuel's daughter, Stella. We have to hold on to that. Yes, we made her, but we aren't her parents. You're not her mother, and I'm not her father. Not in the way that matters. We have no legal rights once this thirty-day period is over."

She nods, a fresh wave of tears falling. "I know, but . . . when I look at her. I see you. I see us, and I see . . ."

A family. One that we're not, and it's going to absolutely destroy her when Samuel returns and wants back the little girl he gave to us for safe keeping.

"Stella, you can't go down that road."

She nods, wiping at her cheeks. "It's going to be hard."

"That's an understatement, but we have to keep telling ourselves the truth. This isn't a situation where we come out without scars."

Stella exhales and then looks away. "I know a lot about scars."

"As do I. The wounds heal, but the reminder is there."

I think about the burn marks on my legs from the fire I was in when I was a kid. While I've learned to almost overlook them, some days, I can't. I remember my mother's screams. The way my father called out for her over and over.

The heat, the smell of things burning around me, and the way I couldn't talk for days after because of how hard I'd yelled that night are as fresh in my mind as they were the day it happened.

The scars of that night are always with me. The woman beside me became my light in the darkness that was consuming me. Stella's eyes, the kindness and friendship that was always there.

She saved me.

She has always saved me, and I gave her wounds.

And it looks like she'll once again be hurt because of me.

STELLA

I roll over, feeling like my eyes are sewn shut from the amount of crying I've done. With great effort, I open them and see Jack is already up.

Last night, we held on to each other for hours, just letting the silence fill the air. Words could do nothing to make this any better.

I push myself up and look at the clock, it's still early.

After I fix myself up a little, I head out to see Jack and Kinsley at the kitchen counter. He's drinking a cup of coffee, and she's eating toast.

"Good morning," I say, pasting on a smile.

"Good morning," they both reply.

I walk toward Kinsley. "Did everyone sleep okay?"

Kinsley nods. "I think so."

"Kinsley was just telling me about her math club." Jack was in math club. The hottest guy in school was the biggest geek. It was poetic in some ways.

In my desperation to make him see me as more than Grayson's annoying little sister, I tried to join. I was terrible. Seriously, I couldn't add without using my fingers, and there I was, trying to fit in with Jack who could solve complex equations in his head. It was pathetic.

He grins as though he can read my thoughts.

Kinsley's eyes jump between us. "What?"

Jack chuckles. "I'm remembering this girl who joined math club when I was in high school. She was pretty, funny, smart, and very transparent."

I groan and look at Kinsley. "It was me. The girl was me."

"She is not mathematically inclined."

I cross my arms while rolling my eyes. "Is there such a thing?"

He grins and then sips his coffee. "It seems Kinsley is."

"I like numbers, they're honest and reliable. You can always get the same answer, no matter what. There's no guessing if two plus two is four. It is. To everyone in the world," Kinsley explains.

"There's a fairness in numbers," Jack finishes. "I get it."

Kinsley nods. "I don't . . . fit in, but the numbers don't care."

How different this girl is from me when I was her age. I never struggled to fit in. I don't know if it helped having three older brothers and a twin who would always be by my side, but I had my people. Joshua, Alex, and Grayson made sure that I was always protected. No one would dare to hurt me.

As for girls, I had my fair share of stupid drama, but because I had Winnie, it didn't matter much. Also, they all wanted to sleep with my brothers, so being on my bad side was a surefire way to never get close to the Parkerson boys.

I take the seat beside Kinsley. "Do you have a best friend?"

She nods. "Carrie Ann. We've been friends since we were about five."

I smile. "I have one of those. Her name is Winnie."

She looks to Jack. "What about you?"

"My best friend is also Stella's older brother."

I sigh deeply. "It's a very tangled web in Willow Creek."

"So, you fell in love with your best friend's sister?" Kinsley asks.

"I did."

"Carrie Ann has an older brother too."

"Oh, honey," I say quickly. "It's a bad idea. Trust me."

Jack raises one brow. "Really?"

I nod. "They're horrible," I explain to Kinsley. "They are wishy-washy. They can't seem to decide if they want you or don't want to rock the boat with their sibling. It's a really bad look."

Jack huffs out his laughter. "And here I thought it was sweet that I cared about everyone."

"It wasn't. It was annoying."

Kinsley laughs. "So, I mean, how was I born then?"

The shift in the room is almost tangible, but I promised her answers.

"I loved Jack since I was a little girl. At least, I thought I did. Now I see that what I felt back then wasn't even close to how I feel about him now. I was young, and . . . I was . . . a little broken. I had no reason to be, not really. My brothers, I have four of them, are all pretty great. My parents, on the other hand, well, they're . . ."

Jack clears his throat. "Horrible."

"Yes, they're horrible. But back then, I really thought they could fix themselves if they just tried. I was watching my brothers struggle with it too. It was my eighteenth birthday when Jack and I gave in to those feelings. For one night, we weren't Grayson's best friend and little sister. We were just Jack and Stella."

"And then I came along?"

"Yes."

"Did you want to keep me?" Kinsley asks with a tremble in her voice.

"More than anything."

Jack places his mug down. "We were young. We knew that we couldn't give you a life like this. One where your mother would be at your school events or your father could take time off to go on fun vacations. I was still in college, and Stella hadn't even started yet. We had nothing, and . . . giving you nothing felt like a selfish choice."

I fight back the tears and hold on to the strength we had that day. "Misty and Samuel were wonderful people. They loved you before you were even born, and Jack and I knew they were the right choice."

Kinsley looks over at the wall of family photos. "They never made me feel . . . less."

"Oh, honey, you weren't less. Not in any of our eyes. When we chose your parents, it was because we knew they were the right option. We knew they'd always love you, do the best thing for you, and they did. They honored what we wanted with the open adoption. Jack and I, along with your parents, agreed on that for your benefit."

"So I could've found you if I wanted?" Kinsley asks.

"Yes, and your mom was always gracious to send us updates so we knew about you."

Jack scratches the scuff on his face. "None of us ever saw it going this way. I can't imagine the strength it took for your father to call us. I know it may not seem like it, but admitting he needed help and then asking his daughter's biological parent to help had to have been one of the hardest things he's ever done. There's a lot of trust in that, and we don't take it lightly."

Kinsley runs her finger along the rim of her plate. "So now what?"

I look at Jack, who nods. "We wish we could stay down here for the time your dad needs, but while we're starting with thirty days, Samuel did tell us it could be more if he needs it. We can stay here a few more days if you need, but then we need to get back to Willow Creek Valley."

A tear falls down her cheek. "I don't want to leave my home."

I reach out, placing my hand on hers. "I know, and I'm sorry, but it's only for a short time."

"Can I take what I want from here?"

Jack speaks first. "Of course."

"Will I meet everyone?"

"Slowly, and only if you want," I say quickly. "You don't have to get to know any of them, but . . ." My stomach is in knots. I don't know how to explain that she has a family, a wonderful one, who will love her instantly. "They'll be there if you want to."

"This is my home," I say as we enter.

Thankfully, Oliver already moved into Jack's cabin and brought Jack's things to my place.

Since I have a two bedroom loft, it made the most sense.

"Wow, it's really cool."

I smile. "I like the rustic warehouse feel."

"Do you live here too?" she asks Jack.

"No, I have a cabin, but Stella's brother is staying there, so I'm going to sleep here, if that's cool?"

"It's cool."

Kinsley has been amazing with us so far. She asks questions, wanting to know us, but then backs off when she gets overwhelmed. Jack and I aren't pushing and are just allowing it to happen at her pace.

I have no idea how I'm going to get to know this brilliant

girl and then watch her leave again.

I keep reminding myself not to fall in love with her, but it's already happened. If I'm honest, it happened the first time I held her, and it hasn't ebbed.

"I need to use the bathroom," she says.

"It's right through there." I point down the hall. "The first door is my room and the bathroom is past that on your right. Your room will be back out this way and to the left."

"Okay."

She heads down the hall, and I let out a sigh. "Let's see what mess we have to clean up in her room. If we can get her settled, I can go talk to my mother."

Jack nods. "All right."

I walk over to what has been Oliver's room, which was Amelia's room before that, and open the door. God only knows how my brother left it.

When I enter, I'm both impressed and overwhelmed. It's clean and changed as well. It did have a pink comforter with butterflies all over it. Now, it has teal bedding. There is a bookcase that wasn't there before that is filled with books I didn't own a week ago. It seems my brothers—or Jessica—were hard at work while we were gone.

There's a note on the side table.

I'm sorry. I love you, and I'm here if you both need me.
-Gray

Jack comes to stand behind me and rests his hand on my back. "Oliver?"

I shake my head and hand him the note.

Jack kisses my temple. "He's a hothead who needed to calm himself."

"I still worry he'll see me as Yvonne."

"Impossible. You're nothing like her, and we all know it."

I turn in his arms, resting my head on his chest. "In my head I know it too, but my heart says something different."

"If Grayson thought it for one second, he'd have a line of people ready to punch him in the face. I'd be first, then your brothers would be behind me."

I smile. "I guess, and it was sweet of him to do this."

"It was. He loves you, Stella. They all do. You're the heart of your family."

"Jack? Stella?" Kinsley calls from the hallway, and he lets me go.

"In here!"

She enters the room and gasps. "Wow."

"My brothers were busy while we were in Georgia," I explain.

Kinsley walks around, looking at the bookcase. "Did you read all these?"

Jack snorts a laugh. "Stella? She's more of a movie girl."

"But you have a lot of novels here."

"They're all new. I guess they got a mix of things? I can imagine the fools in a bookstore trying to pick them out," I say with a grin. "Or my sister-in-law handled it, which is most likely the case."

She looks at the desk and picks up a butterfly.

"That was my niece Amelia's," I explain. "Grayson, who is Jack's best friend, has a daughter. She's almost five, her birthday is coming up. She stayed here a lot before my brother got married."

Kinsley looks at the silk wings, rubbing her thumb against one. "I . . . there's a lot of you guys."

Jack steps forward. "There are a lot of Parkerson siblings and family, so it can feel a bit overwhelming in the beginning. But Stella and I mean it, you don't have to meet any of them if you don't want. We're not trying to force you into a family, we know you have your dad."

I have already let all of my brothers know that they are absolutely not to come to my house. I explained what our plan was, and everyone promised they would respect it.

Oliver was the hardest to get to understand, but in the end, he gave me his word.

But they *want* to know her.

They are desperate to connect with their niece who they never knew. There is no way we'll be able to keep it completely just the three of us, but hopefully, we can do this slowly.

"It's like learning there is a whole new set of people I didn't know existed. I wish I was home. At least there, I know basic stuff like where the bathroom is."

I hate this so much for her. If I could take all of her uncertainty from her, I would.

"Kinsley, you've been thrown into a situation that is complicated for an adult, never mind a twelve-year-old. It's okay to feel unbalanced, but if you need anything—whether it's space or you want to sit and eat an entire package of Oreos and wash it down with Chips Ahoy—all you have to do is tell us," I say with a smile, and she closes her eyes for a second before I continue. "Just, please don't feel like you have to do this alone. We're going to all stumble and that's okay."

She straightens her back. "I'm fine. I am going to read now, if that's okay?"

I force a smile and nod. "Of course. We'll be right outside."

"Thanks."

As Jack and I shut the door behind us, I pray to God we did the right thing.

Thirty-One

STELLA

"Kinsley is in Willow Creek Valley," I tell my mother, who's sitting on the sofa in her new apartment.

"What?"

"I think you heard me, Mom."

She looks down at her clasped hands and then sighs. "I knew this would happen one day."

"That I'd find my daughter?"

Her eyes find mine. "No, that . . . I don't know, it was inevitable, I guess."

There have been so many things over the course of my lifetime that I've had to work through. Things that my parents said or did that I had trouble making sense of, but Kinsley was the one I couldn't ever get through. They forced my hand and never seemed to care.

"How could you have done that to me?"

Her lips part. "Do what?"

"Force me and Jack to give her up. You and Dad threatened to take everything from us if we didn't do it. I don't understand, Mom. We were wealthy and could afford to do the right thing."

She tucks her dark brown hair behind her ear. "It was what we thought was best for you, Stella. Contrary to what you think, it wasn't an easy decision."

"It shouldn't have been your decision at all."

"You had a choice too. I know it wasn't ideal for you, but you could've kept her. I didn't force you."

I shake my head, anger surging through my veins. "Are you that stupid? Of course you did! You knew that Jack and I couldn't give her the life she deserved without your help. You made it very clear we would lose all your support unless we fell in line, which is what made us have to give her up."

"No, your father did, and believe me, we fought about it. The truth was that you and Jack made the decision to have sex, without protection. You and Jack made the choice to have her. You and Jack had to deal with the consequences. It was . . . it was absolute hell for me and your father. I suffered with you, Stella. Whether you believe it or not, there were many nights I cried myself to sleep. I would . . ." She stops and has to clear her throat before continuing. "I would listen to your grandmother talk about the baby kicking and hated that I couldn't be there. If I had been, I would've changed my mind, and I knew it was best for you if you allowed another family to care for her."

Tears run down my cheeks. "And now look at us. Look at the lives we've had because of those choices."

"I'm not proud. I'm far from it. However, I'm not the monster you think I am."

I get to my feet, pacing and wiping away tears that fall. "I don't know what to think anymore."

"Who do you think paid for Misty's cancer treatments?" I turn, my eyes locking onto hers as she rises gracefully. "Who do you think helped when they wanted to send Kinsley to a special camp? It was all done anonymously, mind you. Misty didn't know who the money came from and neither did Samuel. You gave up that little girl, but none of us ever let her go."

"Did Dad know?" I ask. A part of me hopes that the man I once idolized isn't such a horrible person. The other part hopes he is because we are about to destroy him in every way.

She shakes her head. "No. He didn't know."

"Why did you do it?"

"Because that little girl is my granddaughter. I know that family is a touchy subject right now, but I did what I could without interfering."

I sit, my legs feeling unsteady. "She's so overwhelmed," I tell her.

"The last few months have been difficult, I'm sure. But do you remember what you were like at twelve?"

Maybe that's the issue. I don't remember any of it. Kinsley isn't like Amelia, who I can distract with shiny things. She's a kid with emotions, and I am really not sure what to do with all that.

"What was I like?"

Mom laughs, and a soft smile plays on her lips. "Well, first, you knew everything. There wasn't a single thing I could say that you didn't already have the answer to. You were wrong most of the time, but heaven knows, we couldn't tell you that. Teenagers are the most infuriating creatures on the planet, and my house was filled with them. You were smart-mouthed—although, that seemed to be something you have been since you could speak." She laughs and sits beside me. "Most of all, you wanted to be heard. You lived in a house with boys who spoke for you, and you let them know how much you didn't like it. She's at a hard age as it is, but couple it with all she's suffered, and it's ten times worse. Give her space and time. Be patient and let her come to you. She doesn't know you or Jack.

She just knows she was given away, and now the people who raised her are gone as well."

My mother and I were close once. A long time ago, before I knew about my father's affairs or his alternate life, I thought my mother was the strongest and most wonderful woman alive. She *tried* to be a good mom when we were young. For a small glimpse, I'm back to that time again. When my mother would brush my hair and talk to me about whatever I wanted. Then, my father's affairs wore her down and my grandmother saved us.

"How did we get to this, Mom? How did we go so far off track?"

Shame fills her eyes. "I don't know, but I'd like to try to do better. I have a lot to apologize for. Things I've said and done to all of you that I want to make right. I have no excuses, just an apology. I was lost. I still am, but I am working on myself."

There is a vulnerability in her that causes my heart to ache. She's been hurt and, in turn, has hurt many.

"That's good because we all need each other, and I hope we can find a way to be a family again."

She dabs at her eyes. "I would like that very much, but first, we need to focus on getting through the next few weeks."

I nod. "I just want to help her through this."

My mother reaches forward, her hand resting on mine. "Just be you, Stella. Be you and she'll come around."

"I hope so."

"She will. You're impossible not to love."

I knock on Kinsley's door with one hand and hold a plate of food for her in the other. It's been three days of her staying in her room, and I'm running out of ideas that will get her to come out for longer than an hour or two. I keep hearing my mother's words to let her come to me, but it's so hard to wait.

"Kinsley?" I knock again. She needs to eat at least.

After a few seconds, she opens it. "Yes?"

"I have some food if you're hungry."

The door opens a bit more. "Thanks." She looks out around the room. "Where's Jack?"

"He had to go back to his place to make sure everything was still okay. My brother, Oliver, is staying there, and he's not exactly the . . . cleanest of my siblings."

"Oh."

"He's my twin and opposite of me in so many ways."

Kinsley takes a bite of the sandwich. I had no idea if she liked turkey, but I figured it was worth a shot.

"I always wanted siblings."

My chest aches at the statement, but I keep my features schooled. "I sometimes wished I was an only child."

"You have four brothers?"

I walk into the living room area and pick up the photo of the five of us from Grayson's wedding and show it to her. "Yup. This is them. Joshua is the oldest, he's seven years older than I am." I point to each as I speak. "Then Grayson, who is four years older. Alex is two years older, and Oliver is my twin."

She nods slowly and then steps out of her room, entering the living room with the photo in hand. "You all live in this town?"

"Now we do, but for the last few years, we've been sort of scattered."

"Why?"

I exhale deeply, deciding to take the opening and show that my family is far from normal. "Do you want to know all the family drama?"

"Sure . . ."

"Come sit," I suggest, and Kinsley does. I tell her about

my life. The parts about my father's business, and how we all came to own shares. I tell her about the drama with Grayson and him, which is what led to my brothers and me wanting to open our own business.

"No way!" Kinsley interrupts.

"Yeah, it was . . . it *is* horrible. My father isn't a good man."

"This is crazy," she notes with a smile.

"No family is normal, no matter what they say."

"My life was normal until now."

"I'm sorry," I tell her with all the sincerity I have. "I hate that this is what you're dealing with, but it will get better. You just need to give it a bit of time."

She tucks her leg underneath her. "My mom was so . . . perfect. She did everything for me and Dad. Even when she had cancer, she never let us feel neglected. I was so angry that, of all the people in the world, she would get sick, but she wouldn't let me be. She kept telling me that it was okay and not to let this change me."

"I think she did an amazing job raising you."

"I miss her."

"I know, honey."

"She wouldn't have let Dad drink. She would've stopped him. I tried to do what she would. I cleaned and ordered groceries, but he was so sad."

The truth is that, if Misty were still with him, he wouldn't feel the need to drink away his sadness at all. "Kinsley, you did nothing wrong. Neither did your dad. He is hurting and sad and he's getting help. For you. His love for you is so strong that he willingly entrusted us so he could make himself better. I can imagine it feels different for you, but I promise, this was not because you didn't do enough."

Her head turns to the side, and she clears her throat. "I just want him to get better."

"I want him to as well. If there's any reason for him to keep trying, it's you. He loves you."

She nods, still not meeting my eyes.

"How about we watch a movie?" I suggest.

After a few seconds, she turns to me. "Which one?"

"You pick."

She grabs the remote and leans back on the couch. Time, patience, and a little luck is all we need.

Thirty-Two

JACK

I rub my hand down my face as I stare at my accounting books. This is something that I loved doing, but now, the numbers are just running together in a blur from staring at them for too long.

All I can think about is Stella at home with Kinsley.

Yesterday, I spent an hour cleaning before explaining to Oliver that I did not, in fact, have a maid. When I got to Stella's place, she and Kinsley were on the couch, huddled under blankets and watching television. I stood there, my heart racing and feeling a mix of emotions. I was happy for Stella. I know she wanted this so much. However, I was terrified because distance is what will save us from the pain of giving her back.

I can't love her.

I can't let myself love her more than I do already.

It will break everything inside me when I have to watch her go again.

Instead of joining them, I went into the office and pretended as if there was a pressing matter at work. And now I'm here, doing the same thing.

I release a deep breath through my nose and try to focus on some of the things I need to do. After a few seconds, I push the papers off the desk and let out a curse.

"You look like shit."

I jerk my head up to see Grayson standing in the doorway.

"Thanks."

He enters my office and takes the seat across from my desk. "I'm going to assume it's the jump headfirst into fatherhood." I glare at him, and he lifts his hand. "Easy, killer, I'm not here to give you shit. I'm here with an apology and some understanding."

"Really?"

"Really. Remember, I've been where you are. It isn't the same place, but it's close enough."

I shake my head. "You have no idea. Amelia was an infant, I have a twelve-year-old who is pissed, alone, scared, and God knows what else."

"Sort of like you were when your dad took off."

I lean back in my chair and exhale. "Maybe that's the worst part. It's like she's living another version of my life."

Only not quite. She has a great family, one parent who is willing to do what he needs to do to give her the life she deserves and birth parents who may have given her up, but are stepping up as well.

"If there's two people on this planet who can handle it, it's you and Stella."

"Who are you and what have you done with my best friend?"

Grayson rubs the back of his head. "When it comes to Stella, I've always been an asshole, you know that. Honestly, the two of you make sense. Maybe I've known that all along. There's not a man alive I trust more than you. I know I was a prick, and I'm sorry. You know how hard it is for me to find out about lies."

"Yeah, man, I do." Grayson has had his fair share of people playing games with him, and after what his father did, I don't blame the guy for having zero tolerance for lies. "Good. So, you have a daughter?"

I sigh. "I do."

"What's she like?"

I take a few seconds to search for words. "She's amazing. She's smart and likes math."

He laughs. "I hope she has a cool friend like you did."

I flip him off. "You weren't the cool one."

"Right, whatever you need to tell yourself, brother."

"She's the perfect blend of Stella and me."

"Then what are you doing here?"

I look at the paperwork all over my desk. "Working."

Grayson shakes his head. "No, you're hiding, and it's not like I blame you for it, but . . . you're being an idiot."

"You're really inspirational."

He shrugs. "I'm not here for that. I'm here to tell you that you don't have to do this just the two of you. I'll always be around if you need to talk."

Those simple words unlock something in me. Grayson, the guy who knows my entire fucking life, was left out of one of the most important things. It's been harder than he can ever know. Keeping this from him ate away at me. Having to endure it in silence was fucking torture.

So here, in my office, I unload.

Grayson listens, allowing me to say shit that I'm not sure even makes sense. I tell him about Kinsley's birth, and how hard it was to give her over to another family. Every few minutes, he asks a follow-up question, and we keep going this way.

It could be fucking hours, days, a week that I just talk.

And once my words dry up, he nods. "You've been through hell."

"And I'm still there."

He laughs while shaking his head. "You have a second chance, Jack. You get to be in this girl's life for however the hell long the time is. Do you know what a gift that is? Not only did you finally get your head out of your ass and get my sister, but also you're in Kinsley's life. What the hell are you doing?"

"I have to give her back!"

"Yeah, you do. You know that, and it sucks, but wouldn't you like to enjoy the time you do get now?"

My chest is tight, and anger starts to simmer. He gets to keep his daughter. He can love Amelia, raise her, give her a life. I have to let her in only to watch her go once more.

"It's not that simple."

"Maybe not. Hell, I've been called a fool more times in the last week than I can count, so what do I know? Here's the one thing I do understand . . . you have about three weeks with a kid you never thought you'd have three weeks with. You do what you need to do, but this time, Jack, you won't get it back."

"It's fleeting."

"Yes, it is, so you want to spend the time you could be spending with her at your office instead? It's an open adoption, it means she and you all get to choose what relationship you have. No one is stopping you from having a place in her life if she wants you to, right?"

"That's not true, Gray." I don't have the energy to explain the rules because when we give her back, it's not up to us. It's not even really up to Kinsley and I'd rather prepare for the worst.

"Well, as a father, I'll tell you this, if Amelia was with Yvonne and all I could get was one day a year with her. That day would be the best day each and every time." Grayson gets to his feet and shrugs. "But what the hell do I know?"

I don't remember leaving the office after Grayson did, but here I am, standing outside the door of Stella's loft.

I didn't get any work done, and I give zero shits about it. Grayson is right. I have three weeks. Three weeks to get to know her and maybe at the end I never see her again. Maybe this will be all we get, and if it is, then I want every second of it.

I push open the door, and Stella glances over to me, smiling. "Hey, you're back?"

"I am."

"Okay. Is everything all right?"

I nod. "Where is Kinsley?"

"She is getting changed. We were going to grab food."

"Oh."

Stella's head tilts to the side. "Do you want to come?"

"She probably won't want me there."

"Jack," Stella's voice is soft, "don't do that."

"Do what?"

"Make excuses when there isn't a need to. Come eat with us. It's the first time I'm taking her out, and . . . I have no idea who will be around."

One look at Kinsley, and anyone will know whose child she is.

Kinsley walks in before I can reply. "Hi, Jack."

"Hey, kid. You guys getting food?"

She looks to Stella and then smiles shyly. "Yeah. Are you coming?"

"I finished work early, and . . ." *Don't be a fucking pussy, Jack. Tell her.* "I would love to come if that's cool with you."

"Yeah, that would be cool."

Stella's eyes are warm, and she walks over, taking my hand. "I love you."

I gaze at this amazing woman, knowing I don't deserve her but am way too selfish to ever give her up, and brush my fingers against her cheek. "I love you too."

She lifts onto her toes and presses a kiss to my cheek.

"What if we go a few towns over and get something?" I suggest.

Stella squeezes my hand and then lets it go. "We were going to Jennie's, actually. I was telling Kinsley about Fred and Bill. She is sort of amazed that they are there every single day, no matter what time we go."

My chest grows tight because it also means her family or any one of our friends could be there.

I walk over to Kinsley. "Are you sure? There's a good chance that there will be people there who will . . . not respect boundaries."

Stella nods. "He's right, and even though we already talked about it, if you aren't comfortable eating there, here's another option out."

"You don't have to protect me, guys," Kinsley says with a bit of steel in her voice. "I'm not scared to meet people, and I don't want to hide away."

"Okay then. Jennie's it is."

And there will be no going back.

Thirty-Three

STELLA

My hands won't stop shaking.

Jack's eyes are on me as he opens the door to the diner, and I swear my heart is going to explode out of my chest.

Kinsley may be ready to see people, but I'm definitely not. This has been what I've avoided since I was eighteen, but I have to face it.

The door chime rings and Jennie walks over. "Hey there, Stella! Jack, it's good to see you. Just because you have a girlfriend now, doesn't mean you can't come here to eat."

Jack chuckles. "Don't worry, Stella can't cook. We were out of town, that's all."

Thankfully the diner is somewhat quiet. Of course, Bill and Fred are at the counter like fixtures of the place, but none of my siblings are here—or Winnie. I release a deep breath and return my attention to Jennie.

Her hand rests on Jack's forearm. "Good thing, Jack O'Donnell, because Vernon would be mighty upset if you found another place to eat."

He leans in. "Never."

She grins and looks over at Kinsley. "Hi there, honey. I'm Jennie, and . . ." She trails off, her eyes looking at the little girl and then back at us.

Surely piecing things together. My nose. Jack's eyes. Our daughter who we couldn't deny if we even wanted to.

I speak quickly. "This is Kinsley Elkins, and she's staying with us for a few weeks while her dad has a work thing."

Jennie blinks, her lips moving without any sound coming out. After another second, she looks to me. "I see, well, how nice. Do you like pancakes?" She directs the question to Kinsley.

"Yes, ma'am."

"Good. My husband makes the best pancakes in the county."

"Could we get the booth over there?" I request. It's not in the back, but I can seat Kinsley so she won't see people gawk.

"Why it's my best booth, and for you, Stella, I'd kick someone out." Jennie smiles and then guides everyone there.

Kinsley takes the spot with her back to everyone, I slide in beside her, and Jack sits facing the door. Once Jennie leaves the menus, the three of us release a breath. "Well, that wasn't terrible," I say.

Jack looks at Kinsley. "How are you feeling?"

She shrugs. "Weird."

"I bet."

"Is there anyone else here you know?"

"Well, if you look at the counter, you'll find Bill and Fred."

"They're actually here?" Kinsley asks with excitement.

Jack laughs. "I think they have this listed as their mailing address."

Jennie returns with our drinks and lets us know what we'll be eating. Pancakes for Kinsley, a ham and cheese omelet for me, and the works for Jack, whatever that means. I would argue, but it's what I would've ordered anyway.

"Do you eat here that much?" Kinsley asks after Jennie leaves.

"Yeah, it's the only place in town other than the Park Inn, but I didn't really eat there unless I was working."

Kinsley chews on the end of her straw. "So, you and your brothers just quit?"

"It's not that simple, but that's the general idea. We're forcing our father to buy us out so we can start our own resort."

"That's kind of cool."

Jack nods. "It's a testament to their strength, and I'm glad they asked me to join the business with them."

"Your brothers seem pretty cool."

"They're pains in the asses," Jack adds with a grin.

"They are both of those things," I agree.

We continue to talk about the people in the diner, mostly the story of Fred and Bill. Jack fills her in on how he comes here after a fire call, and the three of us settle into a comfortable conversation. She's curious about us, how we live, our friends, and my family. Jack and I do our best to answer everything.

"You did not do that," he scoffs after I tell her a story about going to Jack's college graduation and leaving before he saw me.

"I was there."

"There's no way. I saw your brothers there, and I promise, I would've noticed you."

I shake my head and look at Kinsley. "I was there. I was *not* sitting with my brothers because I didn't *want* Jack to know I was there. He wore a blue tie and took his hat off first. He was in the third row on the left side."

Jack's jaw drops. "You were there?"

"I was always there for you, even when you didn't want

me to be."

He clears his throat, and his tone turns joking. "She was a stalker."

In the same moment, three things happen. Kinsley giggles, the door chime rings, and Jack's eyes widen. I don't need him to say anything, it's someone we know, and the small reprieve we were enjoying is going to end.

I turn my head, and there stands Grayson, Jessica, and Amelia.

"Auntie!" Amelia spots us, and before Grayson can grab her, she's running.

I get up quickly and intercept her, hugging her tight. "Hi, Monkey."

"Auntie, I have missed you so much! Where have you been?"

I smile at her as Gray approaches. "I've been working and . . ."

And trying to keep my shit together.

"It's okay. Are you coming to my birthday party? Daddy let me pick my cake, and balloons, and I'm going to have all my friends there."

I kiss her cheek and smile. "Of course I'll be there."

"Uncle Jack!" Amelia yells, hand waving frantically.

My brother's eyes dart to Jack and then back to me. "Sorry, we didn't know you were here."

"I know that."

He scoops up Amelia, who doesn't want that and starts to struggle to get out of his arms. "I want to see Uncle Jack."

"Uncle Jack is having lunch, you need to calm down, and I'm sure he'll come see you."

"I'm sorry," I say to my brother. I'm sorry that what would've been a fun coincidence is now awkward for everyone.

He smirks. "Relax, Stell. It's fine. Go have your lunch, and if . . . well, if you can or want to, stop by the table."

"Why wouldn't she want to?" Amelia asks.

"Because you're a pain in the butt."

I tickle her softly. "And because you're giggly."

She laughs and Grayson winks. "Go."

I nod, and walk back to my table where Jack is talking to Kinsley. When I sit, I'm completely out of sorts. I don't know what to tell her or ask her. "That was my brother."

"Jack said as much. Is that his daughter?"

"Yes, Amelia. She's turning five soon."

I wonder if her thoughts are going as crazy as mine. That's her cousin, and she doesn't even know her. A whole family that she could've had support her that she never knew. The regrets I have just keep stacking up.

Misty wanted us to meet, but I wasn't ready, and I knew Jack didn't want that either. It was easier for us in some ways not to be on the fringes of Kinsley's life. Not knowing her made it so we didn't have to face the choice we made. There's not a doubt in mind that, had we allowed ourselves to love her, know her, I would've wanted her back.

"Are you embarrassed of me?" Kinsley asks.

Immediately Jack and I speak at the same time. "No. Of course not."

"Not at all," Jack says again.

"I know that I was a mistake."

I lean forward, making sure I have her full attention. "Kinsley, you were not a mistake. Please don't think that. My brothers, all four of them, and my mother, want to meet you. They are begging, but they also know you've been through hell the last few months and don't want to force their way into your life. If you want to know them, we wouldn't be prouder than to introduce you."

She lets out a deep sigh. "I have been an only child with no one other than my parents, and now I have this big family.

It's just . . ."

"A lot to take in?" Jack finishes for her.

Kinsley nods.

"Well, if you'd like to meet Grayson, Jessica, and Amelia, they'd be more than happy to come sit with us."

I wait, my heart pounding with uncertainty about which way I hope she goes. Grayson was not my top choice of who she would meet first. I would've started her off with Oliver. He's sweet, funny, and makes everyone feel at ease. Grayson, while being a great man and very sweet, is a bit intimidating.

However, it's her choice.

After another moment, Kinsley gives me a small smile. "I'd like to meet him."

Thirty-Four

JACK

As I walk over to their table, Grayson watches my progress. "Twice in one day."

"It would be your lucky day it seems." I turn to Jess. "Hi, Jess."

Amelia bristles. "What about me?"

"You? I didn't see you there. You've gotten so big, I hardly recognize you."

She smiles up at me. "You're silly, Uncle Jack."

"I am."

I address Grayson and Jessica. "So, Stella, Kinsley, and I would like to know if you want to join us for lunch?"

Jessica's lips part, and she grabs Grayson's hand.

He blinks a few times, briefly cutting his eyes toward his daughter. "What are we saying?"

"I haven't gotten that far."

"Okay then."

I sigh deeply. "Trust me, we're all winging it. However, Kinsley would like to meet you."

Tears fill Jessica's eyes. "Oh, this is just too perfect."

Grayson glances at his pregnant and emotional wife. "It's perfect?"

"Well, maybe not perfect, but she wants to meet you, Grayson. So, yes, I'd say that is damn near close."

He kisses her temple before telling me, "We'll grab our stuff and come right over."

I head to Jennie, let her know the plan, and then move the table over. Kinsley has moved closer to Stella, leaving room for me on her other side.

"What exactly are we saying?" I ask Stella and Kinsley.

Kinsley answers first. "The truth. My mother always said it's the only answer, no matter how hard it is."

"Your mother was one of the best people I ever knew."

She looks up at me with watery eyes. "She really was."

Kinsley goes stiff as Grayson approaches. He does his best not to gawk at her while they all file in.

Stella speaks, but her voice is shaky. "Kinsley, this is my brother, Grayson. My sister-in-law, Jessica, and that little monster down there is Amelia."

"It's really great to meet you," Grayson says first.

Kinsley chews on her lower lip. "You too."

"I'm Amelia Jane Parkerson!" Melia offers up.

"I'm Kinsley Rose Elkins," she says back to her.

"Are you new here?"

Kinsley nods. "Yup."

"Do you like dolls?"

"I used to."

"I love dolls. They're fun. You can play with my dolls if you want. I'll probably get new dolls soon for my birthday. Daddy and Mommy had me make a list for my party. I put a lot of dolls on it."

Kinsley smiles a real smile this time. "That's really smart of you."

"I like to dance too. Do you like dancing? I'm not very good. Mrs. Butler says I'm ex-exhas-ber-ate-eating, whatever that means."

Stella groans. "You are not that, Melia. You are a great dancer."

"Thanks, Auntie." She beams at her.

"I swear, we should run that woman out of town," Jessica says to Stella.

"Who is that?" Kinsley asks.

Jessica turns her attention to Kinsley. "Mrs. Butler is the owner of the dance studio. She's been there since I was a kid, and I swear she was a hundred then. She's mean and made my best friend, Delia, and I cry a lot."

"That sounds horrible." Kinsley looks to Stella. "Did you dance?"

Grayson and I burst out in laughter, which earns us a glare from her.

Grayson is the one to explain. "Stella is the worst dancer I've ever seen. She has two left feet and a peg leg."

Stella sticks her tongue out at him. "Don't listen to him, I was a talent before my time. What they now call contemporary is what I was good at."

Grayson snorts. "That was called flailing around."

Kinsley giggles. "I can't dance either."

"You get that from me, then."

Silence falls around the table, and Jessica breaks the tension. "Kinsley, have you gotten to do anything fun since you got to Willow Creek Valley?"

"No, not much."

"We haven't really gone out because we wanted Kinsley to settle in first," Stella explains.

"Well, you guys should go out to Melia Lake tomorrow. It's supposed to be nice, and I'm sure there's stuff you guys can do. The boat is there, at least."

Kinsley looks to us. "Is that where you're building the resort?"

I nod. "Yup. Would you like to go?"

"Yeah, I would love to. Can we fish there?"

"Of course."

Grayson cuts in. "I will say, I've yet to catch a thing in that lake. I've tried, but nothing bites."

"Grayson sucks at fishing," I tell her under my breath.

"I heard that."

"I wasn't trying to hide it," I toss back.

Kinsley laughs softly. "I fish a lot with my dad."

I see Grayson stiffen just a bit, and I speak quickly. "Hopefully your dad taught you better than Grayson's did. None of the Parkerson boys are very good at outdoor stuff."

Jessica snorts. "He's got you there, babe. You really aren't."

"You're not, Daddy," Amelia offers, her cute face twisting with apology. "You stink, but Uncle Jack can teach you to be better."

"Gee, both my girls threw me under the bus."

We all laugh, and then Jennie appears with our meals. The rest of the lunch settles in, and I breathe a sigh of relief that Kinsley's introduction to the most difficult Parkerson to win over went well.

The three of us drive down the dirt roadway and park up by the old house that will soon be taken down to its studs.

We show her around, and Stella explains what she's hoping to build here. She meets with another contractor next week to see designs. Since their meeting with their father, they've started the ball rolling. Regardless of whether he buys them out or someone else does, no one wants to waste time.

"Where will you work?" Kinsley asks.

"I'm hoping to have an office away from the main property. I'm sort of an add-on to what the resort offers, so it's a separate business."

"And you're going to offer wilderness adventures?"

"It's not that bad."

Stella scoffs. "It's awful. Let me tell you, I spent a night in the woods with him a few weeks ago, and it was hell."

I roll my eyes. "Hell?"

"Well, it wasn't fun. I almost died."

"You did not almost die!" This woman is so damn dramatic sometimes.

"A bear wanted to eat me," Stella tells Kinsley.

"What?" she yells. "There are bears here?"

Oh God. "There are no bears here. Well, there are bears in the woods, but they're not here."

Stella raises her brows and smirks. "See, I'm not the only one who doesn't want to be eaten."

"We are not going to be eaten by a bear."

She moves closer to Kinsley. "If we see one, we throw Jack in front. If he's going to risk our lives, he should be mauled first."

"I would jump in front anyway."

"Such a gallant hero you are," Stella jokes.

Kinsley starts to laugh and then bites her lip.

"Let's go see the inside," I suggest with a smile.

On our way there, Stella explains some of what she wants. "My hope is that we'll cater to families and a lot of weddings. I want us to have everything so that no one ever wants to leave."

I have never doubted that the Parkerson siblings could do this, but listening to her talk, the way her eyes light up, the smile on her lips, and the lift in her voice tells me so much more. She's going to excel at this.

"It sounds amazing," Kinsley says after Stella tells her

about adding a barn toward the back for the horses. And another building she wants where they can offer different outdoor activities.

"Would it be somewhere you'd want to visit?" Stella asks. "I mean, twelve years old is a hard age to sell a kid on going on a family vacation to the mountains of North Carolina. We want this place to be something for everyone to enjoy."

Kinsley shrugs. "I don't know. I'm not normal. I like numbers and math camp. This wouldn't be something we would've done. Mom liked going to see places where there was education involved."

"Like where?"

"For my tenth birthday, we went to Washington D.C. because I was really into history. We spent days in the museums."

Stella smiles. "And coming to the quiet of the woods wouldn't really be educational."

I laugh. "I teach survival skills, remember?"

Kinsley shakes her head. "Not like that."

"Well, maybe we can find some weird artifacts when we start the build and turn it into something."

"Like fossils?" Stella asks with her brow raised.

"Maybe. You never know."

"Great, I was worried about bears, and now we can add on dinosaurs."

This woman is going to drive me insane. I see it now, years of sarcasm and smiles, wearing me down.

The sad part is, I want it all.

I want a life with Stella and . . .

I stop myself. There is no life with Kinsley. She's not ours, and in a few weeks, we will have to give her back.

Anger starts to simmer, at myself more than anything. I have to keep perspective. Yes, I may want to soak up what time I have, but I need to remember that there's an expiration date looming. Kinsley will go back to her father. She'll have a life that isn't here in Willow Creek Valley.

And then, as if to punctuate what I was thinking, Kinsley turns to me. "All of this is cool, but my dad and I like the beach, so I don't know if I'll ever come back to the mountains. But you guys can send me photos so I can see it when it's all done."

This is all I may ever get, and I see now she feels the same.

Thirty-Five

STELLA

The last week and a half has been strange. It's like something shifted between Jack and I when we were at the lake. He's here with us, but it's like he's gone as well. He's still sweet and attentive, but there's a wall that wasn't there before.

Kinsley has been better. She spends time with us, and she's excited about Amelia's birthday that is coming up because she'll meet Alexander and Joshua. Oliver is coming for lunch today, and she's been all nervous energy since I asked her if that was okay.

Maybe that is why Jack has been so reserved—because he doesn't have anyone to introduce her to. If that's the case, I wish he would talk to me about it so I could make him feel less isolated.

I lie on my side, facing him as he sleeps. The sun hasn't fully risen, but I can't sleep and am desperate for him. He had a fire call last night, which must not have been anything crazy because he was only gone for about two hours. Tentatively, I reach my hand out, touching the scruff on his cheek.

He shifts, eyes slowly opening, and his lips turn up. "Hi there, gorgeous."

"Hi." My cheeks burn at the compliment.

"It's early," he notes.

"It is, but I missed you."

"I wasn't gone that long last night." He lets out a long stretch, and I smile at the sight of what dips below the sheet.

"Maybe not, but I still worry when you go out."

Jack rubs his thumb along my lip. "We're always careful, and trust me, I take far fewer risks since I fell in love with you."

"Awww," I say, snuggling against him a little deeper. "You're so sweet. But I still miss you."

Jack smiles softly. "I'm right here."

"You are, and you're not. It's been hard for us, and we haven't had a lot of time for just the two of us."

"No, we haven't. I've missed you too, Stella."

"You have?" I ask, feeling stupid and shy.

"Most definitely. I love you even more."

Maybe I'm imagining it all. Maybe Jack isn't being weird, and I'm reading into things.

"I love you more."

"Not possible."

"Wanna bet?" I challenge, then laugh and rest my head on my hand before adding, "I think you'd lose."

"Are either of us losing when it comes to this?"   •

"Nope."

His hand moves to my hip and then slides to my ass. "Did you sleep well?"

"I did, even with your snoring."

Jack laughs, his hand cupping my butt and pulling me toward him. "You're one to talk."

I move in closer, my hand on his chest. "I'd rather not talk."

"No?"

I shake my head. "No."

"What would you rather do?"

The tips of my fingers make patterns against his skin. "I can think of a few things."

"I'm all ears."

"Would you rather talk about it or have me show you?"

Jack's eyes blaze with desire, and I realize just how much I need this. I've missed him, needed him, and I am desperate to feel his touch.

"I've always learned better by doing," Jack says, pushing his erection against my core. "Show me what you want, baby."

I lean in, kissing his chest and pushing him down onto his back. I kiss his pecs and then playfully bite his nipples, which he groans at. I explore his abdomen with my mouth, kissing and sliding my tongue down the ridges and valleys.

I love his body.

I love his heart and soul.

I love everything about this man, and I never want to lose him.

As I slide lower, his hand moves to my hair, and I don't tease him. I want him far too much for that.

In one movement, I take his cock deep.

Jack groans, tangling his fingers in my hair. "Stella," he says on an exhale.

I do it again, going up and down, taking him as far back in my throat as I can go. Jack's grip tightens as I move my hand to his balls, massaging them gently.

"Stella, baby, fuck, I can't." His voice is dark and husky.

I moan around his cock, doing it again. He pulls a little harder on my hair.

After a few more seconds, I lift up. My plan is to ride him, but Jack grabs me quickly, tossing me onto my back and parting my legs.

I go to say something, but his mouth is on my core, stealing whatever words of protest I might have uttered, and it's my turn to grip his hair. "Oh, God!" I moan quietly.

He slides his tongue against my clit in a steady rhythm. I hold on because letting go is the last thing I want to do.

Jack, right here, is everything.

He's power and sex with sin wrapping around him. I want to stay in this bubble forever.

"Jack." I call his name softly, allowing the pleasure to lap at me like waves against the shore.

"That's it, baby, feel what I do to you."

My back arches when he hits the spot that always drives me wild. He does it again, causing my breathing to accelerate.

"I need you," I tell him.

His tongue is rougher as he adds more pressure with each stroke.

My climax is right there, I can see it, but I don't want it yet. I want more of him and us and love. I want to fall apart with him inside me. "Jack, please. I . . . want you . . . us."

He lifts his head, kissing the inside of my thigh. "I want to make you lose control."

I take advantage of the moment and slide out from under him. When I try to push him down, he doesn't budge.

"Let me ride you. Let me fall apart with you inside me."

He lets out a noise that sounds like a growl. "Jesus. You're going to kill me."

I grin. "Not until after."

He lies back, and I straddle him. In one swift move, Jack is seated to the hilt inside me. My head drops back, hair falling in waves down my back. His hands move to my breasts, and he kneads them.

It doesn't take long.

I can feel myself getting close. I move faster, and Jack's hands move to my hips. "Stella, you feel so good."

"I can't last long," I tell him.

"Ride me. Take what you need."

I do, feeling my orgasm coming closer and closer. Our eyes lock, and I see everything there. The love he has for me, the need and desire raging through him. I love him. I love him so much.

With that thought, I fall apart. Tears fill my gaze as I crest over the top and start to fall. But I don't hit the ground because Jack is there, holding me, keeping me safe, loving me beyond measure.

He jerks his hips a few times, following me in a sea of pleasure.

I lie on his chest, both of us struggling to breathe.

After a minute, I start to move off him, but he grips me tighter. "Don't. Not yet."

I lift my head to look at him. "What?"

"Just stay here."

I smile and tuck myself into the crook of his neck. "You smell good here."

"My neck?" he asks with a soft laugh.

"You smell like the woods and Jack."

His fingers move to my back. "Stella?"

"Hmm?" I ask, feeling rather content.

"We didn't use a condom again."

I push back just enough to see his face. "I had an IUD put in after we had Kinsley. I've been . . . rather crazy about always making sure I'm protected. We don't have to worry."

He pushes my hair back over my shoulder and then cups my cheek. "I figured as much, but we've never talked about it. I didn't want you to think—"

My finger presses against his lips. "I know. It was me who took advantage of you."

He raises one brow. "Is that so?"

I nod. "Oh, most definitely."

Jack flips us so he's on top, staring down at me. "Then maybe it's my turn to take advantage of you."

"So soon?" I ask with a smirk.

I can feel him growing hard inside me so I roll my hips.

"If you do that again, you'll feel the answer to that question," Jack warns.

Little does he know that's not much of a deterrent. "I'm hoping that's the case," I say and then repeat the motion.

After we finish, we lie in bed and watch the sunlight start to filter through the curtains. I listen to his heartbeat, which is strong and steady beneath my ear. "Will you talk to me?" I ask a few minutes later.

"About?"

I turn, resting my chin on my hand. "You've been distant this week."

"I just have a lot on my mind."

"Such as?" I prompt.

"Well, Samuel is supposed to call Kinsley today. Oliver is coming tonight, and we're going to Amelia's party next weekend. All of this . . . I don't know, Stella, aren't you worried? We have a little over a week left with her. That's it." He sighs deeply, the serene look he had is gone, replaced with frustration.

I sit up, pulling the sheet with me. "I know, but worrying about it doesn't change that. What I don't know is why you're being distant with me."

Jack shakes his head. "Worrying about it is all I do. Someone has to."

"What does that mean? You think I don't care?"

He sits up, exhaling and rubbing his forehead. "I didn't say you don't care. I'm saying that if you know what's to come, what is after that? What exactly do we do?"

I blink a few times, bristling at the change in his tone. "What we have to."

He laughs once. "What we have to? How do you see this playing out, baby? Do you think we're going to just give her back without it tearing our hearts out? That I'm not going to go to Melia Lake and remember the time we took Kinsley out there?"

"Why is remembering her a bad thing?"

Jack sits up, running his fingers through his thick, brown hair. "You asked me why I'm being distant. Well, that's what's on my mind. I'm fucking terrified and doing what I can to make sure that, in a week, we're not completely broken."

"Why would we be broken?" I fling another question at him, which seems to be all I'm able to do at this point.

"Because you're falling in love with this kid." I pull the sheet higher, and my lip trembles. "You can't deny it. You are going to fall apart, and what am I supposed to do then? How do I watch you struggle? How do I make it right? Tell me."

This has always been reality. I knew it from the start, but I've also done what I could not to think about it. It was easy the first week when it was still new and we didn't really know her yet. Then she started to come out of her shell and spend time with us. We have a routine where we have dinner, talk about our day, the plans for the lake, and play some weird math game she likes, which Jack is amazing at.

I've gotten to know her.

And I've let my guard down.

"I don't know, but I can't keep her at arm's length. Not when we have this chance with her. We knew what the rules were when we agreed to help."

He gets out of bed and starts to get dressed. "I'm not asking you to. I'm just answering the question you asked me and being honest about my concerns. We are going to have to let her go again. Today is going to show us that, and I want you to be ready for it."

I appreciate his concern, and it's not without merit, but I

know she's not ours to keep. I don't have some silly fantasy about her wanting to stay, and even if she did, I couldn't do that to Samuel.

He's getting help to be better for Kinsley, so to take her from him would be cruel.

"I'm not living under false pretenses, Jack."

"That's not what I said."

"I know, but just because I refuse to keep her at a distance, doesn't mean I'm not aware of the situation. Regardless of what we all say, I am her mother and you are her father. We may not get to raise her, but there hasn't been a day she's drawn breath that I haven't loved her." I get to my feet, throwing my shirt on and then jamming my legs into my pants. "I loved her the day I knew she was in my stomach. I loved her the day I gave birth to her, and I have spent every day since then loving her enough to let her go. You are the one who is fooling yourself," I say to him, watching his eyes flare at my last words.

This isn't the discussion I thought we'd be having, but here it is.

He turns his back on me, looking out the window. "You're wrong about this, Stella. You're going to end up hurt."

"Of course I am, but I think you're the one who's wrong." I look at his tall frame, the slight drop in his shoulders as he carries the weight of the world.

This has always been Jack's greatest problem. He thinks he's responsible for everyone he loves, and he's failed them. His mother, his father, me, Kinsley, we're all the links in the chain that he's somehow failed to repair.

Instead of just loving us for whatever time we may have together, he pushes against it. I thought—I hoped—that last week was a turning point, but now we're back here again.

I start to walk out of the room, unable to watch him pull away. It hurts, and I need every bit of strength I have today.

"How so?" he asks as I get to the door.

I stop, not turning toward him. If I see his beautiful eyes, I'll crumble. "By thinking you could stop loving her even if you wanted to." I leave him with my words and walk out of the room, ready to face whatever lies ahead.

Oliver meeting Kinsley was exactly as I hoped, hilarious and easy. His easy smile and the warmth that only my brother possesses had her warming up to him immediately. He's so damn likable it's gross.

Since our talk, Jack has been here, but he's still aloof. I wish I could shake him until he saw that our time is slipping away. As upset as I am with the way he's handling it, I have to remember that we each have our own way.

He will be the one with regrets, not me.

It's nearing the time we'd typically put on a movie before bed, but the elephant in the room has grown so large that it's hard to breathe.

We got an email from the facility earlier this week, stating that Samuel was slotted to call today, but the email cautioned us that things could change. Jack and I weren't sure what to do, but we decided telling Kinsley was the right move.

None of us have mentioned it all day, but Samuel still hasn't called.

Kinsley looks out the window and then turns to me. "Did you get another email?"

I shake my head. "No."

Her chin drops a bit. "Oh."

"Don't worry, if it doesn't happen today, I'm sure he'll call another day."

Jack walks over and pulls her against his side, surprising

us both. "I know you're sad, but he'll call. There's nothing in this world he loves more than you, Kinsley."

She gives him a hug back, and I have to fight back tears. There's nothing that Jack loves more either, but he won't allow himself to see that even if he's hugging her and giving more of himself up.

"What if he needs more time? What if he needs another month?" The panic in her voice threatens to shatter me.

"Then we'll figure it out."

"I have to go back to school! I was supposed to be at camp this summer, not here!"

"I know," Jack says. "And I'm sorry your plans got messed up. We don't know anything about your dad's treatment. He may be doing great and be home in a week. Until we hear otherwise, there is no reason to worry about it."

I watch as her lower lip trembles and her eyes fill with unshed tears.

"Why don't we make popcorn and watch a movie?" I suggest. A distraction sounds like what we all need.

"I'm not really in the mood," Kinsley says, pulling away from Jack and wrapping her arms around herself.

Sometimes, it's amazing how much of us I can see in her. Jack's quiet stubbornness. The way he would rather lock himself away than admit he's hurting. My strength in the way she can face the world, her troubles, and forge ahead, no matter how hard it is.

She could've fallen apart when everything unraveled, but she didn't. She stayed strong when I don't know I could've at her age.

"Would you rather be alone?" Jack questions.

Kinsley inhales deeply a few times. "I'm going to read."

"Okay."

When the door clicks shut behind her, I look to Jack, whose eyes are where she last was. "We shouldn't have told her," Jack says.

"We did what we thought was best."

He turns to me while rubbing the bridge of his nose. "What the hell do we know about what's best for her? We barely know her, and everyone she's loved has left her."

I go to him. "No one left her. Her mother died and her father went to get help. We didn't leave her, we gave her a life we couldn't't provide."

I have to keep telling myself that as often as I tell him. There are days when the guilt is so thick I can't see through it. There are nights when I wonder about the nights I could've held her, read her a book, or taken her to dance like I did with Amelia.

Giving her a loving and secure home was the right decision. No matter the cost to me or Jack.

But watching Kinsley struggle through another round of disappointment makes my heart ache.

"I know what she feels, Stella." The edge in Jack's voice tells me he's back to being her age.

The loss of his mother. The abandonment of his father. The hurt of losing everyone he loved.

"Then who better to comfort her than you?"

"What am I supposed to say?"

"The truth," I suggest. "You know more than anyone what she's going through. You lost your mother, and because of that event, your father spiraled out of control and left. It's history, and it's playing out in front of you. Talk to her. Show her that how she feels now is temporary." I rest my hand on his chest.

"I'm . . . I'm fucking this all up."

I shake my head. "No, you went to her. You comforted her, even when I know you're trying to put space between you."

Jack's thumb grazes my cheek. "How can I stop myself from loving her when all I see is you. Your strength, your love, your heart and soul are all there in her. It scares me because I know how impossible it is to resist. I also know what losing you feels like. Life without you, Stella, well, it's not life. It's hell, and when she goes, she's going to take part of that with her."

"I know, but the more we push her away now, the more we're going to punish ourselves later."

His lids lower, and when they open again, something feels different between us. "You're right."

"Go to her, Jack. Give her what she needs."

"I'll try." He gives me a brief kiss and walks toward her door.

Just as he's about to knock, the phone rings, and we both freeze.

Thirty-Six

JACK

I swipe my finger against the screen that shows an unknown Georgia number. "Hello?"

"Hi, Jack."

As much as a part of me hates it, I'm glad he called. Two parts of me are tearing at each other. The one that says I am her father and I want this family we're pretending to be. The other saying it's best for the little girl I love to go back to him.

I was worried about Stella, but it's me who is struggling.

"Samuel. It's good to hear your voice."

"I'm . . . I wasn't sure I could do it. It took me all day to work up the courage to call. To talk to her. If she hates me . . ."

Sympathy flows through my body at the sound of his voice breaking. I, too, know that level of fear. I felt it sitting in his living room three weeks ago right before we were going to meet Kinsley.

"She doesn't hate you. I promise you that."

"Is she okay?"

"She's doing well. She misses you and is worried about

you."

He releases a deep sigh. "I've been sick over it. I know you and Stella would never hurt her, but leaving her, knowing I was too—"

"Strong, Samuel. You were strong and what you did was nothing less than Herculean."

Stella comes to stand beside me and rests her hand on my arm. I let her strength and love wrap around me.

"I appreciate you saying that, but I don't feel all that strong right now."

I can respect that, and I won't diminish his feelings. I can't say that I feel all that strong right now either. "Well, we're here to do whatever we can to help."

"I know." He sucks in a breath. "Before I lose my nerve, can I talk to her?"

"Of course."

Stella is already moving toward Kinsley's door.

A second later, Kinsley practically runs to the phone. I hand it to her, feeling a pang of jealousy that I shouldn't.

"Daddy?" she says quickly. "Daddy! How are you? I miss you. Are you okay?" Kinsley's grin is wide as she rattles off the questions. She looks so happy to hear from him. "Yes. I am. Uh-huh." Time stretches out before us as she talks.

I look to Stella, who is staring back at me. This phone call is doing exactly what I warned her it would do, which is reminding us of our place.

Regardless of whatever lies I've told myself, a piece of me has clung to a hope that she was getting attached to us as well.

I stand here, listening to her excitement to talk to Samuel, and watch Stella turn. She looks out the window, her shoulders slumped, and her arms cross in front of her. I've known her long enough to understand what she's feeling.

Lost.

Stella Parkerson is one of the strongest women I know, but

looking out at the mountain tops and the vast expanse in front of her is what she does when she doesn't know where to turn.

I hate this for her. I want to take all the pain she's feeling and make it mine. She doesn't deserve to hurt.

My heart is pounding against my chest, and I hear the word over and over: *stupid, stupid, stupid.*

Kinsley's voice filters around the room. "That's so great, Daddy. I can't wait. I'll help you, I promise."

Stella moves her hand across her cheek, and I want to rage at the fact that she's crying. If we give in to our feelings and allow ourselves to break down in front of Kinsley, it will only make things worse.

I make my way over to Stella and grip her shoulder. She doesn't say a word as she rests her hand on mine. I lean in, my front to her back, absorbing the hurt that's radiating off her. My lips move to her ear, offering her whatever support I can. "I know this is hard, but we have to be strong."

She nods.

"Once she goes into her room, you can fall apart in my arms. I'll hold you together."

Stella leans back into me while we listen to Kinsley's voice fill with pure joy.

"I will, Daddy. I love you so much, and I can't wait to see you. Okay. Here's Jack."

Two names in the same sentence that should be mine, but only one applies. I close my eyes for a beat, step away from Stella, and grab the phone with a sad smile because that's about all I can muster.

Oblivious in a way only a kid can be, Kinsley smiles and rushes off into her room, and I clear my throat before pressing the phone to my ear. "Hi, Samuel."

"That went better than I hoped. Thank you for everything. I know I asked an incredibly hard thing of you both, and I wish I didn't have to, but I'm thankful that you were willing to step in for me."

"You have nothing to thank us for. We are . . . well, we would never have said no."

He's silent for a moment. "I leave in a week. I will have a long road to go, but I'm at least going the right way now."

"I'm glad."

"I'm hoping that you can bring Kinsley home right away, I want her to be there and get her ready for school to start back."

My throat is tight, but I force the words out. "Not a problem," I lie. I lie because it is a problem. But it's my problem, and that's why I have to say what I don't mean. I don't want to return Kinsley.

I don't want to give her back. Not now that I've gotten to know her. Not now that I can no longer pretend that I'm okay not having her in my life.

No, I have to give her back, not knowing if we will ever see her again.

Stella slams into my side, wrapping her arms around my middle. I love that she knew and came to me. We may never be the same after we drop Kinsley off, but if we can hold on to each other, we may survive.

Samuel speaks again. "I want to focus on finishing the program for the next six days so I'm ready to go home at the end of the week. But I get a phone call the day before I leave, so I'll call you if something changes."

"Okay. We'll plan to bring her back in a week unless we hear from you. Just let us know."

"I will. Please tell Stella I said thank you, and I'll be in touch."

He disconnects, and my arms are around Stella instantly.

Seven days left until we, once again, face pain like we did twelve years ago.

THIRTY-SEVEN

STELLA

My brothers and I stand next to each other in front of our father's desk. We were summoned here today to get the final news regarding his precious company. My brothers and I granted him another two weeks when Kinsley came to stay with us. "I've come up with the capital to buy you all out."

"Great. We expect the process to take no more than another two weeks for you to have the money," Josh says with a perfunctory tone.

"I taught you well, son."

Josh laughs with a smug smile. "You taught me nothing. I left the minute I could and haven't listened to your 'advice' since."

"Yes, and you became a man because of it."

"Sure, we'll go with that. It's all because of you that we're banding together in order to leave the company. Great play, Dad. Real smart business move."

Our father turns his head in my direction. "You think the

five of you can start a new career?"

"I think we're smart enough to do what we must. However, we're here about the money. Our lawyers have drawn up the sale papers, and as soon as you sign them and hand over the money, you'll have back all the equity we owned."

It's not an insignificant amount of money. Between the five of us, it is well over two million dollars. How our father was able to come up with the money, I don't know, but it appears he's prepping the house for sale.

"Not that it'll be worth much," Oliver says as he throws me a grin.

Our father glares at him. "You think you're all so smart."

"We are," Ollie tosses back.

Dad laughs once. "We'll see about that. When you're all back here, begging for your jobs back because you see how hard it is out in the real world. You five are in for the surprise of your lives."

Grayson, who looked bored a few moments ago, scoffs. "You think we'll be back? You think any of us want a damn thing to do with you? Even now, when your own kids are forcing you to find money they know you don't have just so they can get away from you, you think you've won. Not only is your business about to crumble, but your kids—let me rephrase that—at least I'm done with you. Once that paperwork is signed, that's it. We're through. We have no business together. No relationship. You almost cost me everything, and I will never forgive you for it."

Our father's composure cracks just a bit. He has been a horrendous parent the last twenty years, but for a time, he did love us. I believe that, in some part of his mind, he thought gifting us parts of the company was a show of that love. He wanted us to share in something he built.

Now we're telling him we want no part of it. He didn't think of this option. That all five of his kids would walk away.

That he'd lose the managers of all the properties in one swoop, leaving him unable to handle it.

I'm sure he's already hired someone, but there would have been weeks where he lost a ton of money simply because no one who worked for him knew what to do.

"So, you take everything from me?"

Alex, who is normally the last one to speak up, does. "We are taking no less than you deserve. For years, we've allowed you to control our lives in some form or another. We've made you a lot of money, haven't we?"

Dad's eyes focus on him. "You've made a lot as well."

Alex steps closer as he continues. "It was never about money for me. I couldn't have cared less if I had nothing. I wanted to make you proud, and for what? You didn't care about us."

"The hell I didn't!" our father yells. His hand swipes across the desk, sending papers flying.

Josh's hand grips my arm when I instinctually move to clean it up. He shakes his head, and I hate that I did that. But that's how it's always been. We clean up his messes. We fix the broken in the family and hope that will be the time it stays together.

It never does.

Joshua's calm voice sends shivers down my spine. "If you did, Stella wouldn't be in the position she's in. Grayson wouldn't have almost lost his wife and child. I wouldn't have gone through half of what I did. You've hurt every one of us."

"I gave you everything."

"Sign the papers so we can be done," Gray says.

Our father's eyes move to mine. "So, I'm the villain in all this?"

"No, you're the fool. You thought you could control us forever, and now you can't," I say. "Sign the papers and do one thing we're asking of you."

That is the most important thing. Once he signs them, we

know we'll have the money coming to get started. Together, my siblings and I have the knowledge, land, and meetings set up with builders for a few weeks from now. Everything is ready, we just need this done.

"Fine." Our father leans down, signing his name on each of the five sets of sale papers. "You'll have your money in two weeks."

I can feel the tension drain from the five of us. We needed it to be him who bought us out. Yes, if pushed, we would have had an investor come in, but it wouldn't have been as satisfying. When we become the premiere resort in this area, I want our father to be who suffers, not anyone else.

Oliver plops down in the chair beside me. "I like this desk."

"Excuse me?" our father asks.

I stare at Ollie, unsure of where in the world he's going with this. "The desk. I like it. I think we should all get these for our office at our new resort."

"Resort?"

And now I see what Ollie is doing. "What? You didn't hear?" Our father's eyes move from one of us to the other, and then Oliver goes in for the kill. "We're opening a resort just around the corner. Isn't that great?"

Dad doesn't say a word, he just chuckles. "I look forward to watching you all fail."

Now it's my turn to laugh, and I push on Oliver's shoulder, indicating it's time to leave. "Oh, Daddy, there's nothing funny about this. We're going to make this hurt, just like you've made sure to do to us."

"You made a mistake," Grayson says, rising to his full height. "You forgot that we haven't needed you around to run the inns in . . . well, ever. We'll be just fine doing it on our own."

Joshua grins. "And if you back out now." He lifts the papers up, jostling them slightly. "We'll sue you for breach of contract and take the entire company anyway."

We all exit the room, not looking back, ready to start a life without him in the driver's seat.

"She seems to fit in like she was born into it," Jessica notes, staring at Kinsley, who is hanging out with my brothers.

I should be happy about the fact that it's true, but it just hurts a bit more.

Four days until we send her back to Georgia.

I shake off the thoughts, refusing to go down this hole again. I fell asleep last night in Jack's arms with tears running down his chest. He didn't say a word, just allowed me to be sad about what's to come.

"She is."

"Of course she adores Ollie."

I smile at my brother as he performs some stupid card trick for her. "Everyone does." Jess rubs her growing baby bump. "How are you feeling?"

"Good. We're excited for the baby and Amelia is beside herself."

"I'm sure. She loves things she can boss around, so a sister is going to be right up her alley."

Jessica laughs. "She definitely owns her father and uncles."

"Always has."

I look at my niece, who's sitting on Josh's lap with a smile. "It's funny that Josh seems to be the uncle Amelia loves most."

I grin. "She loves whoever is giving her what she wants. Josh has always been under her spell. I don't know if it's because he claims he'll never have kids of his own so he could love Amelia with his whole heart and not worry."

"Why is that?"

"Josh took being the oldest as a great responsibility. When he left for college, he was really guilty over it. I thought he was just being stupid about being away, but when I look back on it, I can see how much Josh shielded us from the ugly shit in our family," I explain. "Gray did too, but Josh really did until he left. Knowing what I do now about my parents, it's clear that he was aware of things between our parents and shielded us."

"So he's going to punish himself now?" she asks.

Both of our gazes move to Delia, the girl Joshua has refused to admit he has loved since they were kids. The saddest part is that she loves him too. However, Josh will never be like my father. He won't enter into marriage, have kids, or let his heart be open to it.

"He thinks love is a punishment."

She snorts. "He might not be wrong."

I sigh and take a sip of my drink. "Maybe, but I would rather suffer from loss and remember the joy while it happens."

She lifts her glass of apple juice. "I'll drink to that." Jess's hand rests on my arm. "But seriously, are you okay?"

"I'm sad because I don't know if she's sad at all over it, which is crazy. Mostly, I'm worried about how I go forward."

"What do you mean?"

I drop my voice to a whisper. "Do I call her or wait for her to call me? Do I ask her if she wants to see us again? Will Samuel want that after he knows we've had her in our care? Does she even want to talk to us after?"

"What did your adoption paperwork say?"

I wipe away the tear that fell. "Basically that we would get yearly updates and that legally, our names be listed on her birth certificate if Kinsley ever wanted to know who we are. I remember the agency explaining it wasn't really a contract so much as a nonbinding agreement between Misty, Samuel, and us. There's nothing that we are legally afforded."

Jessica lets out a heavy sigh. "So, you might send her back

and never see her again."

I nod. "It's possible. I don't think he would, but he might. He is her father—legally."

She pulls me in for a hug. "I'm so sorry."

"Don't be. The thing is, Kinsley comes first. I feel like giving her back though, it's like reliving it all over again. For the last month, I've had this little girl in my home. I've cooked, washed clothes, and been like a real mom. I'm going to give that up."

"She seems to really like you and Jack."

I turn to look at her, my throat closing when I imagine not being able to just look at her again. "She seems to. But once she goes back to her father, I don't know what we'll become. Before, it was almost easy because the rules were defined."

Jess's gaze follows mine. "My dad left when I was twelve. I remember that age and the anger and confusion. No matter what she shows, that girl is feeling the same thing. She's just as confused and unsure. She wants to make her father happy, so she's not going to approach it with him, no matter what she wants. Talk to Samuel, and then . . . talk to her. She's your daughter, Stella, and she'd be so lucky to have you and Jack in her life."

Kinsley laughs deeply at something, and I turn to look. She is smiling up at Jack as he holds Amelia upside down. All the people I love are gathered here with varying degrees of joy on their faces.

She belongs here.

She is a Parkerson, and yet she belongs to someone else.

Jack looks over at me and gives me a wink.

I smile and shake my head before replying to Jessica. "Luck sometimes isn't on my side."

"I know that all too well, but sometimes fate is, and that always wins. Don't give up on her or anything you want, Stella. I've learned that in my two near-death experiences."

"It'll be good if you keep it at that number."

Jess grins. "That's the goal here. Hey, did you set up the call with the builder I emailed you about? Odette came highly recommended and her profile is outstanding."

In all of the craziness of this month, I feel like I've been lost in regards to everything with the resort. I've done almost nothing, and my brothers haven't been dicks about it, which is a very nice change.

"I emailed her, but I haven't done more."

Alex walks into the kitchen, eyeing Jessica and me. "What are you talking about?"

"You."

He shrugs. "I wouldn't be surprised. I am the best-looking Parkerson here."

I roll my eyes. "You're the dumbest."

"If you were the best-looking, I wouldn't have dated your brother, I would've gone for you. What does that say?" Jessica teases him.

"That Alex definitely wasn't the best-looking," I back her up.

Josh's voice carries over from the other room. "Who is the best-looking what?"

Oh, God, here we go.

"Nothing, Josh!" I yell before this becomes a thing.

"Is Alex saying he's the best-looking brother?" Oliver, who could never resist a chance to annoy anyone, chimes in.

"Nope, he said he was the best-looking *Parkerson* here!" Jessica, who I thought was my ally in this, betrays me.

Jack laughs. "Well, that's where we know he's a complete idiot." I raise a brow at him, surprised he's entering the fray. "Stella is the hottest Parkerson."

My brothers all start ribbing him, calling him whipped and slapping his chest or back. I don't know that I've ever loved him more.

"And since Jack is not a Parkerson, he's right and wins!" I say with finality.

"What about my vote?" Jessica asks.

"You're a Parkerson now, you have no vote," Josh says.

One day.

Twenty-four hours left.

Jack's arm tightens around my middle, drawing me back against him. "Don't go there, Stella."

I close my eyes, hating that he knows me so well. "It's like a bomb ticking down in my heart."

"I have the same one, but we cannot fall apart. I can't lose both of you in the same day."

I turn over, my finger touches his lips. "You're not going to lose me," I vow.

"Good."

At least, I really fucking hope not. I am going to need him more than ever. "Now what do we do?"

"I think we do something fun with her. I don't want to spend the day counting down. Do you?"

"No."

"Then let's spend the day not thinking about it and having fun."

If I could turn back the clock, there are a million things I would've done with her. We could've gone to the beach house, spent more time at the lake, or gone shopping. I feel like I've been robbed. I lost the first week, and I want it back.

Only, it's not mine to have.

"Yeah. I'm sure that'll be possible with her packing and talking about going home."

The email came late last night that told us Samuel is doing

well enough to leave rehab and take back his life, which means his daughter.

Jack kisses my temple. "I didn't say it would be easy, just that we need to try. Do you want her to remember us this way?"

I close my eyes, sinking into him. "No. I want to keep her. I know I shouldn't, and I swore I wouldn't, but how could I stop this? She's our daughter. I have you, and now—God, I'm selfish and want her too. I want this family."

His hands move up and down my back. "I wish I could lie to you and say I don't feel the same. I want her too."

"And I did that to you."

He pulls back, lifting my face to his. "You didn't do anything. You were right when you told me that it was the only option, and even though I don't know how we will survive this, I don't regret it."

I don't either.

I nod, unable to speak.

"I'm going to shower, and then we can figure out what to do for the day."

Jack releases me, and I blow out a deep breath before getting out of bed.

Once dressed, I head into the kitchen.

What a mess my life is. A month ago, Jack and I were new and having fun. It was easy. Now we've been living together, which I don't want to change; we had our daughter with us, which is going to change; and the inn is taking the next steps.

I can't stop any of what's to come. Tomorrow we will drive Kinsley to Samuel, and the rest of the world will go on, oblivious to the pain Jack and I will be in.

"Stella?"

I turn to see Kinsley standing there, watching me.

"Yes?"

"Are you okay?"

I look down at the glass of orange juice in my hand, not

remembering when I poured it. I paste on a smile, using all my years of projecting false happiness, and look back to her.

"Yeah, I'm fine. Why?"

"You've been standing there for five minutes."

"Have I?"

She nods. "Yeah."

I place the glass onto the counter and walk toward her. "I'm good. Just didn't sleep well."

"Did you get the email yet?" she asks.

"I did. It looks like you'll get to go home tomorrow."

"I just want him to be better. I'm so glad he got the help he needs."

"Jack and I want the same."

And we want you. Please, don't walk out that door and cut us off. Please see that we love you.

Kinsley wrings her hands. "What time are we leaving tomorrow?"

"Early, I'm guessing."

"Okay. I just want to get the house perfect before Daddy gets home. I'm going to need to be there for him."

I nod.

"I'm just saying that I want to clean up and make sure he's not alone."

"We would never let that happen," I reassure her. "We care very much about Samuel. We love you, and we wouldn't . . . don't worry, we will make sure you're home."

Kinsley steps forward, her hand lifts as if to reach out to me, but then she lets it fall back to her side. "Thanks, Stella. You have been so nice, and I've had a great time with you and Jack. I know that's weird because it shouldn't be . . . fun, but it has been. I'm glad that, if I had to go anywhere, it was here with you guys."

My chest grows tight, and I fight back the urge to cry. I don't want to lose it now, not when I have so little time left with her. I want to hold her tight, never let her go, and spend every day getting to know her more.

I hate myself for ever giving her up.

"We've really liked getting time with you too, Kinsley."

She smiles. "I know. Where's Jack?"

"In the shower."

She nods. "Is he going to spend the day with us?"

I pause, not sure what the hell to say. All of this is so awkward, which it wasn't before.

The truth it is. "I think so. Do you want breakfast?"

"Sure."

She comes around the counter and I gather the ingredients to start making my famous waffles—which aren't famous but are the only thing I can cook.

Kinsley hands me ingredients while I combine the batter, and we work as a team. Jack emerges from the bedroom, looking all too delicious.

"Jack!" Kinsley calls in greeting.

He chuckles, looking at the pair of us. "You are covered in flour."

She looks down at her shirt and shrugs. "Stella is really not careful when cooking."

I tilt my head at her with a grin. "Hey! I'm careful."

"The kitchen would say otherwise," Jack says with a snort.

"We did get a lot on the floor."

"There was no way I could've predicted the bag would rip," I defend myself since they're ganging up on me.

Kinsley snorts. "I said it was ripping!"

"I don't recall that."

Jack takes a few steps closer, inspecting the kitchen. "Is that egg on the cabinet?"

"No. It's . . . not."

It's totally egg. I dropped one of those too.

Kinsley laughs. "It's egg."

"Traitor," I whisper.

Jack walks deeper into the kitchen, looking at the carnage. It's bad. I mean, there's flour everywhere, and the egg thing is just one of the issues. I turn, putting my back against the counter so he can't see the batter that spilled when I closed the lid on the waffle maker.

"Stella?" Jack peeks around to see what's behind me.

"Yes?" I ask with a smile.

"What are you hiding?"

"Me?"

Jack's gaze turns playful. "Yes, darling. You. What are you hiding?"

I bat my eyelashes dramatically. "I have no idea what you mean."

His arms cage me in. "What's behind you? More of a mess?"

Kinsley lets out a snort.

"Nope. I don't make messes."

His deep throaty laugh fills the room. This is the man I love. The fun, playful one who likes to tease me.

Two can do that.

I reach into the batter behind my back and then press my hand against his cheek, grinning as the mixture slides down his face. Kinsley gasps, and Jack just stares at me. "Oh, no. Did I make a mess?"

I am so in for it.

At the first chance of escape, I better run and pray he doesn't catch me.

Jack doesn't miss a beat. He turns, and I dart out, but his arm wraps around my middle, hauling me to him as flour rains down around me.

I squirm, laughing as he covers me with the dust.

There's no way I'll let this go. I grab my own handful and toss it blindly over my shoulder at him.

Jack lets me go, and I move to the other side of the counter so I'm in front of Kinsley. "Stay behind me," I tell her.

"You think you can protect her too?"

"I think you're slow and covered in batter and flour."

He raises one brow. "Is that so?"

"What do you think, Kinsley?"

"You want me to choose who will win?" she asks, amusement in her voice. She steps out from behind me and slides to the right.

I don't take my eyes off Jack, knowing he'll pounce if I do. "Pick my team so we can destroy him."

She laughs, and when I turn my head, Jack attacks. She stands beside him, tossing flour at me, so I fire back with an egg. The three of us laugh as we cover each other and the kitchen in waffle ingredients, battling back and forth until the bag is empty, eggs are gone, and there's no batter in the bowl.

Kinsley lands a perfectly thrown splatter on Jack's face, and we laugh.

He moves around, looking for anything he can use as ammo and then stops.

Kinsley and I freeze, waiting and watching. He smiles. "Give up now, my love," Jack taunts as he raises his hand to reveal the last egg.

"Never."

Kinsley backs away, leaving Jack and me in a standoff.

I move around the island. Jack watches me, measuring each of my steps.

I keep going, a smile on my face as he lunges for me, but I quickly step out of his reach. "Nice try, babe."

"I'll catch you," he warns.

"You can try, but you'll never win."

"I already caught you once."

I take a step to the left, which he counters. "Yes, but this is different."

"I will always catch you. Always. You can run. You can hide. You can throw flour at me, but you will never escape me."

While the words are meant to be playful, I hear the underlying current of what he's saying. It's a promise, the truth of his feelings at the core of it all. Jack loves me. I know this, and regardless of what we have to go through, he'll always be here. I don't deserve this man, but I'm going to keep him anyway.

My hands rest on the cool marble countertop, and I lean in. "I don't run from you, Jack."

"No?"

I shake my head. "No."

I've been doing exactly that, but now, I'm right here. Unmoving, wanting and waiting for him to catch me.

He takes two steps, eyes bright with amusement. "I'm going to catch you."

"I'm counting on it."

"One."

"Two."

Jack lunges before hitting three, bringing me down to the ground in a cloud of white.

I burst out into laughter. We squirm on the floor, and I grab whatever flour and God knows what on the floor, tossing it at him.

After a second of fighting, he gets ahold of my arms and pins me. I shiver at the feel of his lips at my ear. "I love you. I love you both, and I'll do whatever I can to make this okay."

I turn my head the best I can to get a glimpse of his face. "I know. I trust you."

Kinsley walks over, hands on her hips as she stares down at us with a smile. "I guess we're not having waffles."

"No, I think we all had something much better—fun." I smile and extend my hand for her to help me up. When she does, I pull her down, and we laugh again, rolling around in the mess, and I know this memory will carry me through all that's to come.

Thirty-Eight

JACK

I hold Stella's hand as we sit in the house, watching Samuel and Kinsley reunite.

I thought I knew pain before.

I thought I understood loss, struggle, sacrifice.

I knew fucking nothing.

Stella's arm shakes, contradicting the look of joy that hasn't left her face. There are other tells. The way her eyes crinkle just at the edges. How her smile is too tight—too practiced.

She's dying inside.

Hell, I am too.

"I can't thank you both enough," Samuel says, and we both stand.

"It wasn't any trouble." Stella releases my hand, clasping both in front of her. "If anything, I feel like Jack and I should thank you. We got . . . we got time with her."

I clear my throat, swallowing the emotions threatening to choke me. "You've done an amazing job with her. She's really a great kid."

Samuel looks at us, his eyes saying much more than the words. "I'm sorry. I know this can't be easy for you."

Stella shakes her head. "Please don't. Please don't say that. It's hard, but I'm not sorry. Thank you for calling me for help. Jack and I both aren't sorry."

"She's right, and while I hate to bring this up now, I'm not sure I'll ever get the chance again." I force myself to say more. "Stella and I would like to be here for you both if you need us or even if you want us around. We'd like to know Kinsley and talk to her." Stella's brown eyes find mine, and I can see the tears brimming. "None of us need to decide anything today, but . . ."

"You and Stella are always welcome, Jack. Misty and I promised you'd get letters, and if Kinsley wanted more, we'd discuss that. The gift you gave us, well, we cherished it. Maybe after a few days, we'll talk and come up with a plan that works for everyone?" He looks toward Kinsley's room. She went in there right away to unpack so she could help Samuel with whatever he needs. "I have a lot of things to do over the next few days, and I need to get to a meeting tomorrow."

"We understand," I assure him.

And I do, but I can't stop the constant tearing of my heart.

"There's just so much to think about. I have an interview lined up—I don't know if I told you."

"You hadn't. That's great." The words feel thick in my throat.

Stella smiles. "What's the job?"

Samuel's leg bounces as he talks. "It's just construction, I was the foreman before, but since I got let go for drinking on the job, I'm doubtful I'll get anything like that again, but this one is a good starting point. It's a good company."

He failed to mention that's why he got fired, but . . .

"We both wish you luck," I say, meaning every word. Kinsley needs Samuel, and he needs to work to provide for her. Not that Stella and I haven't already decided to help in some way as well.

"And if you need anything, please call us," Stella emphasizes.

I get to my feet, feeling the dread starting to weigh me down. It's almost time. The conversation is leading to us going, and we have to leave her.

There is no more denying or avoiding it. Stella and I will get into our car and return to Willow Creek without Kinsley—again.

I turn away, running my fingers through my hair, working to get myself under control. I have to say goodbye to her. This time, she's not a tiny baby I can pretend isn't mine. She's grown, smart, funny, beautiful, witty, and I can't fucking keep her.

I have to drive away, leaving her behind, and . . .

Stella's hand touches my shoulder. "Jack?" Her voice is soft, full of understanding about the battle raging inside me. When I turn, she's blurry, and I realize that I'm about to lose it. She moves her fingers to my face. "Not now. Please, not yet. If you . . . I can't."

I inhale deeply and wipe away the tears. I have to be strong for Stella and for Kinsley. She's so happy to be home that I don't want to taint that with having her see Stella and I fall apart. I want her to remember how happy she makes us and know we loved her. We loved her with a force that has allowed us to let her go yet another time.

When I exhale, I let it all go and erect whatever walls I can around my emotions so that I can get through this.

"We should go home." My voice quivers.

I can see the war raging within Stella. She wants to go, to get this over with so we can start to figure out this new version of our lives, but she also wants to stay. If we can be here, we have her still, it's not over.

But it is.

It's over, and I need to get the hell away from this before those walls I built crumble around us.

Stella hiccups. "Right. We should."

Samuel blows out a hard breath. "Okay. I'll get Kinsley and give you guys some space. I need to call my sponsor."

A small whimper comes from Stella, but she turns her back and starts to pace. After a second, she straightens her spine and pushes her shoulders back. This woman is a warrior, and she's ready to battle even though she knows she'll take many blows during the fight.

Kinsley enters. "You guys are leaving?"

"Yeah, kid, we have to get on the road."

She looks down. "Right. It's a long drive. I understand."

I dread the hours in the car with nothing to do but think.

"Are you all settled in?" Stella asks.

"I think so." Kinsley moves farther into the room, looking from me to Stella. "Can you stay for dinner? Or maybe we can watch the last episode of the show? I bet she doesn't get the answer right and leaves."

Stella shakes her head. "I don't think so. You have a lot to do, and Samuel needs some time with you."

Kinsley's voice quivers as she speaks quickly. "Will I see you guys again?"

This. This is going to be our undoing. If she cries, I am not going to be able to hold it together.

Stella steps closer, and her hand goes to Kinsley's face. "I don't know what to say. I keep trying to come up with some-thing that will express how I feel, but I can't. So, I'm going to say the truth and hope it's enough." Kinsley's eyes fill with tears, and I see the crack in her for the first time. "I am beyond honored that you are my daughter. Every minute that I got to spend with you is something I will cherish. Your dad is going to talk to you, and if you want me . . . us . . . we want you to know that we're here. We will always be here. I love you, Kinsley. More than I will ever be able to tell you. I hope we get to see each other. I hope that you want to know me and Jack. I just . . . I hope."

Her lips quiver, and then she wraps her arms around Stella. The two of them embrace, both crying, and I turn away, my chest tight as my own tears fall.

I'm angry at the world that's forcing Stella and me to have to go through this again.

I'm sad because I didn't want to know Kinsley. I didn't want to see her as the beautiful girl she is. If she had stayed a baby in my mind, I could've pretended.

Ignorance gave me bliss, and now it's gone.

"No more tears," Stella says, and I turn as Stella wipes away Kinsley's tears. "We have to be strong and show the guys how to handle it."

Kinsley tries to laugh, but it sounds more like a sob. My mask is in place as I move to her.

"The last thirty days have been some of the best in my life," I confess.

Her fingers swipe under her eyes. "I want to see you again. I would like it if we maybe talked and saw each other."

"There's nothing I'd like more than being in your life, kid."

All these years, I fought against the idea of it, and now I can't imagine a world where I don't get to know Kinsley.

"Is it sad that I don't know when I'll see you again? Is it wrong that I'm crying because I can't have it all?" Kinsley asks.

Stella, who is no longer trying to contain the tears, grips her hands. "No, not wrong. No matter what happens, we had a month, and I'll always hold it close to my heart."

I cup my daughter's cheek and wink. "If your dad says it's okay, we'll make a plan that works for everyone, okay?"

Kinsley nods, and we see the first break of a smile on her face. "Yes. Okay!"

My hand goes to Stella's back, and we head to the front door. When we get there, I feel paralyzed. I have to open it, walk away, leave her behind, and manage to drive back home.

I turn, watching Kinsley as she wraps her arms around herself and watches me right back.

The ache in my chest grows, but I somehow find the strength to pull the door open.

"Jack?" Kinsley's voice causes me to stop. "I'm going to miss you," she says before she moves forward, and I pull her to me. I hold on to her, wishing that I could keep her with me forever but knowing that it's not an option.

Not only because she's legally someone else's but also because it's not the best thing for her.

This is her home.

Samuel is her father.

We let go, and after she steps back, I see Samuel standing in the doorway, turmoil heavy in his features.

Please take care of my little girl.

Samuel nods as if he understands.

With that, I take Stella's hand and lead her outside, our hearts left behind once more.

Thirty-Nine

STELLA

Silence is a terrible thing.

It doesn't allow for the numbness to seep in. It screams in its nothingness. Four hours have passed without a word between us.

Tears have been shed.

Glances have been cast, but not a word.

What's there to say anyway?

There is no solace in words because the actions have brought us to this.

When the Great Smokey Mountains start to rise on the horizon, suddenly it feels like I can't breathe.

My hand goes to my chest because the pain is going through my limbs like fire, burning as it moves. Oh, God. I can't do this.

I can't go back home.

I can't go to that house. See where she slept. The kitchen where we laughed. The living room where we watched shows.

I try to breathe, but I can't. Each inhale is harder than the last, and I start to shake. The edges of my vision go blurry.

"Stella! Stella, look at me!" I hear Jack, but I just keep trying to pull in air. "Damn it, Stella!" I turn my head, not by choice but because he's gripping my face. "That's it, baby. Look into my eyes. Breathe." I try, I swear I do, but my lungs won't cooperate. Jack's eyes bore into mine, and his voice is calm. "Inhale." Forcing myself to listen, I suck in a breath. "Good, now let is out slowly."

The air pushes out, but I suck it back in again quickly.

His gaze doesn't falter. "Again. Inhale, but try to control it."

"I can't."

"You can. Just look at me. Only me, Stella."

He's blurry, but there. Jack is here, and I keep reminding myself of that. He won't let me fall. He won't let me break. I have to be strong. I inhale like he said, and this time it's a little easier.

"Good." His voice is soothing. "You're okay. I'm right here."

I nod as the tears fall. "I can't go home," I croak the words out.

"Then we won't." His thumbs rub my cheeks as he presses his forehead to mine. "We'll go back to my place and work through it there."

My surroundings start to come back into focus. Jack pulled over into some parking lot on the side of the road, but I don't care where we are. The emotions of the day are just too much. I've used every ounce of strength I had to get through leaving Kinsley, and I'm all tapped out. I start to cry again. Ugly, loud sobs come out, and Jack just holds me.

He whispers soothing words that I don't hear. The overwhelmingness of it all crashes around me.

After who knows how long, I settle down enough for Jack to ease back, but he doesn't let me go completely.

I'm being selfish. He's lost as much as I have. We are both dealing with the same thing, and I'm requiring him to be the strong one again. "I'm sorry."

"For what?"

"For falling apart. It seems I'm forever making you be the one to hold it together."

Jack still doesn't let go of me. "If you think you don't give me strength when I need it, then you're wrong. There are times when I'm weak and you are the only thing that makes me want to pick myself up."

"And now? When you've lost our daughter the same as I have."

Jack sighs, allowing his hands to drop. "We haven't lost her, Stella. She's still there, alive, and well, I have to hold on to that."

"I know, and . . . I've told myself over and over. But now, going back home, where she's hours away, it feels wrong."

"It does, but it's what we decided twelve years ago, and it's what we have to deal with now."

He's right. Hell, he warned me over a week ago. I just deluded myself into thinking I would accept it when the time came.

I'm not accepting it. I'm being ridiculous.

I pull down the visor mirror, feeling like more of an ass when I get a glimpse of my reflection. I fix my hair, wipe under my eyes, and fan at my face. I am red, puffy, and look like shit, but I resolve to pull it together.

Jack watches me, and when I turn, prepared to say I'm okay, he pushes back a lock of hair that was plastered to my face, tucking it behind my ear.

"You okay?"

"No, but I have you and that makes me better."

He smiles. "Better is good."

"Better is . . . better."

"We'll keep getting better."

I slide my hand into his. "Together we will."

"We'll go back to my place, stay there a few days, and figure it out."

"Okay." I don't have the strength to argue anyway. "What about Oliver?"

"He's already moving his stuff over to your place."

I chuckle softly, thinking of my poor brother, shuffling back and forth because he would do anything for me. I close my eyes, focusing on the feel of Jack's hand in mine.

"I love you, Jack."

"I love you too."

And I know he does. In the depths of my soul, I believe we can survive as long as I have him beside me.

Oliver did his best to clean up, but the cabin is still a mess. Not that I care. I feel the way this room looks . . . haggard.

"Do you want anything to eat?"

"Do we know if there's anything here?" I ask with a raised brow. "We should remember who has been staying here while you were with me."

"Goldilocks your brother is not."

I try to smile, but I don't know what it looks like. "No, he's not."

"Well, how about we see what we have and then go soak."

I sigh through my nose and nod. "Okay."

I'm doing a really shitty job of keeping it together. I wish I had the emotional capacity to care, but I don't. The truth is, I left part of my heart in Georgia today, and the new rhythm is off balance.

We enter the kitchen and find some cheese in the fridge,

so I grab the crackers from the cabinet. Tomorrow, we'll need food, but for tonight, this will be perfect.

Jack and I toss it onto a plate, giving zero fucks about how it looks. When we get to the back deck where the hot tub sits on, he turns on the jets.

The sound is loud as the bubbles come to life. I stare at them, thinking of how I feel the same. The air forcing the water to move the way it doesn't want to. I'm not sure how long I stare before I feel Jack behind me.

"Let me help you," he says softly. His hands move to my cardigan, pulling it down my shoulders and then arms. I've kept it wrapped around me, clinging to it as though it could hold my broken bits in place.

There's nothing sexual about him undressing me. It's careful and measured. Each item gets folded and placed on the chair.

I'm standing here in my bra and underwear, looking at the bubbling water. Jack must've removed his clothes because I feel his hand at my back.

"Come on, Stella. Let's go in."

He's completely naked as he climbs the stairs, which snaps me out of my daze.

I remove my bra and slide my underwear down before hurrying to get in because shivers are starting to run through me.

I sink down into the hot water. Once I'm covered up to my chest, my teeth start to chatter.

What is wrong with me? I'm falling apart, and I'm not that girl.

I'm the one who handles whatever life throws because there's no other choice, not the one who can't think of anything other than the incredible pain in her chest.

Jack is watching me with a look of concern on his face. He's dealing with the same thing and being so strong. I hate that once again, I'm doing this to him. I'm asking him to shoulder all of it. My pain. His pain. The insurmountable amount of anger and frustration with the situation in general.

When I move through the water toward him, he opens his arms so I can nestle against him. Here is where I'm safe. Where I can believe that it'll be okay because I have this amazing man by my side.

My arms wrap around his neck, and I settle a leg on each side of his hips. Any other day, this would be something else, but right now, it's comfort only. Jack clutches me to his chest as I tuck my face against his neck so we can just breathe each other in and cling to one another.

"I miss her," I say.

"I know."

"How do you miss someone you barely know?"

He kisses the side of my head. "You know her. We both do, and that's why it hurts."

I lean back, looking into those hazel eyes that hold so much love for me it's crippling. "I struggle because this is the right thing. Samuel needs her far more than we do, and she needs him, but yet I need her. I want to laugh with her or smile at her facial expressions when she doesn't like something. I want to watch her try to solve some math problem that is far over my head and then witness the joy when she figures it out. When she is sick, I want to be the one to make her better, and yet, I am all too aware that I gave away the right to want any of that when she was a baby."

He lifts his hand, resting it on my cheek. "And Samuel didn't slam the door in our faces about it. We have to hold out hope that he opens that door for us."

A tear falls down my cheek. "I keep telling myself that. Now that she knows that we're not horrible people and that we want her too, she will push for us."

"She might."

I release a shaky breath, and lay my head back down on

his shoulder. "She might, but for now, I can't think about it."

Jack's hand moves up and down my back, lulling me into a state of peace.

We stay like this for a long time, surrounded in the steam and warmth, bare to each other. We don't try to fill the silence, choosing to just hold one another, kissing each other's cheeks, necks, or noses when the moment presents itself.

Even in all the turmoil, I don't drift too far because of him.

He tethers me, and I have never been more grateful for the love we share than I am now. Without Jack, I don't know if I could survive this.

Forty

JACK

Stella and I stay in the cabin, completely alone for two days. The people we love allow us the quiet time, and I'm grateful for it.

There is a level of grief we feel is too prodigious for anyone else to understand it.

On the third day, the peace we've started to settle into is disrupted.

By a very welcome person.

"Uncle Jack? Auntie Stella?" Amelia's small voice causes us both to get up off the couch and head to the door.

But before we get there, her face is pressed to the window, her hands cupped around her face, as she peers in. "I see you!" she yells.

Stella's smile is bright, and she lets out a soft laugh that almost sounds like a sob, but a happy one. "Melia," Stella says as she opens the door before dropping down, pulling her into her arms. "Hi, my sweet little angel."

"Are you sad? Daddy says you're sad."

She looks up at Grayson, who doesn't try to look apologetic. "You are."

Stella's eyes turn back to Amelia. "I am, but I'm feeling much better now that you came to see me."

Amelia's hands frame Stella's face. "Don't be sad, Auntie. It'll be okay because I love you."

"I love you most."

Gray steps forward, his hand clasps my shoulder. "You all right?"

"No, but I will be."

He nods once. "I can't imagine, and I won't pretend to, but just know that you have a family who loves you and is always here to support you. You're not alone, Jack. You don't have to hide yourself away in this cabin. Your family is here to lean on."

I've always considered myself part of the Parkerson crew in some way, but hearing him call me family, it's a feeling I can't describe. With Stella, I am found, as though the world finally makes sense, but when Grayson says I have a family, I have meaning. People who are here.

My father leaving after my mother's death was hard. I struggled to understand what the hell I did wrong.

My father, the strong man who took care of everyone, was gone. He couldn't function anymore. He drank and gambled. He left, giving up everything because it was easier than fighting for it.

I've been lost for a long time, wondering if I could have a family. I hadn't realized that I always have.

"Come on," Stella says, extending her hand to Amelia. "Let's go see if we can find cookies or KitKats."

Grayson groans. "KitKats for lunch? Come on, Stell."

I laugh and watch them go off.

Stella spoils Amelia rotten, but their relationship is so much more than that. She's been there for that little girl every step of the way, never letting her down and being someone she could rely on.

I stare at her, wondering what in the world I ever did to deserve her. How can I ever make things right for her? She should have everything, and I want to be the man who grants every wish she's ever had.

"What's that look?" Grayson asks.

"I love your sister."

He snorts. "No shit."

"I'm going to marry her."

A plan starts to form, and I know exactly what I want to happen. It may take a little luck, but I'm going to make her hopes come true.

"Today?"

I shrug. "I might."

Grayson laughs. "If I know my sister, she might just be crazy enough to do it."

"She should have a wedding. The one she's dreamed of."

"Then I hope you've been very smart with your money, my friend. My sister plans parties like no other, and I would bet my ass that woman is going to want one hell of a party."

"It would be worth it to see her smile. I guess this is me asking you for permission," I say to him, the mood shifting to a more serious tone.

"Stella wouldn't give a shit if you had permission, but I know it matters to you, and you have it."

"Thanks, Gray."

Grayson shakes his head with a grin. "I should've pushed you to her a long time ago."

I look to him, confusion building. "What?"

"You guys are right together, and I think I've known that for a while. I . . . I don't know, man. She's my sister, you know? I didn't want to lose either of you, so it was better to ignore every weird look the two of you shared."

"So you did know?"

"I had a hunch. Especially when you practically became a monk."

"I love her." There really is no other explanation. To be with another woman felt stupid and wrong. I didn't want to find a replacement version of Stella, not when the real thing was right there.

He watches his sister and daughter, who are curled up on the couch together, eating KitKats that Stella had delivered yesterday with a bunch of other groceries. They are busy giggling about whatever they're discussing.

"A stupid man—his name is Jack, in case you're wondering—told me once about moments. How life was all about moments. Well, Jack, the same one I just mentioned, live in the damn moment. If you love her, marry her before she realizes you are, in fact, stupid."

I let out a silent laugh. "You should be a life coach."

"I thought about it."

"Failed the class?"

"Apparently, you're supposed to be optimistic and encouraging, not a sarcastic ogre."

I nod. "Seems we're both out."

"At least we're failing together." Grayson nudges my arm.

"As it should be."

"Have you heard from Kinsley?" he asks softly.

That light feeling I had starts to drift away.

"No."

"I'm sorry, Jack. For more than just that. I wish I had been the friend you needed during it all. If you had told me, I would've been there."

"You would've been livid," I correct.

"Maybe at first because I'm an asshole, but then I would've come around. Still, you shouldn't have had to suffer alone."

"She is who suffered alone."

Stella didn't have anyone other than her grandmother, and she passed away about a year after Kinsley was born. We both suffered in silence because of the threats from her parents.

"Doesn't make it right for either of you."

I let out a long sigh, which causes Stella to turn to me. Her eyes ask a million questions, but I wink, letting her know I'm fine. Her eyes narrow on Grayson, who raises his hands in surrender.

"Hey, I didn't do anything. He breathed."

"You made him breathe with anger."

Grayson rolls his eyes and starts to walk away. "God help Jack for putting up with you."

"I heard that."

He turns back to her. "I'm glad. That man is going to be nominated for sainthood." She sticks her tongue out at him, and everyone laughs. "Mature, as always, Meatball."

"Whatever."

When we step into the living room, Amelia leaps off Stella's lap and runs to me. "Do you have any surprises for me?" she asks with her long lashes moving up and down. She's perfected this innocent and sweet look.

While Stella feeds Amelia KitKats, I usually give her mints. She's not picky about what contraband she gets so long as she gets it. "I might."

Grayson groans. "No more sugar."

"But, Gray, the best part is getting her all hopped up on it and then making her go home." Stella grins, her hands tucked under her chin.

"I'll be sure to have Jessica call you at her bedtime then."

"Go ahead, I know how to silence a call." Stella arches one brow.

He ignores her, focusing his attention back to me. I'm mostly grateful he missed where I gave Amelia a mint and stuck two in her pocket while he was sparring with his sister.

"Are you ready for tomorrow?" Gray asks.

"I will be," Stella assures him.

We meet with two builders tomorrow, and hopefully, one will have the design and vision for what we're looking for. I can't imagine how the hell anyone will be able to pull it off because, when the six of us sat down, it was like a meeting of the minds.

Alexander is adamant we have something for teens because we all remember what it was like to vacation at places with nothing to do.

Stella is dead set on a spa that will appeal to women and those needing corporate retreats.

Josh and Oliver agree that there needs to be a lot of emphasis on wedding options, and Grayson just cares about the food.

And the budget we all anticipated will no doubt be much higher. It always is.

"We're really counting on your instincts, Stell. It'll make all the difference having you to help us see a better vision."

"I know. You fools would have it as a frat house."

Gray shrugs. "Probably, which is yet another reason we're very glad that you're our sister."

"I'm glad too. Even if I would like to beat you with your own arms half the time."

"It's part of our charm."

We spend the next hour talking while Amelia manages to get another candy bar and half a bag of mints out of us.

It's the first time I can breathe, and I have hope that we'll be okay after a little more time and with a little luck, next weekend will go my way.

Forty-One

STELLA

There should be a mediator required for every meeting my brothers are at because today has been nothing short of a damn shitshow.

"You all need a timeout," I say as we enter Gray's house.

Jessica looks just as angry as I am. No one would let the presenters speak before tossing in their two cents. It was chaos from the very beginning.

"The girl was inept." Alexander gives us a scowl as he sits.

"No, she was the only one with a great vision!" I throw my hands up.

"I preferred her design, but Alex wouldn't stop berating her," Oliver says, agreeing with me.

We saw three very different designs and bids. All of them were unique, but there was really only one option that I felt was right. With a few tweaks, it will be perfect. Of course, it's the one my brother couldn't seem to control himself during.

I turn to him. "Seriously, what was the issue?"

"She didn't listen."

I blink a few times, wondering what planet he was on. "You're serious?"

"Yes."

"You think she didn't listen to . . . who?"

Alex crosses his arms over his chest. "Me."

"Oh, and I guess you're just the be-all and end-all? She built you that stupid arcade. In fact, she was the only one!"

"It was half-assed!"

"You're half-assed!" I yell.

"You really think kids are going to want to walk a mile into the fucking woods to play games?"

Again, I'm pretty sure my brother is having some sort of crisis we don't know about. "Yes, Alex, I do. What kid wants to hang out with their friends in the same area as their parents? None that I can think of. If anything, Odette found a place that would appeal to teens *and* make you happy."

He laughs once. "I'm not happy. And who the hell names their kid Odette?"

Grayson shakes his head this time. "We're going with her."

Josh nods. "Hers was, by far, the best pitch, and you know it."

"I wasn't happy with some of the wedding venue things, but they can be worked out. Her design definitely fit more of what we all talked about," Oliver says.

Alexander, who I used to like a lot, groans and walks into the other room. I've never seen him act like this. He is beyond reason, and I'm starting to wonder if there's something other than the resort design that is bothering him about Odette.

Jack finally clears his throat, bringing the attention to him. "Do I get a vote?"

Crap. I speak immediately. "Of course. Of course you do."

"I like her. She has some great ideas, and she was the only designer who already had a crew ready to go. Also, she's the only one who didn't want to clear out way more land than was needed, which preserves the woods."

"A necessity for your job," Josh tacks on.

"Exactly," Jack agrees.

Grayson glares at Alex before speaking. "I think we're all, well, other than Alex, in agreement that this is the best option."

I move beside Jack, taking his hand in mine. "It's more than a best option for me," I say. "Odette had the vision of what we wanted. Yes, there are some small things, but it's nothing that will add to our budget."

Alex returns, running his hand over his face. "I vote no. I think we need more designs."

Joshua raises his finger at me when I open my mouth to argue. Then he speaks. "What aren't you telling us?"

"I've told you everything."

"Bullshit," Josh counters.

A few seconds pass before Alex relents. "I know her."

"I knew it!" I yell and then duck behind Jack, feeling Alex's glare.

"Yeah, whatever. We hooked up a few years ago. She was in Savannah, and I didn't expect her here."

"Do you love her?" I ask, earning a scathing look from Josh.

To which I smile back like the annoying little sister I will always be.

"No."

"Since you hooked up, has she tried to ruin you?"

Alex huffs. "No."

"Did she steal money?"

"No."

"Give you an STD?"

He flips me off.

I raise my hands and drop them. "Then you want to punish her and her company because she realized you're not a catch and broke it off before you did?"

Josh steps in when Alex's glare becomes murderous, and Jack suddenly feels much bigger in front of me.

Oh, I like this caveman feel to my man. That's right, Jack, fight him.

Grayson clears his throat. "Okay, is there any valid reason you can't work with her?"

Alex shakes his head. "No, and you're all right. She has the best design, and I think she'll do a good job."

And it's settled. We'll go with Odette's design and her team.

My first thought is how I wish I could tell Kinsley but can't. I can't tell her or call her because we haven't heard from Samuel yet.

Jack leans down and kisses me softly before I rest my head on his chest, hating that what should be a happy moment feels bleak.

We head to my place first to pick up more clothes and items I want. When we get to the door, I pause.

I don't want to go in there. I don't want to see the room she was in. I don't want to look at the kitchen where flour, batter, and eggs were thrown around. My safe space doesn't feel so safe anymore.

It's lonely because she's gone.

I think I could've handled this better if I didn't think that I'd still get to at least talk to her after we left. It's been four days without a word.

Samuel assured us that he was completely fine with us having a relationship with Kinsley. So, the lack of communication must be from her. She doesn't want us, and that's a far harder blow than I was prepared for.

"Ready?" Jack asks.

"Yeah, I'm being stupid."

"You're not. I'm remembering it all too."

I look up to find his hazel eyes watching me. "It'll get better." I'm not sure if I'm asking him or reminding myself.

"It will. You know, at some point, you're going to have to decide whether we're going to live at my cabin or back here."

My lips turn into a grin. "So, we're officially living together?"

"I moved into your place for a month, and now we're staying at mine. I don't know what you call it, baby, but I'd say we took that step."

"I guess we're not really a normal couple anyway."

Jack laughs. "You mean it's not normal to love someone for fifteen years, finally get together at her brother's wedding, and then move in a few months later?"

I shake my head. "I don't know many couples who follow that trajectory."

He leans in, his lips just above mine. "Dumbasses."

I laugh as he kisses me, it's awkward and filled with me giggling, but I don't care. His big arms wrap around me, plastering me to his solid chest. I hold on, loving how it feels with him. Grateful that, even with the loss we feel, we've found strength in each other.

He pulls back, and before I can stop myself, I say, "Marry me."

"What?"

Okay, I didn't mean to propose to him, but as we've already established, we're not normal.

"I want to marry you, Jack. I want you to be my husband, and . . ."

"Did you just propose to me?"

I bite my lower lip, feeling a little stupid. "I guess I did."

He chuckles loudly and then rests his forehead against

mine. "You insane, silly, amazing woman. I couldn't love you any more if I tried."

"I'm feeling a little dumb."

"Why is that?" he asks.

"Because I proposed, which . . . well, you know isn't the way it goes. More than that, you haven't answered."

I can't imagine how men endure this. Usually they plan it out, get a ring, and get down on one knee. I've seen a few proposals at the Park Inn, and when you're not the one asking the question, it's sweet and amazing.

This is fucking torture.

Jack releases me, and my heart plummets. Oh, God, he doesn't want to marry me.

Okay. I'm okay. I'll be okay.

I'll probably throw myself off a cliff later, but that'll be fine.

He doesn't let me go far before he's cupping my cheeks. "I planned to propose to you next weekend."

My lips part and I inhale quickly. "What?"

"Yeah, I've been working on something and was already planning to ask you to marry me."

"I ruined it."

He shakes his head. "Your proposal was much better than mine will be."

"I doubt that."

"Would you like to wait for that one or do you want to be the one who pulls my man card?"

I let out a nervous giggle. "I think I can wait."

"Good."

Lifting up onto my toes, I wrap my arms around his neck and grin. "After this, I don't want to wait for things, Jack. I want to live with you, love you, and grow old and happy together. We've waited forever, and I want it all now."

Jack kisses my nose, my lips, my cheeks, and then my

forehead. "I plan to give you everything, Stella."

Forty-Two

JACK

I f Stella knew what I was up to, she'd probably kill me, but to save her the heartache, I'm going to do what I can and keep her out of it.

This morning I called Samuel. I didn't know how it would go, but he was doing well and said that he would be open to my coming down to talk to him. I have one thing I have to do before I hit the road tomorrow though.

Three days ago, we signed the contract with Odette's company. She already sent us the proposals and the information for the crew. However, I think I have an idea that will help everyone.

I knock on Odette's office door, and a second later, she opens it, a warm smile on her face. "Hi, Jack, please come in."

"Thank you."

I enter her office, it's warm and inviting. There isn't much furniture other than a large desk and a couch that acts as the only seating in the room. Odette motions for me to sit and she leans against her desk. "What brings you here? Your email was very vague."

"I wanted to talk specifically about my section of the build."

"Of course. I know we covered it in the initial meeting and the follow-up, but I'm happy to discuss any concerns. Although, when we signed the contract, everything seemed to be in order."

"It was."

She smooths her skirt and then smiles again. "Okay, that's good to know."

I nod. "First, I need this meeting to stay between us. Stella has enough going on, and I don't want her aware of this talk. Is that a problem?"

Odette seems to pause at that, but it's the only real contingency I care about. "I'm . . . I'm slightly hesitant."

"I understand, but it's imperative."

She pushes off the desk and heads to the other side of the couch. "Why?"

"Because it's for her."

"Oh," Odette squeaks and then her entire demeanor shifts. "Well, that's okay then. What do you need?"

"In four days, I am going to propose to Stella. It's all exciting, but Stella and I have a very complicated past. I'm only telling you this because I want you to understand why this request is extremely important to me."

She shifts a little and then clears her throat. "Okay."

I launch into a bit of our history, telling her the story of how we met, the relationship we had, and then about Kinsley. To Odette's credit, she doesn't say anything, just allows me to explain the way I need to. After I'm done and have told her about the current position we're in, her hand is covering her lips.

"Wow."

"Yes, but the thing is that I want to make this right for

Stella. All I've ever wanted is to do whatever she needs. And what she needs right now is our daughter. I can't do that without your help."

Odette's eyes widen. "How in the heck am I going to help?"

And then I fill her in on my plan and pray that she says yes.

Forty-Three

STELLA

One would think that I would be done crying, but I'm not. It's not the torrent of tears that it had been the first three days, but they still come.

Sometimes it's brought on by a song, but right now, it's this stupid show about a woman who lost her daughter.

It's been over a week, and we haven't heard a word from Samuel or Kinsley. I've dialed the number, written out a dozen texts, and I even wrote a letter I'll never send. I am desperate to talk to her, but we told them before we left that we were here, so it's up to them whether or not they take the hand offered.

The door is kicked open, and I jump, turning quickly to see Jack struggling to get in the house with groceries.

I get up and laugh. "What the hell is wrong with you?"

"A little help would be nice."

I raise my brows and smirk. "And miss this entertainment? Never. How did you expect to get all of this inside?"

"I'm in the cabin, aren't I?"

Yes, I guess that would be accurate, but only just. He has about twenty bags hooked in his fingers. I have no idea how he got them on his hands to begin with, but he sure has.

"You're going to lose your fingers," I toss back before moving to help. I unhook the bags, setting them on the floor and countertops. "Are we preparing for a zombie apocalypse?"

He rolls his eyes. "I'm a growing boy."

"You're something."

I swear he bought everything they had at the grocery store. I'm seriously confused about why the hell he needs all this, but I've bought ten different pairs of shoes this week because I thought they may make me cry less. We're coping however we can.

When I pull out the box of fruit snacks that are Kinsley's favorite, I lose it.

Tears fall, and I sink to the ground. I hate this. I want to stop this shit already. I got to love her for a little while, and that should be enough, but it's not. All I want is more of everything. I want her all the time, and I *know* . . . I know it's not possible.

"Stella," Jack says, his hands on my shoulders.

I wipe the tears away. "Why haven't they called?"

"I don't know."

"Were we not clear enough? Do they know we want to be there for them and help? Does Samuel understand that I love her and won't try to take her? I just want to see her."

Jack's shoulders drop as he sighs deeply. "We have to be patient. You and I both know that what they're dealing with isn't easy. We have to give her the time she needs, just the same as maybe we need."

My head jerks up at that. "What time do we need? I don't need time, I just need some damn hope! I need to know that we haven't lost her for good. What if he doesn't write? What if he cuts us off?"

"I don't think Samuel would do that. He came to us and asked for our help. We aren't the bad guys, and I don't think he believes that either. He just has a lot going on."

I get to my feet and start to pace, not wanting to hear his damn logic. "I feel like I'm coming apart! I argue in circles, knowing that none of this makes sense. I didn't feel this way twelve years ago, why the hell is it so hard now?"

"It wasn't easy then, but we were kids. We didn't know her."

"She's perfect."

"She is."

"I want to call her," I say before I lose my nerve. "Or at least text her. Something. She needs to know we care."

Jack's eyes don't leave mine, and I know him well enough that the silence is him trying to work through it. "Maybe text Samuel first. Ask him if it's okay. If we start going behind his back, we can't get out of that."

I release a heavy sigh, feeling a little bit of hope and reach for my phone.

Me: I hope you're doing well. I'd really like your permission to text Kinsley. At least to let her know we're thinking of her. If she doesn't want to talk, that's fine, but it would mean a lot to me if you'd be okay with that.

I send the text, and then Jack takes the phone from me. "Hey!"

"No, you're not going to sit here and stare at it. If he texts back, I'll let you know. Until then, we're going to enjoy some time together before I have to leave tomorrow."

"You're leaving?" I ask with surprise.

"I have to work and keep my income stable."

I've been such an asshole not to even think about Jack's

company. "Of course you do. I didn't know you had another trip planned."

"It came in just recently."

"How long will you be out in the dirty woods for?"

Jack laughs. "I think about four days. Depends on how they survive."

I smile. "Can you imagine if you took my brothers and me out?"

"No. I would rather not," he says with a smile to soften the truth. It's probably one of his biggest nightmares.

"Maybe I'll book you for it."

Jack steps closer, resting his hand on my hip. "Is that so?"

"Just us though."

"You want to get lost in the woods with me?"

I shudder. "Not unless the woods come with turndown and room service."

Jack laughs. "I'll turn you on."

His thumb rubs my hip as his eyes fill with lust. My fingers move to his strong, solid chest, feeling his steady heartbeat between us. "I don't think you'll have any problems with that."

"You're so beautiful, Stella."

I smile, feeling his words penetrate deep in my heart. I don't feel beautiful. I'm a mess, crying all the time and trying to keep myself together. I haven't done very well, but he doesn't see that.

The way he looks at me, the warmth in those hazel eyes makes me beautiful. Jack has always seen past the scars and imperfections, choosing to love me despite them all. His love allows me to shine.

"Only in your eyes."

He shakes his head. "No, baby, you're beautiful to everyone. The way you smile makes my chest ache. When you look at me like that, I want to fucking fall at your feet. You, Stella Parkerson, are the most breathtaking and wonderful woman

I've ever met. I love you so much."

My heart rate quickens, and I wonder if this is it, the proposal I've been not-so-patiently waiting for. He grins as though he can read my mind.

"This isn't your proposal. It's coming though."

"You know, this whole taunting me with marrying you is cruel."

"I spent twelve years pretending I didn't want to marry you. After that long of perfecting how to go without, a few more days won't hurt."

I roll my eyes. "That logic is ridiculous. It should be that you went that long and you don't want to wait another minute."

"I want this to be special. I want the day I got down on my knee and asked you to be my wife to be something you talk about for decades."

Now that is something I can't argue with. "Fine."

He laughs. "Only you would be petulant that you aren't getting a shitty proposal."

I lean in, brushing my lips on his. "Only I would be petulant because I want the marriage, not the proposal."

Jack lets out a deep moan and then kisses me. We cling to each other, his tongue sliding against mine, and I lose myself in him.

"I want you," I say.

His warm hands move over my body, touching me exactly the way I like.

"I want you always. I want to kiss you, make love to you, take you over and over until you forget the rest of the world and it's only us."

"Yes," I say as his mouth moves to my neck, kissing and nipping his way down to my shoulder. He moves my shirt down, exposing more skin.

"For years, I've thought about being able to do this."

Jack's husky voice is layered with sex. "I've dreamed of coming home, finding you in my cabin waiting for me."

I bite my lower lip and step back. "And what was I wearing?"

The heat in his eyes is enough to burn me. "Nothing."

"What if I was cold?" I ask as I start to undress slowly. I lift my shirt, easing it over my head.

"You wouldn't be."

"No?"

He shakes his head, watching as my fingers play with the waistband of my leggings. "No because I would make you warm."

"How would you do that?" I ask as I start to push them down.

"I'd lay you down in front of that fire." His head jerks to the enormous fireplace with a rug in front of it. I move there and then lie down. "Take off all your clothes, Stella. I want you naked."

His voice brokers no argument, not that I would fight him on this anyway. It's incredibly sexy, watching him be broody and turned on. I do as he says, pulling my clothes off.

"And then?" I ask, a shiver running over me.

He moves closer, standing there, his eyes trailing over every part of me. "I'd let you lie there and watch your breathing grow heavier. I'd maybe come closer." He does, dropping down. He hovers over me, resting on one arm, his hands so close but not touching me. "I wonder where I should touch you first."

I'm so turned on, it doesn't matter. He could touch my hair, and I bet I would feel it.

"Hmmm," he muses, and then the tip of his finger slides against the seam of my lips. "I could kiss you."

I nod.

"No, I've already done that." His hand moves down my

neck and slides to my breastbone.

I'm panting. My lungs are struggling to draw air as he looms over me. His finger drifting from side to side, just barely touching my breasts. "Jack . . ."

"Are you cold?" he asks.

"No." I'm on fucking fire.

"I didn't think so, but if you were, I would find another way to warm you."

My eyes close, and I silently beg him to find that way.

"How?" I ask on a breath, opening my eyes.

"Oh, there are so many ways."

I stare into his molten eyes and push the air from my chest. "Show me."

Jack pulls his shirt over his head, throwing it to the ground. His abs ripple as he moves closer, and he doesn't tease me any longer. His lips close around my nipple, sucking it deep into his mouth. God, it feels so good.

He moves his tongue around and then goes to the other, doing the same. My back bows off the ground and then his hand is between my legs. He breaks away to stare down at me as he parts my folds, finding my clit.

Just a small touch has me moving toward my climax.

"You're so wet, baby. You aren't the least bit cold. You're fire and strength. You're beauty in every meaning of the word. Look at me," he commands when my eyes close. "I will never let you be left in the cold, Stella."

My throat goes tight because the way he vows that tells me everything I already knew. He would never let harm come to me, and he will always be my shelter.

We become frantic, both desperate for one another. What started as a sexy game becomes more. His lips are on mine, and the kiss becomes hurried as the emotions between us reach a new level.

I need him.

I need him to know how much I want him, love him, and that I'll never leave him.

"Jack, please," I say quickly as he pulls his pants and underwear off. "Jack, now."

"I . . . fuck, Stella." He thrusts so quickly I can barely breathe.

His love and warmth fill the cracks left from the last week. Every part of me feels put back together again.

He moves slowly, as though I'm so precious and delicate he worries I'll break.

"I love you." I place my hand on his cheek, forcing his eyes to meet mine.

"I love you too."

"I will never leave you, Jack."

As Jack knows my fears, I know his. Everyone in his life has abandoned him, but the idea of me ever walking away is impossible.

He is my heart and soul.

Jack's forehead drops to mine, as if the words were too much for him to hear. I push up on my hip, rolling us so I'm on top.

I ride him slowly and give him what I think he needs. "I will always love you. I will always be your safe place, where you can come when you're lost," I promise. "You're not alone anymore, Jack. You never were. I'm here, and while you may keep me warm, I will wrap you in so much love that you can't feel anything other than that."

He grabs my hips, moving me faster. "Fuck, Stella, I can't hold back."

"I'm close," I tell him. Between the words and the sensations, I'm not going to be able to hold on either.

His thumb finds my clit, and we start to move faster together. The moment too great to look away, and I come. I cry his name, forcing my eyes to stay open, knowing he'll catch me.

And then I realize I'll catch him too.

He follows me over the cliff, and then we both hold each other as we fall to the ground.

"You know that sounded an awful lot like marriage vows," Jack says as he plays with my hair.

We're still in front of the fire, only now we have a blanket around us and I'm blissed out on his chest.

"Maybe I was practicing," I muse.

"So, when I hear that again, should I act surprised?"

I lift my head, resting it on my hand. "If you ever actually propose and marry me, maybe you'd know."

He rolls his eyes and chuckles. "You're so cute when you're a headcase."

I sigh and go back to listening to the sounds of the fire crackle and his heartbeat. His fingers continue to glide through my hair, lulling me into a serene place.

My eyes close, and I start to drift until the sound of my phone pinging with a text has me wide awake and sitting up.

Jack does the same, moving to burrow through his clothing to find my phone. After what feels like forever, he pulls the phone out, handing it to me. When I see Kinsley's name, I practically drop it because I'm moving too fast to swipe the screen, anxious to see what she said.

Kinsley: *I miss you guys. I have a test to study for tonight, but maybe we can talk tomorrow?*

Tears fill my eyes, making it hard to type out a response, but I will them back.

Me: We miss you, and absolutely. Call anytime.

I look up at Jack, a smile on my lips. "She wants us."

"I knew she would."

I breathe again, feeling a sense of happiness that is overwhelming. Jack pulls me back to his chest, and the tears that come this time are happy.

She wants us.

Forty-Four

JACK

"Thank you for meeting me and thanks for not telling anyone. I lied to Stella."

"Lied?"

I nod. "She thinks I'm in the woods for work."

Samuel smiles. "Instead of being in Georgia for some mystery conversation."

"Exactly."

Samuel is calmer than I expected.

We caught up on our pleasantries, ordered our food, and talked a little about Kinsley. She's supposed to call Stella and me today, but I'm here and am hoping I might get to see her and set my plan in motion.

"On a normal day, I'd love to sit and have a meal with you, but I'd be lying if I said I didn't want to know more about this proposal you said you were planning."

"I am, in three days. I'd like for you and Kinsley to be there. I have it all planned and I really want the people who matter to Stella and I there. Her brothers, all of whom Kinsley has already met, will be there."

Samuel nods. "I see."

There's more, and while I'd like to ease into this, I can see from his body language that this is actually worse than me just coming out with it.

"More than that, I'd like you to stay in Willow Creek Valley."

His eyes widen and he sputters. "Wh-what? How? I'm not charity."

"I don't think you are," I say quickly. "The truth is, I need your help. We are opening a resort. Stella and her brothers are building it on land they own. I'm moving my business into the Firefly Resort, but I need a foreman to oversee my part of the construction."

Samuel leans back. "You're kidding."

"I'm not. I already spoke with the contractor, stating that I wanted my own crew under their umbrella because I have people who I'd like working on this with me. You being one of them and then if it works out, she has other projects lined up."

He opens his mouth to speak and then stops.

I decide to continue on. "I won't lie and say that a part of the offer isn't because I'd like to have Kinsley close to us. We love her, Samuel. The same way you do. I'm not her dad, I know that, but I am her father, and I'd like to be in her life. Stella is dying inside, and it's killing me. The benefits, in my opinion, are worth it for both of us. You get an amazing job and a support system in Willow Creek Valley that you don't have here while we get to have a very dysfunctional family dynamic."

Samuel leans forward. "This is a lot to take in."

"I know, and I'm not asking for a decision now. It's just that, my father was an alcoholic, and after my mom passed away, he left. I think a big reason he did was because he felt alone." I tell him, not to sway him, but to let him know that

I understand. "You don't have to be alone. You'll have me, Stella, and her entire, invasive family no matter what you decide. They love Kinsley too, and believe me, they will be there, even when you wish they weren't."

He cracks a smile. "During my treatment, I kept wondering how I was going to do this once I got out. I would lay in bed, wondering if Kinsley would be better off without me."

"She wouldn't be." There is not a doubt in my mind about that. "She needs you, and honestly, Samuel, we do too. You saved Stella and me at a time when we were drowning. You and Misty were a life raft, and I'm asking you to let us be the same for you. Come up this weekend, stay at my cabin. You and Kinsley will be comfortable there. Stella and I will stay at her place, and you can just . . . feel it out. But you have a job up there waiting if you want it."

I've said all I can, offered a hand that I pray he'll take. If he doesn't, then it's on him and I have to respect that. This option gives us all what we need—each other.

"How would it work?" he asks.

"What do you mean?"

"With Kinsley."

I release a heavy sigh. "I really don't know. My hope is that we—you, me, and Stella—could be there for her in whatever capacity works. You're her dad, that'll always be the case, but Stella and I could be there, too, as her friends. We love her, and getting time with her changed things. I don't know how we could ever go back to pretending otherwise. It may not work or it might be the best thing in the world for us. I don't know, but I have got a job, support, and friendship to offer you."

Samuel's eyes fill with tears, and he sniffs. "I don't know what to say. I really don't. I've been struggling a lot with what the hell I'm going to do. I can't find a job, I want and need to stay sober, and I miss my wife. I don't know how to raise a teenage girl."

"Neither do I," I say with a laugh. "But I know a woman who will move heaven and Earth to figure it out for us."

He nods, takes a sip of his coffee, and then sighs. "I'll think about it."

"That's all I ask, well, and that you come this weekend."

"That I can do."

"Good."

"Jack!" Kinsley runs toward me and then wraps her arms around me. "You're here! Is Stella?"

I will never forget this moment, not even if my memory goes. Seeing my daughter run toward me with excitement, it is . . . well, it's the best goddamn thing I've ever seen.

"No, kid, just me this time."

"Is she okay?"

I nod. "She is, but I'm not sure I will be when she finds out I got to see you."

"Why?"

"Because she misses you," I say with a grin. I missed her too. I didn't realize just how much until I caught sight of her. It's been just over a week, and I swear it's been years.

"I miss her too. Did you watch the end of the show?"

"No, we didn't."

She shakes her head. "It was stupid. And predictable. I guess math is supposed to be that though."

The show we started watching was a dating game based on math equations. Everything was done by answering a questionnaire and seeing your score to match you with whoever was the same as you. Kinsley and I had a lot of fun trying to decipher their scoring of algorithms and basic equations. Stella did not give a shit about the math but liked the show.

"Did you figure it out?"

She grins. "Maybe."

"You're going to leave me hanging?" I ask.

Kinsley shrugs. "The fun of it is the math. I wouldn't want to spoil it for you."

Jesus, she sounds just like Stella.

"Whatever. I drove down to let you and your dad know that I'm going to propose to Stella in a few days. I know you have school tomorrow, but . . . I was hoping maybe you'd be willing to skip it and come back to Willow Creek Valley for it? You could keep her busy while I work on the other stuff?"

Kinsley's entire face lights up with a smile so bright she could blind me. "Really?"

I nod, and Samuel grins. "I guess you want to go?" he asks.

"Yeah! If that's okay, Dad? I would love to see her face. I'm sure she's going to be so surprised."

"Not entirely," I tell her.

"What? Isn't that the point?"

I huff. "Stella . . . well, that's all I can say. Stella. She sort of knows already, and she's being an incredible pain in my ass, er, butt."

Kinsley shakes her head. "She loves you."

"She does, and I'm incredibly happy for that. So, you'd like to come?"

"Can I?" she asks Samuel.

"We both are. We'll head back with Jack in the morning and spend the weekend there."

Thank God, this might actually work.

Forty-Five

STELLA

"Coming!" I yell toward whoever is pounding insistently on the door. "Jesus, give a girl a minute to put some pants on!"

I hurry over, yanking it open to see Winnie there, holding a bottle of wine in one hand and a cake in the other. "You could've skipped the pants."

"Win," I say almost as a breath.

"Can I come in?"

I pull the door open, wishing her hands were free so I could wrap her into a hug. She enters, setting the wine and cake down before throwing her arms around me and holding me tight. "Are you okay?"

I nod, forcing back the tears. "I'm okay."

"What about good?"

"Not there yet."

"You will be."

I smile. "Yeah, thanks to people like you."

Winnie looks around. "So, you're moving in here?"

"No. No way. This is temporary. You know, until thinking about my place doesn't hurt so much. Jack is in the woods now, so we're going to talk about it when he gets back."

I love Jack, and his place is great . . . for a single guy, but I miss my house. I love the fact that my microwave doesn't make that grinding noise, and I miss central heat and air. It's rustic, and I really don't *do* rustic, even if it has a hot tub.

I'm more of a modern girl who likes to think she's rustic.

"You could always come stay at my house."

I roll my eyes. "Yes, that would be super comfortable while you're still banging that Easton guy."

"I know you didn't love him when you met him, but he's good to me."

"That's good. And it's not that I didn't like him, I just hated the guy you were trying to set me up with."

She laughs. "In my defense, I didn't know you were completely in love with Jack."

I sigh. "I'm sorry I never told you about any of it."

Winnie shakes her head. "I'm not mad, Stell. I get why you didn't tell me. I think I was more upset that you have gone through all this on your own for this long."

"It wasn't easy."

"I'm sure it wasn't. You and I have never kept secrets, and yet you had a kid with Jack."

I wanted to tell her so many freaking times, but I couldn't. It wasn't just my secret to share.

"We made promises, Jack and I, when she was born. It was better to keep the circle as small as possible."

She gives me a soft smile. "Still, it was a lot for you to handle on your own."

"Yeah, but . . . I survived." I decide to switch topics because the longer we go down this road, the more likely it will be that she'll ask about Kinsley, and I really want to stop hurting for a bit and enjoy my best friend. "Tell me more about

Easton . . ."

She launches into a discussion, telling me about how great he is and the dates they've gone on. I've never seen her so animated and happy before. It's sweet, and there's no one in the world who deserves this more than she does. "I don't know, I can't explain it," she says all dreamy-like. "I think about him all the time. He makes me smile, and he's just a great guy."

"Why didn't you bring him to Amelia's party?" I ask.

"And have him meet my sister and Gray for the first time with your entire family? No thanks."

I laugh, understanding all too well.

"He hasn't met Gray and Jess yet?"

"No, I'm avoiding that until I decide we might get married, and even then, I may keep him away from Gray."

Grayson is very protective of anyone he thinks he should be. Winnie never fell into that category until he married her sister. Now she's enjoying all the "benefits" that come along with it.

"He gets better," I lie.

"Yeah, I don't believe you." We sit on the couch, and Winnie's hand rests on my arm. "I would've come by sooner, but I figured you might need time."

"I did. Your texts were appreciated, though, and I know you would've come if I asked."

"In a second. How is Jack doing?" Her voice takes a weird tone as she draws the question out slowly.

"He's better than I am—or, at least, he's better at pretending he is. I always thought of myself as strong, and then this happened, and I don't know who I am."

I've grappled with this so much. I don't cry. At least not like this. I may get upset, shed a few tears, and then move on. Having panic attacks? Not me. It was just too much. Like the weight of the world landed on me, and I couldn't get out from under it. I knew what the outcome would be from the minute we agreed to help Samuel, but leaving her again, it tore my heart from my chest.

It's been over a week since I've talked to her, and I am struggling with that too.

"You're the same, Stell. I can't imagine what you're feeling, and I won't pretend that I can, but you're allowed to feel and cry and be angry. It was a horrible situation that you and Jack knew wouldn't be easy. But you are a far better human than I ever could be."

I give her a look that says I don't believe that. "You'd do the same."

"No, I don't know that I would."

I exhale and look out the window at the horizon. "You would. There's nothing a mother won't do for her kid, even if it means staying away."

"I'm sorry."

I give her a half-hearted smile. "Don't. She's a great kid, and I'm proud that I brought her into this world, even if I don't get to walk beside her."

"That's beautiful, Stell. And you never know when she may want that door opened."

I think of her text and the call that never came. "I know." I grip Winnie's hand and smile. "Cake?"

She nods. "And wine."

We get up and grab plates, forks, and then she's scouring for something. "Does he have a wine opener?"

I think I saw one. "Maybe?" We both open drawers, rummaging around. Jack has zero order to this place. Nothing goes where it should, and I find myself starting to rearrange his drawers while I'm looking for the wine opener. "Why the hell is there a deck of cards in with the silverware?"

She laughs. "No idea, but you can't live like this."

"No, I definitely can't," I agree and bite my lip. "It would be a really nice thing to make his house a little more organized, right?"

"Most definitely. It's like your love language."

"What? Being invasive and rearranging his home?"

"I think of this more as an act of service. You know, you're donating your expertise on how to live like an adult to your overgrown man-child of a boyfriend."

"He's been doing just fine without me."

She looks around. "Has he?"

I laugh. "Well, he's been surviving."

"And now you're here to set him free!"

"Thank God for that," I say with a smile and empty another drawer.

"Oh, move this over there. That way the plates, cups, and silverware make a triangle."

I nod. "Good idea."

"He's going to kill you, you know this?"

I shrug. "It's worth it."

We pour wine, laugh, and talk of nothing but nonsense. The music is blaring in the background while we sing along to the music legend, DMX, and for a few hours, Winnie lets me just feel normal again.

I'm lying on the couch after a long day of hanging out with Winnie, cleaning, and making Jack's place look pretty fantastic if I say so myself. Winnie and I ate the entire cake, and I— and I do mean me—polished off two bottles of wine. She had one glass, I had the rest of the bottle she brought plus one of the bottles I found in Jack's cupboard. He never drinks wine, so it could even be from the previous owners, but it was still good, so I don't care.

My head is swimming, and it feels fucking glorious. I like

this floaty-no-pain-and-everything-is-fine place. It's nice here.

The fire is going because the weather is starting to cool after the sun goes down and I need more warmth. Jack's cabin is only heated by this glorious fireplace, so I keep the blaze going.

My phone is somewhere. Winnie took it away from me around the fourth glass of wine because I kept checking it.

I wonder where it is.

Maybe in a drawer?

Whatever. No one is calling anyway. Jack is off in the woods, Kinsley is never calling, and everyone else can fuck off.

You know what has never failed me? Wine.

Wine is a good friend. It takes all my pain away.

My head lulls to the side, and I look for the third bottle I opened but didn't finish. After bottle number one, bottle number two tasted just fine.

Well, the few sips I had before I forgot where I put it.

Probably with the phone.

"Stella?" I hear what sounds like Jack calling my name outside. I sit up quickly, which is totally a mistake because the room tilts a little to the left.

"Oof!" I yell as I roll from the couch to the floor. I rub my backside and then call out to him. "I'm here, Jack! In the cabin in the woods!"

The door jingles a little. "Baby! Come open the door."

"I can't."

"Why?"

"Because I've fallen and I can't get up!" I laugh, remembering the commercial. "I should get a button," I say to myself.

"A what?"

"Nothing. I'm coming," I say as I roll over and then get on all fours. He's home early, I muse to myself. He said he was going to be gone for four days, not two. Maybe someone got eaten by a bear.

"No one got eaten by a bear," I hear him say.

Huh. I said that aloud.

"Yes, you did. Are you okay?" Jack asks with concern in his tone.

"I'm wine, Jack. I am so wine that I don't even care."

"Oh, Jesus."

I climb the door, at least that's what I think I'm doing because now I'm upright and clutching the metal doorknob to steady myself. I wrench the door open and blink a few times. Because behind him, there are people.

I step back, eyes wide as my hand covers my lips because it's not just people. No, it's so much more than that.

It's Kinsley.

And I'm going to kill him.

Not only did I not know that he was coming home—with her—but also I'm drunk in front of her father, who is battling addiction.

I use every single ounce of self-control I have left to sober up enough that I'm not being a fall-down drunk. Tears fill my eyes, and Jack steps forward, steadying me.

He whispers in my ear, "While this isn't what I planned when I told Winnie to come here to check on you, I think you still comprehend why I needed to lie to you about my location."

"You didn't go to the woods?" I ask.

"No, baby, I didn't."

When Kinsley steps forward, her smile is warm, and I have to remember that I can't fall apart. I can't pull her into my arms and never let her go.

"Hey," she says.

"Hey."

"I know I said I'd call, but . . ."

"This is better," I say as Jack's arm tightens. "This is so

much better."

STELLA

I'm eating a bowl of soup, staring at Kinsley and Samuel as Jack shows them around. I'm still in shock. He wasn't working, he was in Georgia picking them up. I don't think there are enough words to describe how much I love this man.

They come down from the loft area, and Jack's eyes are warm. "You feeling okay?"

"I'm not really sure I can explain how I'm feeling."

He walks over and presses his lips to my temple. "Good."

I dip my bread into the soup until the bread is gone. I regret that wine now, but I never would've guessed this would be how the night went.

Kinsley sits beside me, and I nudge her. "How long are you here for?"

"The weekend. Jack said Daddy and I can stay here for a few days."

"He did?" I ask, eyeing him.

"I did. Samuel is going to go fishing with me tomorrow, so I thought maybe you and Kinsley could spend some time together."

I could cry. I could literally throw myself into his arms, sob for days, and still feel overwhelmed by him. Instead, I bite my lower lip and nod. "I'd like that."

Kinsley speaks up. "I need a dress."

"A dress? For what?"

She looks to Jack, panic in her eyes. "Umm . . . for something."

And then, even in my wine-addled mind, I piece it all together. Jack is going to propose, and he went out of his way, driving hours to go get the one person I would want to be here.

Jack is going to get one hell of a reward.

I look at Kinsley. "It's hard to get a dress for *something*. You need to be specific so I know where to take you."

"Right!" Kinsley laughs nervously. "It's a bat mitzvah for my best friend."

Shit. Maybe I'm wrong then.

"Oh! I went to a few of those when I was your age."

"My friend, Lana, is having hers next month. I was going to go shopping with my mom, but . . ."

Misty died.

"Of course I'll take you," I say quickly. "Tomorrow we'll head a few towns over. There are a few stores I like, and if you don't find anything, we could head to Charlotte."

Heck, I'd head to the moon if it would make her happy.

"I'm going to turn the grill on," Jack announces. "Would you help me, Samuel?"

"Sure."

The boys head out, leaving me and Kinsley here. "Is this weird?" she asks as soon as they're gone.

"A little. What about for you?"

She looks out the back door to where, essentially, both her fathers are. "Yes, but Dad seems to be really okay with it. I asked him a few times because I don't want him to get upset and then want to drink again."

"None of us want that."

"I know, but I'm worried."

"Worried about what?" I ask.

"That he's not really okay, and . . . that I'll have to choose."

"Kinsley, you don't have to choose anything, sweetheart. Jack and I, well, we . . . we're your biological parents, but Samuel is your dad. We aren't trying to force anyone's hand."

She worries her bottom lip. "But I want to talk to you. I wanted to call, and I was so scared."

"Oh, honey, you don't have to be scared. Jack and I will talk with your dad, and we'll figure it out. We all want what's best for you. If Samuel didn't want to be here, he wouldn't have come. So, whatever you're afraid of isn't worth getting worked up over."

She wraps her arms around my neck and hugs me tightly while I hug her back. I fight the tears because my emotions are just a damn mess, but really, I'm so damn happy right now. I have everything, and I don't know how it's real.

I keep waiting for the dream to stop and to wake up on that couch, hungover and hateful. If this is a dream, though, I'm going to stay here as long as I can.

Kinsley pulls back, wiping at her eyes. "Thank you, Stella."

"There's nothing we won't do for you. All three of us, and your mom too. She would've loved this, you know?"

"You think?"

I nod. "Misty was always open with us. She could've stopped writing me, sending photos, but she didn't."

"My mom was the best person I knew."

"She was one of the best people I knew too."

"If she was here, it would be easier for my dad," Kinsley says, looking back toward the porch. Jack is standing at the grill, a wide smile on his beautiful face as he and Samuel talk.

If only this could be our lives.

The three of us being able to help Kinsley through the rough road she's on.

I hope we can find a middle ground because the dead end is not an option.

"Time sometimes is what we all need. I loved Jack for a long time before we got our chance. I used to wish that things could be different. That he'd just love me because I was here and was so desperate for him. In my heart, I couldn't understand why we couldn't be together, but it wasn't our time. We needed to wait, grow up, be ready to love each other the way we do now. Your dad needs time. He has to figure out what life is like without your mom, and that's something that's incredibly hard. As for all of us, we have to allow for things to settle down."

She looks up at me. "If I never met you, it wouldn't be a thing."

I laugh once. "I get that. Before I knew how amazing you were, it was easier to watch you grow up in pictures. Now, I don't know how to go back to it, but if it's what's best for you, Kinsley, it's what I'll do."

"It's hard because I loved my mom, but now you're also my mother."

My chest aches with wishing and wanting to be that for her. I love her. It doesn't matter that I missed her first words or steps. All those things that I wasn't there for are Misty's, but I want to be there going forward. I want to hold her when a boy crushes her heart, help her find her prom dress, and be the mother she'll need in the next phase of her life.

I don't say it, though. I don't know what role I'll get to play because it's not my choice, it's Samuel's.

We don't have visitation or contact unless it's in the best interests of the child. One thing I do know is not in her best interests is a lawsuit to try to prove otherwise.

"I don't want it to be hard for you," I tell her. "Just . . . let's give this time and let everyone talk, maybe we'll find a way."

"Maybe."

I pull her to me. "We'll work it out, Kinsley. I swear."

"Surprised?" Jack asks as we're driving back to my place.

"That you kicked my brother out again or that you lied that you were going to be in the woods?"

He laughs. "Either one?"

"Yes, and I'm glad about both."

Jack gives me a side glance. "I figured you'd forgive me."

"I guess I will." I lean back, feeling like I can breathe again.

"Well, don't expect me to forgive you for reorganizing my entire house."

I laugh. "You'll love it later."

He takes my hand. "What if . . ."

"If?"

"What if we make your place . . . ours? We can make it more official since we both know you're going to marry me."

I smile at him, loving him more each day. "I'd like that. Maybe we can let Oliver stay at your place until he finds his own?"

Jack nods. "Yeah, we can talk about it, figure out the best plan."

"I'm sure he was none too happy about moving out again."

"No," Jack agrees. "I think he was ready to kill us, but he understood in the end."

I sigh. "Where did he go?"

"I think Grayson's."

I burst out laughing. "Oh, I'm sure Jessica wants to kill us now too."

Jack's slow smile is filled with mischief. "As long as he's driving Grayson crazy, I'm happy."

We pull into my place, and the anxiety about walking through that door again is gone. I'm not scared. I'm not worried. Kinsley is okay, and for now, she's here.

Jack and I get inside, toss our bags into the hallway, and collapse onto the couch. His arms are tight around me, and while it's only been over a week since we've been here, it feels like a lifetime.

So much has changed.

"Just so you know," Jack says quietly as my eyes were closing, "I'm going to ask you to marry me this weekend."

I tilt my head back to get a better look at him. "I figured."

"You did?"

"You went and got our daughter."

"How do you know I didn't do that just because I missed her?"

I shrug, tucking my head back against his chest. "I didn't, but I think you knew I needed her, and you always give me what I need."

Jack's lips press against the top of my head. "I always will, Stella. Always."

Forty-Seven

JACK

"You nervous?" Josh asks from beside me.

"Not really. She'll say yes."

"Stella is a mystery," Oliver chimes in. "That girl never does what we expect."

She'll say yes. I know she will. I mean, she better.

I turn and glare at him. "You're not helping."

"What makes you think I was trying to? You booted me out of a perfectly nice living situation—three fucking times—and stuck me with the worst person. Amelia climbs on my bed every morning before the damn sun is up, and apparently, if I'm still there when the baby comes, I'm the nanny."

Alex laughs. "You're looking for a place then?"

Oliver nods. "Damn right. I might just move in with Delia."

Josh tenses. "Delia?"

"She said she has room at her place."

Oh, this is going to be excellent. I step back, letting the Parkerson brothers face off. Josh doesn't disappoint. "I'm sorry, but why would you move in with her?"

"Because she . . . has . . . room."

"Find somewhere else," he warns.

Oliver, being the asshole he is, grins. "Why would I do that? She's single. I'm single. It's not like we have to worry about that." He turns to me. "Is she still single?"

I put my hands up. "I have no idea."

"Well," Oliver continues, "I don't give a shit either way. She has that house she just bought, and I need a place."

Josh's eyes flare with anger. Oliver is such a shit stirrer, but it's fun to watch. "You can afford your own place."

Oliver shrugs. "Doesn't matter. I also want to save what little I'll have left after we break ground. Plus, why the hell do you care?"

We all know why he cares. He just won't admit it. "I don't."

"Then what the hell is this conversation about, Josh? Hmm? Is it because you're dumb and refuse to accept the fact that you've been in love with Delia for years and pretend you have no idea what we're talking about when we call you out?"

Alex sniggers. "You're asking for trouble, Ollie."

"What else is new?" I tack on.

Josh lets out an almost silent laugh. "You all have no idea what you're talking about, and whatever is or isn't between Delia and me is none of your concern."

This is going to turn ugly if I don't stop it. "All right, guys, let's leave this be. Today is a happy day, and I'd like to keep it that way."

We are deep in the woods at the same spot I took Stella camping when we first started dating. There's a huge tent with lights strung up, her brothers and friends are already here, eating and hanging out. Everything is arranged, and we are just waiting for Stella, Kinsley, and Samuel to get back from town so I can go meet them at the main house.

It's a party. Our celebration of being engaged even though

I haven't gotten a yes from her.

And hopefully, tonight, I'll be able to give her even more good news about Samuel and Kinsley.

Yesterday, while the girls went shopping, Samuel asked to meet Odette. We spent hours with her, meeting the other fore-man and discussing the plans as well as his work experience.

Samuel got a text from Odette an hour after we left that said she'd be more than happy to have him on board.

He thanked me again, not saying whether he was going to take it, and I dropped him back off at my cabin. I haven't seen him since, and I'm fucking down on my knees that he accepts it. It would give us Kinsley and allow us to help Samuel.

Alex and Oliver walk away, leaving Josh with me. "You know that they're right."

"They don't get it."

"Neither do I," I tell him. When he was living in New Or-leans, it made sense. They were living in different states and she wasn't going to leave, not with her mother sick at the time and then it just became too late. Now, he's here, and there's no reason why they can't try. "Delia is a great girl. She's had feelings for you since . . . forever. It's not like the age gap is a thing."

"I know that."

"Then what's the issue?"

He sighs. "I can't do it, Jack. I can't get involved with a girl who wants a life I will never be able to give her."

"Why can't you?"

He looks over at Delia, who's laughing at something Win-nie and Jessica are talking about. When I turn back to him, I shake my head. He's so fucked. I've seen that look. He's broken up, trying to pretend otherwise, and doing a really piss poor job at it.

"I just can't."

My phone pings with a text, and as much as I'd like to keep

this conversation up, I have something I need to do first.

Kinsley: We're almost there.

Me: Thanks, kid. I'm on my way. Is she suspicious?

Kinsley: Of course she is. She keeps checking her hair and saying that she needs to practice her surprise face.

She wouldn't be Stella otherwise.

I look back at the crowd and yell, "I'm going to get her!"

They raise glasses, and I earn a few hoots from people. I grab the four-wheeler and head out. God only knows what shoes she has on this time.

When I get to the entrance, she's just pulling in. She exits the car, a smile on her lips, and she's wearing a white dress, heels, and her hair is in waves down her back. She is breathtaking, and she's going to kill me when she realizes she's about to walk in the woods.

I didn't think this through completely.

Still, too late to back out now.

"Hey. How was your day?" I ask as she looks around.

"Good . . . why are we out here?"

"We're camping."

"Jack." Stella's voice is low and full of frustration.

"Yes, my love?"

"I am *not* camping."

Samuel laughs and grabs a bag from the back. "Jack said he wanted to take us out. I'm sure it'll be fun."

She turns to him. "You knew?"

"I'm sorry, Stella," Kinsley says. "I asked Jack if we could see Melia Lake again because I wanted to check out more of the woods."

Oh, I love this kid. Stella, who is way too hopeful that Kinsley will want to be in her life, isn't going to disappoint her.

"Right. I just . . . I'm not dressed for it."

"I have some clothes in my truck," I offer.

The soft, sweet woman who was just talking is no more. No, now she's looking at me as if she wants to rip my eyes out and feed them to a bear. "Clothes?"

"Yeah. I always have a change of clothes. Don't you keep something in your car?"

I know she doesn't, but this is fun.

Stella sighs. "No, Jack, I don't because . . . well, I just don't."

Kinsley laughs and then covers her mouth. I give her a wink. "You can stay back if you want," I suggest.

"Stay? What?" she sputters. "Why would I stay back . . . and why . . . ugh."

"I don't know, but do you want the clothes?" I walk over to my car and pull out a sweatshirt and a pair of pants.

She takes the offered clothing and then walks behind the car, dragging me with her. "You are in so much trouble," Stella warns. "I thought you were proposing! I got all dressed up."

"I can't propose to you here," I say as though she should understand that already. When she doesn't say anything, I continue. "You know it's where Grayson proposed to Jessica."

She rolls her eyes. "Right. Makes total sense."

"Aww, don't be mad, baby. I promise I'll propose at some point this weekend."

"I'm wearing a dress *now*."

"I see that. I like it." I pull her close to me, my hands moving toward her bare legs.

Stella slaps me. "No, no touching for you."

"It starts already. We aren't even engaged yet, and I'm being punished."

"You have no clue . . ."

"I'm sure I don't," I agree. I've seen Stella pissed off at others, and she's . . . scary. But in about thirty minutes, if I'm not dead, she'll have a ring on her finger, and hopefully, all her ire will be forgotten.

She puts on the extremely large pants, rolling them and then groaning. "Jack, I can't wear these."

I smile. "I know. I was kidding."

"So, I'm supposed to hike in a white dress and heels?"

"No, you're going to put on the leggings that are in the bag Kinsley has and we're going to ride out."

"Ride?"

I nod. "I have two ATVs . . . you'll ride with me."

"I hate you."

"I know you don't." I walk out from behind the car, and the pants she just had on hit me in the back of the head.

"I should!"

I laugh, turning toward her with a grin. "But you don't."

As we head toward the clearing where everyone is waiting, nerves start to build. I know this is what she wants, hence her dress, but I really want today to be perfect. The sun is just setting and these woods are special to me.

It's where I kissed her at her brother's wedding.

It's where I fell asleep under the stars, holding her close.

It's where we've laughed, and in truth, it's where it all began.

When we were kids, the woods is where we played. Willow Creek Valley is all mountains and trees, and Stella has always been the ground that kept me steady.

However, right now, she's tapping my stomach and just pinched my side. "Yes?" I call to her, turning my head to the side.

"Can you stop?" she yells.

I stop where there's a break in the trees, and Samuel comes beside me. "If you go up just a little bit, the trees open, that's where we'll camp. I have a tent already there. Go on ahead, I want to talk to Stella."

"All right, I'll unload and get ready."

Samuel and Kinsley drive off, leaving the two of us.

When I turn to her, she's grinning. "You're taking me to the spot we were at last time, where I almost died from a bear attack, because everyone is here and you're going to propose."

I stare at her as she raises her brows. "Seriously? You stopped me here, right here, before we got to where you believe that was going to happen, to what?"

She shrugs. "Prove that I'm right."

"You couldn't just let it go?"

"Does that sound like something I'm able to do? Admit it. You got me all dressed up so you can propose."

I groan, getting off the quad. This woman, this absolutely maddening woman who I love more than anything in the world, is a pain in my ass. Still, there's no other pain I want besides her.

Suddenly, I don't want to ask her in front of the world. Because the world never mattered. She's what does.

She watches me. "What's wrong? You're mad? I've practiced my surprise face all day, so don't worry, I'll get it right. Look." She opens her mouth, and her hands go flying up.

I laugh and shake my head. "You look ridiculous, and nothing's wrong."

"Then why are you making that face?"

"What face?"

"It's a mix of: I have to poop and I'm thinking so hard my head might explode."

Stella climbs off the ATV and walks over to me carefully since she has freaking heels on. I take her hands in mine and then drop to my knee.

"Stella Parkerson, I love you more than I have ever known another could. I've never been worthy of you. Not the day I met you when we were kids. Not the day I kissed you and made love to you. Not the day you gave me a child or any day in between or since. I have always loved you, but have never deserved you. Today, I kneel before you, despite all we've been through, and ask you to let me try to be worthy. That you give me your heart and your hand, knowing that I will always fight to be more—for you. I wasn't going to do this now. I planned for this to happen just through those trees, but this isn't about anyone else but us. I choose you, Stella. I love you, and I am asking if you will be my wife?"

Tears fall down her cheeks as she drops to her knees with me. Her hands cup my face, and she kisses me. "Yes, I'll marry you, you stupid, amazing, wonderful man. I have always been yours, Jack. No matter what you think, you are better than anyone in this world."

I kiss her again, clutching her to my chest.

"Now, I'm going to have to do this again when we go through those trees," I tell her.

"Why?" she asks, rubbing her thumbs along my scruffy jaw.

"Because everyone you love is there, and they're desperate to watch me grovel."

She laughs. "Well then, let's not keep them waiting."

"One more thing," I tell her.

"Yeah?"

"I'm not waiting long to marry you."

"Good. Let's run away tomorrow," Stella says with a grin.

"Tomorrow sounds perfect."

STELLA

One Month Later

Marrying Jack in Vegas was the best and easiest decision I ever made.

For the last month, we've enjoyed being husband and wife. However, Jack gave me the best wedding present ever—Kinsley and Samuel moving here.

"Can you help me with this?" Samuel asks.

Jack rushes over, grabbing the box from him. We gave them Jack's cabin to live in until they want to move, and Samuel started working for Odette last week.

Kinsley comes over, wrapping her hands around my arm. "I love what you did here."

I smile at her. My big surprise for them was a renovation. One that included enclosing the loft area as a bedroom for Kinsley and converting a space downstairs into a bedroom for Samuel. It's not five-star, but it gives them each the privacy they need. No kid wants their dad to see them when they're sulking.

Not only did we do that, but also we redecorated Kinsley's room at my place however she wanted. We're not complicating things, just giving her a space wherever she wants.

"I love it too. So much better than Jack had it before."

She nods. "Especially now that we're living here all the time."

God, those words just make my heart race. I have everything, and I'm still not sure how it's possible. I got the most amazing husband any woman could wish for, my kid who has been missing from my life for far too long, and a friendship with Samuel that I think would make Misty happy.

And, of course, we broke ground on the Firefly Resort.

"Do you like your teacher?" I ask.

"She's fine. I got into the advanced math program, which is what I wanted."

"I knew you would."

Jack yells from the other side of the room. "Damn right we knew."

He is so proud of her.

"Do you think we can go look at the Firefly today?" Kinsley asks.

"Not today. Jack and I have to meet the design crew in about an hour, and you have a lot of unpacking to do."

"I really want to see it," she complains.

Samuel speaks up. "Maybe another time, Kins. I need you here. Plus, they're going to be busy since Odette has big ideas."

She huffs. "Fine."

Odette is amazing. She's on top of everything and has contingency plans on top of each other to make sure we're able to open and be fully functioning within the year. I don't see how it's possible, but she swears it's going to happen, and Samuel agrees.

"Tomorrow we have that girls' spa day," I remind her.

"That's right!"

Jack puts another box down and gives me a look. "I'm not going."

"You weren't invited."

"I'm just saying that Stella is known to torture people at the spa," he warns Kinsley.

"I do not. He's just a big baby."

"A baby?"

I nod. "Yes, husband, a big baby who doesn't keep his pants on."

He glares and then leans in, kissing me quickly. "You're lucky I love you so much."

"I know."

Kinsley makes a gagging noise. "You guys are so gross."

The two of us chuckle, and then Jack heads off to see if Samuel needs help before we head out. "I'll pick you up around noon, okay?"

"You're leaving now?"

I nod. "We have to if I want to make it over there on time. I'll see you tomorrow, though, okay?"

She gives me a hug before I head outside where Jack and Samuel are leaning against the car. "You ready?"

"Yeah," Jack says before turning to Samuel. "I'll come back tomorrow and help out after the girls leave for the spa."

He nods. "I appreciate it. Maybe Kinsley can spend the night with you guys tomorrow? I want to go to a meeting, and I have to leave for work before she will get up. That way, you can help her off to school?"

"Of course," I say quickly. "We can do that."

On the way to the Firefly, we talk about how things have turned out. It's really sort of magical.

"You're happy?"

"Aren't you?"

Jack grabs my hand and kisses my palm. "Blissfully."

"Me too. Well, other than when it comes to this wedding we have to plan."

Apparently, I've stolen this moment from my brothers, and they're not having it. I am *required* to marry Jack in front of them. According to Grayson, we're not legally married unless he witnesses it.

He's an idiot.

And so are the others.

Or maybe I'm the idiot since I'm actually having the fucking wedding they demanded.

"I don't know why you're so against this," Jack says as we near the property.

"Because we're already married! Now we have to spend money on a wedding that is literally just for their benefit."

"And Kinsley's," he reminds me.

"Yeah, yeah, I guess . . . I don't know, I just didn't think she really cared about it. When we left that morning, she was fine."

"What was she going to say?"

I sigh. "I don't know. I just—I loved our cute little wedding in Vegas. It was perfect, and it's the vows that matter, not the rest of it."

Jack lifts our entwined fingers, my ring glittering in the sunlight. "I love you, Stella, but we're having this wedding because I will not listen to your brother bitch for another minute about it."

"He's such a jerk."

"He is, but there's a part of me that wants to see it too," he admits.

"What?"

"The white dress, the flowers, you looking at me all lusty as you see me in my tuxedo."

I roll my eyes. "You're ridiculous. I don't look at you all lusty."

Jack laughs and pulls into the construction site before putting the car in park. "You do. Admit it. I leave you in a perpetual state of horniness."

"Oh, yeah, don't you know it. I'm just walking around, wishing that you were there to satisfy me," I say with so much sarcasm I could choke.

I get out of the car before he can give me a lame retort and walk around the car. When he gets to me, he scoops me into his arms, walking through the mud as I laugh. "Put me down!"

"And let you ruin your shoes? Not a chance. I'm a smart man, Stella O'Donnell, and I am aware of what those things cost."

I smile. "You are going to have to do a lot of wilderness trips to keep my shoe collection happy."

"Is that so?"

"It is, Jack O'Donnell." I grip his face and pull him in for a kiss. "And you promised to cherish me. Shoes are the way to my heart."

"Here I thought I was."

I grin. "You rank high, but not above my Jimmy Choos."

He puts me down, and just as I get my footing, I catch sight of someone sneaking out of Joshua's RV and almost fall on my ass.

I grab Jack's arm, pulling him behind one of the stacks of wood.

Jack lets out a chuckle. "Well, how about that?"

"Delia," I say softly.

Not only is she sneaking out of there, but also her hair is a damn mess and she's struggling to get her arm through her sleeve.

"We both know how this goes," he says, shaking his head.

"Yeah, my brother is a freaking mess. He's never going to commit, and she's going to be crushed."

"Or they fall in love and your brother gets his head out of

his ass."

That's never going to happen. Josh is . . . different. He doesn't want love, a family, or anything in his life worth losing. "I think not."

"Well, this isn't our business."

I look up at him. "You don't know me very well."

"Stella, you cannot get involved."

I shrug because . . . I can, and I probably will. "If you say so, husband."

Jack's eyes close as he lets out a heavy sigh. "You're already planning something, aren't you?"

"Me? Never."

"What are we watching?" someone asks, and I jump, pushing Jack in front of me.

When I see who it is, I work on calming my heart.

Jack speaks first. "Nothing, just trying to get my wife to see the scenery differently."

Odette looks over at the RV and then back to me. "Did your brother have a visitor?"

I grin and walk toward her, hooking my arm in hers. "Why don't you tell me everything you know."

"Great. Just freaking great," Jack says from behind us. I ignore him, hoping I can get some dirt from Odette that I can use on our girls' spa day in two weeks.

"To Stella and Jack!" Winnie says, raising her glass.

Everyone does the same, and I smile. Today has been a load of fun. We've been pampered to the max, Kinsley has had a great time, and I have kept my promise not to say a word about Delia doing the dirty with Josh.

They think they're so sly. Pfft. They're idiots, and once

today is done, I plan to call them out. It's only fair since Josh spent a good portion of time tormenting me as a kid. Plus, I don't want to see Delia hurt.

"Thank you, girls, for being here today. I'm glad we were able to have some fun, leave the boys, and spend some much-needed time together," I say. "I love you all so much, and I can't believe I have to have this big, expensive wedding just to make my siblings happy." They all laugh. "But in all serious-ness, I want to thank you all. Each one of you played a vital role in my life. Whether it was being a friend, a sister I never had, or the reason Jack and I finally got it together, you are the best bridal party anyone could have." I look at Kinsley. "And to my beautiful maid of honor, thank you for letting me in your life."

Winnie raises her glass again. "To the bride!"

Everyone toasts as I wrap my arm around Kinsley. "Do you think . . . do you think I can call you something other than Stella?"

I look down at her, blinking and trying to form an appro-priate response that isn't just sobbing and incoherence. "Yes, I mean, whatever you want to call me is fine."

"I talked to my dad about it. I didn't want to hurt him."

"Of course. Kinsley, you don't have to. You can call me Stella. It doesn't upset me."

I mean that, and even with wanting so badly for her to think of me as her mother, just having her near is enough.

"I know, but, now that I'm here, it's really hard to say, 'Oh, that's my birth mother,' you know?"

"I don't, but I'll take your word for it. Well, whatever you want to call me is fine, and if you're not always comfortable and need to flip around until you settle on a name, that's fine too."

"Thanks."

"You're welcome." I let out a long sigh. "So, did you have

fun?"

"I did. I've never been to a spa before, and this was really cool."

I know that things between her and I won't always be so fabulous. There will be times when she might hate me, and that's okay because I'll love her enough for the both of us. All that really matters is that I'll be around for her life.

"Hey, you two!" Jess calls us. "The limo will be here soon, and we have some shopping to do."

I groan. "Can't we just stay here?"

"No, you need a wedding dress and that's that."

I give her a salute. My sister-in-law offered to help do a lot of the wedding planning since she had hers not all that long ago. It's hard because I always dreamed I'd get married at the Park Inn. Not only did my relationship with Jack start there, but also it's beautiful. Instead, we rented a huge chateau a few towns over. It has floor-to-ceiling windows and is stunning. It'll house everyone and give us the best of both worlds: quaint but also bougie. "Fine, fine. Let's all get changed."

We head into the changing area, everyone laughing, talking, and moving around. The spa gave us a subsection to ourselves.

I enter the bathroom to find both Winnie and Delia coming out of stalls. I go to wash my hands and panic hits me.

Oh my God.

"Shit!" I yell when I look down at my hand, realizing my engagement ring is gone. "My ring!"

"Relax," Winnie says, "we'll find it."

Jess comes rushing in. "You lost your ring?"

I nod. "I had it on when we did toasts."

"Okay." Jessica is calm. "Did you have it when you got changed?"

I think, trying to retrace my steps. "Yes. It has to be in here."

Everyone starts to move around, checking the floor, and I go through the stall. When I reach around the trash basket, I feel it. "It's here! It must've flown off."

A few sighs of relief sound, and when I step out, Jessica is standing there, holding something in her hand that I know very well.

A pregnancy test.

"Why are you holding a pregnancy test?" Winnie asks.

"It was right here," she explains. "I'm . . . I mean, I'm seven months pregnant so we know I wasn't taking it."

"Is it positive?" Delia asks.

"Yes," Jess confirms. "So, which of you guys is pregnant?"

"How do you know it was one of us?" I ask.

"Because this room was spotless when we came in and we've been the only people here." Jessica looks at Winnie, Delia, and then me.

I do the same, scanning the faces of my two close friends. "Is it you, Win?"

"No!" she says quickly. "I have an IUD and Easton wraps that shit up."

"Deals?" Jessica asks.

"No, definitely not. I'm not having sex, so I can't really get pregnant."

My gaze darts to her, and she stares at me. Well, I know that's a lie since yesterday she was sneaking out of Josh's RV. All eyes turn to me. My lips part, but I know it's not mine, which means it's Delia's or Winnie's. Both of them are watching me, but where Winnie looks as though she's about to pee herself with joy, Delia looks like she might break down in tears.

I turn to Jessica. "Yeah. I mean, you found out. It's me. I'm . . . pregnant."

"Oh my God!" Winnie rushes toward me, pulling me into her arms. "I am so happy. Does Kinsley know?"

Shit. Shit. Shit. "No, no one does, and you can't tell her. Please. Not until I figure things out."

Because I'm not pregnant.

"This is amazing." Jessica smiles, her watery eyes brimming. "Our babies are going to be just a few months apart, and they'll be best friends."

I force myself to smile. "For now, can we not talk about this—at all?"

They all nod. "Of course, we'll be quiet."

"Thank you."

"Come on, let's get back before Kinsley gets curious," I suggest.

God, if she heard any of this, I will be in so much trouble. I'll have to explain that I lied, and then if Jack somehow catches wind of this before I have time to give him a heads-up. Just . . . not good.

As we all exit, I hang back, pretending I need to look at something in the mirror. As soon as Jess and Winnie are gone, I grab Delia's arm, pulling her back in.

I keep my voice to a whisper. "We are so going to talk about this."

Tears fill her brown eyes. "I know, just not today. Can you give me a few days?"

"Is it Josh's?"

The tear falls. "A few days, Stella. I just need a few days."

I pull her in for a hug and make her a promise. "A few days."

I'll give her the time she needs, but there are not enough minutes in the world to change the struggle she's about to face if this baby is my brother's.

Thank you for reading Jack and Stella's story. I don't know how to express the joy I had writing it. To be honest, when I finished Return to Us, I had no idea this was direction the story would go, but it unfolded, and I've learned not to fight the characters.
Now, I'm giddy over Delia and Josh.
Josh is . . . well, he's really special and Delia is so much fun.
Their romance is sure to take you on a ride you're not ready for!

Preorder A Moment for Us and be ready for a love story that will leave you speechless!

Acknowledgments

To my husband and children. You sacrifice so much for me to continue to live out my dream. Days and nights of me being absent even when I'm here. I'm working on it. I promise. I love you more than my own life.

My readers. There's no way I can thank you enough. It still blows me away that you read my words. You guys have become a part of my heart and soul.

Bloggers: I don't think you guys understand what you do for the book world. It's not a job you get paid for. It's something you love and you do because of that. Thank you from the bottom of my heart.

My beta reader Melissa Saneholtz: Dear God, I don't know how you still talk to me after all the hell I put you through. Your input and ability to understand my mind when even I don't blows me away. If it weren't for our phone calls, I can't imagine where this book would've been. Thank you for helping me untangle the web of my brain.

My assistant, Christy Peckham: How many times can one person be fired and keep coming back? I think we're running out of times. No, but for real, I couldn't imagine my life without you. You're a pain in my ass but it's because of you that I haven't fallen apart.

Sommer Stein for once again making these covers perfect and still loving me after we fight because I change my mind a bajillion times.

Michele Ficht and Julia Griffis for always finding all the typos and crazy mistakes.

Nina and everyone at Valentine PR, thank you for always having my back and going above and beyond. I love you all so much.

Melanie Harlow, thank you for being the Glinda to my Elphaba or Ethel to my Lucy. Your friendship means the world to me and I love writing with you. I feel so blessed to have you in my life.

Bait, Crew, and Corinne Michaels Books—I love you more than you'll ever know.

My agent, Kimberly Brower, I am so happy to have you on my team. Thank you for your guidance and support.

Melissa Erickson, you're amazing. I love your face. Thank you for always talking me off the ledge that is mighty high.

To my narrators, Jason Clarke and Ava Erickson, I am so honored to work with you. You bring my story to life and always manage to make the most magical audiobooks.

Vi, Claire, Chelle, Mandi, Amy, Kristy, Penelope, Kyla, Rachel, Tijan, Alessandra, Laurelin, Devney, Jessica, Carrie Ann, Kennedy, Lauren, Susan, Sarina, Beth, Julia, and Natasha—Thank you for keeping me striving to be better and loving me unconditionally. There are no better sister authors than you all.

Books by Corinne Michaels

The Salvation Series

Beloved

Beholden

Consolation

Conviction

Defenseless

Evermore: A 1001 Dark Night Novella

Indefinite

Infinite

The Hennington Brothers

Say You'll Stay

Say You Want Me

Say I'm Yours

Say You Won't Let Go: A Return to Me/Masters and Mercenaries Novella

Second Time Around Series

We Own Tonight

One Last Time

Not Until You

If I Only Knew

The Arrowood Brothers

Come Back for Me

Fight for Me

The One for Me

Stay for Me

Willow Creek Valley Series (Coming 2021)

Return to Us

One Chance for Us

A Moment for Us
Could Have Been Us

Standalones
All I Ask
You Loved Me Once (Coming 2021)

Co-Written with Melanie Harlow
Hold You Close
Imperfect Match

About the Author

Corinne Michaels is a *New York Times, USA Today, and Wall Street Journal* bestselling author of romance novels. Her stories are chock full of emotion, humor, and unrelenting love, and she enjoys putting her characters through intense heartbreak before finding a way to heal them through their struggles.

Corinne is a former Navy wife and happily married to the man of her dreams. She began her writing career after spending months away from her husband while he was deployed—reading and writing were her escape from the loneliness. Corinne now lives in Virginia with her husband and is the emotional, witty, sarcastic, and fun-loving mom of two beautiful children.